FIRST THE DREAM

A NOVEL

BY

ELAINE ULNESS SWENSON

FIRST THE DREAM

First Printing, August 1998
Second Printing, December 1998
Third Printing, August 1999

International Standard Book Number 0-9642510-5-1

Printed in the United States of America

DEDICATED

TO

MY GRANDPARENTS AND GREAT- GRANDPARENTS
WHO FOLLOWED THEIR DREAM WHEN THEY LEFT
THEIR HOMELAND OF NORWAY AND SETTLED IN
THE MIDWEST, THE LAND THAT I CALL HOME

CHAPTER 1

1976

It was the eve of her 90th birthday. Anna sighed and looked out her window. Tomorrow the place would be filled with family and friends. Her whole family would be together, down to the last great-grandchild. What a long, full life I've had, she mused.

She looked around at her living quarters, which consisted of this sitting room and an adjoining bedroom and small bath. How she loved these rooms. She loved this whole house, which she and her husband built so many years ago. Now her son, Frank, and his wife shared it with her and she occupied the two rooms on the west side.

The last sunbeams of the day were streaming through her lacy curtains, making the old mauve flowered carpet look more faded than ever. She smiled as she thought back to the day when her dear husband brought that rug home. She asked him why he wanted to put such a beautiful and expensive rug in the bedroom where nobody would see it and he answered, "Anna, dear, when I saw this rug in the window with its delicate pink roses, I thought of you, and just knew I had to buy it. We will see it and enjoy it every day of our lives in this room". And so they had.

Anna had been widowed about ten years ago now and her son wanted to put new carpeting in her room but she just couldn't part with the dear, old rug. She wasn't an overly sentimental person, but there were some things she just had to keep the same.

A soft rap on the door interrupted Anna's thoughts and granddaughter, Kari, popped her head in.

"Hi, Grandma. May I come in?"

"Of course, dear. Come and sit here and keep me company. Your mother and aunt shooed me out of the kitchen and told me to go rest. I told them I'll have lots of time to rest when I get old."

"Oh Grandma, you always say that!"

"So tell me, dearie, how is college going? And have you found a special fellow yet?"

Kari was Anna's youngest grandchild out of five, in her second year at the university in Ames.

"College is going great and, no, I haven't found a 'fellow' yet. But then I'm not really looking for one."

"Nonsense, my dear. Girls are always looking for boys and boys are always looking for girls, whether they admit it or not!"

Kari knew better than to argue with her grandmother so she changed the subject.

"What does it feel like, Grandma, to be ninety years old?"

"Well," she laughed, "I guess I'll find out tomorrow. I"m still only 89, you know."

She sat and reflected a few moments and then said, "You know, Kari, this old body of mine may look old but inside me still lives a young girl. Inside of me I feel about your age. You won't understand that until you get old yourself."

"Well, I hope I can pack as much living in the next 70 years as you did, Grandma. I love hearing your stories about the 'old days'. You know, you should have written a book about your life. In fact, someone could still do it."

"Oh, there's nothing very remarkable about the life I've lived. Who would want to read about that?"

"Your family, for one. And friends and future generations. I think you should do that, Grandma. Have someone write down things as you tell it to them and they could even use a tape recorder." Kari was getting more and more excited about the idea.

Just then Kari's older sister, Barbara, stuck her head in the door.

"Can I come in," she asked, "or is this a private party?"

"Oh, come in, Barb dear, it's so good to see you," Anna said.

"We just got here," Barb said as she gave her grandmother a hug.

"Well, I don't know who's all coming or going here today because I can't see the driveway from my room. And I was banished from the kitchen."

Barb laughed knowingly and said, "Grandma, you look great and not at all like someone who is going to be 90 tomorrow!"

"Bless your heart, dear girl," Anna said. "Let me have a good look at you though. My, you are really getting big!"

Barb was five months pregnant with her first child and did look extremely big already.

"I have something exciting to tell both of you. I saw my doctor again today and he thinks I may be having twins!"

"Twins! Oh, my," said Anna. "That would keep you awfully busy. When I had your mother and your uncle Frank only two years apart, that seemed like having twins!"

"Does Mom know?" asked Kari.

"I just told her now when we came," answered Barb excitedly. "The impact of all that that implies may not hit her till tonight when she's lying in bed! She and Aunt Betty are so busy in there that they can hardly think of anything else but salads, sandwiches and cakes!"

"Oh, dear, I hope they don't wear themselves out. I told them to have this party catered but they wouldn't hear of it."

"How many people are you expecting tomorrow, Grandma?" asked Kari.

"Well, I guess they are planning food for about 300," Anna answered.

"Wow! That's a lot of people!" Barb exclaimed.

'Well, you know I've lived in this community a long time and have lots of friends," Anna said.

"Yes, you are loved by many, many people, Grandma," said Barb as she got up to give her grandmother a hug. "I have to go and find out where we're going to sleep tonight and get Dan to bring up the suitcases. See you later."

"You tell that handsome husband of yours to come around to see me."

"I will," laughed Barb, as she hurried off.

Kari was walking around the room, looking at everything. "I love this room, Grandma. It's so 'you'."

Yes, everything in these rooms was from an era long past. But Anna liked it that way. It had so many memories, why should she change it? The bedroom set was from the '20's and the rocker in the corner was even older than that. The beautiful lamp on the nightstand was very old-fashioned looking, too. It had been a wedding gift from Anna's brother,Tomas and family. The many interesting articles on the dresser were things Anna had used and cherished for years. The comb and brush set were from her husband their first Christmas in this house.

An old trunk sat by the rocker. Kari had been permitted to look inside it quite a few times as a child as Anna was always willing to open it up and show her things to her granddaughters. It had been several years since the girls had had time to come visit her and sit in her room like this.

Oh, how precious her grandchildren were to her and how fast they were growing up. Plus she now had three great-grandchildren and one--no, two perhaps-- on the way.

"Can we look in your trunk now, Grandma," asked Kari, "or are you getting tired?"

"No, I'm not tired. We can look now if you're really interested."

They heard tiny footsteps out in the hall and a little girl burst in the room.

"Hi, Great Granny!" It was Beth, Anna's 6-year-old great-granddaughter. She skipped over to Anna and gave her a hug.

"Well, look at you, little girl. Dressed so cute, as always!" Anna said.

"Beth," Kari said, "We were just going to open Grandma's trunk and have a look inside."

Beth's eyes got big and she ran excitedly over to the trunk. She had never seen inside before.

Anna sat in the rocker beside the trunk and the girls sat on the floor. Before Kari could open the lid, little Beth said, "What are those letters written on there? I'm learning to read in school now, you know." She traced the large letters with her little fingers. "A-N-N-A...."

"Those letters say my name: 'ANNA ARNESDOTTER OLSON'. My papa made that trunk for me--let's see, it must be over 70 years ago now--before I came to this country. A neighbor did the painting and wrote my name on it."

In the top drawer of the trunk were some old pictures, a couple of old lace collars, a packet of letters tied with a ribbon and a very tarnished silver cup.

"Yuk," exclaimed Beth, "what is that old cup doing in there? Was that for a baby?"

"My, that is looking quite bad again, isn't it," said Anna, picking up the cup lovingly. "Perhaps we should give it a good polishing." She traced the word BABY with her fingertip several times and then placed the cup on a table and a look of sadness came over her face. Kari had heard the story before about the little baby cup that was never used but she didn't think that now was the time for her grandmother to go into it with Beth.

She lifted the top drawer out and set it on the floor. On the bottom of the trunk was an old quilt, some crocheted dresser scarves, an old petticoat and many tatted handkerchiefs. Each of the grandchildren had received several of these handkerchiefs through the years but Anna still had quite a number of them. She would have to start giving some to the great- grandchildren now.

In one corner was a small, square box. Kari took it out and opened it. She loved looking in this box because it always amazed her how such a long, flowing baptism dress could fit in so small a box. She held it up for Beth to see.

"This is the dress that my mother and your Grandpa Frank wore when they were baptized," Kari explained to Beth.

"Grandpa wore a dress?" Beth asked with disbelief.

"Well, yes," Kari said. "Many baby boys wore dresses for their baptism. The dresses were then passed down for many generations." Turning to Anna she asked, "Did you make this dress for Frank or did you get it from someone in your family?"

"My brother Andrew's children all wore it and then he gave it to me for my children to wear," Anna answered as she fingered the soft, silk fabric and put it lovingly back into its little box.

Also at the bottom of the trunk was an old shoebox. It was full of old pictures which Kari had looked at several times before. She picked up some of them now and turned them over to see who they were .

"Grandma, you should write the names on the back of all your old pictures because we don't know who most of these people are."

"Yes," she sighed, "I know I should do that someday."

"I could help you with that sometime, Grandma," said Kari.

As she stood up and shook the folds of her skirt, Kari said thoughtfully, "You know, Grandma, a whole story could be written about the contents of this trunk. I still think you should write a story of your life."

Anna laughed and shook her head. "Oh, I'm too old now to do something like that."

They shut the cover of the old trunk just as Frank came into the room.

"Well, what's been going on in here, ladies?"

"Grandpa," said Beth as she skipped over to him, "we got to look into that big trunk of Great-Granny's."

"Did you see lots of interesting old stuff?" he asked, stooping down to her level as she slipped into his arms.

"Some old pictures and that dirty cup over there," she said as she pointed to Anna's nightstand.

Frank and Anna exchanged looks and then Frank said, "Well, I was sent here to fetch you ladies and bring you to the supper table." He helped his mother as she attempted to rise from the rocker.

Anna chuckled and said as they walked down the hall, "I didn't think anyone had time to make supper tonight what with all the fussing going on in the kitchen for tomorrow. You'd think the King and Queen were coming!"

As Anna was seated at the head of the dining- room table, the rest of the family members took their places. They all bowed their heads and said the table grace.

"Grandma, say the table prayer in Norwegian for us," Barb said. "I haven't heard it for a long time."

Anna recited the prayer as requested without skipping a beat:

"Jesu Navn går vi til bords,
at spise, og drikke på dit ord,
dig Gud til aere os til gavn;
så får vi mat i Jesu navn."

"You still say that very well, Mother," said Margaret.

"Have you forgotten any of your 'mother tongue', Anna, after all these years?" inquired Dan, Barb's husband.

"Oh, yes, I suppose I have. You know, there aren't many people left around here who speak Norwegian . There are only two or three left down at the Senior Center who still speak it once in awhile."

As everyone was busy with their sandwiches, Anna looked up and down the table at her family; her two children, Frank and Margaret with their spouses, Betty and Ted; four grandchildren, three great-grandchildren and one husband of a granddaughter. The remaining family members would be joining them tomorrow.

I wonder how many more times I will be lucky enough to have all my family around me, thought Anna, as several conversations were going back and forth across the table.

Jana, the youngest great-grandchild, started to fuss and her mother, Pat, whisked her from the table and the rest of the family started to excuse themselves and clear off the table.

"Grandma," said Kari, "if I go and get that box of old pictures from your trunk, we could start putting names on the backs. Would you like me to do that?"

"Well, I suppose that would be all right. We can't put that off forever, not at my age!"

While Kari was digging in the trunk for the shoebox, she also came up with an old Bible and another little book written in Norwegian. She brought these to the dining room and set everything in front of her grandmother.

"This is the Bible, or 'Bibel' that I brought over with me from home," Anna said as she reached for the old, worn book. She caressed it lovingly and opened it to the first page.

"I received this on my Confirmation day. See, here it says 'To Anna from Papa and Mama, 25 June 1901.'"

Beth had joined them by now and said that she thought that Great-granny's book was awfully raggedy.

"All the pages in this book," said Anna, "have been turned many, many times over all these years. The words on these pages have been my comfort and solace through plenty of trying times. You'll even see some tear drops, I'm sure, if you look closely."

"What's this little book, Granny?" asked Beth. "The words look so funny."

Taking the book from Beth, Anna explained that this was her 'sangbok' or songbook and that the words were in Norwegian.

"We would carry these to church with us on Sundays and sing from them."

Kari had started to take the old photographs out of the box and was lining them up in front of Anna.

"Beth, will you go and ask your mother for a good pen?" asked Kari. "I'll start writing the names on the backs. Some of them I already know." Picking up the first one she said, "This is your father and sister, Kjersti, isn't it?"

"Ah, yes," answered Anna, " dear, dear Papa." And poor Kjersti, thought Anna, shaking her head slowly as she looked at this picture for a long time.

Kari hesitated to break into her thoughts.

"What was it that you told me was wrong with your sister Kjersti, Grandma?"

"Well, nowadays I guess you would say that she was retarded. She wasn't real bad but she wasn't normal either. She was such a trial for my mother."

"You don't have a picture of your mother, do you?" asked Kari, already knowing the answer.

"No, and that's one thing that I regret very much. They were talking of having one taken but then she got sick and died shortly after and so, you see,"

Anna said pensively, "that's how it goes sometimes."

Beth returned with a pen and Kari started writing names and dates.

"Some of these pictures I haven't seen before," said Kari. "Who is this young man? He looks so uncomfortable in that suit!"

Anna hesitated before answering and Kari thought that perhaps she had forgotten who it was.

"That is, ah, the son of a couple I worked for at one time. That's his confirmation picture and probably he had to wear a new suit."

"What name should I write on the back and about what year was that?" asked Kari, reaching for the picture. Anna was reluctant to give it to her and seemed to want to look at it awhile longer. Kari had to try and stifle her youthful impatience and to remember that these old pictures were very dear to her grandmother.

Various other members of the family joined them around the table, looking and exclaiming over all those old pictures. After a couple of hours, Anna decided it was nearing her bedtime. Kari had almost finished labeling the photos. Some of the others were going to have coffee, but Anna said she wanted to go to her room. Barb helped her up and walked with her down the hall. She kissed her grandmother good night and said she would see her in the morning.

Anna put her gown and robe on and sat in her rocker for awhile and read from her Bible, as she did every night. She never started nor ended her day without her Lord. She prayed for all her family members, each one by name and there was getting to be more and more of them to remember. She thanked God for one more day and prayed for the doings tomorrow.

She was ready to climb into bed when she heard a soft knock on her door. As she said, "Come in," Kari popped her head in and asked her grandmother if she could come in for a minute. She placed the shoebox back in the trunk and sat down on the bed beside the elderly woman who looked so frail and vulnerable now lying there.

Kari took her grandmother's hand and held it in hers. It was so soft and wrinkled; the skin looked almost transparent. She still wore her plain gold wedding band. It was getting worn thin and it fit rather loosely now.

"Grandma," said Kari, "I just wanted to tell you how much I love you. I probably haven't told you that since I was little."

"Well, I know you love me, Kari, but it is so good to hear the words often. Your grandpa never let a day go by without telling me that."

Kari let go of her hand and gave her a kiss and tucked her in like a child. "I'm looking forward to tomorrow, Grandma. I know it will be a great day."

"I know it will be, too, child. I've talked to the Lord about it."

"Good night then."

"Good night, dear."

Saturday, October 20, 1976, was indeed a beautiful day. The sunrise was gorgeous for those who were up to see it and the autumn colors were at their most splendid. Margaret came into her mother's room to see if she was stirring yet. She opened the blinds and looked over at the bed. Anna was awake and gave Margaret a sheepish smile.

"I guess I slept a little late this morning," she said, "but then when you're ninety, you can do whatever you want."

Margaret laughed as she bent over to give her mother a kiss. "Happy birthday, Mother. I came over early to help Betty out. It's a beautiful day, just like you ordered." She helped Anna sit up on the edge of the bed. "Remember you're going to have your hair done at 9 o'clock so you need to get dressed and eat breakfast. Frank will drive you over there."

"All this hustle and bustle just because an old woman is ninety!" Anna exclaimed.

"A very special old woman," Margaret added. She helped Anna get her clothes on and they went to the kitchen where several of the others were gathered over the morning paper.

"Look, Grams," said Stan, "there's a picture of you and a long article about your big birthday in the local paper!" He rose to give Anna his chair and gave her a peck on the cheek. "Happy birthday, sweet Grandma of mine," he said.

Anna scoffed at this term of endearment, but of course she was secretly pleased. Stan was such a favorite of hers. But then all her grandchildren were her favorites. She looked at the paper and saw her picture. She remembered the day that the lady from the paper called and asked if she could come over and interview her. "It must have been 105 degrees that day!" she said, "and I didn't know that she was going to take my picture. My hair wasn't very nice and I didn't have my good dress on."

"Oh, Mother," consoled Frank, "you look just fine there. Women never get over being vain no matter how old they get, do they?" he teased.

Pat's husband, Paul, came into the room to join them. He had arrived late last night. "Good morning, everyone, and a special good morning and happy birthday to you, Anna," he said. "The girls are all awake and getting dressed. They are excited about the party and are talking about cake and presents!"

Betty took a pan of cinnamon rolls out of the oven and everyone oohed and aahed over the good smell. They cleared off the table to make room for them and Frank poured coffee and passed it around.

Kari and Barb came in at the same time. "We just followed our noses!" exclaimed Barb. They each gave Anna a birthday hug and found themselves a chair.

The first plate of rolls was gone in five minutes flat! "Betty, you still make the best rolls I've ever tasted," said Dan, "and I've tasted lots of them these last few years!"

"Well, you all know where I learned to make them," said Betty, looking at Anna. "When we got married, Frank insisted that she teach me how and I've made them ever since and that's a good many years now."

"Barb," Dan said, "you better get the recipe and keep the tradition alive. I'll be your willing taster." Everyone laughed at this because they knew how true that would be. Dan loved to eat everything and anything!

"Well, Mother," said Frank, "we better be heading over to that 'house of beauty' so you can get beautiful for this afternoon. We don't want you to be complaining how your hair looks on all the pictures," he teased.

As she got into the car, Anna couldn't help but think how like his father Frank was, always teasing but yet making her feel so loved and cherished. Frank was a wonderful person, so kind and gentle; a good son, husband, father, and now a grandfather. Yes, her children had turned out well, thought Anna. She was deep in thought about another child when Frank broke into her reverie.

"Here we are, Mother. I'll help you into the shop," he said as he opened the car door for her.

As they entered the shop, a cheery voice called out, "Well, good morning, Anna. I'm all ready for you."

"Good morning, Marge, dear. What miracle can you work on an old lady today, then?" Anna asked, as Frank helped her up into the chair.

"I'll be back in about an hour, Mother," he said, leaving the two ladies to do whatever needed to be done.

As Marge washed the beautiful, gray hair, she wondered aloud about what it would be like to be 90 years old.

"Well," offered Anna, "the difference between you and me is that most of my life is behind me and most of yours is ahead of you. I live on memories and you live on hopes and dreams."

"My, you are very philosophical his morning, Anna!" Marge said.

"Well, I have lots of time on my hands nowadays, so I think often about the past," Anna said. "You might say I am RE-living my life."

"Are there things you would have done differently in your life as you look back on them now?" asked Marge.

Anna thought about this for a few moments. She nodded her head thoughtfully and answered, "Oh, yes, there are a few things I would do differently." She drifted off into deep thoughts as Marge finished rolling her hair in rollers. She put her under the dryer and Anna soon nodded off.

When Marge woke her up a short while later, she said, "Well, Anna, I see you were resting up for your big party!"

"I am rather tired this morning. I must be starting to feel my age," Anna chuckled.

Frank returned while Marge was putting the finishing touches to Anna's hairdo.

"Go easy on that spray stuff now; you know I don't like too much of that!" Anna cautioned.

"I'll go easy," laughed Marge, "but I want to make sure it lasts through all the hugging and kissing that's going to go on at the hall today!"

"Oh, goodness me," scoffed Anna. "And have you ever seen so much fussing over one person's birthday?"

"I hope to get done here early today so I can stop by and have some of your birthday cake, Anna," said Marge. "There you are now, all done!"

Frank helped his mother out of the chair and was taking out his billfold when Marge said, "This hairdo is on me today, Anna. We'll call it your birthday present from me."

"Well, thank you ever so much, dear. That's real nice of you."

While they were driving home, Frank looked over at his mother and said, "Your hair looks especially nice today, and you still are one very foxy looking lady!"

"Oh, Frank," Anna said, slightly embarrassed, "you sound just like your father."

When they entered the back door, they were met by three excited great-granddaughters, talking all at once about birthday cake and presents.

"A whole bunch of mail came for you this morning, Mother," said Margaret, helping her get seated at the table and handing her some of them. "Barb, why don't you help her open them. The letter opener is on the desk there."

Anna opened and read about a dozen cards with birthday greetings from people who were unable to attend the party.

"We're going to have an early lunch now, everyone," announced Betty, "and then perhaps Grandma can have a little nap before we get ready to go over to the hall."

That will feel good, thought Anna to herself. All this commotion is making me tired already and the party hasn't even started!

Two hours later everyone was dressed and ready to go. Betty and Margaret and some of the others were going over first and it was decided that Anna would come later. Stan and Dan would bring her and the little girls over just before the party was ready to start.

Anna was starting to feel a little excited and the girls were restless and getting a little wild. She decided to go sit in her room alone for a few minutes. She settled down in her rocker and picked up her Bible and turned the book over and over in her hands. She didn't open it but just holding it was a comfort to her.

"Dear Lord," she prayed, "You and I have been together for many years now, haven't we? Help me to get through this big day and then You and I will have a long chat this evening."

Beth came into the room and stopped short and looked at her great-grandma.

"Great Granny, are you sleeping again?" she asked incredulously.

Anna opened her eyes and said, "No, dearie, I was just talking to God."

"You talk to Him alot, don't you?" asked Beth.

"Yes, I suppose I do," said Anna, rising from the rocker. "He's my best friend, you know," she added, with a twinkle in her eye.

"We're learning that song in Sunday School now; you know, that song about Jesus being our best friend."

"Oh, that's my favorite song in all the world!" exclaimed Anna. "I hope it will be yours, too"

Stan came in the room and said, "Hey, you two, it's time to go now. You don't want to be late for your own party!"

Anna was helped into the car and the little girls scrambled in after her. The hall was only a few blocks away. Anna had spent many hours in this building, where the senior citizens came every week for their meetings and social gatherings.

Upon arriving, Anna was given a corsage of fragrant pink roses to wear and had her picture taken with her family members. First with just Frank and Margaret, then one with the grandchildren and then with all the family.

The hall was decorated with multi-color balloons and Anna couldn't ever remember having such a festive birthday party. The first guests started to arrive and the hugging and good wishes began! In fact, people just kept coming and coming. I didn't know I knew so many people, Anna thought to herself.

Anna had to finally give in and sit down and rest for awhile with a cup of coffee and a piece of that wonderful birthday cake. The little great granddaughters were on their second or third piece by this time.

Stan came over to check on his grandmother. "How is it going, Grandma?" he asked.

"Well, I'm holding out pretty good but I finally had to sit for awhile."

"I noticed, Grandma, that you are always glancing at the door. Are you expecting someone special to show up, perhaps President Ford," Stan queried, "or are you looking for an escape route?"

Anna looked up at him without answering, but she thought to herself that there should have been one more special person here to help her celebrate this milestone. Several people had mentioned to her the fact that wasn't it great that her whole family was here today. She would then think to herself that, no, not quite her *whole* family, and then she would look pensively off into the distance.

The hours of the open house came to a close and the crowd slowly started to disperse. After the last one left, Anna was taken home before the others so she could rest. The wicker basket of cards was brought into the house and set beside her on the living room sofa.

"My," she exclaimed, "there must be hundreds of cards there. How will I get through all of them?"

"You don't have to do it all in one day, Grams," said Dan. "In fact, you can take the next whole month to open them if you want to. There's no hurry. Open them slowly and enjoy them."

"Do you want to lie down on the sofa there for awhile, Grandma, before the gang all gets back?" asked Stan.

"Perhaps I will just do that," Anna said, and she proceeded to lie down and Stan covered her with the afghan. He left the room so it would be quiet for her.

Ah, what a wonderful day this has been, thought Anna, but so very tiring. She soon drifted off to sleep.

About a half hour later, the rest of the family began to return home after cleaning up things at the hall. Anna awoke and sat up to receive the family members as they drifted into the living room.

"Grandma," said Barb, "I have counted all the names in the guest book and just take a guess at how many people came to your party today."

"Oh, I suppose about 200, or so," guessed Anna.

"You're not even close," said Barb. "There were 372 people who signed the book!"

"Oh, my, oh, my," said Anna, shaking her head back and forth. "Why would so many people want to come to my birthday party, anyway?" Tears starting to form in her eyes.

"Because so many people love and admire you, Anna," said Betty as she came into the room and went to sit next to her mother-in-law. "We almost ran out of cake, too, but it might have something to do with the fact that there were some little girls and some not- so- little boys who kept coming back for seconds and thirds!" she said, laughing and looked pointedly at Stan and Dan.

"Well, it was so good," said Stan in defense, not looking one bit ashamed.

Everyone was by now in the room, each one getting himself comfortable by kicking off shoes or loosening ties or belts. Anna looked at them all and was so glad that they all enjoyed being together and got along so well with each other. Not like some families she knew.

It might be a long time before everyone could be together again, Anna thought. Even at Christmas time sometimes one or two were missing. Perhaps the next occasion would be her funeral. She dismissed this thought immediately. It wasn't as if she feared dying but she wasn't quite ready yet, God willing. She knew she had something left to do. Perhaps now would be the time, when everyone was here, gathered around her.

The perfect moment slipped away when little Jana began to fuss and Pat took her upstairs and Betty and Margaret went to the kitchen to put leftover food away. Barb and Dan announced that they better get ready to leave for home soon. Barb was feeling very tired and it was a three hour trip.

Frank suggested that Anna move to the table and he would help her open up some of her birthday cards. Margaret came to help and the trio worked at it for some time before Betty suggested they come into the kitchen for a bite to eat before everyone else left.

As they sat around the kitchen table, Kari asked her grandma what part of the day she enjoyed best.

"I enjoyed hearing so many people say what a nice-looking family I had and of course I agreed with them and I said that I was a very lucky old lady."

The family members laughed at this and Stan told her that the reason that her family was so good looking was because she was such a beauty.

"That's not true and you know it," she said, "but I think beauty comes from within and I hope that I am beautiful inside. That is the important thing."

Pat went to get the girls' things packed up so that they, too, could be on their way. Anna said that she thought she'd go to her room for awhile.

Kari found her there a little later, sitting in her rocker by the window with her Bible in her hands. "I have to leave now, too, Grandma," she said, "but I have to talk to you about something first." She sat down on the bed and started in on the subject that had been brewing in her mind for the last two days.

"Grandma, for my English class at school I need to write a paper and one of the suggested subjects was family history. So," she took a deep breath and continued, "I've decided I am going to write your story and you will need to help me. What do you think of that idea, Grandma?"

"Well, what all do you have to know?" asked Anna.

"Everything," said Kari, "from the time you were born to the present. All ninety years of your life."

Anna was silent for awhile, apparently thinking over something in her mind. There was something that she had kept to herself all these years.

"Well, what do you think, Grandma?" Kari continued. "I'll come here and stay for a couple of weekends next month and we'll try and get all the facts written down. I'll bring my tape recorder, too, and you can just talk and I'll write it up later back at school."

She jumped up and said, "I have to get back to Ames now, Grandma. I have plans for tomorrow. I'm glad I could be here to celebrate this special day with you." She gave Anna a big hug. "Goodbye, Grandma. I'll see you in a few weeks then." She bounced out of the room, full of the energy and enthusiasm of youth.

She's just like I used to be, thought Anna, and I enjoy her so. It will be good to have her come and spend time here with me.

Anna leaned back in her rocker and closed her eyes. My life story, she thought. How can one's lifetime be summed up on a few pages of paper? All their feelings, their emotions, their joys and sorrows, their happiness and disappointments.   Rocking back and forth slowly, she allowed her mind to wander way back into the past, until finally she dozed off.

CHAPTER 2

Anna was born in 1886 in Norway, near the village of Nesbyen. Her parents were Arne and Ragnild Olson. Her family lived on a small farm in the scenic Hallingdal valley, a long, narrow valley with steep mountains on either side. Their farm was close to the river.

Anna remembered her childhood as being relatively happy. She was the youngest out of eight children born to her parents. Her family worked hard to make a living, and all the children were expected to pitch in and help. They raised cattle, sheep and goats and tried to grow a little grain in the small patches of soil available.

Anna loved the summers in Norway. The days were long and wild flowers grew everywhere. It was her job to gather kindling wood every day for the kitchen stove, but she usually gathered more flowers than wood. There were fresh flowers on the kitchen table almost every summer day in their house.

All the children had to help with the large garden her mother kept if they wanted to eat during the long winter months. Helping pick apples was another of Anna's specific chores. She loved any job that would take her out of the house, however.

Her very favorite thing was when she was allowed to go with her older sister, Sigrid, whose job it was to take their cattle up into the mountains to their saeter, or outfarm. The grass was so much better up there and so their milk produced the very finest butter and cheese. Sigrid would spend most of the summer up there in a little house and Anna would get to stay with her for a week or so now and then. Sigrid was ten years older than Anna but the two became very close during those times.

Anna dreaded the coming of winter. The days were short and the nights so long and cold. The bright spot in the middle of winter was the Christmas season, which they celebrated for over a week. Neighbors and relatives would stop by, morning, noon and night, and there were always such good treats which she and her sisters had helped their mother bake. She, as the youngest, was given the honor of carrying out the 'julenek', or sheaf of wheat, to the barn to leave as a special treat for the birds.

The family would bundle up on Christmas Day and travel the six miles to her grandparents' house, riding in two wagons. The horses wore sleigh bells on their harnesses and their tinkling sound was sweet and clear as the horses trotted along the snow-covered path. Her grandmother would always have the same menu for this special day: pork ribs, meatballs, mashed rutabaga, lutefisk, and for dessert, cloudberries and cream.

The wintertime also meant that the children had to go to school, which Anna actually loved very much. She wanted to learn and had an insatiable appetite for it. Her teachers were challenged to keep up with her desire to learn more than the textbooks provided. Anna and her sister Barbro and brother Erik had to walk two miles to the school building on the edge of the village.

Sometimes, if they were lucky, their father would take them in the wagon. Their older brothers Tollef, Tomas and Andres and sister Sigrid were now too old for school. Their sister, Kjersti, who was four years older than Anna, didn't go to school because she wasn't quite 'right in the head' everyone said. She was also rather unruly and quite a handful for Anna's mother.

Years of hard work and childbearing had taken a toll on Anna's mother. She was always exhausted and these last years she had become impatient and short tempered. She had very little time left for Anna as most of her energy was spent on caring for Kjersti and just doing the necessary work around the house. She no longer had time for work outside so those jobs were taken over by Sigrid and the older boys.

Anna always had the feeling that she had never been wanted by her mother. After Kjersti was born, Anna concluded that her mother most likely was not happy to find out that she was going to have another baby. Sigrid, the oldest daughter, seemed to sense this, also, so she took to mothering Anna more than the rest.

Their father, on the other hand, seemed to love Anna the most. Perhaps this was because he, too, sensed his wife's attitude toward Anna, or maybe it was simply because Anna was such an easy and lovable child. She was the 'apple of his eye' and the rest of the family knew it but didn't mind because Anna was the favorite to all of them.

Kjersti was a challenge for the whole family. The doctors said she was mildly retarded and probably uneducable. She also had behavior problems so everyone gave in to her demands, thus making her a very spoiled child. She was, however, a beautiful child, with dark, curly hair and deep blue eyes. Her father would stand over her sometimes when she was sleeping and just look and look at her. She looked so innocent and perfect that it made his heart almost break with grief. Anna was too young to understand, but her father's sadness was not only due to Kjersti's condition, but to the change in his wife over the last few years.

Economic conditions in Norway were not very good and "Amerika Fever" swept the land. Norwegians by the thousands had been leaving their country for America since the middle 1800's. Everyone seemed to know of someone who had gone in search of a better life. Letters from America were eagerly awaited and passed from family to family.

The year 1895 brought a big change to the Olson family. Tollef, the oldest son, had married two years earlier and would be taking over the farm. Tomas, now 22, was thinking seriously of going to America, as there seemed to be no future for him on the farm helping Tollef. His brother, Andres, who was 18, was considering it also. They knew of a family nearby who was planning to leave in the spring and the boys spent many a long, winter evening with them, discussing the venture.

Their father would hate to see them go, but he knew in his heart that if he was young again, he would be doing the same thing. Meanwhile, the doctor told Ragnild that her heart was bad and that she would have to take it easy. Mr. Olson decided that he would move his dwindling family into town and perhaps make life a little easier for his wife. Tollef would live on the farm and Erik, now 15, would stay and help him.That left the four girls, Sigrid, Barbro, Kjersti and Anna to move with their parents.

Tomas and Andres had made up their minds for sure that they were going to leave and their ship would be sailing in April. Tomas decided that he couldn't leave his sweetheart, Bergit, in Norway so they would marry a few days before the ship was scheduled to sail. Everyone was busy packing and making plans for their moves. There were trunks to be made for the overseas travelers and provisions to be gathered together.

Sigrid had been harboring thoughts that she, too, might want to go but never mentioned this to anyone until a friend of hers said that her family had decided to go and would be leaving on the same ship as the Olson brothers. Sigrid was the adventurous type and was feeling the excitement of beginning a new life in a new land.

The evening that she broke the news to her family was one that Anna remembered vividly. Her father looked surprised and sad, but her mother's reaction was quite different. She looked alarmed and betrayed. She knew she was losing her best helper. "Is my whole family leaving me to go to some far-off, God-forsaken land?" she wailed. "Who will help me with all the work?"

Anna's father tried to calm and console her. "You will have plenty help, my dear. Anna and Barbro will help you, and anyway, things will be easier in town. I promise you."

Anna's reaction over the next few weeks was one of grief, as if a loved one had died. She was feeling Sigrid's absence before she even left. Sigrid tried to comfort Anna and ease her pain. "How will I get along without you?" Anna cried in near desperation.

"Oh, Anna," Sigrid said soothingly, "I'm sorry to leave you and I will miss you very much, but I just have to get away, can't you see? I'm 19 years old now and I feel if I don't go now with the rest of them, I may never go. Then I'll end up being stuck here and getting married and having babies and work, work, work."

Sigrid took her little sister in her arms and stroked her hair. "I'll write to you real often and maybe when you get older you can come, too." This seemed to calm Anna and, young as she was, she now seemed to understand what was driving Sigrid to leave her family and country.

Tomas and Bergit's wedding was a small affair at the home of Bergit's parents in Nesbyen. There was a dinner served afterwards for those attending. Tomas' Uncle Olaf took out his small accordion and there was music and dancing. Everyone seemed to know that this was the last time that everyone would all be together. Nobody wanted to see the good time end so it went on til late that night. Finally the guests left and the newly married couple retired to Uncle Olaf's little house which he said they could use for the next few days. He went to stay with his sister.

A flurry of activity took place those last few days before her brothers and sister were going to be leaving. There was food to get ready---dried meats, flatbread, dried fruits, smoked herring, butter and cheeses, coffee and other things that would keep during the long voyage. New trunks were packed with the food, clothing, bedding, some small tools, books, a little brandy, and many other things that might be needed.

At last the day of departure came. The little group numbered 13. Besides Tomas and Bergit, Andres and Sigrid, there was the Ruud family, whose two oldest boys were friends of Tomas and Andres, and Sigrid's friend, Magda Amundson and her parents and two brothers. The whole community seemed to have turned out to bid them farewell. Pastor Smedstad led them all in prayer. He read from Psalms 121: "I lift mine eyes unto the hills. From whence cometh my help? My help comes from the Lord...." Little did Anna know that this passage would be of great importance to her many times in her life. There was both excitement and sadness in the air as goodbyes were said and handshakes were exchanged all around.

The group left in three wagons which would take them to the Halling River a short distance away from Nesbyen. There they would board a small boat which would take them down river to Drammen. Here they would have to wait a day or two for their boat, the "Angelo," which would take them to America. And so it was that on April 30, 1895, this little band of Hallings left their home and families to seek a better life in a promised land which was called America.

Anna, with typical child-like impatience, started expecting a letter from Sigrid within a week's time. She wanted her father to go to the store every day to check the postal box. He tried to explain to her that the trip across the big ocean would take many weeks and then it would take many weeks for the first letter to arrive back in Norway. Finally, as day after day and week after week went by without a sign of a letter, she stopped talking about it.

Her family's move into town was a long process. First the little house that they were to move into had to have some repairs. Her father and Tollef and her Uncle Olaf had to fix the windows and the roof. All the rooms then needed a good cleaning. Anna helped her mother and Barbro sweep, wash and scrub.

Finally their furniture was loaded on the wagon and the final move was made.

Anna claimed a little alcove as her very own room. Barbro shared a room with Kjersti, and Erik stayed on the farm with Tollef and his wife. Within days they were all settled and cozy in their new surroundings.

Anna loved living in town. Every day she would skip down the street and visit everybody and stop into all the shops and talk with the shopkeepers. Everyone got to know Arne Olson's youngest daughter if they didn't know her before.

She especially liked going into old Mr. Leikvold's store because he would often give her a piece of licorice. She soon began to feel guilty getting so much free candy so she would bring some home to Kjersti every other time.

After Sigrid left, Anna found herself taking over the role of "mothering" Kjersti. This was not an easy job as Kjersti was a big girl for her 13 years and was very willful and stubborn. Anna tried to teach her sister some basic things that Anna thought that she could do for herself if she really wanted to. Previously, most everything had been done for her because nobody had had the time or patience to teach her.

One warm summer day Anna took Kjersti down by the river. They sat along the bank tossing small stones into the water. Kjersti started throwing them at Anna and Anna got angry and tried to stop her. They were both standing up and Kjersti grabbed Anna by the shoulders and was quite plainly trying to throw her sister into the water! Anna lost her balance and as she felt herself heading for the water, she grabbed Kjersti's skirt and both girls tumbled into the river's edge. It was not deep but Kjersti began screaming hysterically. For a fleeting moment, Anna felt like leaving her sister to get herself out and maybe that would teach her a lesson, but Kjersti looked so frightened that Anna helped her out. It was not easy since it was slippery and Kjersti was so heavy when she was sopping wet.

Eventually they both made it up the bank and headed for home about a half mile away. Their mother was very upset when she saw them come into the house dripping wet. She made them change their clothes immediately and sent them back outside where they sat in the sunshine to warm up. Anna was very peeved with her sister and would not talk to her or even look at her. They sat there without talking for quite sometime. At last Kjersti put her arm around Anna and looked her full in the face. Anna could see that Kjersti had tears in her eyes. Anna's heart softened as she realized that her sister was trying to say she was sorry but didn't know how. She embraced Kjersti and the two girls sat like that for a long time, holding onto each other and rocking back and forth.

This incident seemed to be a turning point in the girls' relationship. Kjersti tried harder to do the things that Anna attempted to teach her and Anna was more patient and understanding with her. Kjersti learned many things that long summer and, in learning to do things for herself, she became more calm and manageable. Perhaps her behavior up to this point was partly due to frustration with herself. She knew that she was different from everyone else.

The long-awaited letter finally arrived about the middle of June. Papa brought it home from the post office and carried it into the house like it was an important document. The family gathered around as he opened it and began reading it aloud. It was post-marked May 25 and mailed from New York. Sigrid wrote the following:

Dearest family,

It took us three long weeks but we finally arrived here on the 18th. The voyage went pretty well. We were a little seasick about three times. The winds were favorable with no major storms. We were almost running out of food but with close rationing the last week we made it just fine. We all shared what we had with each other.

Magda's mother was not too well for most of the trip but is feeling much better now. One old man died on the way over and one baby was born. Her birth came way too early and she died also. That was really sad as we had come to know this young mother quite well. Both the man and the baby were buried at sea.

When we sailed into New York Harbor we had to all get off the boat and go into a big building on an island where we were examined by the immigration inspector and had to fill out forms and finally got on a small boat and taken to the mainland. We passed another small island where we saw the big statue of the lady holding the torch, welcoming people to America. You remember reading about that, don't you, Papa?

How exciting to finally reach American soil! Mr. Ruud's brother met us at the pier and helped us get loaded up onto some wagons and led us to a hotel where we could stay for a few days until we found some-place to live. Many other immigrants were also staying there, from many different countries of the world! There were some from Ireland, Italy, Germany and several other places.

I have never seen so much hustle and bustle in any city as on the streets of New York. Magda and I ventured out several times to have a look around but Mrs. Amundson wouldn't leave her hotel room. She was scared, I think. Mr. Amundson and his brother went looking for housing for us. After two days they found a walk-up flat for the Amundsons and myself. The Ruuds and Tomas and Andres found a place nearby. Very small, but they will keep looking for something else. We will stay in our place for awhile. It is not too bad. It has two bedrooms, one for Magda and me and one for her parents. The boys will sleep on the floor and sofa for awhile.

We are getting by and are all looking for work. I will write you next week again when I have more news.

My love to all and pass this letter around to all who may be interested.

Your loving daughter and sister,
Sigrid

This letter was read and reread many times in the next couple days. It was then brought over to Bergit's parent's home. They had received one from Bergit the same day and so that letter was brought home and read to the family over and over again. Then the two letters were passed around the community to anyone interested. And that's how it would go until another letter came from someone who had left for America.

Back at the farm, Erik was now taking the cows up to the saeter for Tollef and staying there. Anna's father knew how much she missed this so one day he told her to pack up some things and he would drive her up there in the wagon and she could stay a few days.

How excited she was! She chattered all the way up and Erik actually seemed pleased to see her. "It gets lonesome after awhile with just the cattle for company," he told her.

Anna ran and played and hugged almost every cow and picked flowers. She found some wild strawberries which they ate for their evening meal, along with fresh bread that her mother had sent, and some cheeses.

After they ate Anna said, "Papa, can you stay the night with us?"

"No, my little Anna, I best be getting back to your mother now." He took his leave and they watched as he wound his way back down the mountain. They could see two different villages and many little farms scattered below.

"I like it up here because I can see everything!" Anna exclaimed to Erik. "But I wish I could also see beyond the mountains. I want to know what's on the other side of them."

Anna had not been beyond the mountains of her little world more than twice in her short life. Once was on a trip to Drammen to visit relatives and the other time was when she was allowed to go with her father and brothers to Christiania, the capital. This was the most exciting thing that had ever happened to her. She was 7 years old and it happened to be at the time of the Syttende Mai celebration. She had never seen it celebrated in such a big way and would never forget it. There was a parade and people waving little Norwegian flags everywhere. Everything about the city was so big and exciting to a young child. When she returned home, she couldn't stop talking about it.

Anna and her brother passed the next few days watching the cattle and doing the milking twice a day. The milk wagon came up every morning to take their milk down to the village.

One afternoon, a few days later, Anna saw a wagon coming up the path toward them. She could see that it was her father and he had someone with him. "Could it be Mama?" she wondered aloud. When they got closer, she could see that it was Kjersti. She ran to them and helped her sister down from the wagon.

She couldn't recall that Kjersti had ever been up here before. She led her around and showed her everything. They spread a blanket on the ground and had a meal with food that Mama had made and sent along. Kjersti seemed to enjoy the outing but soon it was time to be heading back down the mountain.

They said goodbye to Erik and the three or them got into the wagon.
They rode in silence for awhile, taking in the wonderful view and thinking their own thoughts. Of course, no one knew what Kjersti was thinking, but Papa was thinking about how much he loved this valley and would never leave now. Anna was thinking how much she loved this same valley but she might want to leave someday and see what's out there in the big, wide world.

A second letter from Sigrid arrived about two weeks after the first. This one read as follows:

My dearest family,

I have not had time to write before this, but today is Sunday so I have time to catch my breath! Since my last letter there have been many changes. First of all, Tomas, Bergit and Andres decided to head west along with the Ruuds. They are planning to go to Wisconsin. They know several families from back home who have settled there.   They did not like the big city very much! We were sad to see them go.

Magda and I love the city and we both have found employment at the same place. It is a pattern factory. Patterns are made for women's and children's clothes and we help assemble them.   We work 5 1/2 days a week. Our wages are not very good but it is a start.

Mr. Amundson is working with a man who is a carpenter. He is from back home, near the Valdres area. It was strange how Mr. Amundson got the job. He had gone down to the street market to buy some fish and was asking the man who was selling the fish if he knew of a carpenter in the area who would be looking for help. Standing next to him was the man who ended up hiring him!

Leif has found work with a boot maker but Olaus is still looking.
We are getting along in our cramped little quarters for now. I will write more later. I hope all is well with my dear family. Give this letter to Tollef and Margit. I hope she is feeling well by now.

Your loving daughter and sister,
Sigrid

That afternoon Anna and Kjersti rode with their father out to the farm to show the letter to Tollef and Margit. They were excited to hear news, as was everyone else, from those adventurous souls who had left this valley to find a new life elsewhere.

Margit was expecting their first baby and was getting very big. She had been feeling very poorly for quite some time but she now seemed to be doing fine. She was a happy, out-going person and she and Sigrid had become close friends after her marriage to Tollef. She missed Sigrid very much. The days got very lonely sometimes but, with the coming of a baby, she would soon be kept busy enough! She said she would sit right down and write a letter back to Sigrid.

"I'm sure Sigrid misses us all very much," she said, "and maybe she'll come back here someday. I can't imagine just picking up and leaving one's family and homeland."

I can, thought Anna, but she didn't say anything. Margit suggested they pick some apples to take home with them. Anna and Kjersti ran outside with a basket and started picking. By the time they were ready to go home, they had also picked wild strawberries and flowers by the armload. Mama would be pleased, thought Anna. She misses her flowers and fruit trees. Margit hugged them goodbye and insisted that they come back more often to keep her company.

Fall seemed to come all of a sudden to the valley. The trees were sporting their autumn colors and there was a chill in the air in the evenings. And of course the days were growing shorter. But Anna loved this time of year because it also meant that she was back at school. The village school was a two- room building with two teachers and this year there were 27 students in all.

Anna liked her teacher, a Mr. Narveson. He was very tall and lanky and rather funny looking, but he seemed to understand Anna's quest for knowledge and he always assigned her extra work to keep her busy and interested. She thrived on this. He also gave her books to take home and read in the evenings. Sometimes she would finish a book a night until Mama put a stop to it.

"You can't read all night and expect to do well in school during the day, Anna," she scolded.

One Sunday morning in mid-October, Tollef came to their house to tell them the news. Their baby, a boy, had come during the night. He was very small but seemed to be doing all right. Margit was weak but very happy. He had to hurry right back home to her, he said.

Later that afternoon, the family was getting ready to take a drive out to the farm to see the new arrival when Anna heard someone come galloping up in front of their house. She looked out her little window and saw Tollef running up to the door. She ran downstairs to hear him tell Mama that the little baby boy had died earlier in the afternoon. He was sobbing so that it was hard to understand him. He said that Margit was taking it very hard and that maybe the family should come out to see her.

Tollef left immediately and the family got ready to follow in the wagon. Anna was silent and shivering all the way to the farm. She didn't know what to expect or what to say to Margit.

Margit was lying in bed when they came in and she started crying afresh when she told them about the precious little baby who had lived such a short time. The baby was lying in a small wood box that Tollef had quickly made for the little body. He had dressed him in a gown and cap that Margit had made. Anna forced herself to look down into the box. The baby looked like a tiny, wax doll, she thought. This was the first time she had seen someone dead. She stared at the body, transfixed, until her father came beside her and led her away, into the kitchen to help her mother make a meal for Margit.

Margit didn't want to eat; she was too distraught. Tollef did not know how to console her and could not find relief from his own grief. He finally went out to the barn to tend to the horses. Anna's mother went into the bedroom with a bowl of porridge and closed the door. After about a half hour the door opened, Anna's mother came out carrying an empty bowl and Margit was composed and resting comfortably.

Anna looked up at her mother as if to ask, " what did you say to her?" but her mother had a look about her that stopped her from asking. She never could talk to her mother. How she longed for a closer relationship with her.

When Tollef returned to the house, the family left. On the ride home, Anna saw her mother wiping a tear from her eye and her father put his arm around his wife to comfort her. Anna couldn't understand why an innocent baby had to die; he hadn't done anything wrong.

The next afternoon, the family gathered around the grave site as the tiny box was put into the ground. Margit was not able to be there, but her parents and brothers and sisters were all there, along with the Olson family. Kjersti could not understand what was going on as she watched everyone sobbing as the little box was lowered into the earth. Anna could not remember a time when she had felt more wretched. This was worse even than having to say goodbye to Sigrid and her brothers. This was so final. And all this heart-wrenching sadness for a little being that she had never even held or seen alive!

Upon returning home, nobody talked about the loss of the baby, but instead threw themselves into their work. Anna read the night away and was glad to return to school the next morning.

Winter came and so did another letter from America. In fact, two letters came, one from Bergit and Tomas and one from Sigrid. Bergit's letter was written from Wisconsin where they were now living:

Dear family,

We are now living in Rock Prairie. It is a little settlement of mostly folk from back home. We are living in a little cabin on a farm and Tomas is helping the farmer who owns it. We like the people here and of course, we all speak the same language. Not like in New York! We did not like it there. We can't understand why Sigrid wants to stay there. Maybe she will join us here later.

I'm sure Andres is not very good at writing letters so I will tell you about him, too. He is working on another farm several miles from here for a farmer who owns two farms. He is kept very busy and makes pretty good wages. Better than Tomas but we can't complain too much. We see him about every other Sunday. We share our letters with him from you all back home and he has shown us some of his. With winter coming he says that he may have to go into town to find some work. The farmer that Tomas works for says that he has enough work to keep Tomas busy all winter if he can stay here. I guess he likes him and thinks he is a good, strong worker.

I help Mrs. Grinde, that's the farmer's wife, with her big garden and also to keep her house up. She is getting old and her children have all moved away from here. She is nice to work for and she appreciates the help.

We miss you all very much. Tomas is taking a nap. He is so tired on Sundays that he sleeps all afternoon! Share this letter with my family and I will write again when I get time. We enjoy getting letters from you. Anna, you are getting to be quite the little letter writer. You tell us more than anybody else! We are glad that you are doing so well in school. We felt bad to hear about Tollef and Margit's baby. I will write to them soon.

Love, your children,
Tomas and Bergit

After reading that letter several times, they then turned to Sigrid's letter. It was postmarked December 1, 1895, and read as follows:

My dearest family,

Thank you for your last letter. We are so excited when we get a letter from back home. We were so sorry to hear of Tollef and Margit's baby. We hear from Bergit and Tomas about every month or so, but not much from Andres, except through Bergit.

We are moving to a bigger place next week. It is a two-story brick row house. It has three bedrooms and a kitchen and front room. Mrs.

Amundson is so happy about it. She plans to take in washing and ironing then to make a little money. The house is in a pleasant little neighborhood. It will be a little closer for Magda and I to go to work but farther for Mr. Amundson and the boys. Olaus has found work now down at the docks but he doesn't like it much. He is keeping his eye out for something else.

We took part in our first American Thanksgiving last week. We all were invited over to Mr. Amundson's brother's home. It's just him and his wife now as their children are all grown and have moved away, so his wife, her name is Caren, thought it was fun to fix a special meal for a big family again. And did we eat! It was a real feast. We had turkey which I had only tasted once before, and many other good things. Magda and her mother and I made some things, too, and brought along. We had a very pleasant day. The weather was fine and it was good to all have a day off work.

Anna, I miss you very much and keep sending those very nice letters. Barbro, write and tell me more about your plans. I will write you more when we get moved.

Your loving daughter and sister,
Sigrid

When Anna went up to her bed that night, she lay awake a long time thinking about Sigrid and her brothers. She missed them and now Barbro was thinking of leaving home and going to Drammen to find work. It would just be Anna and Kjersti left at home then. How her large family had shrunk!

Since moving to town, Mr. Olson had been working at the blacksmith shop for old Mr. Vigen who had recently taken ill and and not been back to the shop for a long time and probably would never be able to work again.   He wanted Mr. Olson to take over the business so that kept Anna's father very busy. He would have to look for help, come spring.

Anna would stop by there every day after school. It was a good place to warm up when it was cold outside. If a letter had come from America that day, Anna's father would not open it until Anna got there and then they would sit by the stove and read it together. This day a letter had come for Barbro from their relatives in Drammen.

"Can we open it, Papa?" asked Anna.

"Oh, no, Anna, we can't open someone else's mail. Here, you can carry it home and let Barbro open it for herself."

She skipped home and ran to Barbro with the letter. Her sister opened it quickly and read it to herself first and then shared it with her mother and little sister.

"They say here that I can come and stay with them while I look for a job there!" 'They' were Mrs. Olson's cousin and family, the Pederson's, who lived in Drammen. Mr. Pederson had a good job and they had a nice, big house so they had plenty of room for kinfolk. Barbro danced around excitedly while Anna and her mother looked on in despair.

"Another one leaving home," Anna's mother said quietly, shaking her head.

When Mr. Olson came home in the evening, they all crowded around him while he read the letter aloud. He looked at Barbro and saw how excited she was. He couldn't very well deny her this chance. After all, she was 17 now and there was nothing here for her except to stay at home and wait to marry somebody. He was silent for awhile and everyone held their breath to see what he would say. Anna hoped that he would tell her that she couldn't go, that she had to stay here and help Mama.

Finally he said, "Well then, Barbro, when do you plan to leave us?" She smiled and looked relieved.

"I thought right after Christmas, or maybe early spring," she answered. "What do you think, Papa?"

"We'll think on that for awhile, Barbro. Perhaps it would be better to wait for the snows to melt before you go."

Supper that evening was a quiet one. Anna went to her room early and read a book til she finally fell asleep. It was hard for Barbro to fall asleep, too, as she couldn't stop thinking about the adventure before her.

Christmas that year was a quiet affair. They were all lonesome for Sigrid and the boys. They received letters and gifts from all of them. Sigrid wrote that they liked their new house and how nice it was that the Amundsons treated her like one of the family, and how she missed her own, dear family back home, especially at Christmas time. She said that she and Magda were taking English lessons from a neighbor two nights a week for twenty-five cents a lesson. It was worth it, she said, because she and Magda decided they didn't want to sound like such "newcomers" and wanted to speak good English and get better jobs uptown.

The family went out to Tollef and Margit's on Christmas Day and tried to make a festive time of it. Margit was trying hard to put on a happy face and had cooked and baked several family favorites. Uncle Olaf was there with his accordion so they had music in the evening. Margit suggested that they write a letter to Sigrid and the others and they all signed their names.

When they left for home the moon was shining brightly on the new-fallen snow. It was a beautiful night and Barbro started them all singing some favorite Christmas songs. The next few days were busy with friends and family dropping by and so it was that Christmas of 1895 ended on a happy note after all.

CHAPTER 3

Anna's school years sped by. She and her father became closer than ever. Every evening after supper they would have lively discussions about things that were happening near and afar. Tomas, who was now living in Minnesota, would send his father the Decorah Posten, a weekly Norwegian-language newspaper. Anna and her father would devour every word of news from it and then pass it on to Tollef and Margit.

Anna helped her mother with all the household chores. She had also learned to sew clothes for herself and had turned out some very nice dresses. Sigrid would send her patterns and also Barbro would keep her posted on the newest fashions for women. Barbro worked in a dress shop in Drammen and was very happy there. She tried to come home about twice a year to see her family.

Tollef and Margit had a fine, healthy son a year after their first one died and, three years later they had another boy. There was much news from America. Sigrid had married Louis Anderson in 1898 and they had just had a daughter named Annie. Sigrid told Anna that she just had to have a little "Annie" to take care of again. Tomas and Bergit were living in Minnesota in a town named Mankato and he was working for a carpenter and liked it very much. They had just had their first child, a boy whom they named Arne after his grandfather. Tollef and Margit's first boy was also named Arne. Andres, who now went by the name of Andrew because it was more American, had moved to Iowa and was working on a farm there. He wasn't married yet.

Barbro was getting married to a man named Peder Haaken and she wanted the family to travel down to Drammen for the wedding. It would be in the Pederson's home. The women packed their "bunads", the dress worn for all special occasions. For the women of the Halling region, these were long, black wool jumpers with rows of colorful embroidery along the bottom and across the bodice. A long-sleeved white blouse was worn underneath.

The wedding was in June so the weather was very nice. Barbro and Peder seemed very happy and well suited to one another. Peder was a professor and Barbro planned to work for awhile longer at the dress shop because she loved it so much and they could use the money to buy a house.

Anna's mother stood the trip pretty well and Kjersti was on her best behavior so the trip was great fun for everyone. They stayed about a week at the Pedersons'. Papa thought it was about time to get back to the blacksmith shop, even though he had a very reliable man working for him now. Anna was thinking to herself that one day she would like to come back here and stay.

When Anna was 15, she was confirmed in the little church in Nesbyen with 12 other young people. This was a milestone in a young person's life as well as a religious rite. Anna had sewn herself a new bunad and her mother had spent hours doing fancy embroidery work on the bodice.

Anna wanted to go on to more school but she would have to go away to do so. There was a higher school in Hŏnefoss which Papa was willing to let her attend. She had been hoping that he would let her go to Drammen and stay with Barbro but he thought she was too young to go away to the big city. Mama didn't think it was necessary for her to go at all. She thought Anna had had enough school for a girl.

Papa understood her longing for more education but he knew he would miss her very much when she was gone.

That summer there was more interesting news from America. Bergit had just had a baby girl and they named her Hannah, and Sigrid was expecting a baby very soon. Barbro had had a baby girl shortly before this and Anna thought to herself that the babies were sure coming fast, one after another!

In the fall, Papa drove Anna to Hŏnefoss where she boarded with a family that they knew, the Larsons. It was a fairly big school and Anna had some fine teachers. Papa would come and get her once a month on a Friday and bring her back on Sunday night. By the end of the year she had decided that she would like to become a teacher. There weren't many female teachers at that time but Anna knew that was what she wanted to do. She had to convince her parents of this, however.

On the wagon trips between Hŏnefoss and home, she and Papa had long discussions about the subject. Mama felt that she should just stay home and help her until she got married someday. That is exactly what Anna did not want to do and she told her Papa that.

"Anna," he said, "you are so much like me when I was young. I wanted to travel and learn and go beyond these mountains, too."

"Why didn't you do it then, Papa?" she asked.

"Well, I was thinking of going to America when I was about 20 years old when some people were first starting to leave here."

When he didn't explain further, Anna asked, "What happened then? Why didn't you go?"

"I met your mother and we wanted to get married and she didn't want to go away from here, so we stayed and I started helping my father on the farm."

Anna was silent for awhile before asking, "Did you ever regret not going and doing what you wanted to do, Papa?"

"I married your mother. That's what I wanted to do," he answered with a finality that stopped further questioning.

When Anna finished the year at Hönefoss, it was decided that she should remain at home for a year and then see if she still wanted to go off to more school to become a teacher. Anna didn't know if she could stand to wait a whole year here at home. She wanted to go to Drammen and stay with Barbro and go to the school there. Her parents said, "Wait till you are a little older."

Anna decided to make the most of that year. She made herself some new "grown up" clothes appropriate for the city. She read books and wrote letters to her brothers and sisters. Andrew wrote back that he was planning to get married to a girl named Alice Parkins. Her father owned the farm that Andrew worked on. She was an only child and Mr. Parkins said that Andrew could take over the farm sometime in the future.

Sigrid wrote, encouraging Anna to go to Drammen and study to be a teacher. She said she hoped Anna would come to America someday. She also told about little "Annie" and how cute she was and how she adored her new little brother Arthur. Sigrid said that she was very happy with her life in America. Her husband had a good job working on construction, mostly of bridges. The pay was quite good so they had bought a little house in Brooklyn.

"I wish the whole family could come for a visit," she said.

Anna would go out to the farm and help Margit a couple days a week. She was kept busy with two small boys and so much work to do and she was expecting another baby so she was tired all the time. Anna loved going out there because Margit was such a fun person to be around. Erik was still living with them. He had a girlfriend now so they all teased him about getting married.

After Christmas, time seemed to go slow for Anna, but her former teacher, Mr. Narveson, lined up some tutoring jobs for her with some of his young students. Anna enjoyed this very much and was more convinced than ever that she should become a teacher.

Margit had her baby in the spring, a little girl, and they named her Signe after Margit's mother. Anna stayed out on the farm for almost a month. The day she returned to town, there had come a letter from Barbro asking if she could come earlier than planned as she was not feeling well and needed help with little Ragna. Anna became very excited with this prospect and her parents agreed that she could go early.

She spent the next week gathering up all the things she would need for the next school year and on a beautiful June morning they set out for Drammen. Mama and Kjersti accompanied Anna and Papa.

They wanted to go along to see Barbro and her family. Upon arriving at Barbro and Peder's, they soon learned the reason why Barbro was not feeling well. She was expecting another baby! Mama and Anna made her rest while they caught up with the neglected housework and did all the cooking. After a week Barbro was feeling better and Anna's parents and Kjersti left for home.

Anna and Barbro had such a good time that summer. Shortly before her

16th birthday, Anna enrolled in her new school. There were only three other girls but she didn't mind that. She did well in her studies and could keep up with all the boys.

In early November, Barbro's baby was born. It was a tough delivery but another dear little girl joined their family. They named her Annetta and she was a good and happy baby.

Papa came to get Anna in December for the Christmas break. She enjoyed being home and seeing all the family again and they had a joyous Christmas with Tollef and Margit's little ones. She was glad, however, to return to Drammen and her school.

They received one or two letters each month from America. Sigrid and Louis had sold their house and bought a little bit larger one as their family was getting bigger with the addition of baby Sylvia just before New Year's. She said they had heard from Andrew and his new wife Alice several times. They seemed to be getting along all right on the farm and they had a baby boy named Alfred. Tomas and Bergit were still in Minnesota and little Arne and Hannah were doing well.

Anna was finding it hard to remember Sigrid and her two brothers. It had been almost 8 years ago that they had left Norway. She wondered if she would ever see them again.

That summer she went home to see her family and help out for a couple of months. Mama's health seemed to be in a better state and Papa was kept busy in the blacksmith shop. The man he had hired was a young widower with two small children. His name was Anton Simmons and he lived in a tiny cottage near the shop. His older sister who had never married came over to help take care of the children in the daytime and do the cooking. Anna would see the children running around by the shop when she stopped by and they looked like a couple of "ragamuffins." They would stop and stare at her but would never talk to her. Papa said that he thought they needed a mother and told Anton that he should remarry. Anton would just shake his head sorrowfully at this suggestion.

In the Fall, Anna returned to Drammen and her last year of school. By spring she had to start looking for a teaching position. Papa wrote to tell her of several openings that he had heard of, one in Gol, which was close to Nesbyen, and another in Mjöndalen, which was not far from Drammen.

Within a month, she had heard from the school in Mjöndalen and they had already filled the position. She finally received word from Gol that they would consider her but would like to see her first. She wrote back that she would be coming home as soon as school was out and that she could come to Gol and meet with them.

She packed up all her belongings and reluctantly left Drammen and went home to Nesbyen. Papa drove her to Gol the following week. She was interviewed and shown around the little one-room school. They said they would let her know soon. She went home to wait. Meanwhile a letter had come to her from Sigrid:

Brooklyn, New York
June 10, 1904

Dearest sister,

We are having a most beautiful spring here this year. The children have a nice little backyard to play in and they want to be out there all the time. I don't get much else done but to watch them! They are so healthy and rosy and are such a joy to us.

Louis finished the job he was working on. I think I told you he was helping build a subway system in the city and that has been completed now. He is back to building bridges again. They are always needing a new bridge!

What are you planning to do now that you are done with school? Will you find a job there someplace? I was thinking that maybe you would like to come to America and stay with us and get a job here. What do you think of that idea, little sister? We would love to have you and I long so to see you. At least come for a visit. I know it costs plenty of money but perhaps we could send you the fare. We are doing well here.

I suppose you have heard that Bergit and Tomas are going to have another baby soon. It would be fun to take a trip out to Minnesota to see them and also to Iowa to see Andrew but that is just too hard with the children. Maybe someday we will all get to see each other again.

You can tell that I am lonesome today with all my talk about family! I am sitting outside on the steps writing while I watch my dear children and wish so that you could see them.

Your sister, Sigrid

Anna waited all through the month of June and still no letter from the school at Gol. When July came and went, she was really starting to wonder what she should do. Maybe they had hired someone else and had forgotten to inform her. She wrote them a letter asking about the position and told them she needed to know very soon.

Finally, in the second week of August there came a letter from Gol. She hardly dared to open it. She waited til she got home and she went straight up to her room. She held her breath as she opened it and started to read. They said that they were sorry to have made her wait so long but that the job was hers. She got the job!

She ran down to tell Mama and then ran out the door and over to the blacksmith shop. "I got the job, Papa!" she cried. "I got the job in Gol."

Papa put down the bellows and came to her and swung her around. He was happy for her. "Did you hear that, Anton? Little Annie here is going to be the teacher over in Gol." Anton looked up from his work but only mumbled something that sounded like a reluctant congratulation.

He just thinks that women shouldn't be teachers, Anna thought to herself. Well, Papa is proud of me, anyway.

And proud he was. He took Anna outside and down the street and told everyone they met about her new job. Mama's reaction was somewhat like Anna expected. At the supper table that evening, her mother did not have much to say about the subject except to inquire about when she would be starting and where she would stay.

Papa said, "Anna and I will make a trip over to Gol tomorrow and look for a place for her to stay."

Early the next morning they set off in the wagon. They arrived before noon and began inquiring about lodging. The town was soon buzzing about the new teacher who was looking for a place to stay and it was a woman! She was told to check with old Mrs. Barstad at the edge of the village. Maybe she would take in a woman boarder.

They stopped first to eat their lunch which Mama had packed. They sat under a big chestnut tree. It was a warm day and they rested there awhile. Then they went knocking on Mrs. Barstad's door. She answered warily but let them in.

Yes, she said, she had a room available and arrangements were made for Anna to move in the beginning of September. The room was a nice size and had plenty of windows. This Anna liked. They thanked Mrs. Barstad and paid for the first month's rent before leaving.

The rest of the summer passed quickly for Anna. She spent some of the time out at the farm helping Margit with her gardening. The boys and little Signe were growing so fast. Signe followed Anna everywhere and hung on her skirts till Anna picked her up. She was so chubby and rosy and so lovable. Anna would miss her very much.

There came a letter from Tomas and Bergit and a picture of their whole family which now included a new baby girl named Sarah. They were so excited to have this picture that they took it around and showed everyone and then they placed it on the mantel and would look and look at it.

The letter which accompanied the picture said that they were all happy and healthy and they had moved into a larger house. Tomas was doing well in the carpenter trade. He worked for a man who had a really good business and they were busy all year long. They wished that somebody from home would come and visit them. They saw Andrew and Alice about once or twice a year. They would sure like to have Sigrid and family come for a visit but that was too big an undertaking, Sigrid had told them. They were very lonesome for family,

They asked if Anna was thinking of coming to America. When Papa read that, he said to Anna, "I hope you aren't thinking of leaving us too, Anna." She didn't answer him and couldn't meet his eyes.

Early in September, Papa was to drive her to Gol but he fell ill with the flu so Anton said that he would drive her over. Anna was not too happy with this arrangement but what could she say? So off they went, the wagon loaded with her boxes of clothing and books.

It was a beautiful, autumn day and the weather was very pleasant. Anton was not a very talkative man but Anna, with her steady chatter, finally got him to open up a little and he talked about his youth and about his wife's death and about his children. His wife had died of milk fever about a month after the birth of their second child. He had had a difficult life, growing up in a very poor, large family. He was glad to have his job at the blacksmith shop and liked working for Anna's father.

The trip went fast and soon they were in front of Mrs. Barstad's house. Anton unloaded her boxes and carried them up to her room. Mrs. Barstad asked him to stay and have a bite to eat with them, which he did, and then he said he must leave. Anna thanked him, they shook hands and he left.

Mrs. Barstad bustled around helping Anna get settled in her new surroundings. There were a couple of days until school started so Anna wanted to go over to the school and get things organized there. That afternoon she walked over, carrying a few of the books with her. The school room was not too clean so she went back to Mrs. Barstad's and asked her for some rags and a pail. Mrs. Barstad offered to come with her and help her a bit. She carried a broom and followed Anna back to the school. By the end of the afternoon the two had the room clean and in order. They returned home tired and hungry.

Anna was rather nervous the first day of school. She was told that she would have 19 pupils, ranging in age from 6 to 15. When they all arrived and found their seats, the room was filled to capacity. There were 21 children! They could not have squeezed in one more. This was going to be a real challenge, she thought to herself, all the while smiling at her young charges, trying to look confident. She knew that she wasn't much older than some of them and hoped that would not present a problem.

They were seated at tables and benches. She had two sweet 6-year olds, who seemed like they were scared stiff to be in school, three 7-year- olds who seemed to already be in love with her, and six 8- and 9- year olds who were looking at her in expectation. As for the remaining older children, they seemed to be saying that she would have to prove herself to them before she would have their respect.

Anna knew that this first day was really important to the relationship between teacher and students. She started by having each one stand and introduce themselves, beginning with the oldest and telling what their favorite subject was and why. She told them about herself and said that she hoped that they would have a great year, learning together.

That evening at the supper table, Anna was exhausted both emotionally and physically. Mrs. Barstad kept quizzing her about her day, but Anna was almost too tired to answer. She hoped that it would not be like this every day.

She excused herself and went to her room and lay down on her bed and fell asleep in a matter of minutes.

After a couple of weeks, Anna got used to the routine and was really enjoying her children. She only had one or two who were sometimes a problem. She had not had the time or the energy to write letters home or to America, so she took a Sunday afternoon to do just that.

Occasionally, Mrs. Barstad had other boarders for an evening or two so sometimes there were others at the supper table. One evening when she came down to supper there was a man already seated who rose when she entered the room and Mrs. Barstad introduced him as Mr. Ness. While eating, Anna learned that he had just come back from America! He had gone over there two years ago and lived in Wisconsin in the city of Milwaukee where he worked as a clerk in a store and liked it there very much. He had returned to get his wife and children who lived in Christiania and they would be returning with him next month. Now, though, he said, he was on his way up to Hemesdal to visit his aging parents for possibly the last time. Anna asked him all kinds of questions about America and they sat and talked for a long time after the meal was finished.

"Miss Olson," he said, "it sounds like you are interested in going there yourself someday."

"Perhaps I shall," she answered. "Perhaps I shall." With that she excused herself and said that she had work to do before tomorrow.

A letter came for her from Sigrid one day in early November. She ripped it open and began to read:

> Brooklyn, New York
> October 20, 1904

Dearest Anna,
    Today is your 18th birthday, dear little sister! How I long to see you. How do you like teaching? I hope it is going well for you. I heard from Mama and she said that you hadn't been home since school started and had not had time to write very often.

    We received the family picture from Tomas and Bergit and it was such a joy to see. It gave us the idea that we should have one taken, too, and so by Christmas time you shall have a picture of our little family.

    I still think, Anna, that you would love it here in America and you should think seriously about coming here. I know you think that you should not leave Papa and Mama as they would then have so little family left there, but you need to think about what would be good for you sometimes. You are the adventurous type and I don't think you would be happy until you have given it a try. You could always go back home if you did not like it.

You have not told me if you have a special fellow that you are sweet on and then, of course, that would be a different story. You would not want to leave him!

Andrew wrote and said that little Alfred had been very ill and they almost lost him but he is doing better now. Alice is expecting another baby early next year. Her father, Mr. Parkins, is very ill now, too, so Andrew is taking over the farm and has had to hire a man to help him. They did not have a very good crop this past summer. It was too dry.

I do not hear much from Barbro. She is not a very good letter writer. Margit isn't either; I suppose she is too busy, but I hear news of them from Mama.

I hear my little Sylvia crying so I have to close.

Your loving sister,
Sigrid

The days and weeks went by fast for Anna. School was going quite well and soon it was time for Christmas vacation. Papa said that he would be coming for her the Saturday before Christmas. She was ready and waiting by noon that day when she saw their wagon drive up in front of the house. But it was not Papa driving. It was Anton Simmons. Was Papa is sick again? she wondered.

When he came to the door Anna ran to open it. He told her that her father had asked him if he could go and get her. Her father said he had something else he had to do. Anna was disappointed but at least her father was all right. She invited Anton in to have a bite to eat with them before they started out.

After they finished eating, he loaded up Anna's things and off they went. Anna had been looking forward to having a nice, long talk with her father on the journey home. In her disappointment, she tended to be a little more quiet than usual. After several miles Anton noticed this. "I suppose you wish that your father had come for you," he said, "but he asked me to do it and I said I would be glad to."

"Oh, I'm sorry if I'm not being very sociable," she said, "but I guess I'm tired today. The children have been so excited this last week about Christmas that they have worn me out."

They rode in silence for quite sometime. He's probably thinking that teaching is not for women and if I am tired it is my own fault, Anna thought to herself. She started asking him questions about back home and about his children and she soon had him talking more openly.

It seemed like it took longer than usual to get home but finally she could see the edge of the village and she was much relieved. She thanked him after he had helped her carry her things in the house and then Mama offered him a cup of coffee so he stayed for awhile. She politely excused herself and went to her room.

After he left she came back down and then her Papa came in and they sat at the table and talked while he had some coffee. "What did you have to do today, Papa?" she asked. "I was wishing it had been you that came to get me."

Her father did not look at her when he answered, "Well, I just had some things to do in the shop, that's all." He rose from the table and said that he had to get back to work.

Anna helped Mama get supper started and they talked about Christmas plans. Mama had baked numerous things already and Kjersti had been helping her. Perhaps Kjersti had decided that if she was the only one left at home, maybe she better try to help Mama a little. She was very proud of the things she had made. Together they had made 14 kinds of goodies, one kind for each day of the holiday season.

Mama said that Margit could use some help out at the farm so the next morning Anna went out there and spent the day. They were going to have a Christmas tree this year for the first time. Mama had never wanted to fuss with that. Tollef and the boys, Arne and Knut, had gone out the day before and cut down a small spruce tree.

Anna helped the boys make decorations. They made little baskets out of paper which would be filled with candy on Christmas morning. She showed them how to make ornaments out of straw. She and her school children had been making them just last week. They made heart and star-shaped ones, and while the boys' creations were quite crude, Anna told them that they looked wonderful.

Anna tried to keep little Signe busy with different things, too, to keep her out of her mother's way for awhile. Margit had much to do to get ready for her Christmas company. Anna drove home late that afternoon before dark. She had some Christmas gifts to finish up and only two days to do it.

When she walked in the house, Anton and his two children were sitting at the supper table with Papa, waiting for her to come home.

"We've been waiting for you, Anna," her mother said, and motioned for her to sit right down so they could start. She noticed that the children, a boy and a girl, did not seem to have much in the way of table manners and they looked rather dirty and neglected. Anna tried to engage them in conversation about Christmas but they were very shy and unresponsive. She told them about the tree she had just helped to decorate and about Tollef and Margit's three children. Their little eyes showed curiosity and some excitement but they said little.

After the meal, Anton excused himself and said he should get the children home. Anna helped her mother with the dishes. Her mother said, "What those two little ones need is a good mother." Anna got the impression that her mother was directing that remark at her, as if she could do something about it.

"Next year the boy will be in school," Anna said, "and that should help him get over some of his shyness."

"I don't think that sister of Anton's is of much use over there by the looks of the children," Anna's mother went on. "He needs a good, strong wife."

Papa came back into the house and sat at the kitchen table and opened the paper, the latest Decorah Posten which Tomas had just sent. Anna joined him and they discussed some of the articles. Anna decided that this might be a good time to bring up an idea that was foremost in her mind these days.

"Papa," she said, "Sigrid has been writing me and asking if I am going to come to America."

"Why would you want to do that?" Mama said in an outburst. "You have a good job here."

"Yes, I do, but I want to see more of the world," Anna explained. Before she could continue, Mama started in on a tirade.

"I need you to stay here and help me!" she said, hands on her hips. "Everyone else has left home. There's no reason for people to leave this country to try and find something better." Her voice was getting louder and louder. "People should be satisfied with what they've got!"

She started to weep. "Is America going to take all of this country's sons and daughters?" she wailed.

"Now, now, Mama," Papa tried to soothe her, "Anna didn't say that she was going for sure, she just said that Sigrid wants her to come and that she is thinking about it. She's a young girl, and she has dreams, like we all did when we were young."

"You mean, like you did, when you were young," Mama ranted. "I didn't have any dreams. I just did what was expected of me. I had to work hard at home for my parents until I got married and then I've worked hard ever since. What is all this nonsense about dreams anyway?"

Anna left the room and ran upstairs while Papa calmed her mother down. She opened a book and read until very late and then fell into a restless sleep.

The next morning was Christmas Eve day. She went downstairs and her mother was already baking some last minute things. She was rolling out lefse so Anna started helping her without a word passing between them for sometime. Finally Anna said, "Mama, I'm sorry if I upset you so last night. I won't talk about it again." She wanted to keep peace, especially during Christmas.

Papa came in later that morning, bringing the mail. A letter and package had come from Sigrid. Anna and Kjersti opened it excitedly. In the package there was the family photograph that Sigrid had promised. "Oh, see how darling the children look!" Anna exclaimed.

"Little Annie looks like you, Anna," Papa said, "and Sylvia looks like Barbro with that dark hair and big eyes. Arthur looks like his father."

They couldn't get enough of looking at the photo. They finally put it on the mantel beside Tomas and Bergit's family picture. The women went back to their baking and Papa went back to the shop.

They wouldn't be going out to Tollef and Margit's til the next day but tonight they had a special Christmas Eve meal. Mama and Anna had made sotsuppe (a fruit soup), lutefisk, boiled potatoes, and home-canned carrots. Lingonberries were served for dessert. Then they bundled up and walked over to the little village church for services. It had been snowing heavily all day so it was slow walking. Anna hoped the snow would stop so that they could get out to the farm the next day.

When they got home from church, they opened the little packages that had been coming from America the last week. Anna got a leather- bound journal, a beautiful pair of combs for her hair and a pretty lace collar, which was made by Bergit. From her parents, she got a beautiful søljer. This is a "lacy-like" brooch which is part of the Norwegian costume and worn at the neck of a white blouse. Mama then served a tray of assorted cookies and fruit cake and coffee. They all retired early in anticipation of the big day to come.

Christmas Day dawned bright and beautiful. They had to pack the wagon with all the packages and food and soon they were off for the short trip to the farm. When they arrived, Tollef was walking up from the stabbur, or storehouse, with a package of meat which had been stored there. They unloaded everything and each carried something to the house. The children came running to greet them and were so excited. They told Anna they had found candy in their paper baskets which were hung on the tree.

Anna and her mother began to help Margit get ready for the big meal which was to come. Besides the Olson family, Margit's family was coming, too. There would be almost 20 people. Another table had to be set up and Papa had brought along some chairs from town. The children were so excited that they were just in the way so Anna and Kjersti took them to the bedroom and told them some stories to calm them down.

When all the guests arrived they sat down and Papa led the table prayer. Then Anna helped Margit serve all the food. There were pork ribs, sausages, meat balls, mashed rutabagas, lingonberries and lefse. For dessert Margit served rice pudding. An almond was placed in one serving and there was much excitement to see who would find it because that person would receive a little gift and would have good luck for the coming year. Everyone dug into their pudding eagerly.

For awhile it looked like nobody was going to be the lucky person when finally Anna found it in her very last spoonful! Her gift was a piece of marzipan in the shape of a pig. There was also a raisin put in the pudding and the one who found that had to do the kitchen clean-up chores. Finally Erik admitted to finding the raisin and they all had fun teasing him about having to clean up. His girlfriend was along and she said that she would help him.

They teased Anna, too, saying that her "good luck" would be finding a husband. She answered that she did not think that would be too lucky. They all had to help with the clean-up or it would have taken all day. The children were getting anxious to open up the gifts that their grandparents had brought them. Papa had made a little rocker for 2-year-old Signe. She just loved it and claimed it for her very own from the start. She sat in it all day and would not let anyone else touch it. For the boys, he had whittled horses and made miniature wagons which could be hitched up to the horses.

Margit's father had brought along his fiddle and Uncle Olaf had his accordion so they had an afternoon of music and singing. The young people also went out to play in the snow for awhile. After the men had finished milking the cows, another meal was spread out on the table. This consisted of rullepolse (rolled meat) sandwiches, lefse, fattigmann, julekakke, fruit cake and many, many kinds of cookies and other sweets such as sandbakkels, spritz and krumkake.

Everyone was in such a happy and jolly mood that Anna thought that perhaps this was the most enjoyable Christmas that she could remember. It was one that she would remember for many years to come. The evening was spent playing games and telling stories. When it was time to go home, everyone did so reluctantly. Echoes of "God Jul" and "Gledelig Jul" rang in the evening air as the guests departed.

Papa, Mama, Kjersti and Anna bundled up for the wagon ride home. Thoughts of the wonderful day kept them warm all the way home as they talked about the good time they all had had. Still Anna had the nagging feeling that this was probably her last Christmas here with her family.

The holiday season lasted until Twelfth Night, or January 6. Friends and relatives came calling at least once a day and Mama's cookie supply was dwindling. Anton and his children came again once or twice and they ate cookies til she thought they would burst!

A couple days before Anna was to return to Gol, Papa came home for supper and told Anna that he had something important to discuss with her. "Anton lingered after work today," Papa began, "and I knew he had something on his mind. Finally he came out and asked me if he could have your hand in marriage, Anna."

Anna froze and was speechless with surprise. "What!" she finally uttered. "He wants me to marry him? Wherever did he get the idea that I would be even remotely interested in such a thing?"

Anna looked at her mother who was standing like a statue with a plate in her hand, unable to move or breath until she heard Anna's answer. "Mama, did you know anything about this? Were you encouraging him, by always asking him over for meals and things?"

When her mother didn't answer and Papa started to say that maybe this wouldn't be such a bad idea, Anna lost her temper and shouted, "How can you even think that I would marry a man that I don't love and have no interest in whatsoever? I have plans for my life and they do not include marrying young and having baby after baby and never leaving this valley!" With that she ran up to her room and stayed there the rest of the evening.

After she had calmed down somewhat, she began to formulate a plan in her mind. She now knew what she had to do. It was maybe just a dream before, but now it was going to become a reality. She would go to America. She would tell her parents in the morning. She didn't sleep well that night, but tossed and turned with her head filled with thoughts and plans. She would write to Sigrid tomorrow.

When she came down the next morning, her father had already gone to the shop and Mama and Kjersti were busy with morning household chores. She wanted to talk to Papa but she didn't want to go to the shop because Anton would be there. She helped her mother in silence for awhile. Kjersti kept looking at her sister, waiting for her usual bright chatter. When none was forthcoming, Kjersti finally said, "Anna talk." With that, Anna could not keep silent any longer.

"I'm sorry, but I am too upset to talk," she said to both Kjersti and her mother.

"Well," her mother said, "I think you could have at least given it some consideration."

Just then they heard Papa coming in the back door, stomping his boots to remove some of the snow. He sat at the kitchen table and Mama brought him a cup of coffee. He had been to the store. "No mail for us today," he said.

Anna sat across from him and said, "Papa, I'm sorry for my outburst last night and I have come to some decisions. I am going to America when school is out. She saw her mother stiffen and Papa's shoulders seemed to sag when she said this. He looked at her and she could see the sadness in his eyes. He couldn't speak. He finished his coffee and left again for the shop

She found some stationery and went up to her room and began a letter to Sigrid. She told her that she had decided that she would be coming to America as soon as she could after school dismissed. She would write later with more details.

The letter was very brief as she was not in the mood to tell her sister about the happy Christmas they had just had or to thank her for the nice gifts. She signed and sealed the letter and went down and got her warm coat and boots on and trudged through the deep snow over to the store. She stood and looked at the letter for a short time before actually posting it. There, that's done, she thought to herself. Now nothing will be the same again.

That evening she told her parents what she had done and they didn't have much to say. She felt anger from her mother, but from Papa it was more of a resignation. Tomorrow she had to go back to Gol so she needed to get started packing up her things.

"What time are we leaving for Gol in the morning, Papa?" she asked.

"We'll leave about noon. It won't be quite so cold then," he answered in a flat tone. Anna retired to her room. What if Papa asks Anton to drive me to Gol tomorrow, she thought. No, he wouldn't do that to me, she reassured herself. She fell into a troubled sleep.

The next day, she and Papa loaded the wagon and bundled up and headed for Gol. They rode in silence the first few miles. Finally Anna said, "Papa, did you actually want me to marry Anton?" His answer was very important to her.

He sighed and said, "No, I guess not, knowing you the way that I do. But it would have been a way to make sure that you didn't leave. Perhaps I have always known that you would be leaving us someday."

"Yes, that's always been a dream of mine. Do you think I'm crazy to want to leave here for America?" she asked.

He thought for awhile before answering. "You know, Anna, you are so much like me. In fact, of all my children, you are the most like me. And so I understand your wanting to leave, to satisfy the longings of your heart. If a person doesn't follow their dream, they can become dried up and bitter inside sometimes."

"Then you do understand, Papa. That's so important to me."

"Yes, I understand only too well, but I will miss you so much. I am feeling sad already. You and I, Anna, have become very close and when you leave, some part of me will shrivel up and die."

"Oh, don't say that, Papa. You will make me feel so terrible about leaving. Don't let a part of you shrivel up; instead let that part of you go with me. I will take that part of you across the sea with me and we will experience new adventures together."

Anna's father was silent again for many miles, deep in his own thoughts. When they arrived in Gol, they unloaded Anna's things. Mrs. Barstad asked him to stay for supper but he said he better turn right around and head for home. He had a quick cup of coffee and warmed himself by the stove in the kitchen. He turned to Anna before leaving and said, "My dear Anna, I want only the best for you. You are a fine, young woman now, and I can't tell you that you cannot go. You will do what you have to do." With that he left and she watched him as he hitched up the horses and started down the road.

She plunged herself into her second term of teaching. Letters between Anna and Sigrid passed back and forth over the Atlantic. She saved every penny of her teaching wages to buy her ticket to America. She told the school board at Gol that she would not be returning. They had been reluctant to hire her, they admitted, and now they were sorry to see her leave as she had proved to be a very adequate teacher.

At the end of May, her brother Tollef came to get her as he had an errand near Gol. It was nice having this time alone with him.

"What do you think about my leaving, Tollef?" she asked.

He shrugged and said, "If that is what you want to do then you better do it. I know it will break Papa's heart to see you go, though."

She would be leaving the end of June so there was much to do. Papa was making her a big trunk. When it was finished, they had a neighbor lady do some painting on it and she also wrote Anna's name in very large letters. When the heavy domed lid was opened, there were two removable drawers on the top and room for lots of things on the bottom. It stood in the middle of the floor in the front room and Anna started to pack things in there as she thought of them.

The last week she had to go around and say goodbye to everyone. She spent a day at the farm. Margit said that she had heard that Anton was seeing a widow from over near Al and she supposed he would be marrying her. Anna often wondered what Papa had told him in answer to his proposal. She had hardly seen him since she returned. She avoided the shop and Mama never invited him over anymore.

It was difficult to say goodbye to Margit and the children. She had grown so fond of them all. Margit gave her a piece of Hardanger embroidery to remember her by. Tollef and Erik came in for supper and she bade them farewell also and then she returned home. She laid the piece of embroidery work in the top drawer of her trunk. Kjersti was curious as to what was going on and seemed to sense that Anna was going away for good this time. She was fascinated with the trunk and what was going into it.

Her last night at home, Anna packed her 'bibel' and 'sangbok' as well as several of her other favorite books. She put her clothes on the bottom and laid her bunad, which was her national costume, on top of the pile. She carefully wrapped her brooch in a handkerchief and put it in one of the top drawers. Mama had made her a beautiful apron with rows and rows of tatted lace on it. She laid this on top of everything else.

The next morning she had breakfast with the family. No one seemed to want to talk about her impending departure. Leaving the table, she made a last minute inspection of her trunk and closed the lid. Papa locked it and gave her the key to keep in her hand bag. Papa needed help loading the big trunk into the wagon so he had to get Anton to give him a hand. Anton would hardly look at Anna and he left without saying anything.

Anna said goodbye to Kjersti upstairs in her room. She embraced her older sister for the last time but could not say a word because of the lump in her throat. Mama followed them out to the wagon and Anna turned to her to say goodbye. She and her mother looked at each other for sometime and then Mama took her hand and shook it and said "farvel Anna" and turned and hurried into the house. She shook my hand! Anna had hoped for a warm embrace from her mother. She was so devastated by this that she started to cry in great sobs that came from deep within her. Papa took her by the shoulders and tried to get her under control. Finally he put his arms around her and he held her tightly until he could feel the sobs subsiding. He helped Anna up into the wagon and they started off slowly, away from this place forever.

They traveled part way by wagon and then transferred to a small boat to go down river. They were going to spend a day at Barbro's in Drammen. This was out of the way for them but Anna wanted to see her sister and family once again.

Barbro and Peder were so happy to see them but the little girls were shy at first. Ragna was five now and little Annetta was almost two. They had a good visit but the next morning it was time to say goodbye. The two sisters clasped each other for a long time, promising that they would see each other again someday.

Anna and Papa traveled most of the day before getting to Christiania. They stayed in a hotel that night. They had a tasty supper in the hotel dining room and then retired to their room. Papa was reluctant to turn in for the night; he seemed to want to make this evening last longer. They had talked of many things the last two days traveling together so there was not much left to say. Finally Anna said she was tired and could not stay awake any longer so they both went to bed. Papa, tired as he was, could not get to sleep right away. There seemed to be something nagging at him that he should talk to Anna about.

"Anna, are you sleeping?" he inquired quietly.

"No, I'm just lying here thinking. I'm too excited to sleep after all, I guess."

"I have to tell you something," he said into the darkness. "I know you are disappointed in your Mama and perhaps you think that she doesn't love you, but I know that she really does." He paused and reflected awhile.

"She used to be happy and full of life," he went on, "but something seemed to have died inside of her many years ago and I don't know what it was. Especially after Kjersti was born. She really changed then and all I can do is reassure her that I still love her. But I feel so bad that you never knew your mother the way she used to be."

Anna had left her bed now and was sitting beside her father who had also sat up. They were both weeping and Papa said that that was why he was going to miss Anna so much. She was his ray of sunshine. This made Anna feel so bad that she said, "Maybe I shouldn't go then, Papa. I could still change my mind. I don't want you to feel so bad."

"No, Anna, I would never forgive myself if I stood in the way of your dream. You go and know that you have my blessing."

They wiped their tears and said no more, each returning to their own beds.   After awhile, Anna could hear her father's gentle snores so she knew that he had finally fallen asleep but Anna was still troubled and she tossed and turned most of the night.

Father and daughter stood on the pier the next morning. The trunk had been loaded and the passengers were starting to go up the gang plank. Papa tried to be cheerful but he felt in his heart that he would never see his dear daughter again.

"Papa, you can come to America to see all of us someday!" Anna exclaimed.

"Well, maybe we could do that someday," he answered, only to give her some hope and to put a smile on her face. Before she turned to leave, he gathered her in his big arms and held her for a long time and then released her and gave her up to her dream.

CHAPTER 4

June, 1905

Anna stood at the railing and watched England fade from view. She had done what Sigrid suggested. She took the boat from Christiania to Liverpool, England, where she got on a new and faster steamship. This had cost her more money but it would be worth it. She should be in New York within a week and a half or so.

What have I done? she asked herself over and over again ever since she had bid her father goodbye on the pier in Christiania. She stood on the deck for a long time, until she could no longer see land. Well, it's too late now to undo what I have done, she told herself. From now on I have to look forward and not backward. With that thought in mind, she walked around to the front of the ship, the part that was facing America and her future. She would not look back again.

"First comes the dream, and then comes the doing," Anna said aloud, looking over the railing. Anna made a striking figure, standing there. Although she would maybe not be considered beautiful, she was an attractive young woman. Her long, regal neck made her look taller than average, and she had thick, brown hair, worn piled on top of her head. She had big, brown eyes which shone with merriment. She would not have trouble attracting the young men on board ship, or in America, for that matter.

Her accommodations aboard ship were quite comfortable even though she was traveling 3rd class. She noticed several other young ladies on board and also a family with two daughters about her age. She would have to make their acquaintance, otherwise it would be a long, lonely trip without anyone to talk to.

Over the next few days she came to realize that there was only one other young woman who spoke her language! This is something I will have to get used to; this is what happens when you leave your country behind, she told herself. She almost had to chuckle, thinking about the fact that she had been talking to herself quite a lot these days. The other passengers were either

English or German or Irish.

The young woman from Norway was going to join her brother in America, she told Anna. He lived in Wisconsin and had a dairy farm there. He had been there for five years now. Her name was Caren Anderson and she and Anna enjoyed many long days together. They strolled the deck and in the evenings there was music and dancing topside.

There was bad weather only a couple of times but Anna never had any problem with sea sickness. Her friend Caren did, so on those days Anna would try to get acquainted with others. She and a young English girl tried to communicate but it was very difficult. She knew that her name was Margaret and they would walk together sometimes. Margaret understood that Anna was going to America to live and so she taught her some English words, like "hello", "goodbye" and "thank you" and also the names of some of the foods that they ate. Anna vowed that she was going to try and learn English as soon as possible.

On the twelfth day out, the captain announced that they would be seeing land by the next afternoon. Everyone became excited about this and they started to pack up their things. The next afternoon, everyone was on deck straining their eyes to the west. Shortly before supper, someone with binoculars shouted that land had been sighted. That night the music and dancing were more spirited than usual. Anna did not lack for dance partners. She even learned an Irish jig!

The next day the ship entered New York Harbor. All the passengers were on deck, pointing and shouting excitedly in several different languages as they passed the Statue of Liberty. The immigrants disembarked at Ellis Island and each had to have a quick physical examination and go through other formalities before being allowed on the mainland.

Anna was so excited and nervous. She and Caren stuck together as they walked down the gang plank to the pier. Would Sigrid be there to meet me? she wondered. Will we even recognize each other? They craned their necks and kept looking about them in all directions. There were so many people moving to and fro around them. Caren had a cousin living in New York who was supposed to meet her. They both wondered what they would do if no one showed up to meet them.

They had looked and waited for almost an hour when Anna saw a man and woman looking at them closely. It was Sigrid! Or was it? The woman came closer and said, "Anna?" But she was looking back and forth at both Anna and Caren. Anna had grown up and changed so much that Sigrid didn't know for sure which girl was her sister. But Anna could tell that it was Sigrid so she called out, "Sigrid, is that you?

"Yes, it's me," she cried and the two sisters fell into each other's arms. They leaned back to have a look at each other and then embraced, again and again. After wiping their tears of joy, Sigrid introduced her husband, Louis, whom Anna recognized from the photo. Anna had almost forgotten Caren so then she drew her into the circle of family members. Caren said that she was worried that no one was going to meet her. Sigrid said that they would wait with her awhile longer to see what happened. Caren didn't know what the cousin looked like and he had never seen her before so it was not a good situation.

Louis went to see about Anna's trunk and the three women found a place to sit down. Sigrid said, "After the crowd thins out somewhat maybe we'll see someone who is looking for a young woman from Norway!" And that is exactly what happened. A middle aged man came walking by slowly and heard them talking Norwegian and so he stopped and asked if one of them was a Miss Anderson. Caren jumped up and introduced herself and soon they were gone. Louis came back and said that everything was ready and loaded into their carriage. The sisters, walking arm in arm, followed Louis and he helped them into the rig which would take them home.

Anna and Sigrid talked and talked all the way so that Anna hardly had time to look about her to see the city. They arrived at their home after about a half hour and the children came running out to meet them. A neighbor had come over to stay with them while their parents had gone down to the pier.

"Well, goodness, let's go on inside," Sigrid said as she hustled them all through the front door. Louis went to seek a neighbor's help to unload the trunk. The women removed their hats and Sigrid went to get some glasses of lemonade. It was a warm day and the house was very hot. They took their glasses and went out into the back yard.

"I'll show you the house later, Anna, but first we'll sit out here in the shade and cool off a bit," said Sigrid as she found chairs for Anna and herself. The children sat on the ground by Anna's feet and stared up at her. Louis joined them a short while later and Sigrid went in to get him a glass of the cold drink.

"It sure is nice to finally meet you, Anna," he said. "And Sigrid has been so excited ever since she heard you were coming here that she has everyone else excited, too, including the whole neighborhood!"

Anna noticed that his Norwegian was not very good but she could make out what he was saying. The children talked among themselves in English but would switch to halting Norwegian when they talked to her. Anna liked Louis right away. He was a big, jolly man, friendly and outgoing and he seemed very kind and gentle. Just the kind of man I'd like to marry, thought Anna.

Suddenly she thought of Anton. To think that he was almost a possibility sent a shiver down her back. If she had been a meek, obedient daughter it could have happened.

Sigrid returned with lemonade for Louis and refills for the rest of them. The children were all excited to meet their Aunt Anna from the "old country" as their mother always called it

Annie, who was now almost six years old, was a forward little lass, but

Arthur was shy and little Sylvia was a bouncy, wiggly two-year-old. The children played on the grass with their father. You could tell that they adored him. It was apparent that Sigrid did, too. How lucky she is, thought Anna. I want this someday. A home, a good man and some children.

That evening Sigrid and Anna talked til way into the night after the rest of the family had gone to bed. They sat at the kitchen table drinking coffee. Sleep would have been impossible for either of them as they were still so excited to be together again. The talked about Papa and Mama, Tollef and his family, Kjersti, Barbro and her family and everybody else back home.

The next day, Sigrid took Anna around the neighborhood. They put Sylvia in the perambulator and the other two children followed and they went from house to house so all Sigrid's friends could meet her sister from Norway. When Sigrid spoke to her friends, she used English and she also spoke to her children mostly in English.

When they returned to the house, Anna spoke to Sigrid about this. "I would like to learn English as well as you speak it, Sigrid," she said. "How long did it take you and where did you learn it?"

"Magda and I started learning it shortly after we arrived here so that we would sound more like we belonged here. We took some lessons from a neighbor lady. They give lessons to newcomers now down at the school in the evenings. If you would want to go there, we could inquire about it. I don't know how much it costs or anything."

"I would be very interested in that," said Anna. "I noticed Louis' Norwegian is not very good. Why is that?" she asked.

"His parents came from Norway back in the 70's but he was born here and went to school here. He and I speak English all the time, except with the old timers. We see the Amundsons once in awhile and Magda's mother never did learn a word of English."

On Sunday, the whole family attended church, located within walking distance. Then Sigrid packed a picnic basket and they all loaded into the carriage and set out on a sight-seeing tour with a stop at a park where they spread out blankets and enjoyed lunch. Anna was enthralled with everything she saw and she said, "I don't know why Tomas and Bergit disliked the city so. I think I am going to like it here."

A couple of evenings later, Louis went down to the school to check out the possibility of Anna taking English lessons. When he returned, he announced, "New classes will be starting in two weeks and I signed you up for them, Anna. The cost will be $5 for ten weeks of lessons, two evenings a week." Anna thought that sounded all right. In the meantime, Sigrid and Anna sat at the kitchen table every evening and Sigrid tried to teach Anna some words and phrases.

"You know, Sigrid," said Anna, "maybe I could just learn from you."

"Well, I can speak it pretty good now but I don't do very well when it comes to writing it. You better take the lessons that are available. You'll need to know it very well if you ever plan to teach here in this country."

Anna pondered this for a few minutes and then said. "I do hope to teach again someday. I did so like it, but it will probably be a long time before I'll be ready for that."

She and Sigrid spent the rest of that evening writing a letter back home to their parents. Anna would write to Barbro in a day or so. "I need to write to Tomas and Andrew, too, and let them know I got here safely."

Anna had spent the first week getting unpacked and settled. She had a room of her own as Sylvia had been moved in with Annie. It was such a pleasant room with lace curtains on the windows and pretty flowered wallpaper on the walls. It had been decorated for little Sylvia so it was really a little girl's room but Anna loved it.

One evening at the supper table, Anna announced, "I think that I shall look for a job. Louis, do you have any idea where I could find one?"

This took Louis and Sigrid by surprise. "You don't have to look for work yet, Anna." said Sigrid. "You will need to learn English better first."

So Anna was persuaded to wait awhile. She helped Sigrid with the house and the children and Sigrid said she really appreciated this. The children loved her and hung around her all the time.

One Sunday after church, Anna was introduced to a young woman about her own age. She had come from Norway about two years before and her name was Emma Flaten. She lived with her parents several blocks down from the Andersons. They got to talking and Emma said she would like to visit further with Anna so she said she would walk over to visit her in the afternoon.

Emma arrived about midday and it was such a beautiful day that she suggested that they take a walk. Annie and Arthur wanted to tag along but their mother said that they had to let Anna go alone with her new friend. Anna grabbed her hat to protect her face from the bright afternoon sun.

The two young women walked and talked for many blocks along the pretty residential street. Emma said that she had a job in a hat factory and had been working there for about a year. When she learned that Anna was thinking about a job in the near future, she said that maybe she could arrange for Anna to get a job at the same place. Girls were quitting all the time, she told her. They got married and then they would leave.

Anna and Emma found themselves back in front of the Anderson house so Anna invited Emma in for a glass of lemonade. They sat out back and visited with Louis and Sigrid. Sylvia was napping and Annie and Arthur were playing next door. What a peaceful, beautiful afternoon, reflected Anna. I think I made the right decision to come here.

Reluctantly, Emma said that she had to go home and Anna walked her to the front of the house. They made plans to meet again soon.

"When you're ready to look seriously for a job, Anna, let me know,"

Emma called from the end of the sidewalk.

"I'm so glad you have found someone your own age, Anna," Sigrid later said. "Emma seems like such a nice, young lady."

"Yes, I like her. We seem to have much in common," said Anna as she helped set the table for supper. "She said she could maybe help me get a job at the hat factory where she works."

Anna started her English classes and after several sessions, she declared that she thought the language was very difficult. "I don't know how I'll ever learn it," she complained.

"You'll learn it soon enough, Anna," said Louis. "You just keep studying and it will become easier."

"Yes, Anna," said Sigrid encouragingly, "you are a bright student and it will come easier by and by."

So Anna worked diligently at her lessons and the family decided that they would speak English to her most of the time. This would help greatly, her teacher agreed.

Anna and Emma continued their friendship throughout the summer. One Sunday after church, Emma said that she had news for Anna so she walked her part way home. Emma said that there was a job opening at the factory in the same department where she worked and she talked to her boss and he said that Anna should come in and talk to him.

At the Sunday dinner table, Anna told Sigrid and Louis what Emma had said. Anna decided to go down there the very next morning. She talked with Emma later and it was decided that she would go to work with her the next day.

Anna was up early and walked down to the corner grocery store where she was to meet Emma. After only a few minutes, her friend arrived and they walked about three blocks more to the street car. They paid their fare and found a seat. Anna was a bit nervous but Emma said that her boss was a nice man and that she need not worry.

Mr. Sampson, Emma's boss, was indeed a nice man and he asked Anna some questions which she was able to understand fairly well and she answered in passable English. She had the feeling, though, that he would surely want someone with some experience who could speak the language fluently. After the interview, he asked her to wait outside his office for awhile. She saw two other young women come and go. Finally he called her back into his office and told her that the job was hers and if she had nothing else pressing for the rest of the day she could start immediately! She was flabbergasted to suddenly find herself employed.

Emma was informed and chosen to be the one to show her around and to train her for her job. The factory made men's felt hats and employed about 50 people, about half of them women like herself. Anna's job was to work with the lining, sewing it and fitting it into the completed hat. Another girl sewed in the label and stamped on the size and the hat was then ready to be packed for shipping.

The girls took the street car home again and talked excitedly about Anna's first day at work. She was tired out from trying so hard to do everything right. At the supper table that evening she had to go over every detail of the day for the rest of the family. Sigrid said that she decided that Anna must have gotten the job being she never came home.

Summer came to an end and so did Anna's English classes. She spoke English almost all of the time now. She was very proud of that fact and remembered back to the beginning when she thought it was so difficult. She enjoyed her job, mostly because she liked the people she worked with. Besides Emma there were two Italian girls, a Jewish woman and an Irish woman in her department and she got to know them well. She and Emma put in five and a half days a week, Monday through Saturday morning.

Brooklyn had a beautiful September that year and she and Emma took many Sunday afternoon excursions throughout the city. About six blocks from their neighborhood were two very exclusive residential areas, Brooklyn Heights and Cobble Hill. They would walk down there, along the East River, and dream of living in one of those big houses someday. "We will have to marry somebody very rich," they would tease each other.

Early October brought her a second letter from her father. Everyone was well and he missed her very much. He brought her up to date on the political situation in Norway. Before she had left in June, the Norwegian Parliament had ended their union with Sweden. Sweden had almost gone to war with them in the meantime but, he wrote, Sweden finally recognized Norway's independence. He wished that she was still home to discuss things like this with him because Mama had no interest in the subject.

Anna missed her Papa, too, so she sat right down and wrote him a letter that evening. She told him that she was happy and liked it here and thought that she had made the right decision. She didn't know if that would make him happy or sad!

Both Tomas and Andrew had written Anna, asking when she was coming out to visit them, or better yet, to live with them. They couldn't imagine that she liked the city! Andrew said that they were doing well now; they had been having good crops the last two years. A baby girl had been added to their family and they named her Berta. Tomas was still in Mankato, Minnesota, and was doing quite well in the carpentry business. Anna longed to see them and their growing families.

Time passed quickly and soon Anna was experiencing her first American Thanksgiving which she had heard so much about. She helped Sigrid bake and cook for two days prior as they would be having a table full of guests that day. Louis's family, which consisted of two sisters and their respective families would be there, and Sigrid had invited a neighbor family who otherwise would have been alone. There were 12 around the dining table and the smaller children were fed in the kitchen. What a big turkey they had! And all the trimmings. Things that Anna had never had before, like pumpkin pie.

Christmas time was fast approaching and Sigrid was striving to make this a very happy holiday for Anna so that she wouldn't get so lonesome for home. They cleaned and polished and baked and baked some more. They had shopped early for gifts to send to Norway. Anna was able to help Sigrid decide on just the right thing for everyone back home.

Even though the hat factory was owned by a Jewish man, he gave the girls two days off for Christmas. That was his gift to them, he said. Anna and Emma were delighted. The Irish woman that they worked with, whose name was Mary Catherine O'Connell, was having a rough time at home. She belonged to a very large family and her father was a drinker and not a good provider. Anna and Emma went shopping on Christmas Eve morning for little gifts for Mary Catherine and her younger brothers and sisters and they delivered them to her house.

"What joy ye've just brought to our whole family!" exclaimed Mary Catherine. "Mum has not been well but she was tryin' her best to make a nice Christmas for us."

Anna and Emma left the house with mixed feelings. Feelings of satisfaction because they had brought some joy to an otherwise bleak situation, and feelings of guilt because they themselves had it so good at home . They each hurried home to help with preparations for Christmas Eve observances in their own homes.

Tonight it would be just the immediate family. They had a traditional Norwegian supper of lutefisk, lefse, sotsuppe, and mashed potatoes. Sigrid could not get lingonberries that year so they had rice pudding for dessert. After eating their meal they bundled up the children and took them to the church service. Anna had never heard such beautiful singing. Some of the familiar Christmas songs from home were sung, too. She had to brush a tear aside as she thought of her parents and Kjersti sitting in their own little church singing the same song.

Her nostalgic mood did not last long when they returned to the house, however. The children were so excited that it was easy to be caught up in their spirit. Louis lit the candles on the tree and everyone sat down and listened while Louis read the Christmas story from the Bible. Then everyone was allowed to open one present each. Before bedtime, Sigrid served coffee, milk and cookies. Sigrid and Anna stayed up after the rest of the family had gone to bed. They had preparations to make for the next day. Only one of Louis's sisters was coming with her family so there would not be as many people as at Thanksgiving.

They awoke on Christmas Day to see that it was snowing heavily. The children awoke early and were wanting to open the rest of their presents. Sigrid said they had to wait till the afternoon. It continued to snow all morning. They were wondering if Louis's sister and family, the Norgaards, would be able to make it. They were planning to eat their Christmas dinner about four o'clock. About noon, the snow diminished and finally stopped and they remained hopeful that their guests would make it.

About two o'clock, they heard stomping on the front porch and they opened the door to find the Norgaard family, all bundled up, trying to get the snow off their feet and legs. "You look like snowmen," laughed Sigrid as she opened the door wide and ushered them into the nice, warm house. Louis's sister, Mabel, said that nothing would have kept them from getting there! They gave up on trying to take the horse and carriage. Instead they walked to the street car, which could barely make it through the snow, Mr. Norgaard said, and then they walked the eight or so blocks from there! They each carried gifts and food and were very tired and worn out from the journey.

Louis took their wet clothes and told them to sit down in the front room and Sigrid brought them something hot to drink. Their two children, Greta and Theo, who were 14 and 12 years old, put their gifts under the tree and sat and admired it. It was so tall that it reached the ceiling. They did not have one at home themselves this year, they said.

The women busied themselves with the meal preparation and soon everyone was seated at the dining table. Louis led everyone in the table prayer, which was always spoken in Norwegian, even by the small children. Everyone got plenty to eat and the meal was topped off by pumpkin pie.

"Sigrid makes the best pumpkin pie!" Louis said, patting his stomach, and everyone had to agree. After dinner, the children played while the women cleaned up the dishes and the men napped because they were too full to move.

By the time everyone gathered in the front room again, it was dark outside and Louis lit the tree candles. The children sang some Christmas songs and Sigrid and Anna sang some old Norwegian favorites. Sigrid said she hoped that she could get a piano someday. She would like to take music lessons and she thought that Annie would soon be old enough to take them, too. The gifts were passed out and opened one by one.

While the children occupied themselves with their new things, the grownups talked about many things. Mr. Norgaard told Anna about coming to America when he was only eight years old. Inside of just one year both his mother and his father had died and so had his little brother. His mother and brother had become ill and died shortly after arriving here. He and his father moved on to the Dakotas to join some friends and then his father was killed in an accident with a horse. He was then raised by friends and when he was old enough, he set out on his own. He worked for the railroad for awhile in Dakota Territory and then he went to Pennsylvania to work and then he was sent to New York where he now was employed by the B & O Railroad.

He ended his storytelling by recalling some amusing incidents in his years of working with all kinds of people. Everyone, even the children, laughed till they almost hurt! Some more Christmas songs were sung and then Sigrid served coffee and cookies and then the Norgaards said that they had to start for home. Louis said that he would drive them home in the carriage. He thought that the horses would not have any trouble now. He and his brother-in-law went to hitch up the team while the others gathered up their things and put on their coats and boots.

After the last "Merry Christmas" and "God Jul" were exchanged, Anna and Sigrid sat down by the fireplace and reflected on the past two days.

"Anna," Sigrid said, "I hope that you were not too homesick for the family back home on your first Christmas away."

"No, it was a wonderful time and thank you, Sigrid, for all the extra things you did to make it so. I guess people can have wonderful times wherever they are when they're with people they love and care about."

Two days after Christmas, a package came from Norway. In it were little gifts for everybody. There was a hand knit scarf for Anna from Kjersti. It was a sorry-looking scarf, but Anna almost cried when she saw it because she knew the pains Kjersti must have gone through to make it. In the letter that came with the gifts, Papa said that Mama had been teaching Kjersti to knit and this was her first attempt. She worked on it fervently and she would hold it up and say,"for Anna," all the while she was working on it. Anna knew the love that had gone into it so it was very precious to her. She wore it to work under her coat all winter.

Papa also wrote about the political situation again there. He said that the people had approved of a new king. He was a Danish prince and he became Haakon VII.

"We have a new king now, King Haakon," Anna told Louis that evening.

"When you say 'we', Anna, do you still think of yourself going back to Norway or do you think you would like to remain here and become a citizen?" asked Louis.

"Well, I hadn't given that any real thought, I guess," answered Anna thoughtfully.

"Yes, Anna," chimed in Sigrid, "maybe you should think about that. You could apply for citizenship here."

That evening, feeling lonesome for her family back home, Anna wrote a letter to Kjersti, thanking her for the scarf, and to Papa telling him how much she missed them all. Later, in bed, she asked herself, "Do I want to stay here and become a citizen of this country or would I want to go back home?" Time would tell, time would tell, and she drifted off to sleep.

As winter stretched on towards spring, Anna began to think that it was time for her to make a visit out to see her brothers. As much as she liked the city, she would probably never be able to get a teaching job here, but Tomas and Andrew both assured her that teaching jobs were plentiful out there, especially in the country schools. She was beginning to tire of her job at the hat factory and the desire to teach was surfacing again.

Anna discussed these feelings with Sigrid over their late-evening coffee time at the kitchen table. Sigrid said that she would hate to see Anna go but she knew she was anxious to see the rest of their family and understood also her love of teaching. Anna wrote to both of her brothers telling them that maybe she would come out to see them this summer.

Within a month, she received letters from both Tomas and Andrew telling her how delighted they were that she was going to come out to visit them. They would be waiting to hear from her again.

Spring burst out in full bloom in the city about mid-April. Anna and Emma both had spring fever and were getting tired of working in the stuffy factory. There was a young man named Toby Mund who worked there also and he was always teasing the girls and wanted them to go out with him. He was a likable fellow but nobody took him too seriously. One day he asked Emma and Anna if they would like to go out dancing with him and a friend. There was going to be a big dance at the new Crystal Ballroom down on Flatbush Avenue. He told the girls that they needed to go out and have some fun for a change.

Anna and Emma decided that maybe they should take him up on his offer. It was about time they got out a little and did something different. The dance was about two weeks away so the girls had lots of time to talk about what they would wear.

As the day of the dance approached, plans were solidified with Toby and anticipation mounted. On Saturday morning, the big day, Emma sent word to Anna through her younger brother that she was sick and did not think she could go. In the afternoon, Anna walked over to Emma's house to see if she was feeling better. In fact, she was feeling worse, she said. It was decided that Anna would go anyway as it would be impossible to let the fellows know at this late hour of any change in plan. They were to meet them at the street car stop where the girls went every morning.

Anna got herself ready for the evening but it would not be as much fun without Emma, she thought. Sigrid did not like the idea of Anna walking alone to the street car stop but Anna assured her she would be all right, especially since it was still light out. She said that she would have the guys walk her all the way home after the dance. This made Sigrid feel better about the situation and she bid Anna goodbye and told her to have a good time.

When she arrived at the stop, the fellows were not there yet but after only a few minutes she saw Toby get off another street car and there was someone with him. As they approached her, she thought that Toby looked nice all dressed up for a change. The young man with him was dressed very suavely and Anna had the first impression that this was a slick character. Toby said, "Anna, I want you to meet my friend, Mr. Joseph Alexander Morrissey, but just call him Joe." Joe shook her hand and tipped his hat and said, "I'm very pleased to meet you, Miss Olson."

Toby looked around and said, "Where's Emma? Didn't she come with you?"

"No, she can't make it. She's been sick all day." Anna answered. "Perhaps I shouldn't go either, then. You fellows maybe want to just go on your own now."

"Nonsense," said Joe. "We three will have a good time anyway."

With that, the street car approached and Toby said, "Let's be off then," and he helped Anna up the stairs and paid her fare. Toby was his usual jolly and entertaining self on the ride uptown so they all did a lot of laughing. Maybe this will be fun anyway, Anna thought to herself.

They got off the car a couple blocks from the Ballroom and joined the other young people walking towards it. It was crowded but they managed to find a place to sit along the wall. Both Toby and Joe were good dancers so she never wanted for a partner. Toby taught Anna the Fox Trot and Joe was a great waltzer. Toby said that he would go and get some punch while they danced. Joe grabbed her and out they went for another waltz. This was a slow one and Joe was holding her closer than she felt comfortable with but he was so strong that she couldn't push herself away.

When that dance ended, Toby was back holding two glasses of punch. He gave one to Anna. Joe excused himself and Anna and Toby sat down to rest. She thought her punch tasted strange but she was so thirsty that she drank it down quite fast. She and Toby went out to dance another dance and when they came back to their seats, Joe was coming back. Anna thought she could smell liquor from him. He grabbed her and whirled her out onto the floor for another waltz. With his face only inches from hers, she could smell the liquor again. "Have you been drinking, Joe?" she asked.

"What if I have?" he answered. "Does that bother you if I have a little something to whet my thirst?"

Not wanting to make a big deal about it, she answered, "No, I guess not," and she fell silent for the rest of that dance. Toby had returned with another glass of punch for Anna and she drank it thirstily again. When she got up to dance again she felt a little dizzy and then It finally dawned on her what was happening. "Toby Mund, did you put something in my punch?" she asked angrily.

"Well, I just put in a little gin to give it some zip," he said defensively. About this time Joe suggested that they go and take their party elsewhere. Anna didn't want to leave but she didn't have much choice but to go along with them. They got on the street car and she thought maybe they were going to take her home because she was being a 'wet blanket' about the drinking. After several blocks they got off the car but Anna said, "This isn't my stop yet."

"No it isn't," Joe said. "We're going up to my place for awhile." Anna became alarmed now and she said she wanted to go home.

"We'll take you home after a little while, Anna," Toby said reassuringly. They went up three flights of stairs and Joe led them into his small apartment. He told them to sit at the table and he got three glasses and started pouring whiskey into them.

"None for me," Anna said as she tried to cover her glass with her hand.

"Oh, you must have a little bit, my dear," said Joe. "You don't want to be a party pooper, do you?" So Anna let him pour the liquid into her glass. I'll just sip a little, she thought to herself.

"Down the hatch," said Joe, and he and Toby drained their glasses in one swallow. "Come on, Anna," they coaxed. "You do the same."

She didn't want to but she was afraid of being made fun of again so she tipped the glass to her lips and tried to drink it fast. It burned all the way down and she started choking. They laughed at her and filled her glass up again.

"Please," she said, "I'm not feeling very good."

Joe suggested that she go sit on the sofa.

"I'm going down to the corner store and buy some gin," Toby said, as he grabbed his hat from the table. Anna wanted to go home but Toby said they would wait till she felt better.

She settled herself on the sofa and after Toby left the apartment, Joe pulled her up by the arms and said, "Here, why don't you go into the other room and lie down. Maybe that will make you feel better."

She went reluctantly and could hardly walk, she was so dizzy. He helped her into his bedroom and she laid down on the bed. She curled up on her side and wished the whole evening had never happened and just wanted it to be over with.

She thought Joe had left the room but suddenly he grabbed her and turned her onto her back and was looming over her. She didn't like the look on his face and she tried to push him back. He started fumbling with her clothes. She felt like she was going to be sick; she tried to get up but she fell back dizzily and passed out.

When she came to a short time later, she hardly dared open her eyes. Joe was gone but she felt that something was terribly wrong. She felt searing pain in her lower abdomen and her clothing was all askew. What really did happen, she thought wildly. She cried out and Toby came to the door and looked down at her. She tried to get up but was too weak. "Toby, I have to get home. Will you help me?" He was not too steady on his feet himself but he knew he had to help her. Joe was sleeping on the sofa and couldn't be roused.

"I'll make us a little coffee, Anna, and then maybe we'll be able to get you home," Toby said. He put the coffee pot on and then came and helped her from the bedroom to the kitchen. She had managed to straighten her clothes. She sat down and put her head in her hands and wept silently. He gave her a big cup of steaming coffee but he didn't sit down. He drank his coffee while he paced the kitchen floor.

Every now and then he would look in on Joe but it didn't look like he would be awakening any time soon. Anna finished her coffee. "I think we should go. Perhaps I can make it now."

They helped each other down the three flights of stairs and walked slowly to the street car stop. They boarded and rode silently all the way to Anna's stop. Toby got out with her and she asked if he could walk with her to her home. He said he would if she led the way. He didn't know where she lived. They were again silent with their own thoughts as they walked the few blocks to Anna's house. Toby left her at her door and looked like he was going to say something but then he just said, "I'm sorry, Anna. Good night," and he turned and retraced his steps.

Anna knew that it was very late and so she tried to be very quiet when she entered the house. She stumbled several times going up the stairs but finally found her room and tumbled into bed without even undressing.

The next morning Sigrid peeked into her room and found her sound asleep so she didn't disturb her. Several hours later the bright sun on Anna's face awakened her. She sat up quickly to see what time it was and her head hurt so much she had to lay back down immediately. She lay there trying to think why she was still in bed and why she had her clothes on. Then it started to come back to her. The dance. The punch. Joe's apartment. Oh, no, it can't really have happened, she tried to tell herself. I am having one big hangover this morning. How did I get home and in my bed? she wondered. Oh, yes, Toby brought me to my door. Sigrid must wonder why I am not up yet. Why is it so quiet downstairs?

She tried to get up again, this time more slowly. She thought she would change clothes and go downstairs but she started to feel sick so she just took off her dress and lay back down again. Soon there was a light knock on her door and Sigrid came in and stood beside the bed. Anna looked up at her with a miserable expression.

"What happened, Anna?" she asked quietly. She sat on the edge of the bed carefully. Anna rolled over and groaned into her pillow. Sigrid sat there for awhile and then said, "Do you want to talk about it?"

Anna turned and looked at her older sister. "They put something into my punch and I guess I have what they call a hangover and I feel so sick I want to die." With this she started to cry softly. This is all she could tell Sigrid.

Sigrid took pity on her sister and said, "I'll bring you some tea and you just stay in bed till you feel like getting up. I'll make some excuse to the rest of the family and I'll try to keep the children quiet."

About a half hour later, Sigrid returned with a cup of hot tea and set it on the bedside table. Anna opened her eyes and Sigrid told her that Emma had just stopped by to see her and asked about last night.

"I told her you were sick and she said that you must have gotten sick from her. I let her believe that that was what happened."

Sigrid pulled the shades on Anna's windows and left the room. Anna groaned and turned her face into her pillow. I just want to die, she kept thinking to herself. I should have stayed in Norway and done what was expected of me. How can I face anyone after what has happened? It's mostly my fault, she thought. I should never have gone up to Joe's apartment. I should never have had those drinks. She finally fell into a fitful sleep.

Sigrid told the children and Louis that Anna had the flu and that they should stay away from her room. When Anna awoke it was late afternoon. She laid there awhile and then thought she would try to get up. She slowly raised herself and for the first time that day, she did not feel sick to her stomach. Her head was feeling better, too.

She went to her washstand and poured water into the bowl and took a clean cloth and washed her face. She hardly dared to look into the mirror. What she saw startled her. She was not the same person anymore and she could tell it in her eyes that something terrible had happened to her. She started to take off her underclothes and was alarmed to see blood stains on them. She thoroughly washed herself and put on clean clothes. She hid her soiled undergarments in the back of her drawer. She would wash them out herself later. She didn't want Sigrid to see them. Then she would know what had happened to her and no one must ever know, she told herself.

She lifted the shades and sat down in the little rocker by the window. I will just have to try to put this out of my mind, she told herself. Her eye fell on the Bible on the night stand. She picked it up and started paging through it. I feel too sinful to even pray, she thought with despair. She automatically turned to Psalm 121. "I lift mine eyes unto the hills. From whence cometh my help? My help comes from the Lord...."

She sat in the rocker for sometime. She heard a slight noise outside her door. Annie slowly opened it and looked inside. She saw Anna sitting by the window so she thought it would be all right to go in. "Auntie Anna, are you still sick?" she asked.

"I feel better now. Come here and tell me what you have been doing all day."

Sigrid poked her head in a few minutes later. "Oh, Annie, you musn't bother Anna now. She doesn't feel well."

"That's all right," Anna said, "I feel better now so she can stay."

"Do you feel like eating anything yet?" asked Sigrid.

"Well, maybe some biscuits and tea, but nothing more than that."

"I"ll bring some up in a few minutes. Annie, you go and wash up for supper."

Later, while eating her biscuits and sipping her tea, Anna wondered if she would be able to go to work in the morning. She stayed in her room the rest of the evening. She just couldn't seem to face anyone yet. She heard the house grow quieter and quieter as the family, one by one, went to bed for the night. Sigrid came to her room after Anna had settled back in bed for the night. She came and sat on the edge of the bed and took Anna's hand in hers. She looked into Anna's face for a long moment.

Looking back at Sigrid, Anna said with surprise, "Sigrid, I didn't realize how much you look like Mama!" She choked back a sob. Sigrid leaned over Anna and took her in her arms. "My dear, little Anna," she said and rocked her back and forth for quite some time.

"Why didn't Mama ever love me?" she asked between sobs.

Sigrid let go of her sister and straightened up. She looked down at the figure lying there and felt so much compassion for her. "I'm sure she loved you in her own way, Anna. I know she never showed it but she wasn't always that way. I don't know what happened to her but when I was little and it was only me and Tollef and Tomas, Mama used to sing and laugh alot. I was very young but I just remember that she was very different then."

"I wish I could have known her then. Why did she have to change?" Anna started to sob again and she turned her face away. Sigrid pulled the top quilt up snug around Anna's shoulders and softly said good night. She turned out the lamp and closed the door. Anna laid awake thinking about Mama and Papa. I wish Papa was here now but it would break his heart to know what happened to me, she thought to herself. He must never find out.

Monday morning Anna awoke early and felt she just had to go to work even if she didn't want to. She needed the money. She got dressed and went downstairs. Louis had already left for work and Sigrid was alone in the kitchen.

"How are you doing this morning, Anna?" asked her sister.

"I feel all right, I guess. I must go to work today," answered Anna. Sigrid had made oatmeal. She poured cream on it and sprinkled sugar on top. It tasted quite good. She lingered over her coffee for awhile and then looked at the clock. She grabbed her coat and hat and hurried to meet Emma.

Emma was waiting for her. "I was going to wait another five minutes for you. I didn't know if you would be coming today or not."

"I feel pretty good today and knew I just couldn't miss work," said Anna. They boarded the street car and settled down for the ride. Emma was bursting with questions. Anna knew she couldn't avoid them forever so she might as well get this over with.

"Did you have a good time Saturday night?" asked Emma. "Tell me all about it."

"Well," started Anna, measuring her words, "the dance was fun. The new ballroom was beautiful. Toby and Joe are both good dancers."

"What were all the girls wearing?" Emma wanted to know. "What time did you get home? When did you start feeling sick? Not at the dance, I hope."

Anna skillfully answered all her questions and soon they came to their stop. They still had to walk some blocks to the factory.

"What was Toby's friend, Joe, like? Was he handsome? Do you like him?" Emma continued.

Anna tried to answer matter-of-factly. If I can get through this day, she thought to herself, then maybe I can make it.

At work she didn't run into Toby until late in the afternoon. He couldn't look her in the eye and he only mumbled a hurried greeting. I"m glad Emma didn't see that, Anna thought.

When Anna got home that evening there was a letter waiting for her from Andrew. He was wondering if he should send some money to her to help pay for her trip out west. He said they were so anxious to have her come. His wife, Alice, was anxious to have another female in the house, he said. She's tired of talking only to hired men. Little Berta had been a colicky baby but was fine now and a real joy to them. They hoped to hear from her soon.

That letter was very timely, Anna thought, because she had been wondering what she should do now - stay here, go back to Norway or go out west. I guess I'll go ahead with my plan to go see my brothers, she said to herself, and then we'll see.

At work one day later in the week, Toby finally stopped and told her he had to talk to her, so they made plans to meet outside during the noon break. They sat on the back steps of the building and ate their sandwiches, making very little small talk.

Toby finally cleared his throat and said, "Anna, I am so sorry about Saturday night. Joe just told me the other day what really happened while I was gone to get more liquor. I am just sick about it," he continued. "Joe was kind of bragging about it and I was so mad at him I almost hit him. I said I didn't want to ever hear him talk about it again."

Anna didn't know what to say. She tried to choke back her sobs. He awkwardly put his arm around her shoulders to try and comfort her. The bell rang, summoning everybody back to work. Anna tried to compose herself before she went in. Toby was silent. He didn't know what else to say or do. Anna turned to him and said quickly, "We won't speak of this ever again," and she hurried to her post.

On Friday, Anna gave her boss two week's notice, telling him about her plans to go out west to visit her brothers and about her desire to maybe teach school again. He told her that he would miss her and that she had been a good, reliable worker.

Emma was heartbroken when Anna told her that she was actually leaving New York. "I'm going to miss you so much. You've been such a good friend and we had some really good times together, didn't we?"

"I will miss you, too, Emma. I hope that you find another job that you like. You will have to write me often."

Emma thought that her friend had not been the same lately, ever since that dance, but she attributed it to Anna's preoccupation with plans for leaving her job and the city.

Anna once again packed her big trunk and after hugging Sigrid and the children a tearful goodbye, Louis drove her into the city to Penn Station to catch the train. They went in to buy her ticket while the red caps took care of her trunk. It would be about an hour wait before her train would leave. She told Louis he could go because he had the horses and buggy outside. He gave her a big hug and told her to hurry back and stay with them again. She wiped away a tear and said goodbye and thanked him for all he had done for her and for letting her stay with them for so long.

After he left, she found a place to sit where there weren't too many other people. She was glad to sit down. She had not felt well this morning when she got up. It must be the excitement of packing and leaving a place I love again. She was hungry as she had not been able to eat breakfast, so she took out an apple and ate that. Sigrid had packed food enough for several days. She could also buy some on the way.

Her train was called and she almost missed the announcement. She had been deep in thought so she jumped up and had to hurry through the crowd to her gate. The conductor helped her board the train and she found her seat. Nobody had come to occupy the seats next to her by the time the train pulled out of the station. That was all right with her, she thought. She put her bag with her lunch and some books on the seat next to her. She took off her hat and settled down for the long ride and whatever awaited her at the end of the line.

CHAPTER 5

The train seemed to stop in every little town along the way. Anna enjoyed looking out at the countryside as the train passed through eastern Pennsylvania. Toward evening they reached Harrisburg where they stopped long enough for the passengers to get out and walk around a bit. Anna thought it felt very good to stretch her legs. She walked over to a lunch counter where they were selling coffee. She ordered a cup and sat down to drink it. That tasted real good, she thought, as she finished it. Not as good as Norwegian coffee but it was something hot anyway.

She boarded the train just at the last minute, not wanting to be seated longer than necessary. It was starting to get dark and she dozed off and on. Still no one occupied the seats next to her. About 6 a.m. they chugged into Pittsburgh. They were still in Pennsylvania! What a wide state, she thought. She got up to use the lavatory at the back of her car. When she got in there, all of a sudden she didn't feel good. She felt so nauseated. Have I got the flu again, she wondered. She managed to get back to her seat and she sat down hard, perspiring heavily. She fanned herself with a newspaper. Oh, what a miserable trip this will be if I am sick the whole time, she lamented. She thought she would keep the newspaper handy in case she had to throw up.

The train pulled out of the station and Anna rummaged around in her lunch sack and pulled out some biscuits to nibble on. She leaned back in her seat and tried to sleep some more. She started thinking instead. I didn't feel good yesterday morning either but I was all right in the afternoon. Why am I sick again this morning? A thought struck her and she sat bolt upright! Sick in the mornings! Then she remembered that she hadn't had her "monthly" yet either but she thought that was because of all the excitement of leaving and everything else. Oh, no, she thought, it can't be. It just can't be that. Her heart was pounding wildly. What if it was true? What would she do?

She tried to calm herself and reassure herself that everything was fine and she just had the flu again. She dozed fitfully off and on during the day. By late afternoon she heard the conductor announce that the next stop was Canton, Ohio. They could get out again for awhile. She took advantage of this and walked around the station. I feel fine now so I'm sure everything will be all right, she told herself.

She saw a pleasant looking couple waiting to board the train. She got on behind them. The conductor led them to their seats, right next to hers. Now she would have company the rest of the way. They all sat down, with Anna by the window.

When the couple was all settled and the train was beginning to move again, the gentleman turned to Anna and introduced himself and his wife. They were Sam and Amanda Martin and they were on their way to their new home in Toledo, Ohio. Mr. Martin had been there and secured a house and he had returned to Canton to get his wife.

The couple looked like they were in their mid-thirties. They were very pleasant company and kept Anna distracted from the thoughts that would enter her head now and then. A shiver of dread would then come over her.

"Are you cold, my dear?" asked the kindly Mrs. Martin.

"No, I am fine, thank you," Anna answered. "In fact it is rather warm in here, I think."

"Yes, these trains are always so warm in the summer and cold in the winter. I have traveled on them so many times," volunteered Mr. Martin.

Anna ate some more of her lunch and then she settled back to try and sleep through the night. The train stopped at Akron but she didn't get out. Towards morning the train stopped again, this time in Cleveland. Anna got up and made her way to the back of the car. She got into the lavatory and there she felt sick again! She had to throw up this time. Finally she felt a little better and got herself composed enough to go back to her seat She had to disturb the Martins again to get past them. She almost fell into her place; she was so anxious to sit down. She closed her eyes to discourage Mrs. Martin from making conversation. She had to have time to think. She was quite convinced by now what was wrong with her. She was going to have a baby!

What on earth was she going to do now? She was very distraught and could only lift her thoughts unto the Lord and ask for His help. "I will lift mine eyes unto the hills. From whence cometh my help? My help comes from the Lord." My God, what shall I do? My God- what shall- I do? She repeated this over and over again in rhythm to the clickety, clickety clack of the train.

She fell asleep for awhile and when she woke up she felt calmer and was able to think. I can't go out to Andrew and Tomas now. They can't know about this. I can't go back to New York because Sigrid must not know either. Where can I go then? she asked herself.

Anna sat up and gazed out the window at the passing countryside. Mrs. Martin said, "Did you have a restful night, Miss Olson?" When Anna said that she hadn't, Mrs. Martin said, "I can never sleep on these things, either. I am always so tired when I finally get to my destination."

The Martins ate some breakfast from their bag and offered some to Anna. It looked so good that she took some and tried to eat it. It was an interesting looking biscuit of a type she had never seen before. "It's a doughnut, my dear," said Mrs. Martin. "Haven't you ever had one before?" Anna said that she hadn't but that it tasted very good.

After they all had enough to eat, they settled back as the train began to roll again. Mr. Martin turned toward Anna and asked her where she was headed. She didn't know why she said what she did but she answered, "I don't know for sure. I need to stop someplace and get a job and make some money. And then I am headed farther west to see my brothers." Later she excused herself to go to the back of the car again.

After she returned and got back in her seat, Mr. Martin said, "My wife and I will be needing a maid when we get to Toledo. Maybe you would be interested in staying with us for awhile." Anna looked at him and the thought crossed her mind that the Lord had already answered her prayers! When she didn't answer, Mr. Martin went on to say, "We'll be in Toledo soon, by this evening, in fact. If you think you would be interested in this offer, we would be delighted to have you. It would save us the trouble of finding someone after we get there. My wife will have so much to do to get everything unpacked. All our household things have been shipped and will be waiting for us."

Mrs. Martin looked at Anna hopefully and Anna said that she would think about their kind offer. She leaned back and began to do just that. These seemed like very nice people and if it works out, maybe I can stay there for awhile till I decide what else to do. Thank you, Lord, for providing an answer for me. I don't know what else to do right now.

She sat forward later and addressed Mrs. Martin. "I think I will take you up on your offer. I'm sure I can be of some help to you, at least for awhile." Mrs. Martin seemed delighted with her answer and the two women chatted for the next few miles. They each opened their lunch bags and finished what was in them.

It was almost dusk when the train pulled into the station in Toledo. Mr. Martin went to see about their luggage and also Anna's trunk. It was all loaded up in a wagon and a driver was secured to bring it to the house. The Martin carriage was waiting for them and there was just room for the three of them plus a driver. Mr. Martin said that the drive would take about a half an hour. When they passed the glass factory, Mr. Martin told Anna that that was where he worked. He was general manager and it was owned by a Mr. Libbey. It had been built about eight years ago, he said.

The Martin house was on the west bank of the Maumee River. There were many large, pretty homes there. They pulled up in front and Anna thought it looked like a very lovely house. Mr. Martin said that he had bought it from a railroad baron who had gone bankrupt. The carriage driver helped the wagon driver unload all the baggage and the trunk into the foyer. Mr. Martin asked the men if they would be so kind as to carry the trunk to one of the upstairs bedrooms, the one on the west end, he told them.

Mrs. Martin had never seen the house before so her husband took her and Anna on a grand tour. It was wonderful! Large but not too large. There were boxes everywhere so she knew that she and Mrs. Martin would be very busy in the coming days. The workmen who delivered the furniture a few days before had set up the beds in the bedrooms. Mrs. Martin found the box labeled "bed linens" so she and Anna got busy and made up the big bed in the master bedroom and also a smaller bed for Anna in the room which was to be hers.

They all were so tired that they went to bed almost immediately. Tomorrow would be a busy day, Mrs. Martin said. Mr. Martin was staying home for the next two days so he could help get settled. Anna was so tired that she fell asleep instantly in spite of the fact that this was a strange place and also the turmoil of her emotional state.

Anna awoke to the smell of coffee the next morning. She jumped out of bed and the nausea hit her immediately. She lowered herself back down on the bed and laid there for awhile. What am I going to do; I have to get up and help Mrs. Martin. That's why I'm here, she told herself. So she slowly lifted herself up to a sitting position and sat there for a minute and then she stood up and started to get herself dressed. There came a light knock on her door.

"Anna, dear, are you awake yet? I have some hot cereal ready for you." It was the cheerful voice of Mrs. Martin.

"I'll be down in a minute," answered Anna. She knew that there was no way that she could eat hot cereal this morning but what excuse could she make to her new employer? When she entered the kitchen the smell almost overpowered her but she managed to keep from running from the room. "I'll just have the toast and coffee, Mrs. Martin. I'm sorry but I am not a big breakfast eater."

"Well, that's all right, Anna. You just eat whatever you want," she said, "but we'll need all our strength to tackle the big job ahead of us today."

Mr. Martin came in from outside and sat at the breakfast table. "Good morning, Miss Olson," he said as he reached for toast and a bowl of the hot cereal. "It's going to be a fine day today. I was just taking a walk around the place. When you two get finished with breakfast we'll all take a look around the yard."

Anna felt better when she got out into the fresh morning air. They walked down to the river's edge behind their house. There was a little gazebo much in need of a coat of paint and a shed full of garden tools and flower pots and things of that sort. There was a dock extending out into the water about twenty feet.

"The people who had this place before us used to have a little row boat but I guess they must have sold it," said Mr. Martin.

Mrs. Martin was enchanted with everything she saw. She found the perfect spot for a vegetable garden and she could tell that at one time there had been many flowers growing here and there in many different flower beds. There was plenty to do in the yard, both front and back, she remarked to no one in particular.

Mr. Martin told her that maybe they would have to hire a yard man. He would look into that tomorrow. They returned to the house and started moving furniture and emptying boxes. Mrs. Martin said that she would have to go to the grocery store and buy some food so Mr. Martin took her in the carriage and they were gone for about an hour. Anna went to her room and laid down on the bed for awhile. She was feeling better but was so very tired.

When she heard the back door slam, she got up and went down to help Mrs. Martin put the groceries away and start lunch. After they ate, she mentioned that she should get a letter off to her brother, Andrew, right away because he was the one who was going to meet her and he would wonder what happened to her. Mr. Martin found some paper for her and she went out to sit at the dining table to compose her letter.

She just wrote a short note saying that she had decided to get off in Toledo and was going to work for awhile for a very nice couple that she had met on the train. She would write later with details. She gave the letter to Mr. Martin and he said that he would go and post it right away as he also had some other errands downtown. She returned to the kitchen to help clean up.

The two women worked all day on the boxes and the house did indeed look better by nightfall but there was still much work left to do. Each room had to be cleaned before things could be permanently put away. When Mr. Martin came home again, the women started supper. Mr. Martin announced that he had found a yard man, a Scot named Mac Donnelly. He worked for one of the owners of the Libbey plant who said that he would share him with the Martins. He would be starting next Monday and would put in three days a week. Mrs. Martin was delighted and was already planning things for him to do, like painting the gazebo, digging up a garden spot, planting flowers, trimming trees.

"I'd say we have enough work for a full time man," remarked Mrs. Martin.

"Well, we'll get along with a part time one for now," said Mr. Martin. "Mr. Lorentzen said that this guy is very good and gets the job done in short order so I think he'll work out just fine. I was looking more closely at the outside of the house before I came in now and I think that maybe it needs a coat of paint, too."

"Oh, I just love this house," exclaimed Mrs. Martin, "and I think it will look so nice when it gets all ready and the yard work gets done!

"I'm glad you like it, my dear," said Mr. Martin. "You know it was really hard picking out a house by myself. But then I only had about three choices and this was by far the best."

"You did a very good job, dear," she said, giving him a peck on the cheek and then she started to clear up the table.

Anna jumped up to help her and when they had the dishes done they went outside to cool off. It had been a warm day and they had worked so hard. They went down by the river's edge and sat on the dock. Mr. Martin joined them later. He asked Anna to tell them about her life in Norway and so they talked until the darkness drove them inside.

Anna excused herself and said she thought she would retire early. I have to write to Sigrid, she told herself, but I am too tired tonight. It's good that I am kept so busy, she thought, for then I don't have much time to think about what I am going to do in the months to come. I'll just take one day at a time. She soon fell into an exhausted sleep.

The days and weeks passed quickly because there was always so much to keep them all busy. She was feeling better in the mornings now. One day in early July, Mrs. Martin announced that they would be taking the next day off as it was the Fourth of July and they would be taking in the parade downtown and then the Libbey plant was having a picnic for all the employees on the company grounds. Anna was welcome to come along if she wished. She said she would see.

In the morning Anna decided that she would like to go with the Martins to see the parade. The streets were swarming with people from far and wide who had come to town to take part in the celebration. After the parade there were speeches by some of the city's dignitaries. It was getting hotter and hotter and they had been standing so long that Anna thought that she might just faint. She told Mrs. Martin that she did not feel well and that she just had to sit down someplace. They helped her through the crowd and found some shade under some trees. She sat down right on the grass. After resting awhile, she felt better but she said she didn't think she would go with them to the picnic.

The Martins dropped Anna off at the house on their way to the picnic. She went upstairs and laid down for awhile. When she got up she decided she could no longer put off writing to Sigrid. She found pen and paper and went out to sit in the newly painted gazebo. Sigrid would surely wonder whatever made her decide to stop in Toledo, of all places, instead of going straight out to Andrew's. She would have to think up something convincing to tell her.

It took Anna most of the afternoon to finish her letter. She told Sigrid that she decided she needed to make some more money so that if she needed to go to school before she could get a teaching job here, then she would have the money. She had her letter sealed and ready for mailing by the time the Martins came home. They had a light supper that evening and Mrs. Martin told Anna all about the picnic.

Mac, the yard man, was a friendly, happy fellow. He whistled while he worked and the work seemed to go so fast. He got more done in one day than most people would in three or four days. He was invited into the house for morning and afternoon coffee, where he would be bombarded by a great array of cookies and cakes, none of which he could refuse. He said that he had to work hard so that he wouldn't get so fat from the ladies' sweets. He brought his own lunch to eat at noon and then he would lie down on the grass and take a nap that would last for exactly 15 minutes. Anna and Mrs. Martin, just for fun, would time him and it was like he had an inner alarm clock that would wake him at just the right interval of time.

Mac had made the yard come alive with flowering blooms everywhere and now he was giving the big house a fresh coat of white paint.

As the weeks went by, Anna finally received a letter from Sigrid. She was almost afraid to open it. She put it in her pocket and waited until a break in the afternoon's chores. She took it and went out to the gazebo. As she slowly opened it she wondered what Sigrid was going to say to her. She read as follows:

Dear Anna,

What in the world did you stop in Toledo for? I thought you were so anxious to get out to see the boys. I was waiting and waiting to get a letter from you, thinking all the time that you were at Andrew's by now. I thought perhaps you had written and that the letter had become lost. Oh, well, I guess you are old enough to know what you are doing. How long do you plan to stay there?

Anna put the letter down for awhile as it was hard to read through her tears. Mac happened to walk by just then and saw her crying.

"What have we here, Lass?" he asked in his thick Scottish brogue. "No one is allowed to be unhappy on such an afternoon as this!"

Anna tried to wipe her tears with her apron and decided it was useless to pretend that she had not been crying. He saw that she was reading a letter.

"It's not bad news from home, I hope," he said, his tone now becoming gentle and concerned.

"No," she managed to answer. "It's just a letter from my sister in New York. She's wondering what I am doing in Toledo. I wonder myself, sometimes."

"Ah, getting a little bit of a scolding from the older sister, eh?"

"I guess you could say that," Anna answered.

Mac decided he would pry no longer and he went back to his painting. Anna finished reading her letter. She felt wretched. She felt like she was deceiving her sister and everyone else. If only I had someone to talk to, she thought. Perhaps I need to tell someone. She had always been taught to take everything to the Lord in prayer and that's what she had been doing every night in her prayers. The Lord will show me the way but I need to be patient. Maybe I need to tell Mrs. Martin. I will soon start to show anyway and then she will guess.

Several evenings later she and Mrs. Martin were walking down by the dock. They sat down on the bench that Mac had made.

"Oh, how I love this place now!" exclaimed Mrs. Martin. "Hasn't Mac done a wonderful job? You know, I wasn't very happy when Samuel told me that we would be moving from Canton. I had so many friends there and I liked living there. I haven't had the time to make very many friends here yet, but I think I am going to be very happy here."

Suddenly she looked very wistful and sad. "There's only one thing that would really complete the picture for us and that is if we could have a child. We've been married for almost fourteen years now and I've almost given up hope of ever having one. I pray about it every day." With this said, Mrs. Martin dabbed at the corner of her eye to catch the tears that would always begin to fall whenever she thought about her childless state.

Anna was also trying to hold back her tears but she lost the battle. She burst out crying so suddenly that Mrs. Martin gave a start and looked at Anna and said, "Oh, Anna, I didn't mean to distress you so with my problems." She put her arm around the young girl and Anna cried all the more.

"Oh, Mrs. Martin," she started, "I have to tell you something, and it's not going to be easy but I have to tell someone. I"m going to have a baby and I don't know what to do!"

Mrs. Martin was struck dumb for a moment or two before she could find her voice. "Anna, my poor dear, I am so surprised! I never suspected. Oh dear, oh dear, what are we going to do?"

"It's not your problem, Mrs. Martin. It's all mine and I don't know what to do. That's why I agreed to work for you for awhile so that I would have time to think about what to do. I couldn't go out to my brothers in this condition. I would be so ashamed."

"Does your sister in New York know? Did she know before you left there?"

Anna calmed down and took a deep breath and started to tell Mrs. Martin the whole story. When she finished, it felt good to have simply told someone. Mrs. Martin did not condemn her or make her feel like she was a bad girl.

"Anna, I feel so bad that this had to happen to you. You are such a good person. We will stand by you and help you all we can. Don't worry about what's going to happen to you. We'll think of something." Mrs. Martin held Anna for a long time and Anna felt a sense of peace come over her.

"I'm so glad I finally told you. It's been so hard carrying that burden all by myself for so long," Anna told her.

"I wish you had told me sooner, but I guess I can understand your reluctance to do so."

Mr. Martin came walking down the path and called to them. "Hey, you two, what are you so absorbed in? I called to you from the back door."

Mrs. Martin jumped up and said, "Oh, just some girl talk. Goodness, we need to do the supper dishes, don't we, Anna?"

Anna was very quiet that evening and she knew Mr. Martin would be wondering why. Mrs. Martin would no doubt tell him everything later but I guess that is just as well, Anna thought to herself. He will have to know sooner or later.

The next morning after her husband left for work, Mrs. Martin told Anna that she had told him everything last night. "We don't keep any secrets from each other," she said. "He said that you are not to worry. We will help you in any way that we can. He said that he will make an appointment with a doctor for you soon."

"Oh, no, he musn't do that. I don't want to see any doctor!" exclaimed Anna.

"Why ever not, my dear?" asked Mrs. Martin with surprise.

"I don't know...I...I..." she stammered, "I guess I just never thought of having to go see a doctor."

"Well, we will see that you get the best care possible."

That night when Mr. Martin came home, Anna could hardly look at him. After supper he finally said, "Anna, come into my study. I want to talk to you for a bit."

She followed him into the room and he indicated she should sit in the chair opposite him. He started a fire in the fireplace as the evenings had begun to get chilly. He sat down and looked at her with compassion and concern. Anna's fears of a stern lecture faded.

"Anna, my dear, my wife told me about your predicament and that you feel so bad about it. I just want you to know that I certainly do not condemn you and we want to help you in any way we can. Have you given any thought as to what you will do after the baby is born?"

"I think about it all the time and I don't know what I should do. I don't want to keep it. It was not a baby conceived out of love. I have no feelings for it because I loathe the man who did this to me."

Anna could not believe that she was talking so frankly to Mr. Martin but he had always been so kind to her, almost like a father. She choked back a sob when she thought about her father, and how disappointed he would be if he knew, but he would be just as kind and forgiving as Mr. Martin.

Anna wept into her hands. "My father must never know because I was his favorite daughter and he would feel so let down."

"Anna, you must never feel that this was your fault and your father would not feel that way either. You couldn't help what happened."

Winter would soon be upon them. Mac finished his fall yard work and said that he was heading south to find work for the winter months. He didn't know if he would be back or not. Mr. Martin said that if he did come back, they would like him to work for them again. Anna was beginning to show now quite a bit. She found Mac looking at her strangely several times but nothing was said between them.

One chilly evening Anna was sitting in the study with the Martins. Mrs. Martin put down her needlepoint and looked at Anna. "Anna, after the baby is born, do you think you will want to take it with you out to your brother's?"

"Oh, no," answered Anna quickly, "I can't do that! I've told you that I don't want to keep the baby. Every time I would look at that baby, I would be reminded of its father!"

Mrs. Martin hesitated a moment before continuing. "Do you want to put the baby up for adoption then?"

"Well, yes, I suppose that is what I'll have to do," Anna answered.

Mr. and Mrs. Martin exchanged glances. Mr. Martin pulled his chair closer to Anna's. "Anna," he started gently, "Mrs. Martin and I have been talking and perhaps we have found a solution for you. As you know, we have been childless for quite a long time now and we would very much like to adopt your baby if that is what you would want."

Anna looked at them and saw their expectant faces. "Why didn't I think of that? You two would make the perfect parents." She fidgeted momentarily before asking, "But how could you want this baby when you know how it was conceived?"

Mrs. Martin got up and stood close to Anna, her hand on her shoulder.

"You can't blame the baby for that, Anna. We would love it all the same, like it was our own child, conceived in love, after many years of trying."

Anna stood and walked around the room, then returned to the warmth of the fire. "I think God has just answered my prayers again, and perhaps yours, too." Anna and Mrs. Martin, still standing, embraced each other, neither needing to say anything further.

The next morning after Mr. Martin left for work, Mrs. Martin told Anna to sit at the table and they would have a second cup of coffee. "I need to talk to you about something," she said. She poured the coffee and sat down.

"Anna, you know how long I have wanted to have a baby. I felt like such a failure before my family and friends. I would very much like them all to think that I gave birth to your baby. That it was our child, not an adopted child. Do you think we could do that?"

Anna looked surprised at this suggestion. "Well, I suppose that we could try, but don't people around here know about me yet? I haven't told anyone but then I don't really know anyone. Except Max, and he did look at me funny a few times. Then there's the milkman and the grocery delivery boy. Perhaps they could see that I am very much with child."

"Well, from now on you and I will stay out of the public eye as much as possible. My parents have written and want us to come to Canton for Christmas but I will tell them that I do not feel well and don't want to travel. They can draw their own conclusions."

And so it was that Anna and Mrs. Martin kept a low profile, not letting anyone see them up close. When they went to church on Sunday mornings, both women wore long, flowing cloaks. They kept a quiet Christmas, not entertaining or accepting any invitations. Anna wrote and received letters from her family. A long letter came from Papa. She read it over and over again through the quiet days of waiting. Papa asked her if she was ready yet to come back home.

The family doctor, kindly old Dr. Rhinehart, came to the house every week towards the last. He thought that the baby would be born sometime the first of February. The Martins told him of their mutual agreement with Anna to say that Mrs. Martin was the one actually giving birth. He said he had never been party to this type of deception before but if all parties agreed, he said that maybe it would do no harm. He would not be able to lie on the actual birth certificate, though.

On the morning of February third, Anna awoke and felt that things were not just right. It felt like butterflies in her stomach she said, but by noon it started to feel like more than that. The doctor was notified and Mrs. Martin sent Anna to bed.

Dr. Rhinehart did not make it over to the Martin house until late afternoon. He examined Anna and said that it would be quite a while yet. He said he was going home and they should send for him when things began to happen in earnest. Mr. Martin came home while the doctor's buggy was still in the driveway. He hurried into the house and ran up the stairs, calling for his wife. He met her and the doctor at the top of the stairway.

"What has happened, Amanda?" he asked his wife.

"Oh, Samuel, thank God you're here. Anna is in labor and I sent for the doctor but he says it will be awhile yet."

Mr. Martin saw Dr. Rhinehart out and returned to join his wife by Anna's bed. She had just had another contraction and Mrs. Martin was wiping her face with a cloth. They both left the room for awhile. Mr. Martin put his arm around his wife and held her close. "Soon now, my dear, we will become parents."

"Yes, and I am so excited and nervous. I just hope everything goes all right. I hope Dr. Rhinehart gets back here when we really need him."

"Don't worry about a thing, Amanda. Everything will go just fine." He wasn't as sure as he tried to make himself sound. He was nervous, too, he realized.

The evening wore on and Anna's contractions became stronger and closer together. Mr. Martin drove over to Dr.Rhinehart's and asked if he could come now.

"I was just thinking that I may be needed at your house about now," the doctor said. "I have delivered hundreds of babies and you can just about tell. I think her delivery will go very smoothly and routinely. Let's be off, then," he added as he grabbed his coat and muffler and, of course, his black bag.

When the two men arrived up in Anna's room, things were happening very rapidly. Amanda Martin was never so glad to see two people before! Dr. Rhinehart took over and Mr. Martin went out in the hall to begin pacing. It took another half hour, though, before he heard a baby's cry through the closed door. He waited for what seemed like an eternity before his wife opened the door and motioned him to come in.

"It's a boy!" she told her husband. "We have a fine son!"

Anna, looking totally exhausted, had tears rolling down her cheeks. Tears of relief that the ordeal was finally over, and tears of joy for the look of total happiness on the faces of Samuel and Amanda Martin, the new parents of her child. They were holding the baby, wrapped in a blanket and seemingly staring up at them. They looked like a picture, Anna thought, a picture that she would never forget.

Then the baby began to fuss. Anna had already told Mrs. Martin that she did not want to nurse the baby, so Mrs. Martin had bought bottles and she hurried now to prepare one for the newborn. The doctor told Anna that she had done well and that the baby was healthy and normal in every way. They had weighed the child on a baby scale that Mrs. Martin had ordered and it weighed a little over seven pounds.

The doctor said that he had to fill out the birth certificate and he needed to know the name of the real father. Anna hesitated a few moments and finally said, Joseph Alexander Morrissey. She never wanted to speak that name again. That chapter of her life was now closed. She would only look forward.

Anna convalesced while Mrs. Martin took over the complete care of the baby. The Martins named the baby Samuel, after his new father, but they called him Sammy. Sammy was a good baby, eating and sleeping most of the time. Anna didn't hear him cry very much. She stayed away from him as much as was possible. Both she and Mrs. Martin secretly feared that Anna could possibly become attached to him if she was around him too much.

After about a week in bed, Anna started to return to normal life as much as possible. She wrote to Andrew to tell him that her job here in Toledo was finished and she would be coming out to stay with them about the first of March. Mr. Martin had put an advertisement in the local newspaper for a housekeeper.

Anna began to pack her trunk and once again prepared for a move. She and Mrs. Martin had some tearful conversations over late night cups of coffee after Sammy was settled in and Mr. Martin had retired to his study. She said that she hoped that she was doing the right thing and she said she knew that the Martins would be great parents for little Sammy.

"You can't possibly know the happiness you have brought to us by letting us be the ones to raise your baby, Anna," Mrs. Martin said. But I understand, too, that this has been an extremely trying time in your young life. You have handled it very well."

On the day of her planned departure, with Mr. Martin waiting out in the carriage, Anna said her final goodbyes in the house. It was a house that she had grown to love as she had the people in it. She thanked Mrs. Martin for being so kind and understanding. She held little Sammy in her arms one final time. Mrs. Martin left them alone. Anna gave him a kiss on his soft, sweet forehead and said that she hoped he had a wonderful life with his new parents, a life that she just couldn't give him herself.

With tears in her eyes, she handed him back to the waiting Mrs. Martin. She held him close and told Anna that she need never regret giving him to them. With that, Anna left the house quickly and almost ran to the carriage.

They rode to the train station in silence. She never looked back at the house because she knew she would see Mrs. Martin standing in the doorway holding the baby and waving goodbye.

She could never look back now. It was agreed upon between the two women that Anna would not try to contact them but they would send word to her from time to time regarding little Sammy's well being. A chapter in her life was drawing to a close and another one was ready to open before her.

CHAPTER 6

Anna had been dozing when she heard the conductor call out South Bend. The passengers were allowed to get out and stretch here. Anna went inside to buy a cup of coffee to go with her lunch that Mrs. Martin had packed. Twenty minutes later the whistle blew and she hurried back on board. The next stop would be Chicago and there she would change trains. She hoped she wouldn't have any trouble getting on the right train. She felt lucky that she knew English as well as she did but sometimes people talked so fast that she still had trouble understanding them. She had to listen very carefully to the conductors, she had found out.

She had a new seat mate for this leg of the journey. He was a talkative young man who was getting off in Chicago. He was going there to try and get a job on the newspaper. It had always been his dream to work for the Chicago Tribune. He was curious about Anna, where she had come from and where she was going. He was interested in people and thought her coming to America would be a good human interest story.

"Someday maybe I'll be able to write articles about people like you and it will sell papers," he stated enthusiastically.

She told him that she was worried about catching the right train and he said he would help her. They arrived in Chicago about midnight. True to his word, he led her to the right platform and told her she had to wait about a half hour for her train. He helped her find a bench and she thanked him for his kindness and wished him good luck with his job hunting.

The train was on time and she boarded right away and found her seat. She was very tired by now and hoped to be able to get some sleep during the night's ride. She had an elderly man sitting on one side of her and an empty seat on the other side. The train made several stops during the night but she did not pay too much attention to them. She slept off and on. She only needed to listen for a town by the name of Davenport.

The morning sun woke her up fully and she felt fairly rested. She made her way to the back of the car and then returned to eat something from her bag. About noon they came into Davenport. This was in Iowa, she believed. I'm getting closer, she thought to herself. She had to get off here because she had to change to another train again. She stood looking at a big wall map to try and figure out how much further she had to go. Perhaps she should send Andrew a wire from here. She went to talk to a man behind the ticket counter and he helped her figure out what time she would be coming into the station at St. Ansgar, the town where Andrew said that she should get off. She next went to the telegraph window and sent her wire. Then she sat down to wait. Her train was not scheduled to come in until about 3 o'clock in the afternoon.

She would sit for awhile and then go outside and walk for awhile in the cool March air and then return to the station. Finally her train came in and she got on and the train car was almost empty. The rest of the day went quickly. The train made short stops at Cedar Rapids and Waterloo and picked up a number of passengers at each place. A couple hours before dawn, the train came into Charles City where they stopped for about a half hour. They stopped briefly at several small towns throughout the morning. She knew she was getting very close now.

Anna finished her lunch and tried to freshen herself up somewhat. She felt herself getting nervous and anxious about seeing her brother after all these years. She figured out that it was actually about 12 years since her brothers left their homeland. She would never recognize Andrew and he surely wouldn't know her after all this time, she thought.

About half past noon the conductor called out St. Ansgar and she felt her heart almost jump up into her throat! She gathered her things and looked out the window to see if she could catch a glimpse of someone waiting for her. She was the only passenger to get out at this stop. As the conductor helped her down the steps of the train, she saw a man and a small boy walking toward her. She almost stumbled on the step, she was so excited. The little boy came running up to her and calling, "Are you my Auntie Anna?"

"Well, if your name is Alfred Olson, then I guess I am," she answered, looking from the child to the man.

"Anna, is it really you, all grown up?" asked the man.

"Oh, Andrew, I didn't even recognize you!" she exclaimed and she put her bag down so she could embrace him. They stood at arms length looking at each other, trying to find something familiar about each other's faces.

"Well, Anna, I think you have grown up to look a little like I remember Sigrid and also a little like Mama."

"I guess you do resemble Tollef somewhat, Andrew, now that I have looked at you longer," she added. They had been talking partly in Norwegian and partly in English. Little Alfred was getting impatient for some attention so he started pulling on his Papa's pants leg. Andrew picked up Anna's bag and they started for the wagon.

"Oh, I have to wait for my trunk, Andrew," she said. It was just being unloaded from the baggage car. Two men put it on a trolley and they brought it over to Andrew's wagon. He helped Anna and Alfred get up on the seat and then they were off.

"We live on a farm about twelve miles west of here so it won't take too long. I'm glad it is a nice day today for you. Yesterday was very windy and cool."

Alfred sat between them and he kept looking up at her, grinning. She put her arm around him and thought how wonderful it was going to be to get acquainted with Andrew all over again and his new family.

"We will have so much to talk about, Andrew, I don't know how we'll find time to eat or sleep!" Anna exclaimed.

The ride to the farm went very quickly as the two of them were so busy talking. Little Alfred fell asleep, with his head on Anna's lap. When they stopped in front of the farmhouse, he awoke and jumped up and scampered down from the wagon so he could run to tell his Mama that Auntie Anna was here. Andrew helped her down and then Alice came out on the porch to welcome her sister-in-law.

"Welcome, dear Anna, I finally get to meet you!" Alice exclaimed. "Andrew has talked so much about you lately. He was wondering if he would even know you after all these years. He said you were only about 9 years old when he left home."

"Yes, I guess we both had changed so much that neither one of us recognized each other at the train station, except that I was the only passenger who got off there and he was the only other person on the platform!" said Anna.

"Well, come in, come in," said Alice, holding the screen door open for her. "Here, let me take your coat and hat and you just sit down by the table and I'll get us a cup of coffee."

Andrew came in after putting the team away. "I'll need some help getting that big trunk into the house. What do you have in it anyway, Anna, a load of bricks?" he teased. "Maybe you brought me some big rocks from our old farm in Norway!"

He washed up and joined the ladies at the table. "Little Berta is sleeping but she should be getting up from her nap soon," said Alice. "You will certainly hear her when she wakes up."

Andrew put some cream and a sugar lump in his coffee and stirred it slowly, looking at Anna. "I can't believe that you are finally here, little sister."

Alfred begged for a sugar lump. "Just one, young man," said his mother, giving him one and putting them out of reach. Turning to Anna, she said, "You speak English fairly well, Anna. That is good that you caught on so fast."

"I took some lessons in New York, and we spoke it at the factory where I worked. Sigrid and Louis spoke it most of the time, too."

"We speak it all the time here at home," said Andrew, "because Alice never did learn to speak Norwegian very well at home. Her mother was Norwegian but her father was Scottish."

They heard a wail from the other room. "There's Berta," said Alfred, as he jumped off his chair and ran to get his little sister. They came into the kitchen hand in hand and when the little girl saw a stranger sitting there, she started crying all over again. She hid behind her brother but he kept pushing her to go over to Anna's chair. Finally Alice rescued her and set her down in her lap and fed her a cookie and let her get used to Anna from a distance.

Anna didn't know when she had seen such a pretty little girl. She had big brown eyes and her hair was full of ringlets. She was very shy, though, and would hardly look at Anna.

"She'll warm up to you after awhile," Alice reassured Anna.

"It will take you many weeks to tell me everything I want to know, Anna," said Andrew, "but you will have to excuse me for awhile. I have to go and do the chores, but I'll be in by suppertime." With that he put his old chore jacket on and went out to the barn.

"You sure have a nice place here, Alice."

"This is the farm I grew up on. My father left it to me when he died. I didn't have any brothers to take over the farm. It was a lucky day when Andrew came in the yard one day looking for work. My father liked him right away and of course, I did too!"

"Is your mother still living then?" asked Anna.

"No, she died, too. She lived here with us for a couple years and just died about a year ago."

Alice put Berta down so that she could start fixing supper. Anna thought that it was best if she just ignored the little girl for awhile. "Is there something I can help you with, Alice?"

"Well, here's an apron and you can start peeling the potatoes, if you wish." Alice went to change Berta's diaper.

Anna stood at the sink, looking out the window as she started her task. I can hardly believe that here I am, so very, very far from home, she thought to herself. I wonder what Papa and Mama are doing right now. A feeling of homesickness flooded over her. I miss Sigrid and her family, too, she thought.

Then Alice returned and put Berta on the floor and gave her some spoons to play with. Alice said, "I planned a special supper for us tonight to celebrate your arrival."

"Oh, that's so very nice of you, Alice. I was just standing here feeling kind of lonesome for home and thinking about everyone."

"I hope that you will like being here with us. We sure have been looking forward to having you come, finally." Alice opened the oven door to take a peek and a wonderful smell filled the kitchen.

"Oh, what is that good smell?" asked Anna, sniffing the air again and again.

"It's pork ribs," replied Alice, shutting the oven door just in time before Berta got too close.

Anna finished the potatoes and Alice put them on the stove to cook.

Anna sat down by the table and watched Berta and Alfred at play. Pretty soon, Berta came up to Anna to show her a toy. "See! See!" she said. Anna reached for the toy and Berta held out her chubby little arms to be picked up. Anna lifted her onto her lap and she sat there contentedly for quite sometime.

"I think you have made yourself a little friend, Anna," said Alice.

Anna hugged the little girl to her breast and felt her heartache return for the baby she had just given up. She buried her face in Berta's hair and felt the tears coming but she fought them back. She couldn't cry now. Maybe later, but not now.

Sometime later, Andrew came bursting in the back door. "Oh, it smells so good in here and I'm hungry as a bear!" he exclaimed.

"We will soon be ready to eat. I'll just get the table set," said Alice. She took out her good dishes and put them around the table, then she called everyone to be seated. Before eating, Andrew said the table grace and added a special thanks to the Lord for the safe arrival of Anna. Just now he reminds me of Papa, Anna thought to herself as she watched him sitting there, head bowed over the table.

After the wonderful meal, Andrew played with the children while the women did up the dishes. Then Alice took the children up to get them ready for bed. Anna and Andrew settled themselves down for an evening of talking and reminiscing. Andrew had so many questions about the family back home. He had many years to catch up on, he told her.

When Alice came down, she lit the lamps as it was growing dark but Anna and Andrew had hardly noticed, they were so deep in conversation. Alice busied herself in the kitchen for sometime and then came to join them. They then switched to English so she could understand them. Sometime later, Anna started yawning so Alice said that perhaps they had better call it a day. She showed Anna up to her room. It had been Alfred's but they had moved his little bed in with Berta. My trunk will hardly fit up here, Anna thought to herself. A neighbor was going to stop by in the morning to help move the trunk upstairs, Andrew had told her.

Anna changed into her nightgown, washed her face and sunk down into the little single bed which was piled high with soft quilts. The sheets smelled of fresh air. Oh, this feels so wonderful, she thought, as she drifted off to sleep almost immediately.

The next morning she awoke to the smell of coffee. She dressed quickly and looked out her little dormer window. There was a man in a wagon pulling into the yard. This must be the neighbor, she thought, as she hurried down the steep stairs.

"Oh, good morning, Anna," said Alice cheerfully. "I hope you slept well in a strange place."

"I slept like a rock!" answered Anna. "The bed was so comfortable and I was so tired."

Andrew came in the door, followed by a young man who removed his hat when he saw the women.

"Good morning, Peder," said Alice. "Come sit down and have a cup of coffee with us. I suppose you have already had your breakfast."

Andrew led him toward the table and said, "Peder, this is my sister, Anna Olson, and Anna this is Peder Jorgenson."

He held out his hand shyly to Anna, then they all sat down and Alice poured coffee for everyone. Andrew said the blessing and they dug into the pancakes and sausages. Alice had just started on her first pancake when they heard a wail from upstairs. She went to get Berta and came down with both children.

"When Berta decides to wake up, nobody else can sleep," she said, looking at Alfred.

"Here, Peder," said Andrew, "you better have one of Alice's cakes. You'll need the energy to get that big trunk up those stairs!"

"No, no, I'm full up to here," he said, pointing to his chin. "Ma made eggs and bacon this morning and I ate so many biscuits, too!"

When breakfast was finished, the two men went out to get the trunk from the wagon and into the house. Anna started clearing the table while Alice helped Berta with her pancake.

"The Jorgensons are our closest neighbors and they have been dear friends for years. Peder is their youngest son. He's a nice young man, don't you think?" Alice asked Anna. "He's about your age, I think, maybe a couple years older."

The way Alice was smiling, Anna got the feeling that she was going to be the object of some matchmaking. I don't want any of that, not yet anyway, she thought to herself.

The men came banging into the house, hardly able to get the big trunk through the door. They proceeded across the kitchen and started up the steep stairway. "I told you, Peder, that Anna has this trunk full of rocks from Norway, didn't I?" Andrew said jokingly.

"Well, I believe that, all right," answered Peder from halfway up the stairs.

After the task was done, Anna thanked Peder as he left the house for coming to help. After the dishes were done, she went upstairs to unpack some of her things.

The weeks went by with Anna helping Alice with the endless household chores and enjoying late-night talks with Andrew. Spring came early and by Easter, she and Alice had started planting potatoes. Andrew was getting anxious to start planting wheat and corn. He had milk cows and hogs and chickens so there was no end to all the work. His hired man came every day, now. He lived near by with his wife.

"I'm glad he doesn't stay with us anymore," said Alice. "He was a nice enough man but it meant more cooking for me."

"I hope you don't feel the same about me," said Anna teasingly.

"Oh, goodness no! You're family and anyway you help me so much I don't know what I'd do without you now!"

That made Anna stop and think that she needed to get on with her life. She couldn't just stay here forever. That evening she talked to Andrew about it.

"I think it's about time I went to visit awhile with Tomas and his family and then decide what I should do next. I'd like to get a teaching job by next fall."

"Well, we'll miss you very much, Anna. I know Alice really appreciates all you do to help her. I'll have to get a hired girl here for her now," he said, smiling at Alice.

"That would be a good idea, Andrew," said Alice. "Anna did spoil me a bit."

The next day Anna wrote to Tomas and told him that she would be coming to stay with them at the end of May.

It was a very warm day when Andrew hitched up the team to the wagon for the trip to St. Ansgar where she would board the train for Mankato, where Tomas lived. She didn't take her trunk this time. She had bought a small suitcase in town to put just her clothes in. She hugged Alice and the children goodbye. Little Berta clung to her and did not want to let go. They had become fast friends. Alice was trying not to cry as she embraced Anna one last time.

"I will probably be back soon so don't look so sad," said Anna as Andrew helped her into the wagon. She turned and waved until the three were only little specks in the driveway.

"I certainly have enjoyed this time with you, Andrew. You found yourself a good wife and you have two very wonderful children. You are so lucky," she said pensively.

"You will have yourself a wonderful family someday, too, Anna. You are still young but the right young man will come along soon, I'm sure."

"I'm not looking for that 'right young man' yet, my dear brother," she scolded. "I have things I want to do first."

"Yes, I know you want to teach again. I bet you make a great teacher. You seem to have a way with children. I've watched you with Alfred and Berta."

"I hope to find a teaching job somewhere," Anna said, "but maybe no one will want to hire somebody from the old country. They'll want someone who speaks the language better."

The hot sun beat down on the pair as they bounced along on their way to town.

"I should have taken the buggy today, as least we'd have some shade, but I needed the wagon to haul some bags of feed home again," Andrew apologized.

"That's all right," said Anna, "we'll soon be there. I hope the train isn't too hot."

They pulled into the station and saw that the train was already there. Anna got a bit excited. "Are we late, do you suppose?"

They got down and hurried into the station and went up to the ticket counter. The agent said, "No, you aren't late, the train is just early and it is filling on water so you still have a few minutes."

Anna bought her ticket and she and Andrew walked over to the edge of the platform. They embraced and said goodbye. "I'll write soon and tell you if I have found a teaching job. I'm truly going to miss all of you but I am very excited to see Tomas and Bergit again." With this she stepped up into the train and found her seat. It was on the side of the platform so she could see Andrew standing there, waving to her.

The train pulled out of the station right on time. She had no one on either side of her. In fact, the car was only half full. She would stay on this train until they reached Owatonna, Minnesota, and then she would have to change and get on one going west to Mankato. These seats were quite comfortable and she leaned back to rest. It was rather warm in the car, but a man opened some windows further up so maybe that would help, she thought. She dozed on and off throughout the afternoon.

They stopped in many small towns and picked up more people at each stop. By evening, the car was almost full. An immigrant family had boarded in Austin and were sitting across from her. She understood enough of what they were saying to tell that it was Swedish. The couple had three small children who were very hot and tired. She heard the conductor mention Minneapolis to them.

She wondered about this family, where they were going to end up and what they would be doing. They looked very weary and somewhat fearful. They probably just got off the boat recently and have been traveling ever since. She thought back to the day that she arrived in this country and everything that had happened since. I wonder what the future will hold for me.

It was way past midnight when they arrived in Owatonna. She got off the train and waited for her suitcase and headed to another train on the other side of the station. Her seat was next to two men who were headed to the Dakotas, they told her. They were Norwegian and were speaking mostly in that language. They were both from Oslo and had been in this country for about six years. They were going to Fargo, North Dakota, to see their cousin who was in the clothing business. They were hoping to get jobs there, doing carpentry work.

The time passed quickly with someone to visit with. Anna wasn't tired as she had slept so much during the day. She was getting very hungry, though. She had shared some of her lunch with the Swedish family earlier and had run out of food. The sun was coming up when the conductor announced that they would soon be getting into Mankato. I hope Tomas got my wire, she thought.

There were quite a number of people who got out at this stop so she wondered if Tomas would find her very easily. She got her suitcase and walked off to find a place to sit and watch for him. Just then she saw a tall man come hurrying up to her.

"Anna, is it really you?" the man asked. Anna had to look closely to tell that it was indeed Tomas.

"Oh, Tomas, yes, it is really me, finally!" He put his big arms around her and they stood this way awhile. Neither one wanted the other to see their tears!

"Well, here, let me take your suitcase and we'll be off. It's just a short ride to our house."

She followed her brother to his wagon and he helped her up. She kept turning and looking at him on the way. "It sure is good to see you again," Anna said.

"Well, we have been waiting for a long, long time," he said in a voice meant to be stern, but then he smiled at her. "I can't wait for you to see our growing family!"

"Yes, and I hear that Bergit is going to have a baby soon. Maybe I'll get in on that," said Anna.

"Well, it's not until September but perhaps you will at that," he said. He rounded the corner and stopped at a small, white house with a picket fence all around it.

"This is it!" he said, as he stopped the team by the side of the house. He helped her down and she turned to see Bergit running out of the house toward her.

"Oh, Anna, my dear, how good it is to see you!" She gave her a quick hug and then looked at her and then hugged her again.

"Bergit, you haven't changed very much," said Anna. "Not as much as Tomas has."

"Well, he's gotten heavier and has a beard now," replied Bergit as she led Anna into the house. Anna could smell coffee and bacon and eggs. She could hardly wait to eat, she told Bergit.

"Here, let me take your hat and you sit right down, or maybe you'd like to wash up a little first. Over there is a wash basin and I will pour you a little warm water so you can freshen up. I'm sure the train was hot and dusty, if I remember right."

When she was finished, Tomas came in and they all sat down and had some breakfast. The children were all still sleeping, Bergit said.

"Arne and Hannah had their last day of school just yesterday so I will let them sleep a little later. Sarah is still sleeping, too, which surprises me," said Bergit.

"Let's see now, how old are the children exactly?" asked Anna.

"Arne is almost eight and Hannah is six. Sarah just turned three," answered Tomas. "They are a lively bunch so Bergit has her hands full."

"That is for sure," Bergit said, "and here I am in the family way again!" She laughed good naturedly.

"I hope I can be of some help to you then and earn my keep!" said Anna.

Tomas finished eating and took a second cup of coffee and sat back in his chair and looked at Anna. "Bergit, what do you think of our little Annie, then?"

"I think that she's grown up to be a beautiful, young woman! She was only a child when we left the old country."

"Yes, I was only nine at the time and how I hated to see you all go, especially Sigrid. We had grown so close," Anna said, thinking back.

"I bet you enjoyed your stay with her in New York," Bergit said, as she finished eating.

"Oh, yes! I liked the big city. We had a wonderful time together," answered Anna. "I understand you didn't like it one bit!" she said to both of them.

"No," Tomas replied, "We were glad to get out of there and get to the wide open spaces. We really like it here in this small town. Life has been good to us here. We like the people and the carpentry business has been going very well."

We're thinking of getting a larger house, especially with one more child on the way!" said Bergit. "This one is nice, but we are feeling a little cramped with the children getting bigger."

"Speaking of carpentry work, I better get going and make some money for us!" Tomas said, pushing back his chair and reaching for his hat. "We're building a new store down on the main street. I'll take you down there tomorrow."

After he left, the children started waking up and coming down, one by one. First came Hannah, followed by little Sarah. They were surprised to see a stranger in their kitchen so early in the day.

"This is your Aunt Anna, children, from Norway," Bergit told them. They came shyly up to her and said hello and then just stood and looked at her.

"Don't stare, children!" their mother scolded. "Sit down and I will bring you some eggs and bacon." They did as they were told and soon they were joined by the oldest, Arne.

"How do you do, Aunt Anna," he said, and then sat down. Papa told me that you would be here when I got up this morning."

The children and Anna were all speaking in English and Bergit remarked on how well Anna spoke the language. The three adults had been speaking only Norwegian earlier. Anna told Bergit that she would prefer to use English as she wanted to improve on it.

"We speak mostly English to the children because we want them to speak it well by the time they start school, otherwise the other children may make fun of them," Bergit told Anna.

"Did it take you a long time to learn it, Bergit?" asked Anna. "You speak it really quite well."

"Well, It was very hard at first, I tell you!" she said, clearing up the dishes. "When we left New York we lived in Wisconsin for awhile, helping a farmer there. They spoke only Norwegian so I didn't learn much that year. When we came here, I took lessons for awhile and so did Tomas. His boss speaks only English so he had to learn it fast."

After breakfast, Bergit showed Anna the rest of the house. "I'm sorry that you won't have a room all to yourself; you will have to share a room with Arne and Hannah. Sarah sleeps in our room."

The afternoon grew very warm so Bergit told Anna to go outside in the back yard with the children and sit in the shade. "I'll bring some lemonade for everyone in a little while."

Anna could have fallen asleep except that every time she closed her eyes, one of the children would come and want her attention. Soon it was nap time for Sarah and the other two went to play next door. Bergit came to sit down beside Anna for awhile.

"I need to do some ironing, but I'll just sit for a few minutes," said Bergit.

"You work too hard, Bergit," Anna told her. "I think that I won't get married and have children. Everyone I've stayed with so far, Sigrid, Alice and now you, all seem to have to work so hard all the time! I think I'll just be an old maid school teacher," laughed Anna.

"Oh, when the right man comes along, you'll want to get married and then you will want to have children, just like we did," retorted Bergit. "It is alot of work, I will admit that. I wish I had a hired girl for the summer. There is so much to do all the time, I can hardly keep up. If I let things go for one hour, I am already behind!"

"Well, I'm not afraid of work, and I'll help you, but it just seems that things are so hard for the women, taking care of the children and all," said Anna.

"What is the solution?" asked Bergit. "The men work very hard, too."

"Yes, Andrew sure worked hard when I was there. I guess his work was never done, either."

"Well, work never killed anybody, and speaking of work, I better get in and do the ironing and then start supper. It was nice sitting out here for awhile. I usually don't take the time to do that during the day. Once I'm up, its go, go, go all day long!"

Anna jumped up, too, and picked up the glasses and followed Bergit into the house. "I'll do the ironing, Bergit, and you can start supper and we can have a nice chat while we are working. Alice and I did that so much and she said that the work seemed to go so much faster if you had someone to talk to while you were doing it."

By the time Tomas came home, the supper was on the table and everyone sat down at one time. Tomas asked the blessing and Bergit dished up the children's plates.

"So, Anna, tell us about this job in Toledo that was so important that you couldn't come out and see your brothers," Tomas said teasingly.

At that, Anna swallowed her water wrong and started choking so it was awhile before she could speak. This gave her time to think of an answer.

"I met this nice, young couple on the train and they asked me if I could come and work for them for awhile. They were just moving into a new house and needed help unpacking and everything," Anna said, not really looking at either of them.

"You sure stayed there for a long time," said Tomas. "The letters were flying back and forth between here and Sigrid until she finally got your address there! She couldn't understand what had gotten into you. She said that you were so anxious to get out here to see us and then you stop off there for so many months."

Anna didn't know what more to say. Bergit then asked, "Did the couple have any children?"

"Ah, no, but they got a baby when I was there," she said, wondering how she could change the subject.

"Oh, so that's why you stayed an extra long time; they wanted help taking care of the baby," said Bergit, as if that explained everything.

"Well, ah, I guess you could say that," answered Anna. The children were getting restless, listening to the grownups talk, so Bergit said they could be excused. Anna wished she could also be excused. Then Tomas announced that he had some things to attend to outside and they all got up. The women cleared away the dishes and Anna was relieved to talk of other things.

Anna retired early that evening as she was very tired. The children were already in bed when she came into the room. She tried to be very quiet but Hannah said, "Auntie Anna, it's going to be fun having you sleep with us!"

Anna answered that she would read them some bedtime stories but not tonight. She was too tired from her train trip. They were satisfied with that and soon all three of them were sleeping.

The next day was Sunday so after breakfast the family went to church. Anna was introduced all around. Later, at the Sunday dinner table, Tomas and Anna discussed the old country and especially their parents. She told them all about Barbro and her family and Tollef and Margit. Anna always felt lonesome for them all when she would talk of them with one of her brothers or Sigrid.

After the meal was cleared up, Tomas said he would take Anna for a little drive around the town. Sarah was ready for a nap and Bergit said that she would just rest awhile herself, too. Tomas brought the carriage around to the front and Anna joined him. He drove her around to all the recent buildings and houses that he had helped build. His boss, Mr. Hudson, was a good man to work for and business had been very good the last few years so Tomas said that he was well satisfied with his life now in America. He was very glad that he and Bergit had come.

"Do you remember the Ruud family that came to America with us?" asked Tomas. "Their two boys were friends of mine and Andrew's."

"I remember them a little bit, especially Mr. Ruud; he was always laughing!"

"Well, we keep in touch with them a couple times a year. They left Wisconsin a few years ago and headed for the Dakotas. North Dakota, in fact. They have a nice farm now in the rich Red River Valley that we have been reading about in the Posten. It would be fun to see them again someday. The boys are both married and have families."

"It's hard when friends and families get spread out so far apart," said Anna wistfully. "Some of them you never will see again." After thinking awhile she asked Tomas, "Do you think we will ever see Papa and Mama again?"

"Maybe, if we can persuade them to come to this country but I doubt that they ever will. Mama especially would be against that idea." He paused for a moment and then continued, "I would really love to see Sigrid and her family again someday. We don't even see Andrew all that much. It's been two years now, I think, since I was down there."

After their drive, the two returned home and joined the rest of the family who were out in the yard now. Bergit was sitting in the shade, watching the children play. Bergit beckoned Anna to come join her. "I'm really lazy today. It takes me all Sunday to rest up from the other six days!" Bergit said.

"Just when is your baby due?" asked Anna, sitting down on the grass beside her.

"About the middle of September, the doctor thinks." she answered. I'm so much more tired with this one than the others. Maybe it's because I'm getting older," she laughed.

Tomas joined them and sat down, too. It wasn't long before he was lying down with his hat over his face. They could hear him snoring softly so they knew he was sleeping.

Bergit said, "Tomas works so hard, too. He really needs this day of rest." She rose and went to tell the children to play on the other side of the house for awhile so their father could continue napping. Anna got up, also, and the two began walking down the sidewalk.

"Tomas doesn't seem to have any regrets about coming to this country, and I hope you don't either, Bergit," said Anna.

"Oh, no, I'm glad we came. I miss my family and my homeland but we have such a good life here," she answered. "Did I tell you that my parents may come over next year and visit? I'm hoping they will like it here and stay."

"Maybe they can talk Papa and Mama into coming, too," said Anna without too much conviction.

"You never know," replied Bergit. They turned around and came back toward the house.

"I like your house, Bergit, and your yard is so pretty, do you really think you want to move from here?" asked Anna.

"I like it, too, but you can see that it is getting too small. I would like a bigger kitchen, too. I hope we can find something soon."

"Maybe Tomas could build you a new house," suggested Anna.

"Oh, that is my dream, but he doesn't have the time to build one for us now. He hopes to start his own business someday, maybe when Arne grows up and if he is interested in carpentry, they could work together."

They returned to the yard and could see Tomas still lying under the shade tree. They went in the house and Bergit said she needed to start something for supper. "I think we'll just have sandwiches for supper tonight."

The days and weeks passed quickly. Anna had told Tomas that she wanted to look for a teaching job and was wondering where to start. "I know I would never be able to get a job in town here, but perhaps out in a country school someplace near here," she said. Tomas said he would check into it for her.

A few days later, when he returned home from work, Thomas had a list of some names that Anna could contact. He had received it from the principal of the school in town here. It listed the names of several county school superintendents in neighboring areas.

The next day Anna got busy and wrote to each of them, asking about any teaching positions available. She walked downtown and mailed the letters and thought, now there's nothing to do but wait.

Soon the Fourth of July was upon them and the town was planning a big celebration. There would be a parade in the morning, followed by speeches in the park and a potluck picnic. Anna helped Bergit make pies and a cake and they put some beans in a pot of water to soak overnight. Bergit rose early the next morning to mix up the sauce for the beans and then put them in the oven to bake for a few hours.

The children were excited for the big day to begin so they were up early, too. They decided they would all walk downtown to watch the parade and then Tomas and Bergit would return home and get all the food and put it in their wagon and come to the park. Anna would stay with the children.

After the parade, Anna and her little charges started walking over to the park. They found a good spot not far from the serving table and sat there and waited for Tomas and Bergit. After quite sometime, Arne spotted them walking toward them carrying all the food. He ran to help and they brought everything to the big, long table set up for serving. Bergit helped the other women get everything ready.

When the political speeches were over, everyone started flocking towards the table, which was laden with all sorts of wonderful things to eat, like fried chicken, beans, biscuits, jellies, pickles, pies and cakes. Lemonade and coffee topped off the fare. Everyone ate until they were stuffed!

"Oh, that was all so wonderful," said Anna, patting her full stomach. She sat down on the grass and leaned against a tree. Sarah joined her, and even she seemed content to just sit still for a little while. Anna watched all the people, most of them still strangers, and started thinking back to just a year ago, at another Fourth of July doings. She wondered if the Martins had taken little Sammy to the parade in the buggy. I wonder how he is getting along and how he is doing, she continued thinking. Sarah leaned her little head against Anna's shoulder and Anna put her arm around her and held her close. I musn't think about this now, she thought to herself. She usually only let herself indulge in these thoughts when she was alone in her bed at night.

Hannah and Arne came up to her just then to ask where their parents were. Anna replied that their mother was still helping the women and their father was over talking to a group of men. Sarah, who had been almost sleeping, stirred and got up to join her sister and brother. No more quiet time for her!

Anna looked up to see two young men walking toward her. One was a son of a family she had met In church and the other was a stranger.

"Anna, are you coming to the dance tonight?" asked the Halvorson boy, as the two stopped in front of her.

"I don't think so. I may stay home and take care of my nephew and nieces."

"Oh, that would be too bad. We're going to have a good time tonight," he announced. "You should join us." With that the two fellows went off, laughing at some private joke. Anna shuddered, in spite of the warmth of the day, remembering one other dance that had ended so terribly for her.

She got up and found that Bergit was ready to carry their dishes and things back to the wagon. She helped her and then they came back to find the children. There were going to be some games and races starting soon and Arne said that he wanted to take part in them. He and Tomas were going to do the 3-legged sack race for father and son teams. Tomas and Arne started off to get their sack and the women and little girls found a good place to sit down and watch the fun.

Tomas and Arne came in almost last in the race but they had had fun anyway. It was announced that there would be homemade ice cream served near the bandstand so the people started moving in that direction. There was a baseball game going on in the lot next to the park. Tomas said that he didn't care to watch that as he had never caught on to that American game.

The children were excited about the ice cream and even though the grown ups were still full from dinner, they enjoyed the cool treat almost as much. The city band was tuning up in the bandstand for a concert ready to begin soon. When everyone had finished their ice cream, they found places to sit on the chairs and benches brought over for the event.

After the delightful concert, the crowd walked slowly off to their homes or wagons. The Olson family was tired out after a good, fun day. They returned home with one sleeping child and one almost asleep. They laid Sarah on the sofa and Hannah laid right down on the floor. The grownups sat down to rest and discuss the day.

"That was such fun!" Bergit exclaimed. "Did you enjoy yourself, Anna?"

"Yes, I thought it was great fun, too," she replied. "Are you two going to the dance tonight?" she asked, looking from Tomas to Bergit.

"Well, I don't know; are we going, Bergit?"

"I'm pretty tired and I don't know who would stay with the children," she said with a sigh.

"I'll stay with them," stated Anna. "You two go and have yourself some fun."

"You are the one who should go, Anna," said Bergit. "You are young and should be going to dances and things to meet other young people."

"No," she said emphatically, "I want to stay home with them and you go. That would please me very much if I could do that for you."

Bergit could see that she would not be able to change her mind. If Anna was anything like her brother, once she made up her mind, that was that! "We'll see how we feel later on. I need to rest awhile. What do you think, Tomas?"

"Like you said, we'll see later on." He went out to tend to the horses.

As it turned out, Tomas and Bergit did go to the dance and Anna stayed home with the children. She played games with them and read them stories and finally they were ready for bed. Anna herself was about to go upstairs, too, but then she thought she would sit for awhile and read the paper. It wasn't long before she dozed off in the chair and before she knew it, Tomas and Bergit were standing over her as she awoke with a start.

"Oh, dear me, I must have dozed off for a bit," she said. "Did the two of you have a good time then?"

"It was so much fun!" said Bergit. "We haven't gone dancing for several years. So many of our friends were there."

"Thank you so much, Anna, for staying with the children. Were they any problem for you?" asked Tomas

"No, no, not at all. We had fun." she replied. "Well, I think I'll go up and go back to sleep, in bed this time!"

By the last week of July, Anna had replies from two of the letters she had sent and neither one knew of any openings for a teaching position. If the other one comes back negative, what shall I do next? she wondered. Tomas had no advice to give her except that maybe she would have to go back to school here and get some more training.

On August first, the third reply came back, also negative. Later that day, Anna saw a boy on a bicycle turning into their driveway. He hurried up to the door and knocked importantly. It was a telegram, he said, for a Miss Anna Olson. Bergit took it and thanked him and gave it to Anna. He stood there watching, waiting for her to open it. The women looked at him, and he said he was waiting in case there was a reply to send.

Anna opened it and tried to read the message but soon gave up and handed it to Bergit. "It's from Andrew," she said, as she attempted to read between all the "stops".

"What does it say?" asked Anna excitedly and with some dread, thinking something was wrong.

"He says that there is a teaching position open in the next township if you want it. Reply very soon, he says."

Bergit told the messenger boy that he could leave as they would have to think this through first. They showed it to Tomas as soon as he arrived home.

"I wish there were more details, but I assume he didn't have time to spare so that is why he sent a telegram instead of a letter," Anna said.

"What do you want to do?" asked Tomas. "Do you want to take it?"

"I guess I should, being there isn't anything around here and time is going fast. One month till school starts."

Well, then," said Tomas, "we'll go to the station first thing in the morning and send a wire back to him."

That's exactly what Tomas and Anna did. Anna wired that she was very interested and that he should send more details.

"I wonder if I will hear from him yet today," said Anna.

"It's possible but more than likely it will be tomorrow before you hear," Tomas said. "Unless he goes to town especially to see if you have sent him an answer, or if they send someone out to the farm today sometime."

Anna waited two days for an answer and it came in the form of a letter instead of the expected wire. Andrew stated that he had received her wire but that he had too much to tell her so he quickly penned a note and hurried to the train and asked them to rush it to Mankato, which they did. The job is yours, if you want, he said again, but the board would like to visit with you first, Andrew told her. Could you come right away? he asked.

It didn't take Anna long to pack as she did not have much in the first place. The first train that would take her that direction would be early evening. Tomas got home in time to have supper with her and then he took her to the station after she bade some hurried goodbyes to Bergit and the children.

The train was not as comfortable this time and she had trouble catching any sleep. The next day, she had someone sitting next to her who wanted to talk all the time so she could not sleep then either. By the time she reached St. Ansgar and Andrew picked her up, she was so tired she could hardly sit in the wagon without falling over!

It was dark by the time they pulled into the yard. Alice met her at the door and hugged her.

"It's good to see you again, Anna. My goodness, you look so weary, was it a tough trip?"

"I hardly got a moment of sleep!" she answered.

"Here, sit down and I'll get you a cup of coffee. The children are already in bed. I didn't tell them you were coming tonight because then they would have wanted to stay up."

Andrew came in and joined them at the table. "Well, here you are again, Anna! I hope you won't regret coming back on such short notice. A few days ago I heard that a school in the next township was frantically looking for a teacher. The one that they had hired last spring all of a sudden ran off to get married and wouldn't be coming back here. I got in contact with a man I know over there and he told the board that I had a sister who was looking for a teaching job. So then the other morning," he went on, "two men from there drove over here to talk to me about it. That's the day I sent you the wire."

"Tell me a little about this school," said Anna.

"Well, like I told you, it's in the next township, about ten or twelve miles from here. It's a little country school with about 20 children. They all come from Norwegian families so they won't mind if you don't know the English perfectly yet. They want to meet with you in the next few days. I am to let them know when you get here."

"I think Anna needs to get to bed now and we can talk about this more in the morning," interrupted Alice.

Anna couldn't agree more. She rose and went up and fell onto her old bed without even undressing, except for her shoes. I could sleep for days, she thought to herself.

She didn't get to sleep that long, but she did sleep later than usual. Alice kept the children quiet by having them go out to the chicken coop with her to pick eggs. She usually didn't do this as they always riled up the chickens too much.   Anna was up and downstairs when they returned with a basket full of eggs. Alfred and Berta were so excited to see their auntie again. They were full of questions and chatter while their mother made breakfast for them all.

Andrew came in and he told Anna that the man who stops by to pick up their milk also goes out past the school where she will be teaching so he was going to get word to one of the school board members that they would be over there tomorrow afternoon to visit with them. "I'll take you over there right after dinner."

"Oh, Andrew, I know how busy you are right now," said Anna, " and I feel bad that you have to make all these extra trips because of me."

"That's all right, I have my hired hand working, and the threshing crew won't be coming here for another two days to take care of my wheat. Usually we're done by now, but we got so much rain a week ago that we had to wait to finish, " he explained to her.

That evening over supper, Andrew had time to ask her many questions

about Tomas and his family. He would love to see them more often, he said.
Anna told them about her unsuccessful tries at getting a teaching job there and
how she didn't know what she was going to do and then his telegram came at
just the right moment. "The Lord is taking care of me again!" she said.

The next day, after dinner, Andrew hitched up the buggy because he said
that would be faster. They set off for the short drive. He said the school was by
the Cedar River so it was called the Cedar River school. They stopped at the
Overson farm as Mr. Overson was one of the board members. He told them to
come in and another board member would be coming over soon. About a half
hour later a Mr. Larson joined them.

Over coffee the informal interview began. They asked Anna some
questions about her training and former experience. They were impressed
with her command of the English language. They hadn't expected it to be that
good, Mr. Larson said. They discussed salary, school vacations and her living
arrangements. She would board with the families who had children in the
school, staying about two months at each place.

She asked if she could see the school and they said they would be glad
to show it to her. She and Andrew followed them over there. They were
mighty proud of their little school. It was well built and the roof didn't leak, Mr.
Overson told them.

The school was indeed nice and it was nestled in the trees not far from
the river. It had some swings and a little merry-go-round beside it. Anna said
that she thought that it was very nice. They told her that school would start on
September 5 but she might want to come a day or two earlier and get settled.
They would write her and tell her where she would be staying first. They shook
hands and left her and Andrew to look around some more.

As Andrew turned the buggy toward home he said, "Well, Anna, it looks
like you have your first teaching job in America!"

"Yes, I am excited and a little scared, too," she stated. "It seems like a
nice school and those two gentlemen were very kind." She had much to think
about on the ride back home.

The rest of August went by fast. The threshing crew came to finish up
Andrew's wheat. Alice, Anna and the hired girl were kept busy every minute.
First there was a big breakfast to make for all the men. Then before they knew it
it was time to bring out morning coffee. They packed up doughnuts, breads and
coffee. They put the food and coffee cups in a big dishpan and covered it with a
dish towel. The coffee was carried , very carefully, in a big enamel coffee pot.
Anna and the hired girl put everything in the wagon and slowly drove out to
where the men were working. The women could not believe that, after such a
big breakfast, the men were actually hungry again!

When the girls returned to the house, Alice had dinner started. The men
came to the house for this. They ate mounds of mashed potatoes, meat,

vegetables, pickles and jams. And, of course, pie for dessert! Anna and Margaret, the hired girl, washed the dishes while Alice stirred up a cake. The cake was for the afternoon lunch. Then there was supper to make! This cooking and baking marathon went on for several days. Anna didn't know how Alice did it. Alice said she could never do it without lots of help. Some years she had two hired girls during threshing time.

"Well, you have two this year, too!" said Anna. "I'm glad I was here to help you but I sure got played out!"

When the threshing crew left and moved to the next farm, there was the garden produce to do something with. Anna and Margaret helped Alice with the canning. That took many days, but when they were done, they had many jars of wonderful things preserved for the winter.

Anna had checked her wardrobe to see if she needed any new dresses for teaching but she decided that the dresses she had would suffice. The ones she had worn when she worked in the factory would do fine. Her last Sunday at Andrew's, she took time to write letters to Sigrid and to her parents telling them about the busy summer just past and about her new job. She was looking forward to it with growing excitement. What would the year bring? she wondered.

CHAPTER 7

Two days before school began, Andrew brought Anna over to the place where she would be staying for the first two months. It was the farm home of Ben and Mary Benson. When they drove into the yard, they could see that it was a well-kept farm with a nice, big, white house. Andrew helped carry in her things and Mrs. Benson insisted that he stay for a cup of coffee. Mr. Benson came in while he was there. He was a big, tall man, outgoing and friendly. Mrs. Benson was a little woman, perhaps in her mid thirties, and rather quiet, especially when her husband was present.

"I guess I better be going now, folks," said Andrew, getting up from the table. "Goodbye and good luck, Anna. I'll be here to pick you up on Friday after school."

He and Mr. Benson left the house together and Mrs.Benson took Anna up to see her room.

"My, you have such a nice house and so roomy!" exclaimed Anna as they went up the stairway.

"We built the house about eight years ago now," said Mrs. Benson. "You should have seen what we used to live in!"

There were four large bedrooms upstairs. The one at the top of the stairs was Mr. and Mrs. Benson's and the next two were for their four daughters. Anna's room was at the end of the hall.

"Oh, this is wonderful!" said Anna excitedly, as she looked the room over. There was a desk and some shelves and a closet. On the bed, there was a beautiful blue and white handmade quilt.

"This quilt is very beautiful, Mrs. Benson. Did you make it?"

"Yes, I love to make quilts when I have the time. I've made one for each bed now. This one is called the 'Irish Chain' pattern. Well, I'll let you get settled now and you can come down whenever you are ready and I'll show you around some more. I'll have Ben carry up your boxes of books when he comes in for supper."

Anna unpacked her clothes and hung her dresses in the closet and put the rest in the dresser drawers. This room is so nice, she thought to herself.

There were pretty, ruffled curtains on the windows, which faced the east and south. I'll get the morning sun, she thought with satisfaction.

On her way downstairs, she quickly peeked into each room and saw that all the beds had equally beautiful quilts on them, all a different pattern. I'd like to see how she makes them, Anna thought to herself, as she went down the stairs.

"Oh, there you are, Miss Olson. Our girls should be home anytime now so you can meet them. You will have three of them in your school. They walked over to the farm right south of here for a birthday party."

"May I help you with anything?" asked Anna.

"No, I have everything under control for our supper, so why don't we just sit down here in the parlor and get to know each other a little bit," she answered as she indicated for Anna to sit on the sofa.

They sat and visited for almost a half hour before they heard the girls arrive in the yard. Someone had given them a ride home in a wagon. They were laughing and talking as they came to the house.

"Mama, Mama," called one of them, and stopped at the parlor door as she saw a visitor.

"Come in, girls, and meet your new teacher, Miss Olson."

The girls all filed in and stood and took turns being introduced to Anna. The oldest was Rose Ann, who would be in the sixth grade. Next was Sonja, a fourth grader and Grace, a second grader. Last of all was little Marie, who said she was five years old and couldn't go to school for another year.

Anna asked them about the birthday party and they all began to talk at once.

"Girls, girls, one at a time," Mrs. Benson said, laughing. Anna could tell that she adored her girls and just beamed with pleasure looking and listening to them.   They all were so pretty and well behaved.

They heard Mr. Benson come in the house and Mrs. Benson jumped up and said, "I'll get supper on the table. You sit and get acquainted until I call you."

Soon they were all seated at the big kitchen table. Mr. Benson asked Anna questions about herself and about her life in Norway. The girls listened with interest. After the meal, the older girls helped clear the table and Mrs. Benson started washing the dishes.

"Ben, perhaps you could carry Miss Olson's boxes of books upstairs for her."

"Let's see," Anna said, looking through the boxes. "I want to take one of the boxes to school with me. I would like to go over there tomorrow and get things organized. Do you suppose you could drive me over there, Mr. Benson?"

"O course!" he answered. "What time would you like to go."

"Maybe right after breakfast, if that would be all right with you."

"That would work out fine," he said, "then I'll continue on into town for some feed with the wagon.

"Could I go with her, Mother?" asked Rose Ann. "I could help her and show her where everything is."

"Well, I suppose that would be a good idea," answered Mrs. Benson.

The other girls wanted to go, too, but Mr. Benson said, "No, only Rose Ann can go. The rest of you can help your mother." And that was that. No argument.

Mr. Benson picked up the box that Anna wanted upstairs and carried it up for her. She followed him up and he helped her put the books on the shelf and he took the empty box back down to keep for her. Anna sat down at the dressing table and looked in the mirror and said, "Anna, I think you are going to like it here."

The next day, after a hearty breakfast, Anna and Rose Ann rode with Mr. Benson as far as the school. Upon entering, Anna was surprised to see how clean everything was and she remarked on this.

"Some of the mothers take turns cleaning the school and they did it just a few days ago," Rose Ann told her.

Rose Ann showed her where everything was and helped put her books away. They went outside to explore the immediate area. It was a pretty setting for a school, Anna thought. Rose Ann kept up a running commentary on all the pupils who would be coming the next day. Anna felt like she knew them all already!

Mr. Benson had said that he would stop and pick them up on his way back from town, but it was a beautiful September day so Anna and Rose Ann decided to start out walking. It was only a mile from the school. Rose Ann said that she and her sisters walked to school most of the time unless it was raining or very cold. Anna thought that she would do the same. It would be good exercise for her. She used to do a lot of walking in Norway.

They reached the farm house shortly before Mr. Benson, and dinner was almost ready. The girls had set the table and were excited to have Miss Olson back again.

"The girls love it when it's our turn to have the teacher stay with us," explained Mrs. Benson.

"How often does your turn come up?" asked Anna.

"Every other year we have the teacher in September and October. It just works out that way," said Mrs. Benson. "I enjoy it myself, too. There have been so many nice young women. They stay about two or three years and then they get married and leave and we never see them again unless they have married a farmer from around here."

"Were there ever any men teachers?" asked Anna.

"Why, yes, there have been a couple. Only one stayed here, though."

"In Norway, most of the teachers were men but that is changing. I was the first woman to teach in Gol. That's where I taught for one year before coming to America."

Mr. Benson drove in and came inside and washed up and they all sat down for their noon meal. He had brought the mail and there was a package from the Sears catalog, he said, but the girls would have to wait until after they had eaten to get it from the wagon. It was big, too, he teased. The girls were too excited to eat. They were trying to guess what would be in it. Maybe the shoes that their mother had ordered for them.

"Or maybe the yard goods for your new dresses," Mrs. Benson told them.

"I send for much of the things we need from the catalogs," she told Anna. "It isn't very often I get to a town of any size to buy the things I want."

"I take Mary and the girls to Mason City about twice a year," said Mr. Benson. "Sometimes we go up to Austin. That's in Minnesota."

The girls finished eating and said they didn't want dessert. They ran out to the wagon and brought in the package. They ripped it open and sure enough, there were four pairs of shoes in there! Brand new school shoes!

"I surely hope that these fit you girls now. We measured so carefully. Last year I had to send back two pair," said Mrs. Benson.

The girls each found the shoes that were meant for them and they all sat down on the kitchen floor and tried them on. They all seemed to be satisfied with them. Mr. Benson checked each one out and declared them to be perfect fits.

"Yippee!" said the girls as they ran around the house with their new shoes on.

Mrs. Benson let them enjoy them for awhile and then she told the girls that they had to take them off now and help her clear up the dishes.

"Maybe the yard goods will come tomorrow. I ordered four pieces, enough for a dress for each of the girls. They wear hand-me-downs most of the time but once a year or so, I like to make a new dress especially for each girl. And, of course, I always have to make new ones for Rose Ann."

In the afternoon, a couple of the neighbor ladies stopped by with several of their children. Anna didn't know really why they stopped by, probably just to get a glimpse of the new teacher! Mrs. Benson invited them in for coffee and cake. When they left, the children all said, "See you tomorrow, Miss Olson."

Everyone in the Olson household was up extra early the next morning. Mrs. Benson didn't know who was more excited, Anna or the girls! Anna said she wanted to go early so she would start out alone but the three girls said they were all ready so they would walk with her. They set out down the dirt road, carrying the pails of lunch that Mrs. Benson had packed for each of them. They walked past the field where Mr. Benson was working and he waved at them.

There was no one at the school yet, since it was so early. Anna got out her list of the pupils who were expected to come. There were twenty-two in all, if everyone showed up. Sometimes the older boys couldn't come until later in the fall as they had to help on the farm.

Soon Anna could hear voices outside. Sonja looked out the door and said, "Here comes the preacher's kids. Their names are Josie and Lucas. They live about a mile the other way. You'll be staying there next, Miss Olson."

The girls went outside to meet them and tell them all about the new teacher. Soon the rest of the children came and Anna rang the bell and they all came in and found their seats. There were a couple of new first graders who didn't know where to sit so Anna found seats for them up front. She greeted the children and counted noses. There were only twenty.

She began to take roll call and had each child stand when she called their name so she could see who they were, checking off the names as she went along. The two names left were for two boys, one a seventh grader and one an eighth grader. Perhaps they can't attend school yet, she thought.

She introduced herself and told the children a little bit about herself. Then she sat down and looked at them and they were all looking at her expectantly. She had a moment of near panic. What do I do now? Then she remembered what Rose Ann said yesterday. She had told Anna exactly what they did and when.

"I believe it is time to say the Pledge of Allegiance, children," she said. They all stood up and waited for her to begin. She didn't know the Pledge! She quickly thought of an idea.

"Each day we will have a different pupil lead us in saying the Pledge. Today, we will start with the oldest. Raise your hand, whoever is oldest," she said looking toward the eighth graders. Lucas Peterson, the preacher's son, raised his hand. He turned to face the flag and started the Pledge. Everyone joined in. Anna thought to herself, I need to learn that by tomorrow!

The rest of the day went without a hitch, except for another moment of near panic when two of the younger boys failed to come in after the noon break. Thoughts of the nearby river went through Anna's mind. She sent Lucas and Theo out to find them. They had been hiding, hoping someone would have to come and find them. Anna made them stay after school and told the class that if anyone ever did that again, their parents would be notified.

After school, the two boys, Marcus and Ralph, had to write on the board, "I will never do that again" a hundred times. It took them almost an hour. Then Anna walked home alone. The Benson girls had gone home right after school.

At the supper table that night, Anna had to tell the Bensons all about her first day. Rose Ann volunteered to help her learn the Pledge. She told Anna that Marcus and Ralph were just testing her. They did something like that to every new teacher the first day

"It's good that you didn't let them get by with it," said Rose Ann. "You shouldn't have any more trouble with them the rest of the year."

Every day after that went along quite smoothly and soon it was Friday. That morning, during breakfast, Anna thought that Mrs. Benson seemed anxious about something and that mood affected the girls, too. Anna soon dismissed that thought as she left the house for the walk to the school house. The girls weren't ready to go yet; they would come later.

Andrew, true to his word, was at the school at 4 o'clock to fetch Anna. She said that they needed to stop by the house first and pick up her small bag. When she went into the house, Mrs. Benson looked like she had been crying.

"Are you all right, Mrs. Benson?" she asked.

"Oh, yes, yes, it's nothing," she answered, busying herself with something in the kitchen.

"Well, goodbye then," said Anna. "I'll see you all Sunday evening." Mrs. Benson didn't answer her so Anna just let herself out quietly.

When Anna walked into Andrew's house, Alice and the children greeted her warmly. They were excited to hear about her first week of teaching.

"I'll wait and tell you everything when Andrew comes in to supper," she said.

Later, when they were all seated around the table, Anna told them that she liked it very much and that the Benson family was very nice and that she was going to enjoy staying with them. She told them about all of her students.

"I wish I could go to school," said four-year-old Alfred. Anna told him that he had to wait another two years and he almost started to cry.

"Oh!" exclaimed Alice. "I almost forgot. A letter came from Bergit yesterday and she has had her baby! It was a boy and they named him Theodore."

"Well, that certainly is exciting news! How could you wait for two hours to tell me?" Anna teased.

"I guess I was thinking only about you and your school," said Alice.

The weekend went by quickly. The family went to church Sunday morning. The Jorgenson boy, the one who helped with Anna's trunk, came up to Anna and tried to make some conversation, but he was so shy that he couldn't think of anything to say. Alfred came to the rescue by saying that his Papa was ready to leave. Anna excused herself and hurried to the wagon.

"What did Peder Jorgenson have to say, Anna?" asked Alice slyly.

"Very little," laughed Anna. "The poor thing has a hard time making conversation. I don't know how he'll ever find himself a girl!"

Later that day, when it was time to bring Anna back to the Benson farm, Alice and the children rode along. They were anxious to see where it was that Anna stayed and also to see the school. They stopped at the school first and Anna let them in to have a look. Then they drove into the farmyard. No one came out of the house or the barn at first. Soon Rose Ann came up to the end of the walk and said that her mother wasn't feeling well and that her father wasn't home. Anna introduced her to Andrew and his family.

"We better be heading back before it gets dark," Andrew said. "We'll see you on Friday, Anna." She bade them goodbye and she and Rose Ann walked to the house.

"What's the matter with your mother?" she asked the girl. "I hope she isn't sick!"

Rose Ann hesitated for a moment before answering. "Well, she isn't exactly sick. But she didn't feel like leaving her room today."

Anna thought this was very uncharacteristic of Mrs. Benson but she didn't say any more. "Where is your father, then?" she asked, as they entered the house.

"I....I don't know," Rose Ann answered quietly. The other girls came into the kitchen when they heard Anna come in. They didn't say a word, but just looked very sad and anxious.

Anna put her bag down and took off her hat and motioned for them to follow her into the parlor. She sat down on the sofa and pulled little Marie onto her lap.

"All right," said Anna, "tell me what is the matter here." No one said anything. The girls looked down at the floor. Little Marie looked right into Anna's face and said, "Papa hit Mama!" The older girls gasped.

"Marie, you're not supposed to tell!" exclaimed Sonja. Marie started to cry.

"What do you mean, your Papa hit your Mama?" Anna asked all of them.

"Come on, girls," Rose Ann said as she hustled the girls out of the room and up the stairs. Anna was left in the parlor alone, wondering what to do. She went in and picked up her hat and bag and went upstairs, too. She paused by Mrs. Benson's bedroom, wondering if she should knock, but then she went on to her own room.

Anna didn't know what to do, but she stayed in her room the rest of the evening. When she went to bed, she picked up her Bible and read some chapters and then prayed about the situation. Later, she heard heavy footsteps come up the stairs and they went into the Bensons' bedroom. She could hear muffled voices and once she thought she heard a woman crying. Or was it one of the girls?

She got up out of bed and put her robe on and opened her door quietly. She tiptoed over to the first door, Rose Ann and Sonja's room. She hesitated and then knocked softly. She heard a little voice say to come in. When she opened the door, four little faces looked up at her. All four girls were sitting up in Rose Ann's bed. They looked frightened.

Anna came and sat on the edge of the bed and asked if there was something they wanted to tell her. "We can't tell you anything," said Sonja. Grace was crying and Marie looked confused.

"Has something terrible happened?" asked Anna. Grace nodded her head.

"Please tell me about it and maybe I can help," said Anna.

The girls looked at each other, each wondering if that would be a good idea. They were silent, waiting for Rose Ann, the oldest, to decide what to say, if anything. Finally she made the decision, and she began, "Our Pa has been drinking and then he and Mama fight and then he hits her and she cries."

"We get scared then," Grace sobbed. She came closer to Anna and snuggled against her. Anna reached out her arms to all of them.

"Let's pray about it, girls. When I have a problem or something that bothers me, I take it to the Lord in prayer because He promises in the Bible that He will answer our prayers if we but ask." The little group, a teacher and four small girls, huddled together in prayer, asking for God's help for this situation. When they had finished, she told Grace and Marie to go back to their own room and go to sleep and she left for her room, also.

Anna lay in bed for a long while before sleep would come. I can hardly believe this of Mr. Benson, she thought to herself. He always seemed so nice. Poor Mrs. Benson! She is so gentle and kind, how could anyone hit her.

The next thing she knew, the morning sun was coming into her room and she jumped out of bed and began to dress. She almost dreaded going downstairs. She didn't know what she would find. Finally she could put it off no longer and as she passed the girls' rooms, their doors were still closed. She knocked softly on Rose Ann's door and asked if they were ready. A voice said that they were soon ready to go down.

When she entered the kitchen, Mrs. Benson was busy by the stove, making pancakes.

"Good morning," Anna said hesitantly. Mrs. Benson returned the greeting but didn't look at Anna.

"Sit down and I'll have these cakes on the table in just a minute," she said. "Goodness, when are those girls coming down? They'll be late for school."

The girls started coming down then, one by one and took their places at the table. Marie was still sleeping, Rose Ann told her mother. There wasn't much conversation during breakfast. They all seemed in a hurry to finish and get on their way. Perhaps they want to avoid their father, Anna thought to herself.

When they were all ready the girls and Anna said good bye to Mrs. Benson and off they went to school. The girls didn't have much to say on the way so Anna left them alone with their thoughts. I guess I'm glad, too, that I didn't have to see Mr. Benson this morning, Anna thought.

The day went by quickly and soon the foursome were walking back to the farm house. Their steps were slow, as if they were not in any hurry to get there. When they entered the house, the smell of freshly baked bread hit them.

"Come and have some bread and jam," Mrs. Benson suggested. She was trying to sound cheerful. The girls, as if sensing that the crisis was over, for now anyway, gladly sat down and dug into the pile of sliced bread and good, homemade raspberry jam. Mrs. Benson poured big glasses of milk for each of them, including Anna.

"I'm sorry, Miss Olson, that I wasn't up when you came back last night, but...I...ah...didn't feel good so I went to bed early," she said. The girls and Anna all looked at each other over their glasses of milk.

"That's all right, Mrs. Benson, the girls were here to greet me," said Anna.

The girls went up to change clothes and went about their after-school chores. Anna went up to her room and worked on correcting papers after asking Mrs. Benson if there was anything she could help her with.

Anna came back down about supper time and she could feel the tension building up in the girls again. They were dreading to see their father when he came in, not knowing how he would be. Mrs. Benson waited supper a little while and just as she had told them to all sit down, they heard the door open and Mr. Benson walked in. Everyone seemed to be holding their breath.

"Well, I seem to be a little late," he stated in a cheerful voice. I went to town to buy something." He produced a package and handed it to his wife. She hesitated about taking it.

"Go on, take it and open it right now," he suggested. She unwrapped the brown paper and took out a beautiful little music box. She looked at him questioningly.

"A little something for you, my dear, just because you...ah...haven't been feeling well the last few days." All eyes now turned to Mrs. Benson. She turned the crank on the bottom of the box and it played a nice, little tune. She started to cry softly.

"Here, here, my dear," said Mr. Benson. "Don't you cry now. Everything is fine. Isn't that just like a woman to cry when you give her something pretty," he said, trying to cover up the moment.

Mrs. Benson dried her tears with the corner of her apron and tried to smile. She started dishing up the food and Mr. Benson said, "Let's bow our heads for the table blessing." Anna looked over at Mrs. Benson and their eyes locked. She knows that I know, Anna thought, but she won't say anything and I won't either. That's the way it's done.

The next weekend when she was back at Andrew's she told Alice all about the situation with the Bensons. Alice said that she knew of a family where the same thing was happening except that in this case the husband and father beat his wife and children both, even when he wasn't drinking. He had a bad temper and the least little thing would set him off. The wife and children had fled to the neighbors many a time.

"Why does she stay with the man, then?" asked Anna, shaking her head unbelievingly.

"I don't know," answered Alice, "I guess she has no other place to go. He may end up killing her one of these days."

"Did anyone ever talk to the pastor about it?" asked Anna.

"Oh, yes, he came to call one day and the husband ran him off the place with a shotgun. He probably beat his wife twice as hard that night!"

The whole situation bothered Anna immensely, but she could think of no solution. The next several weeks went by smoothly at the Benson home. Things at school were going good, too, even after the arrival of the two boys who were not able to start school right away because they had to help their fathers with the fall farm work. Rose Ann had told her that she might have some trouble with them. They liked to think that they were too old now for this "school stuff." Anna soon learned that the older of the two boys, John Walther, was very bright at arithmetic and figuring, although he had trouble with reading and writing. She managed to keep him challenged and that seemed to help his boredom.

The other boy, Charles, said he was going to just be a farmer so why did he have to have any more learnin' anyway? He said that his mother was making him stay in school until he finished the eighth grade. "Then I'm quittin' for sure," he said. "No high school for me." Actually this was the pattern for most of the boys from farm families who attended country schools. The girls were more apt to go on to more schooling and perhaps become teachers unless they were needed at home.

After school one day a few weeks later, Anna arrived at the Benson home later than usual. In fact, it was about supper time. When she came into the kitchen, she could sense that something was wrong. Mrs. Benson gave her only a hurried nod and the girls looked up from their chores without saying anything. There in the corner, Mr. Benson was sitting in the rocker. He got up and greeted her and she noticed that he was not too steady on his feet and his speech was slightly slurred.

"When's supper ready?" he asked impatiently. He plopped himself down at his place at the head of the table.

"In a minute, Ben," his wife said, trying to hurry things along. She dished everything up and told Anna and the girls to sit down. Mr. Benson tried to say the table blessing but it didn't sound like it should. The girls were very quiet and Mrs. Benson seemed nervous and jumpy. She knew what was ahead of her, Anna thought to herself.

Mr. Benson was carrying on about this and that. It was hard to follow his one-sided conversation. With his mouth full, he gestured at his wife and girls and said, "Look at that woman of mine, she's a good woman but all she could give me were girl babies! A man would like a son, you know?" He looked at Anna. She couldn't look at him. She felt the pain and embarrassment that Mrs. Benson must be feeling now. Not to mention the hurt that the girls were feeling.

Anna couldn't remember a time when she had felt so keenly like she could almost kill someone!

Mrs. Benson jumped up and busied herself at the cupboard. The girls squirmed in their chairs. Anna had all she could do to sit there and not scream at that man. Soon he got up and grabbed his hat and mumbled something about going to town, where he would be in better company, not with a houseful of women!

When the back door slammed after him, you could have heard a pin drop in the kitchen. No one could move or say a word. Soon Marie started to cry. She knew what was coming, too. Mrs. Benson picked her up and sat down in the rocker with her. The other girls started to clear the table. Anna took hot water from the big tea kettle and poured some into two dishpans and started washing the dishes. Marie calmed down and wanted a story so Mrs. Benson asked Sonja to take her into the parlor and read her a story. Rose Ann and Grace finished drying the dishes and left the room, too.

Anna faced Mrs. Benson with a questioning look and was about to say something but then Mrs. Benson turned and went about some other chores. When it was bedtime, the girls all went upstairs. Anna was up in her room working on the next day's lessons. When she finished, she wondered if she should go down and see if Mrs. Benson was still down there and if she wanted to talk. She decided against it and got ready for bed instead. She sat by the desk again and opened her Bible. After reading awhile, she bowed her head and prayed very hard for the Benson family, asking God to protect them all and bring about some solution to the situation that the whole family found themselves in.

When she awoke in the morning, she realized that this was Friday and that she would be leaving again for the weekend. Would the girls and their mother be safe until she got back? she wondered. She went down and Mrs. Benson was preparing breakfast. Before the girls came down, Anna asked her if she thought she and the girls would like to come with her for a visit to her brother's for the weekend. Mrs. Benson looked surprised by this proposal and didn't answer right away.

"Oh, I don't know if we could do that. I just couldn't get away, you know. There's always so much to do."

Then Anna had another idea. "Do you think that the girls would enjoy going, then? It would be a little vacation for them and I would love for them to meet my family, Alfred and little Berta especially."

"Well...ah.. I.. don't know what to say to that," she stammered. "It's kind of short notice, and it would be too much trouble for your sister-in-law to have four extra children for the whole weekend!" That seemed to be the end of that but Anna wouldn't give up. She didn't want the children to go through another weekend like the last time. How many times have they gone through this in their short, little lives? she wondered.

"Oh, please, Mrs. Benson. It would be wonderful for them to get away," Anna pleaded. She knew she shouldn't beg but she did want to get the children away from here, if even for a short while. She could tell that Mrs. Benson was pondering this idea over in her mind and she, too, maybe thought that it would be good for the children to escape what was coming.

"Well, I'll think about it a little bit," she said just as the first of the children started coming down, then the next two, and finally Marie. They looked relieved to see that their father was not here. After everyone had finished and Mrs. Benson was fixing their lunches and putting it into their pails, she turned and looked at the girls.

"Girls, Miss Olson has asked me if you would like to go home with her this weekend for a visit." The girls were so surprised with this statement that they were silent for a moment before it hit them. Then they jumped up and said, "Oh, yes, we'd love to!"

Anna looked at Mrs. Benson, thanking her with her eyes and Mrs. Benson seemed to do the same. "Girls, calm down now. I'll pack your things while you are at school and you can pick them up when Miss Olson comes for her bag. How will that be?"

"Oh, goodie, goodie!" they exclaimed with apparent happiness and glee. They picked up their school books and lunch pails and followed Anna out the door. The girls asked Anna many questions about the family that they would soon be meeting.

The school day went fast. Anna noticed that Grace and Sonja seemed unable to contain their excitement over their upcoming weekend trip. Rose Ann, on the other hand, seemed deep in thought for most of the last hour. When Anna dismissed school, Grace and Sonja hurried to help Anna clean up and get ready to leave. They saw out the window that Anna's brother, Andrew, had just driven up. Anna left them to finish cleaning the blackboard while she went out to speak with Andrew.

"Andrew, I have done something that perhaps you will not be too pleased with," she said. "I've invited the Benson girls to come home with me for the weekend. Their father is beginning one of his drunken binges again and I don't want them to have to go through that all over again."

"Well, I guess that will be all right. Alice shouldn't mind. We'll find room somewhere for them to sleep," he answered. "Are you ready to go then?"

"Yes, I think so. I'll get the girls." With that she went back into the school house.

"That will be good enough, girls," she said of their clean-up attempts. "Andrew is ready to leave now."

The foursome hurried out and got into the wagon. They drove the short distance to the farm. Anna and the girls ran into the house. Mrs. Benson and Marie were in the kitchen.

"I have the girls' things all ready to go, Miss Olson," she said. "What did your brother say?"

"He said that it would be all right," Anna answered as she went upstairs to retrieve her bag.

When she got back down, Rose Ann was standing by her mother. She looked at Anna and said, "Miss Olson, I don't think that I will go with you this time. I'll stay home with Ma. She might need me."

Anna looked at Mrs. Benson to get her reaction to that. "I told her that she should go, that it would be fun for her," she told Anna. She turned to Rose Ann and said, "Please go, Rose Ann. I want you to. Go and have some fun. Please."

Rose Ann looked undecided. Anna didn't know what to tell her. Perhaps someone should stay here with Mrs. Benson. While she was hesitating, she heard Rose Ann finally say, "All right, I'll go, but only if you're sure, Ma. I could stay with you."

"Oh, Rosie, my dear," she said, as she hugged her oldest daughter. "Now, you musn't keep Mr. Olson waiting." She shooed all of them out the door and followed after them to say goodbye. The girls all hugged their mother and she was smiling at their excitement. Rose Ann lingered by the wagon and said, "Ma, are you sure you'll be all right?

"Of course, dear. You all have a good time now." She stood waving after them as the wagon left the yard. Only now did she let the tears come. The family dog came over by her and she sat down on the back step, hugging the animal to her. She was worried what the next couple of days would bring for her, but at least the girls would be safe and happy.

The ten-mile drive to Andrew's went fast. The four girls sat in the back of the wagon and were singing and chattering. Even Rose Ann was starting to show some enthusiasm now. She needed to be a little girl again, not her mother's protector. She had had to grow up fast.

Wouldn't Alice be surprised when they all piled out of the wagon, Anna thought, as they pulled into the yard. The girls jumped out and grabbed their bags and then stood by the wagon waiting for Anna, suddenly realizing what a surprise they were going to be. Alice came out of the house just then and stopped and looked at all the little girls standing there. Alfred and Berta came out, too and were wondering who they were. Anna hurried on ahead to tell Alice about the situation.

"I thought they would be safer and happier here, Alice. I hope you don't mind."

"Of course not, Anna. Bring them on in." Alice motioned for the girls to come to the house and Anna introduced them.

There was a lively crowd around the supper table that night. After the dishes were done, the children played several games of tic-tac-toe and Alice served hot cocoa and cookies later. When it was time to go to bed, Marie started to get homesick, so Anna said that she could sleep with her. The three older girls slept on the floor in the other bedroom.

Early Sunday evening, Anna told the girls that it was time to go back home. Alice put an old feather mattress on the floor of the wagon so it would be more comfortable for them. After many goodbyes, hugs and thank yous, the little group started off. The closer they got to the farm, the more apprehensive Anna felt. She could tell that Rose Ann and even Sonja were feeling that way, too.

When they came into the yard, Anna murmured to Andrew that maybe he should come in with them. He carried a sleeping Marie on his shoulder and followed the rest of them into the house. It was all quiet in the kitchen. No one in the parlor, either. Anna told Andrew that he could lay Marie down on the sofa in the parlor. Rose Ann ran upstairs and called softly to her mother. After a short while, she came back down and said that her mother was in her room. Her father was nowhere to be seen.

As Andrew was preparing to leave, Anna walked him out to the wagon. "Maybe you should go in the barn and check to see if Mr. Benson is in there." Together they went into the big, red building and started to look around. There, they found Mr. Benson, milking one of the cows. When he saw them, he was startled and jumped up.

"Oh, I didn't know you were here," he said. He looked awful, Anna thought, like he hadn't slept or cleaned up for days. He seemed ashamed and couldn't look at them directly. "Well, I must get back to my milking," he muttered.

Andrew left and Anna returned to the house. She looked questioningly at Rose Ann. The girl just hung her head and tears started to flow. "I should have stayed here with her!" she lamented.

"Why, what's wrong, Rose Ann?" Anna asked. "Is she hurt?"

"He really beat her this time," Rose Ann said through her sobs. Anna led the girl out onto the porch, beyond earshot of the other girls. They sat down on the top step.

"Her face looks awful, and her one eye is black and blue. Oh, how could he do this to her? I could kill him!" With this, Rose Ann got up and started down the steps.

"I could kill him!" she screamed and sobbed, almost hysterically now. Anna went to her and held her in her arms until the sobbing subsided somewhat.

Just then, Mr. Benson came out of the barn and walked to the house. Rose Ann saw him and ran into the house and up the stairs, calling the other girls to do the same.

"What's going on here?" he asked Anna, who was still standing outside. "What's all the noise?"

Anna was livid with anger by now and could hardly contain herself. She didn't know what she dared say to him.

"Rose Ann is very upset, Mr. Benson," she said, trying to remain calm. "It seems that she found her mother.....ah.... not feeling... very well." With this, she turned and went into the house. Mr. Benson stood out on the sidewalk, hanging his head in sorrow and shame.

Anna found Marie still on the sofa so she carried her upstairs to her bed. She got her clothes off and put on her nightgown and tucked her in.   She wanted to go in and talk with Mrs. Benson but she was afraid that Mr. Benson would be coming up soon.   She knocked on Rose Ann's door and was told to come in.

"Is everything all right?" she asked.   Rose Ann didn't answer but Sonja said that their mother had told them all to go to sleep and she would see them in the morning.

"Remember to say your prayers then," she told them as she left and shut the door softly.   She lay in bed a long while before she heard Mr. Benson's footsteps coming up the stairs.   Then she fell into a troubled sleep.

The next morning, she was appalled when she saw Mrs. Benson.   You could tell that she had tried to cover it up with face powder but to no avail.   It was just the two women in the kitchen yet, so Anna went over to her and put her arm around her.   This gentle act started Mrs. Benson to crying and she allowed herself to be comforted by Anna.   "I guess I can't hide what's happening anymore," she said.

Anna led the woman to the table and they sat down. "Tell me about it."

"When Ben starts drinking, he changes into a completely different man. He gets violent and beats me sometimes."   She started sobbing again.

"How often does this happen?" asked Anna.

"About every four or five weeks.   He just has to have a drink again and then he can't stop.   It goes on for two or three days and then he stays sober for awhile, until the next time."

"What are you going to do?   You can't let it go on and on.   You could get hurt badly sometime.   Has he ever hit the girls?"

"No, he never hits them, thank goodness.   But they are so scared when he gets like that.   They just can't understand how he can be so mean when he is normally a gentle man.   They don't understand what alcohol can do to a person."

"Ben had an uncle like this," she went on, "who finally drank himself to death."   She started crying anew.   " I can't leave him. I have no where to go and anyway, I love him.   Most of the time he's a wonderful person.   You know that.   Everyone thinks he's a wonderful man, except that I think some people know about his drinking bouts now.   He goes to town to the bar and starts out there and then brings a bottle or two home and drinks in the barn till he almost passes out.   The next night, he goes to town for more."

"Why did he beat you so bad this time?" asked Anna.

"He was upset because I let the children go home with you. I told him that the girls were afraid of him when he was drinking and then he got really violent."

Anna felt bad now, wishing that she had not been so insistent that the girls come home with her.

"He won't show up for breakfast this morning." Mrs. Benson went on. "He's so ashamed and he has guessed that you know about it. By this evening he'll be his old self again and try to make amends."

The girls were coming down now for breakfast so Anna and Mrs. Benson had to change the subject. Grace and Sonja hadn't seen their mother's face yet and were horrified to think that their father had done that. Mrs. Benson tried to mollify them and told them that their father didn't mean to do it but that the drinking made him do things that he wouldn't ordinarily do.

"Can't you make him stop drinking, Mama?" asked Grace.

"I've tried and he's tried but it has such a hold on him. I don't know what more to do," she said, wringing her hands. Sonja went to her and put her arm around her and said, "Mama, we shouldn't have gone and left you. We'll never leave you again."

"It isn't right that you should have to feel like my protectors," their mother answered. She looked at the clock and said, "Oh, dear, look at the time. You will all be late for school." She got up and dished up their breakfast and hurried and made their lunches and off they went, almost running down the driveway. They were indeed almost late for school. Many of the children were already there and wondering where their teacher was.

During afternoon recess, Anna was in the cloak room and she overheard two of the older girls talking. One of them was saying, ".... and how can she expect to teach us English when she doesn't speak it very well herself?"

The other girl answered, "My Pa says that they shouldn't have hired someone who just came over from the old country. She isn't even a citizen of this country."

The girls went outside then and Anna stood frozen to the spot. So that's what people were thinking of her! Tears came to her eyes but she thought to herself, I can't cry now. The children will see me. She brushed her eyes and went and sat at her desk to think. English was the next subject right after recess for the older children. Now she dreaded it. She was trying hard to learn it better and she spent some time almost every evening working on it.

It was time to ring the bell but she didn't want the children to come in just yet so she let them play another ten minutes. Finally one of them came in to see why they were having such a long recess.

"Oh, Matthew, I'm sorry. You go ring the bell, will you please?"

In a few minutes, everyone was seated and waiting for her to begin. Her heart wasn't in it so she said that she was going to give them all some free time to study, read, or practice their numbers and letters. They looked at her for an explanation but none was forthcoming so they finally all busied themselves. Anna pretended to be very busy with something at her desk.

After school, she sent the girls on home ahead of her. She came a little later, walking slowly and thinking about what she had overheard. Maybe she shouldn't have expected to teach so soon in a new country where the language was so very strange and difficult. And here I thought I was doing pretty good, she thought to herself.

She entered the house and hardly said anything to anyone but went straight up to her room. She flopped down on her bed and finally let the tears flow. After awhile she started to pray. "Forgive me, Lord, for indulging in self pity today." It felt good to let the tears flow for awhile. "I can't do this without Your help," she continued. "Show me what I need to do."

There was a soft knock on her door. She called, "Come in." To her surprise, it was Mrs. Benson. Upon seeing Anna's face, she said, "Oh, dear, is something the matter?"

"I was just feeling a little sorry for myself this afternoon but I'm all right now," she said, blowing her nose and wiping the traces of tears from her eyes. "My troubles are nothing compared to yours, Mrs. Benson."

"First of all, why don't you start calling me Mary and may I call you Anna?"

"Why, of course..ah..Mary," Anna answered. She looked at her inquiringly now, wondering why she had come to her room. "Do sit down." She motioned for her to take the desk chair and Anna sat on the bed.

"I'm sorry to have burdened you so with my problems this morning but I just can't keep it all to myself anymore. I'm grateful for your concern."

"That's all right," said Anna. "I wish that I could help you somehow but I don't know what the solution is. As you said, you have no place to go."

"When Ben came home at noon for dinner, he was trying so hard to be nice, but he can hardly look at my face. He says he can't believe that he could do such a thing. He also said that he knows he needs help but doesn't know where to go."

"Have you tried taking the problem to the Lord?" asked Anna.

"I pray about it every night but no answer seems to be coming," Mary said.

"Do the two of you ever pray about it together?" asked Anna.

"No, we haven't," said Mary. "Ben leaves most of the praying up to me."

"How long has this situation been going on?" asked Anna.

"Well, for most of our married life, which is about twelve years now, but at first it was only about once or twice a year. It's gotten so much worse this past year. He never used to hit me."

"Mama, Mama, where are you?" they heard Marie calling.

"I better be going down now. And Anna, thank you. It helps to have someone to talk to," Mary said as she got up and left the room.

Later, just as Mary had said, her husband tried to act normal, as if nothing had happened. It was hard for everyone, however, to look at Mary and not be reminded. The children seemed to relax somewhat, knowing that the crisis was over for now. Their father played some games with them in the parlor while Mary and Anna did up the dishes. He even asked the girls if he could help them with their homework. He's trying to make up for what he had just put them through, Anna thought.

That weekend, when Anna was back at Andrew's, she told Alice about the incident of overhearing the two girls at school talking about her. "Do you think that the girls were right, Alice?" she asked. "Maybe I shouldn't be teaching here yet."

"You do have an accent, of course, Anna," Alice stated, "but I can certainly understand what you are trying to say. And I think that your English has improved since you first came here back in March. It will just take some time."

"Yes, but how much time? Maybe they'll tell me to leave and they'll find someone else.   They never would have hired me if they hadn't been desperate."

"Just do the best you can, Anna, and if they would ask you to leave, that isn't the worst thing that could happen to you!" Alice said.

"Yes, but then no one else would want to hire me if they knew I had been asked to leave."

"You just keep studying and practicing your English and make it through the year. Take one day at a time," Alice told her.

The next week at school, Anna tried particularly hard to pronounce every word just right. She decided on a plan that would involve her pupils, especially the two girls concerned. Their names were Amy and Leona.

"Children," she asked them, "how many of your parents came over from Norway or Sweden? Every one of them raised their hands. "And how many of them could speak English when they first came here?" Not one hand went up.

"Can they all speak English now?" she went on quizzing them. They all nodded their heads to indicate yes. "How many of your parents still have accents?" After some hesitation, all hands went up again.

"Would you be surprised if I told you that every one of you has an accent, too?" They all looked at each other, surprised and puzzled at what the teacher was getting at.

"As you all know, I came over from Norway only a little over two years ago. I knew absolutely no English. I spent about a year in New York. I lived with and worked with people who had been born here in this country. They had what I would call an American accent. When I listen to you children, you do not have an American accent. You still have the accent of your parents, but not as strong an accent. Mine is worse because I have not been here very long. What

I am getting at is this: we all need to practice our English so that when we get out into the world, away from this little Scandinavian community, we will talk like Americans and not like newcomers. So here is my plan. We must all help each other. When we hear each other mis-pronounce a word, we will call their attention to the fact. I'll ask Amy and Leona to keep track of the words that we have the most trouble with and we will all work harder on them." She looked at her pupils as they were all looking at each other and nodding their heads that this would maybe be a good plan.

"We will start right now, then," Anna said. She gave Amy and Leona a pad of paper to write down the words for the rest of them. As the days went by, many words and phrases were added to the list. Anna felt that she, herself, was benefiting the most from this, but the children were, too, and they seemed to like this approach.

At the end of October, it was time for Anna to move on to the next home. She would be staying with the Reverend Peterson and his wife and three children. The Bensons hated to see her go but, of course, the girls would still see her every day in school. Instead of going back to Andrew and Alice's on Friday after school, she stayed at the Bensons' to pack up her things. On Saturday afternoon, Mr. Benson would be driving her over to the Peterson place. Before they left, Mary came up to Anna's room and told her how much she enjoyed having her stay with them. Anna said that she hoped that Mary and the girls would be all right. It was probably soon time for Mr. Benson's next binge, she thought.

Mary could almost read her thoughts so she said, "Ben is trying real hard to lick this problem. In fact it has been about five weeks now since his last drinking bout. He tries to keep himself very busy and away from town. Pray for us, Anna."

"I do, Mary, every night," she answered. "Well, I suppose it's time to go now. I see the wagon is waiting down there," she said, looking out the window.

The girls followed Anna and Mrs. Benson out of the house, each carrying something for her. Mr. Benson loaded each box and bag. Anna turned and gave each of the girls a hug and said to them, "I'll see you on Monday, or perhaps even tomorrow in church." Mary came up and gave her a warm embrace, and said softly, "Thank you, Anna, for your friendship. I'll miss you," and then she let her go.

Anna clamored up into the wagon, avoiding Mr. Benson's outstretched hand. She smiled and waved and felt an unexplainable sadness. Goodness, she thought, I'm only going about two miles away. She tried to shake the feeling. Maybe it's because I'm always leaving someplace, she thought.

CHAPTER 8

Anna had been staying at the home of Reverend and Mrs. Peterson now for about two weeks. They lived in the parsonage which was next to the small country Lutheran church, nestled in the trees by the bend in the river. It was a pretty setting for a church. They had three children, Josie and Lucas, who were in school, and little Willie, who was four. Mrs. Peterson was a very kindly woman and Anna could see that she was a very good helpmate for the Reverend. She never had an unkind word to say about anyone. She believed that there was always some good in every person.

The Reverend was a small man, about mid-forties, who went about his task of tending his flock with great care and concern. They were both very frugal and Anna could see that they had very little to do with but they seemed to manage without complaining. Anna almost felt guilty taking food from their table but she knew that every family was expected to take their turn boarding the teacher.

Anna enjoyed having Josie and Lucas in school, but Willie was the real charmer. He was also very bright; "sharp as a tack" his father would say. He could read any chapter in the Bible that you put in front of him. Anna thought to herself that here would be a real challenge for a teacher, trying to keep ahead of him. She also wondered to herself if she would still be here in two years when Willie would be in school. Actually, his parents were starting to think that they should send him a year earlier and they asked Anna's opinion. She thought that that would probably be the best thing to do.

She enjoyed seeing the Benson girls every day in school. She would inquire about their mother and how things were going over there. She looked for signs in their behavior to give her clues as to whether their father was acting up again.

Sure enough, about three weeks after she left, she could tell, one Friday morning that things were not going well at the Benson home. The girls were withdrawn and quiet. Rose Ann was nervous and anxious. She asked them to stay after school for a little while so she could talk to them. They were not afraid to confide in her any more and so told her the whole story. Their father had come home for supper the night before and he was already roaring drunk. He had been in town all day long. They were so hoping that he was not going to do that any more as it had been about six or seven weeks since the last incident.

They went on to tell her that when their mother tried to calm him down he hit her. He had never done that in front of the girls before. This enraged their mother, who was usually so meek, so much so that she tried to hit him back! This was the most disturbing thing for them to see; their parents fighting right before their eyes.

"I'll walk over tomorrow to see your mother," she told the girls as they were getting ready to leave for home. They didn't seem in any hurry to go.

That evening after supper, Anna asked the Reverend if she could talk to him about something. They went into his study where she sat down by a worn library table that served as his desk.

"Rev. Peterson, I am very concerned about what has been going on over at the Bensons," Anna stated. "Being they are members of your congregation, I was wondering if Mrs. Benson had ever confided in you about the situation over there?"

The pastor sat down in the chair behind the table and didn't say anything for a few moments. Anna began to feel that she shouldn't have brought up the subject.

"Just exactly what situation are you referring to, Anna?" he asked her.

"His drinking and the fact that he hits her when he is drunk. Surely you must know about that."

"Mrs. Benson did confide in me about a year ago when I happened to make a call over at their farm. Mr. Benson was not home and the children were in school. Ben had been drinking the day before and was in town again. She was very worried about what was going to happen when her husband came home."

"What advice did you give her then, as her pastor?" asked Anna.

He looked uncomfortable at her question and he sighed resignedly. "What could I tell her? I said that I would talk to Ben but she said I couldn't do that because then he would know that she had told me. She didn't want people to know what was going on. About all I could do then is tell her that I would be praying for her and that if things got really intolerable, she and the children should come to the parsonage when Ben goes on one of his binges. I haven't heard anything from her about it since."

"She confided in me when I was staying over there," Anna said. "Actually the girls told me first. She said that about every four weeks or so he gets very drunk and then comes home and takes out his anger on her. I don't know what he is so angry about."

"She did tell me that Ben grew up with an abusive father and that he would drink and sometimes beat his wife and children. That anger wells up in Ben and in spite of his efforts not to, he goes out and drinks and does the same thing himself," Rev. Peterson told her.

"I feel so bad for them and I don't know what the answer is," said Anna, "and I just hope that nobody gets badly hurt someday."

"The physical abuse is bad enough, but the emotional scars that the children will carry with them is another matter," he said. "I feel bad that I can't do more, but when people don't want things to be out in the open, one's hands are tied. People are so afraid of what everyone else will think that they choose to suffer in silence." Rev. Peterson looked genuinely disturbed about his inability to do anything about such matters.

"You'd be surprised, Miss Olson, by the things I have seen people suffer through just to keep up appearances." He stood up, indicating that this conversation was over and said that he had to tend to something outside.

The next day being Saturday, she asked Mrs. Peterson if she thought that she could take the horse and buggy for a while in the afternoon to make a call.

"I'm sure you can, my dear," she said. I'll mention it to the Reverend when he comes in."

Anna drove slowly into the Benson yard, not knowing what she would find. She hoped that Mr. Benson would not be around. She was almost up to the door when one of the girls saw her and came running out to greet her. Grace was so happy to see Anna that she wrapped her arms around her waist and would hardly let go.

When Anna stood back and looked at the girl, she noticed that she had been crying. "Why, Grace, what is the matter?" she asked, knowing what the answer would be.

Grace didn't answer but only took Anna's hand and led her into the house. Mary and Rose Ann were sitting by the kitchen table, trying to work on some mending.

"Anna, it's good to see you again," Mary said. "Have a seat and I'll pour you a cup of coffee." Anna could tell that Mary's heart wasn't into entertaining a guest but she was trying her best.

Anna got right to the point of her visit. "Mary, the girls told me that Ben is at it again. I'm so sorry for you. How can I help?"

"Oh, I had my hopes up this time that he was really going to stop drinking. I think that he did, too, but the urge is too strong for him sometimes. He says that he doesn't want to drink but he isn't strong enough to keep away from it. I don't know what to do," she said, pacing the floor by the table. She remembered the promised coffee and brought Anna a cup plus a plate of cookies.

Trying to change the subject and cheer things up, she asked, "So you didn't go to your brother's this weekend?"

"No, I told Andrew that I was going to stay here because he will be coming to get me the middle of next week for the Thanksgiving vacation," Anna explained.

"We will be having a houseful that day," Mary said. "Ben's sister and brother and their families are coming. They all bring food but it still is so much work getting ready for it."

They talked of many things and by the time Anna left, the girls seemed to be cheered up somewhat. Mary said to Anna that about all she could do is grin and bear it and hope for the best. It would soon be over. Until next time.

Thanksgiving was a fun day at Andrew and Alice's. They invited the Jorgensons over for dinner. They had all gone to church services first, where they thanked their Maker for all their blessings. The little church was full on this special day. After a big dinner, everyone rested and then they played cards and games. Peder Jorgenson tried to sit closest to Anna and she caught him looking at her many times but he couldn't think of much to say.

After their guests left and the children were put to bed, Anna and Andrew were sitting by the table having a cup of coffee. They were discussing again how much they had to be thankful for and Anna mentioned that she didn't think that the Peterson family that she was staying with had very much.

"That's true of all the pastors that I've ever known," Andrew said. "I think the congregations try to starve them!"

"Oh, Andrew," reprimanded Alice, "you shouldn't say such a thing."

"Well, it's true that none of them get paid much. The people in their congregations all seem to think that just because they are ministers of God, that they should be satisfied to live on practically nothing." Andrew was getting warmed up on a subject that you could tell bothered him.

"Every year at our church's annual meeting," he went on, "I try to get them to raise the pastor's salary a little but it's like pulling hen's teeth to get them to agree to that!" Andrew got up and got the coffee pot to pour refills for himself and Anna. "I try to do my part by giving our Pastor meat and eggs and cords of wood, and I've helped make repairs on the parsonage."

"Well, the Petersons seem pretty self-reliant. They have cows and chickens and plenty of wood. Mrs. Peterson has a huge garden and sews everything they wear."

"It still isn't right," Andrew insisted.

"I agree with you, Andrew, but what can one do?" asked Anna.

"Keep trying to change the minds of some pretty stiff-necked people, I guess," he concluded.

"It's getting late," announced Alice. "I'm going to turn in." Anna agreed and started upstairs. Andrew went to put more wood in the stove.

As Anna lay in bed that night, she thought about her family back home in Norway and about Tomas and his family. Her thoughts then turned to her new family in this country, the people that had become dear to her, the Benson family and now the Petersons. She hoped things were going all right for Mary and the girls over at the Benson farm.

Lastly, as she did every night, she thought about the Martins, now a family with little Samuel. Her little Samuel. The ache in her heart returned with the thought of him. She could feel his soft hair brushing against her cheek that last day. She fell asleep wondering what he looked like now.

One evening, back at the Peterson house, when they were having supper, Rev. Peterson was telling of his trip into town that afternoon. He mentioned that 'Big Ole' who was considered the town drunk had been put in jail for a few days because he had hit Mr. Jensven and had given him a pretty wicked black eye.

When Anna heard this she said, "You mean that if a man hits another man he can be put in jail?"

"Yes, that is so," answered the Reverend.

Anna, feeling the heat rise to her face went on. "But if a man hits his wife, nothing is done about it!"

Pastor Peterson hesitated a moment. "I guess you could say that."

Anna rose from the table and started pacing. "So in other words, in this country a marriage license is almost like a license to hurt or kill!"

"Well, no, I wouldn't put it like that, Miss Olson," replied Pastor Peterson.

"A man can beat his wife and nothing happens to him but a man can hit another man on the street and be put in jail for it! That doesn't make any sense."

"I know that it isn't right but what can we do to change it?" asked Mrs. Peterson.

The Reverend shook his head back and forth and said, "This is an old problem and I don't know the answer to it. It seems that what goes on inside the walls of one's home is very private and the law can't interfere unless someone is killed."

"The laws need to be changed then," said Anna, still agitated over the subject.

"Yes, they do," agreed Rev. Peterson. "My hands as a pastor are tied, too, if the family doesn't want to come out openly with their problems. And we Norwegians are very good at trying to keep our problems from everyone else. Believe me, I know!"

The subject was then changed when Mrs. Peterson brought dessert and the children asked their father if he had brought home any candy for them from town.

"No, not this time, my dears," he said regretfully, "but maybe next time."

At Christmas time, the school had two week's vacation. Anna's school put on a Christmas program on the last day before the break. The room was full of parents and the children did very well. The children had recitations and sang songs and one of the older boys even dressed up as Santa Claus.

It was good to see Ben and Mary Benson there and little Maria. Everyone complimented Anna on a job well done and said that this program was the best ever!

Mary took Anna aside and pressed a small package into her hands. "A little Christmas gift from me," she said. Anna asked her how things had been going and she said that Ben was trying extra hard not to drink and was succeeding for the time being. She went to town with him every time he went in and that kept him away from the bar.

Anna gave her a quick hug and said she hoped that they would have a very happy Christmas at their house. She went on to talk briefly with all the parents as they were leaving.

This was her first Christmas with Andrew and Alice and it was very busy and fun. The time went fast with all there was to do and all the visiting that went on. The Sunday School children put on a Christmas program at the church on Christmas Eve and the next day they had a big dinner and went over to see the Jorgensons in the evening.

They received Christmas mail from Tomas and Bergit and also from Norway. It was good to hear the latest news from everybody. She missed them all so much and especially so at this time of the year. Anna also received a letter from Toledo, from the Martins. She opened this one with trembling hands and went up to her bedroom to read it in private. Inside was a baby picture of little Samuel! She had to sit down on the bed and she looked and looked at it for a long time. Finally she took her eyes off it long enough to read the accompanying letter. Mrs. Martin said that Samuel was doing very well, thriving and growing like a weed. "He is a very bright and happy child," she wrote.

Through her tears, Anna finished reading and then picked up the picture again. She did not bring it down to show the family. She didn't think she could do that without betraying herself. She put it in her Bible where she would look at it every night for a long time to come. That evening she sat down and wrote a short note to Mrs. Martin, thanking her for the precious picture. "I can't tell you what it means to me to get this picture. I will always cherish it," she wrote.

The remaining weeks of staying with the Peterson family went by quickly and soon she was moved to the next family and then the next. They were all very nice to her and soon it was spring and time for school to be let out. They had an end-of-the-year program and she said goodbye to all the children and parents. She was not coming back even though they had asked her to. She decided that she needed to go back to school herself.

The first of June Andrew put Anna on the train again. She was going back to stay with Tomas and Bergit in Mankato. She would be attending school there and the term would be starting early in June.

Tomas and Bergit were happy to see her again. Anna got acquainted with the new baby boy, Teddy, who was born the September before. The other children swarmed all over her, so happy they were to have her back with them.

"So, Anna," Tomas began, "we were a little surprised that you didn't take that teaching job for another year."

"I liked it all right there, but I felt that I needed some more education to do a good job of teaching. Especially in English and American history. The children knew more than I did much of the time!" Anna answered.

"It will be so nice having you here for the summer, Anna," said Bergit. "I really missed you when you left us at the end of last summer."

Anna thought that Bergit looked very tired. With four young ones and a house to care for, I guess she would be, thought Anna to herself.

The next few days, she got settled in and tried to help Bergit as much as possible before her summer school began. She would be attending classes every morning, five days a week.

The small house was even smaller now with another baby plus Anna staying there. Bergit said that she hoped that they could move into something bigger very soon. "Tomas has been keeping his eyes open for one to our liking," she said.

One evening Anna was in the parlor rocking the baby in the big, old rocker. He had fallen asleep and she didn't want to move him. Her thoughts turned to little Samuel and how it would feel to be holding her own little boy right now. Tears came to her eyes and her heart ached for him. Bergit came in and saw her and asked her if something was wrong. Anna got flustered and started to get up.

"No, no, nothing is wrong," she said. "I was, ah, just thinking about all of my loved ones and how I miss them." She tried to brush her tears aside.

"Here, let me take Teddy up and put him to bed," said Bergit. Anna went up and got ready for bed also. As she opened her Bible, the picture of Samuel fell into her lap. She picked it up and looked at it for a long time again. She read some scripture and then said her prayers, her heart heavy with sadness and longing.

The next week her classes began and she was kept busy with assignments and spent some time each afternoon in the library. It was easier to study there than at the house with four children making noise. Her classes were quite challenging and the assignments were long each day. She was tired out by the time she returned to the house but she tried to help Bergit with making supper and tending to the children.

Many evenings, after the children were all in bed, Bergit would be standing in the kitchen by her ironing board and Anna would be studying at the kitchen table. Bergit would refill Anna's coffee cup as needed to keep her awake. The two sisters-in-law had formed a close bond the summer before and they could work together in companionable silence, each with their own task. When Bergit would finish her work for the evening, she would pour a cup of coffee for herself and sit down at the table with Anna. They would talk for awhile before calling it a day.

"You study too hard, Anna," Bergit would tell her.

"You work too hard, Bergit," Anna would answer. They would laugh and wearily walk arm and arm up to their rooms.

One afternoon when Anna was in the library, she needed assistance in finding something so she went up to the front desk. The woman who was usually there and who had always been so helpful to Anna was not there just then but a young man was standing with his back to her, deeply involved in some task. She waited awhile and then cleared her throat and said "Excuse me, sir, might I have some help, please?"

He whirled around, unaware that she had been standing there for sometime.

"Lawrence Howe, at your service, ma'am," he said, clicking his heels.

"I'm looking for the woman who is usually at this desk. I need help finding something," Anna said.

"I'm taking her place this afternoon. What can I help you with?" he asked.

She told him what she needed to look up and he said that he knew just where to find it. He led her down a side aisle and pointed to some books up on the top shelf.

"Here, let me help you get those down," he suggested as he stood on his tiptoes and reached up for them. They were heavy so he carried them back to the table that she had been sitting at and laid them down.

"There you are then, Ma'am," he said, giving her a big smile.

"Thank you very much. You've been a big help," said Anna, sitting down to begin her search of some information.

"Just leave those books there when you are finished with them and I'll carry them back for you," he said, leaving her to her work.

Anna looked at his retreating back and thought, what a nice, young man and so pleasant and helpful.

Anna would run into this nice, young man numerous times in the library for the next few weeks. He usually managed to find some reason to approach her and talk to her about some subject or other.

One day he said to her, "You have such a charming accent. Is it from Scandinavia?"

"Why, yes it is," she answered.

"I'm pretty good at guessing where people are from by listening to them talk," he said. "But you almost had me fooled." Anna didn't look like the typical Scandinavian who had settled in that area. She was tall, slim, and had dark hair and brown eyes. "Norway, is it?" he asked.

"Yes again, Mr...ah.. I'm sorry but I forgot your name."

"Lawrence Howe, but everyone calls me Lorrie. But you've never told me your name."

"I'm Anna Olson," she said, extending her hand. He shook it eagerly.

"You must be a student here," he said.

"Yes, I am, and you?" she answered

"I'm a student, too, but I work here part time."

When Anna was ready to leave, Mr. Howe stopped her and said, "Would you allow me to walk you home, Miss Olson? I'll be ready to get off in a few minutes."

Anna didn't know what to say to this so she didn't answer right away.

"I could help you with your load of books there," he offered.

"Well, I guess that would be nice, Mr. Howe, but you needn't go to that trouble."

"No trouble at all, Miss Olson, it would be my pleasure," he said.

As they walked the four blocks to Anna's, Mr. Howe kept up a running conversation and soon they were at her door.

"I live here with my brother and his family," Anna told him. "Thank you for helping me with my books, Mr. Howe."

"You must call me Lorrie from now on and may I call you Anna?" he asked.

"Yes, of course you can," she answered and turned to go in.

"See you tomorrow at the library," he called from the sidewalk.

When Anna came in the house, Bergit was standing there.

"And who was that young man, Anna?" she asked with a sly smile.

"Oh, just someone I see at the library every day. He offered to help carry these books home," she answered.

Over the course of the summer, Anna had written to and received letters from most all of her family. Barbro and Peder were doing well in Drammen and they had all just been back home to visit Papa and Mama. Margit wrote that she and Tollef and the children were all doing fine. Little Caren was such a joy; she looked just like Anna, she said. Sigrid wrote from New York, too, and said that she wished Anna would come back there and go to school. They missed her. Papa wrote that Mama was again having some heart spells, and Kjersti was also failing but they did not know why. Anna had suggested to him that he and Mama come to America for a visit but he said that was out of the question.

Alice also wrote and said that she was expecting a baby again and it was due in late December. She and Andrew were both excited about it but she hoped that this would be the last one.

Anna and Lorrie saw each other almost every week day at the library the rest of the summer. He would walk her home sometimes and they enjoyed each other's company. "He makes me laugh," Anna told Bergit. "He says I'm too serious at times."

When fall came, Anna enrolled for the next quarter. She had done quite well in her classes over the summer. Lorrie would come over for supper sometimes and often on Sunday afternoons he would come by for Anna in the buggy and they would go for a ride. They could talk to each other for hours on end.

Lorrie was several years older than Anna. He had taught in country schools for four years but then he decided he wanted to teach in high school so he had to go back to school for more training. His family lived in southwest Minnesota where his father was in business in a small town.

The school year went by quickly. They heard from Alice and Andrew shortly after the new year. The baby, a boy whom they named George, was born New Year's Eve and everything was all right with mother and baby.

In the spring, both Anna and Lorrie were applying for teaching positions. Lorrie hoped to get into the high school right there in Mankato and Anna could only hope to get into some country school.

In early June, Tomas announced that he had found a house that he thought Bergit would like so on Sunday afternoon they all took a ride over to see it. It was on the other side of town in a nice residential area. The house was about twenty years old and would need only some minimal repairs which Tomas could very well do himself. It was a two-story, four-bedroom house and it had a nice size yard and an orchard already started. The man who owned it had just died and his widow was going to live with her son.

Bergit and the children were very excited about it. "There's so much more room!" exclaimed Bergit excitedly. That evening after the children had all gone to bed and the three adults were sitting around the table with their coffee cups, Tomas and Bergit made the decision to buy the house. Bergit was very excited. They could move in at the end of the month.

That next week, Bergit and Anna started packing things up and discarding some, preparing for the move. After the widow moved out, they were able to get into the house and start painting and begin the repairs. Finally, moving day came and it was July 3rd, the day before the big Fourth of July celebration. They were all too busy and too tired to take part in any of the festivities. Lorrie came and helped them, too.

He had just received word that he could have a teaching position in a high school in a town named New Ulm, about 30 miles from Mankato. He would be moving there the middle of August, he said, to get settled in. Anna had still not heard anything yet and was beginning to get worried. What would she do if she didn't get anything? Perhaps she could get a job in one of the stores downtown.

Finally toward the end of July, she received a letter from a school in Cottonwood County. It was a country school named Riverside School #2. That's all she knew about it but they would hire her, sight unseen. Time was running out for her to be choosy. After a day or so, she wrote them a letter accepting the teaching position. Two weeks later she had a reply from them saying they were glad that she had accepted and that they would like her to be out there by the first of September as school started on the 3rd. She was to write or wire them on her time of arrival and someone would be there to meet her train. They sent train fare for her which she thought was very nice.

The month of August was spent helping Bergit with her garden which was back at the old place. They picked and canned many vegetables by the score and also fruit from their new orchard. There were apples and plums and chokecherries. Many colorful jars of newly "put up" fruits and vegetables lined the shelves of Bergit's new cellar.

Anna barely had time to look for new shoes for herself and sew herself a new 'serviceable' dress for teaching. On September 1, Tomas brought her to the train station for her short trip to the town of Windorn and her new venture.

She was met by a man and a woman, Mr. and Mrs. Halvorson, who said that she would be staying with them the whole year. They always boarded the teacher because they lived right next door. They seemed like nice people, Anna thought to herself, and she hoped that she would like them or else it would be a very long year.

When they pulled into their yard, four children came running out of the house toward them. They lined up, oldest first, and Anna met each one of them in turn. There was Margit, the only girl, who said that she was twelve, and Toby, who was ten. Lars and Hans were twins and were going on seven.

Besides the four Halvorson children, there were fifteen others in her school. They were all quite well behaved so everything went smoothly. She liked the Halvorsons and they had a nice house where she had a small room for herself. She didn't go back to Tomas and Bergit's until the middle of October. She boarded the train on Friday evening and the next day was her 22nd birthday so she was able to celebrate the event with family.

Some letters had come for her and one of them was from Mary Benson. She told Anna that Ben had had an accident. He had fallen from the roof of the barn and was still partially paralyzed from a broken back. The doctors didn't know if he would ever walk again or not. It was still too early to tell. Mary wrote, "Is this God's answer to my prayers? Ben can't drink now because he can't go into town to get it. Now I'm praying for him to be able to walk again, but then he will start drinking again." God works in mysterious ways, Anna thought to herself.

Several letters were from Lorrie. He didn't know her new address. He liked teaching where he was and was wondering how things were going for her. She wrote him a letter that evening and would have Tomas post it on Monday. Sunday afternoon she took the train back to Windorn.

The weather was mild up until Thanksgiving. A diphtheria epidemic was raging in the next county. Just before Anna left for Mankato for Thanksgiving vacation, she heard that there were two cases in Cottonwood county and every family was frightened.

Bergit cooked a big Thanksgiving dinner and she had invited their pastor who was recently widowed and would have been alone. They all talked about how many things they each had to be thankful for. Pastor Lingren told how he had lost his first wife on the voyage over to this country. His second wife had died in childbirth. The child, a boy, had grown up and gone out east. He married for a third time and had been married for about twenty years when she died, also. Anna marveled at his strong, unwavering faith in the goodness of God. She told him about Ben and Mary Benson. He said that he would add them to his prayer list.

On Sunday morning when Anna was preparing to go back to her school, a telegram was delivered to her from Mr. Halvorson. He said that they were closing the school for a week because the diphtheria outbreak was hitting their community and everyone wanted to keep their children home. He would let her know when they would reopen. She hoped that none of her families would be stricken with the dreaded disease.

Anna waited all the next week for word and finally on Saturday afternoon she got a wire saying that school would be closed for one more week. They would let her know for sure at the end of that week. One of her families, the Hersch family, had three of their children down with the disease but they seemed to be recovering. There had been two deaths in the little town of Windorn itself so the people were being very cautious.

Anna used the time to write letters and help Bergit around the house. She even went downtown and did a little of her Christmas shopping to get a head start. At the end of the week she got word that her school would reopen on Monday for sure so she got on the train once more and headed back. When the Halvorsons met her, she found out that one of the Hersch children, the youngest, had died but the other two had recovered. They did not return to school for another week.

She heard from Lorrie a week later and he said that he would be going home to see his parents at Christmas. He wished that they could see each other again soon but he didn't know when that would be.

When Anna was back at Tomas and Bergit's at Christmas, she received a letter from the Martins like she had the year before. Mrs. Martin told her all about little Samuel but did not have a new picture to send her at this time. He would soon be two so they would have his picture taken again then. Anna reread the letter many times and memorized everything about him. The old ache in her heart returned again. She threw herself into the festivities going on around her to help keep those feelings at bay.

Back at school, the winter continued to be mild with little snow. One day in late February, however, things changed dramatically. The morning started out gray and cloudy and Mr. Halvorson said at breakfast that he didn't like the looks of the sky. After lunchtime the schoolhouse was suddenly hit by a wind so fierce and loud that all the children looked up simultaneously and all eyes turned toward the window. It sounded like a freight train was descending upon them. Anna and some of the children rushed to the windows. A wall of white engulfed them. It was snowing and blowing so hard that one could see nothing out the window. Anna had never seen anything like this. She had to speak loudly to make herself heard above the noise surrounding them.

Some of the younger children began to cry and Anna was wondering what she should do. Some of the older children said that two years ago there had been a blizzard and all of them had to spend the night at the school and part of the next day. Anna tried to gather her wits about her and not panic when she heard this. She asked an older boy to check the wood supply in the wood box. There was plenty of water, she thought. What about toilet facilities, she wondered. She tried to keep the children's minds off the weather so she read to them for awhile. After a couple of hours, the wind seemed to subside somewhat and she could see the trees beyond the school yard.

About this time they heard some stomping feet out in the entryway. There was Mr. Halvorson, all covered with snow! He told them to get their coats on quickly and he would load them all up in his wagon and take them to his house while they could still see something. Perhaps it would get worse again. The children didn't have to be told twice to hurry. One older girl confided in Anna that she was worried that maybe they would all get lost between the school and the house. She had heard of this happening. Anna looked at Mr. Halvorson and he said that the horses knew how to get home and if they hurried they would make it.

All the little ones scampered up into the wagon and were pulled onto the laps of the older girls. The bigger boys walked alongside, holding onto the wagon's sideboards. They could just barely make out the Halvorson house in the near distance. In a few minutes the wagon drew up close to the front door and the children were hustled down from the wagon and were hurried into the house by Mrs. Halvorson. Her husband went off to the barn to unhitch the horses. Anna counted heads and breathed a sigh of relief when all were accounted for.

"I am so relieved to be here, Mrs. Halvorson," Anna said. "I truly did not know what I was going to do with the children if we had to spend all night at the schoolhouse. The wood supply was getting low and everyone had eaten all their lunch at noon."

"Well, I was really worried about all of you, too. I'm glad that the storm let up a bit. I think it's worse again now," she said as she peered out the window towards the barn. "Theander should have been back here by now," she added, sounding worried. She busied herself getting the children comfortable and went to stir up some hot cocoa for the bunch.

Later, when everyone was almost finished with their hot drink and cookies, Mr. Halvorson burst in through the back door. Everyone turned to look at him. He was very pale and he grabbed a chair and sat down.

"I don't know when I've ever been so scared in a storm before!" he said, shaking his head back and forth. "And I've been in lots of them over the years. I left the barn and halfway to the house, I couldn't see the house at all. I kept walking in what I thought was the right direction but I guess I veered to the left quite a bit. I kept walking and walking and I knew I had walked too far when I finally bumped into the outhouse. Then I knew I was way off track. I had walked way past the house. I went in and waited awhile and hoped that I wouldn't have to spend the night in there!"

"Oh, dear," said Mrs. Halvorson, "I was worried about you; I knew it was taking way too long for you to get back here."

"I finally caught a glimpse of the house," he went on, "and I started towards it, praying all the way, I tell you!"

His wife brought him a cup of cocoa and saw that he was shivering so she told him to get his wet things off and get dry clothes on. He did that and then took his cup and sat close to the stove for warmth.

"What will my Papa think when he comes to the school and we aren't there?" asked a little first grader.

"No one will come to the school until the storm ends. They will know that you are safe, either at the school or here," Mrs. Halvorson assured her. "This happened one other time a few years back. The whole school came over here and had to stay for two days."

"Two days!" cried another little one. "I want to go home now."

Anna went to comfort her and she knew that she had to get the children's minds on something else. She hustled all of them into the parlor and got them started playing games. Mrs. Halvorson was busy in the kitchen trying to figure out what to feed all her guests for supper. She sent her husband down to the cellar to get jars of home-canned vegetables and fruits.

After supper, the storm seemed just as intense as ever. Anna and Mrs. Halvorson went upstairs and figured out where to put everybody when it came to bedtime. They found extra quilts and blankets and pillows and had them ready.

The younger children started drifting off to sleep, one by one, so they were carried upstairs and put on the floor, side by side, and covered up. The older children, plus Anna and the Halvorsons played charades till quite late. With the storm still raging, they all finally went to bed and by midnight the house was quiet inside.

Not so outside. Anna listened to the howling winds. She couldn't remember that there had been any storms as bad as this in Norway. It was almost frightening, and as she snuggled deeper under her covers, she wondered what the next day would bring. She said her prayers, thanking God that she and her charges were all safe and snug. It would have been a cold night in the schoolhouse!

The next morning, it was the silence that awoke Anna. She sensed immediately that something was different. There were no howling winds. Light was starting to filter into her bedroom window. She shook herself awake and went to see outside. What she saw took her breath away. There was snow piled up about as high as the porch roof and it stretched from the house to the barn. She wondered if they could even get out of the house!

She heard someone downstairs so she quickly dressed and went down to the kitchen where she found the Halvorsons. She could smell coffee beginning to boil.

"Have you been outside yet?" she asked Mr. Halvorson.

"No, but I opened the door and the snow is higher than the door!" he answered. "I think I can get out the back door, though. I'll try after breakfast."

Mrs. Halvorson was stirring up a big batch of pancakes and had the griddle almost hot enough. Anna poured herself a cup of coffee and asked Mr. Halvorson what he thought the roads would be like.

"In my experience," he said, "some will be impassable and others will be blown free of snow." He and Anna sat down to have the first two pancakes.

Two of the older boys came down and joined them, loading up on pancakes like they were starving! Mr. Halvorson bundled up and went to try the back door. The snow wasn't as high here. It had swirled around to the front. Still he walked in drifts up to his hips at times. It was slow going, Anna could see, as she watched from the window. Soon she could no longer make out his form. The two boys were anxious to go out and see for themselves what the storm from the night before had left. Mrs. Halvorson found them some extra clothing and they followed Mr. Halvorson's path to the barn.

Some of the other children were now coming downstairs, curious as to what they would find. Anna made Mrs. Halvorson sit down and eat while she made pancakes for her and the assembled group.

By the time the last of the children had come down and eaten, Mr. Halvorson and the two boys came back to the house. The boys had much to tell and they both talked at once. It had taken the three of them about a half hour just to get the barn door open enough so that they could slip in. They fed the horses and milked the cows. They could see that there was a big drift across the driveway. Later they would go out and see what was beyond that. First they had to warm up, they said.

After dinner, all the children wanted to go out and play in the huge snowbanks. It was quite a job getting them all bundled up with whatever extra clothing could be found. They had fun sliding down the big bank by the house. They could actually get up on the porch roof and they slid down from there. There was much laughter and a few snow ball fights. When they finally all came in, cold and wet, Mrs. Halvorson gave them hot cocoa again and she had two freshly baked cakes and not a crumb was left after the children finished eating!

While they were all still sitting at the table, someone noticed that it had started snowing again. The children groaned and began to wonder among themselves if their parents were going to come for them soon. Mrs. Halvorson gathered all of them around the piano and she played and they sang until they ran out of songs that they knew. When the music stopped, they could hear the wind blowing again.

Mr. Halvorson and the boys came in then and said that the wind had picked up and it was starting to snow heavily. "I don't like the looks of this," he said. "I guess this morning was just the calm before another storm." Anna and Mrs. Halvorson looked at each other, reading each other's mind. Will we have food enough for all these children for another day or maybe even two more days?

Anna suggested that the older girls take the younger children upstairs and play "school". The older boys sat around the table and played a card game with Mr. Halvorson. Anna and Mrs. Halvorson started cooking and baking, wondering what the days ahead would bring.

By supper time, the wind was really howling again. "I bet the parents are starting to get frantic, worrying about their children, thinking that maybe we are still at the school," Anna said. She was worrying herself, pacing the floor in front of the window, looking out every few minutes, as if there would be any change that soon!

"There isn't anything we can do about the situation, Anna," said Mr. Halvorson, "so you may as well sit down and not get the children nervous by watching you." She did as he bid, but was soon up again, trying to be helpful in getting supper on the table.

That evening the younger children were getting very tired of this and wanted to go home. Some were crying. The fun of the experience was wearing thin for the older ones, too. Anna had to think up something for them to do.

"Why don't we put on a play for the Halvorsons!" she exclaimed. Her enthusiasm soon spread to the children. It was decided that half of the group would go upstairs and plan a play and come down and put it on for the rest of them. They would need some makeshift costumes as well so it maybe would take some time. The group remaining downstairs was going to plan a treasure hunt and would be making up clues and hiding treasures. Everyone got into the excitement, even the Halvorsons, and the evening passed swiftly. The play, Cinderella, was a success and the hunt for treasures was a fun way to pass the time. Cookies and milk were served and then everyone was tired and went to their sleeping places from the night before.

Before retiring, Mrs. Halvorson started some bread dough to raising so they would have bread the next day. She opened the back door to check on the weather and it sounded just as bad, or even worse than the night before!

The storm raged all that night and into the next day. By noon, it seemed to be letting up and by mid afternoon the wind finally stopped, exhausted and spent. The drifts were even higher and they were hard packed this time so that one could actually walk on top of them without sinking in the snow. The sun came out and the children, cooped up far too long, hurried to go outside and enjoy the novelty of house-high drifts and to run off some energy.

The children thought that, of course, their parents would be coming for them soon, but the adults knew that was unlikely. No one would be able to get out of their own yards to go anywhere for quite sometime. They would perhaps all be spending another night together! Mrs. Halvorson and Anna prepared food and tried to think of something for the children to do in the evening.

It was the afternoon of the third day before the first parent was able to get out and make their way over to the Halvorson's. It was their closest neighbor. They took five of the children, three of their own and the other two were cousins. They had come by horse and sleigh. Soon another sleigh came for more of the children. And so it went until all but two had been fetched by their parents. Anna told everyone that there would be no school the next day, not until Monday. The two remaining children had to stay another night. Their father was finally able to come the next morning. He said he had never seen the likes of this storm.

The four Halvorson children were lonesome after everyone had gone to their own homes. Meal time was less hectic and there were a lot less dishes to wash! Anna and the Halvorsons talked over coffee that evening and Anna said that she was totally exhausted.

"I think it was the anxiety of it all," Mr. Halvorson said, "but all's well that ends well."

"We certainly will all remember the big storm of February, 1909, won't we?" pondered Anna. "I hope I don't see anything like that ever again."

The rest of that year passed uneventfully and when school was out, Anna was not offered the job at the Riverside school for the next year. The man who had taught there for two years previously had returned and wanted his job back. The board was divided on this matter for they liked Anna, too, and hated to tell her she didn't have a job for the next year. A vote was taken and the young man won out.

Anna did not mind too much as she was rather anxious to spread her wings again and go on to the next place. Why am I such a vagabond? she asked herself. I left Norway to see what I could see, and I guess I haven't seen it all yet!

CHAPTER 9

The summer went by quickly for Anna. First she went to visit Tomas and Bergit. Lorrie was also in Mankato for the summer going to school again. Anna realized just how much she missed him when she saw him again. He must have felt the same way because he embraced her much longer than was necessary between friends.

The month of July Anna spent visiting Andrew and Alice. She got acquainted with the new baby, George, who was now about 7 months old. While there, she drove out to visit the Benson's one day. They were all so happy to see her. Mary said that things were going well. Ben's back injury was healing and he could walk some with crutches or by pushing his chair in front of him. Ben even discussed his drinking problem with Anna. He hadn't had a drink since the accident, he told her, and he hoped that he would never take one again.

"I believe that God answered my prayers, Anna," said Mary, "but He sure did it in a dramatic way!"

"Do you worry that Ben will start drinking again when he can get around by himself?" Anna asked Mary.

"We just take one day at a time and hope everything works out all right," answered Mary.

When Anna announced that it was time for her to be starting back, the four girls wanted her to stay longer. She promised that she would come back once more before she left for Minnesota.

While she was still at Andrew's, a letter came from Mrs. Martin. In it was a picture of Samuel taken when he turned two. Mrs. Martin said that he was a healthy and robust little boy. Anna could see that by the picture. She put it in her Bible along with his baby picture, where she would see it every day for a long time to come.

They also received a letter from Norway. Papa reported that everyone was well, even Mama was feeling better than she had for quite some time. Papa said that they all missed their family in America and wished he could see everyone again.

When Anna returned to Mankato, a letter came for her saying that she was hired to teach in a little village school in Courtland. Both she and Lorrie were excited about this because Courtland was near New Ulm where Lorrie would be teaching again.

Early one Saturday morning the two of them took a drive in the buggy over to Courtland so that Lorrie could show Anna the area. He had driven this way many times between Mankato and New Ulm. It was a very pretty drive, especially around the lake area. Swan Lake, which appeared to be quite a large lake, was nearby. They picnicked near the shore at noon and then drove on to Courtland. Anna got to see the school and also the little 2-room house where she would be living. It was right next to the school and it was reserved for the teacher.

The first part of September, the two made the trip again. Lorrie dropped Anna off at the little house and helped her in with her things and then he went on to New Ulm. The house was small but cozy and fully furnished. I think I'm going to like it here, Anna thought to herself.

School began and she had only twelve pupils to begin with. Ten of them were between grades four through six. That was her favorite age group to work with. She enjoyed living in a house by herself instead of always living with a family. In fact, she thought to herself, this is the first time in my life that I have not lived with a family.

Lorrie came by every Saturday or Sunday while the weather was nice. They would often drive out to the lake and picnic there. On Monday morning, the children would tease her about her beau. She would tell them that he was just a good friend. Or was he becoming more than that to her? she asked herself after one particular Sunday outing with him. They had gone dancing at a pavilion by the lake and she was thinking how good it felt to be in his arms. Lorrie loved to dance and they went as often as they could.

The school year sped by and soon it was summer again. Lorrie wasn't going to Mankato this year because he had finished school. He was going to his hometown of Marshall to help his parents in their grocery store. He wanted Anna to come out and visit him and meet his family. She went to Tomas and Bergit's first for awhile and then she took the train out to Marshall the end of June.

Anna fell in love with Lorrie's family and they with her. His mother was a pleasant woman who laughed often and made Anna feel so at home. His father was very nice, too, and his sister, who was getting married in July, was a little younger than Anna and they got along famously. Lorrie's brother was older and had moved to North Dakota a couple of years ago.

Anna was only planning to stay for a week but Lorrie wanted her to stay for his sister Elizabeth's wedding, and she thought that would be fun, too, so she agreed to stay a week longer. The wedding was simple but beautiful and there were many friends and relatives of the family there. That evening, after everyone had left, Lorrie led her out for a walk. It was a warm, moonlit evening and they found a bench in the little town park where they sat down to rest awhile.

Lorrie took Anna's hand and held it in silence for a long moment and then he spoke what had been in his heart for sometime.

"Anna, my dear, I think you must realize by now how I feel about you and I have reason to believe that you feel the same way." He cleared his throat and continued, "Would you do me the honor of becoming my wife?"

Anna caught her breath at this question. She really had no idea that he would be asking this, at least not so soon. Lorrie had stopped breathing altogether, waiting for her answer. Anna looked at him and in the moonlight she could see so much love in his eyes and in his expression that her heart did a leap in her chest. Before she knew it, she answered, "Yes."

Lorrie jumped up and let out a whoop and pulled Anna to her feet. He took her in his arms and hugged her tightly. Then he held her away from him so that he could look into her deep brown eyes. "I love you very much, Anna. We will be so happy together!"

Anna, who was still in a kind of daze, realized that some declaration of love should be forthcoming from her, too. "Lorrie, I thought of you as just a friend for such a long time, but I have been feeling lately that it has become more than friendship. I guess it must be love that I am feeling. I am so new at this!"

He hugged her again and said, "Let's hurry home and tell Mother and Father before they all go to bed. They were so excited that they almost flew down the path towards the house. They burst into the parlor where Mr. and Mrs. Howe were relaxing after a big day.

"Mother! Father!" Lorrie began. "We have the most wonderful news to tell you! We're going to get married! Start planning another wedding!"

The Howes jumped up and embraced the excited couple and said how glad they were to hear that. They had come to love Anna already and were hoping that this would happen. Their son had never been seriously interested in any girl before.

"My family will be so thrilled with this news, too," Anna said. "I can hardly wait to tell them."

A few days later she was able to do just that. Tomas and Bergit were not too surprised but were very happy for Anna. They thought it was time for her to find a husband and start a family, Bergit said.

"When will you be getting married?" asked Tomas.

"We decided on next June," answered Anna. "We'd like to get married here. Just a small church wedding. Will you help me plan it, Bergit?"

"Of course I will," Bergit said. "That will be so exciting." Bergit and Anna went on to talk about such things as bridal gowns and wedding trousseaus so Tomas excused himself and went out to his shop.

"If only Papa and Mama could come for the wedding!" exclaimed Anna. That would make it perfect. I'm going to write a letter right now and ask them to try and come." Anna became more and more excited about her idea. Bergit didn't think that Anna's parents would ever come but she didn't say this to Anna. She didn't want to dampen her enthusiasm.

In the fall, Anna and Lorrie both went back to their teaching positions of the year before. Anna had purchased the material for a wedding gown in Mankato so she spent the long, winter evenings sewing on it. She and Bergit made wedding plans by way of the mail. Lorrie came almost every Saturday or Sunday, weather permitting.

One weekend in April he had some exciting news to tell Anna when he came. He had been offered the principal's job in the school in Marshall, his hometown. This would mean a significant raise in salary and it would mean that they would be living close to his family. After discussing it with Anna, he wrote back to accept the offer.

When school was out, Anna went to Mankato and Lorrie went home to Marshall to look for a place for the two of them to live after the honeymoon. The wedding date had been set for June 28. Anna and Bergit had a few things to do before then. The dress was almost finished but there was cleaning and baking to do. They would have a small reception at the house after the ceremony.

Anna had received a letter earlier that spring from Papa saying that they would not be coming. Papa stated several reasons why they wouldn't be, but reading between the lines, Anna knew that it was because Mama refused to venture out of her safe, little world, and Papa would never come without her. She was heartbroken with this news but she realized deep down that she really had not expected that they would actually have come.

When Lorrie saw how badly she felt about this, he said that maybe some year soon they could go to Norway and visit her family. This helped to lighten her disappointment a little.

Anna was so happy to hear that Andrew and Alice and the children were planning to come for the wedding. They would come several days early and stay at Tomas and Bergit's for about a week. All the little cousins would have such fun getting acquainted with each other. If only Sigrid could come now! She had written her but had not had any answer.

One day about a week before the wedding, as Anna and Bergit were finishing up on the cookie baking, little Teddy blurted out, "Auntie Anna, I have a secret but I can't tell you!" Bergit gasped and said sharply, "Teddy!" as Sarah quickly clamped her hand over his mouth and drug him out of the house.

"My goodness," said Anna, "what was that all about?"

"Oh, nothing," answered Bergit, who now seemed a little flustered. "You know how children are."

After that Anna seemed to sense a growing air of suspense building as the day went on. Tomas came home from work early and Bergit served supper earlier than usual. The children kept looking at each other with sly smiles when they thought Anna wasn't looking. Tomas pushed himself away from the table, excusing himself saying that he had an errand uptown soon. He went upstairs and changed clothes and off he went in rather a hurry, Anna thought. I wonder what's going on here, she asked herself, but soon dismissed it as she got busy with cleaning up after the evening meal.

During the next half hour, she noticed the children kept looking out the window and finally Bergit shooed them all outside. Soon they came bursting back into the house and announced, "They're here, they're here!"

"Who's here?" asked Anna, looking at Bergit for an answer to all this mysteriousness.

Bergit just sighed and took Anna by the hand and said, "Come outside and see for yourself, Anna." Bergit could hardly contain her excitement.

Anna saw Tomas standing beside the buggy, helping a woman down from the high step. Bergit pulled Anna closer and then Anna saw who it was. "Sigrid!" she shouted. "Oh, Sigrid, is it really you?" As the sisters hurried toward each other, both were crying and laughing at the same time as they fell into each other's arms.

"What a surprise, Sigrid!" exclaimed Anna. "I didn't know you were coming." Anna looked at Bergit as if to ask her if she had known and by the expression on Bergit's face, Anna had her answer. "Oh, you people! You knew all along. That's what all the secrecy has been about today."

"We thought it would be fun to surprise you. We told Sigrid not to let you know," said Tomas. "I understand the children almost let the secret out today, though."

The two sisters walked arm and arm into the house with the rest of the family following behind, exchanging smiles of satisfaction with each other. Sigrid said that the children were staying at the home of Louis's sister. "It would have been a long and tiring trip for them," Sigrid said. It was very late that night when the lights went out in the Olson house as there was so much catching up to do.

Andrew and his family came two days before the wedding and then there was more excitement. The house was filled to overflowing with all the children sleeping on the floor. Anna felt sorry for Bergit who was getting the brunt of all the work, cooking for this large family. She and Sigrid helped out as much as possible.

That evening, late into the night, two sisters and two brothers sat around the table talking of their parents and family back in the old country. Alice and Bergit had long since excused themselves, saying that they were too tired to stay up any longer. It seemed that Anna and her siblings could not get enough of being together. She looked at Sigrid and her two brothers around the table, her heart filled to overflowing with love and gratitude that the Almighty had managed to get four of them together again after so long. Tears came to her eyes and she did not bother to brush them back when they started falling.

"This will be such an extra happy wedding day with all of you here!" she exclaimed, and they all smiled at each other in their happiness at being together.

The day before the wedding, Lorrie, his parents and his sister and her husband came. They booked rooms in one of the hotels downtown. Bergit invited all of them over for supper the first evening. Lorrie's family was so easy to get to know and so fun-loving that it was a joy to have them around.

Anna and Lorrie went out for a walk to be by themselves a little. They held hands and talked about the honeymoon they were planning. It would be a three-week trip, which Anna didn't think they could afford but Lorrie assured her that he had been saving his money for quite sometime now and he wanted to do this. They also talked about the little house he had found for them and Anna was already busy furnishing it in her head!

The day of the wedding, June 28, 1911, started out cloudy with the threat of rain but it ended up being a beautiful day by two o'clock in the afternoon, the time set for the ceremony. Bergit and a friend had filled the church with many bouquets of fragrant peonies in several shades of pink and white. Anna was radiant in her white dress and long veil and she carried a bouquet of pink roses. Lorrie looked tall and handsome in his new black suit. His sister, Elizabeth and her husband, Conrad were their attendants.

After the ceremony, the couple stopped by the photographer's studio which was downtown and had their official wedding photo taken and then they hurried to the house for the reception. It was held outside in the back yard. Bergit had planted more flowers than usual just for the occasion. Tables and chairs had been borrowed from all over the neighborhood and set up on the lawn. There was cake and cookies and sandwiches, coffee and lemonade. The couple opened the many beautiful gifts given them.

Later in the day, Anna changed into her traveling dress and amid a shower of rice and many wishes for happiness, the couple hugged their family goodbye and set off in the buggy for the train station to start their honeymoon.

Lorrie had reserved a sleeper car for them. Anna had turned quiet and was deep in thought. She was beginning to worry about the wedding night, hoping that she would not have flashbacks of a terrifying figure looming over her; a memory of groping, struggling, pain and shame.

The next morning, Anna realized that she need not have worried. Lorrie was very gentle and considerate and their mutual desire for each other soon took over and made the experience a wonderful thing for Anna. She was so relieved that she could have cried. She had decided that she would never tell Lorrie about the tragedy that had befallen her. He loved her so much that the knowledge of that long-ago event would cause him much pain.

Their ultimate destination was Fargo, North Dakota, but after a couple days of traveling, they stopped in Detroit, Minnesota, where they would stay for two days. This was a town near Lake Detroit and they stayed in the Hotel Minnesota. This was a beautiful, 4-story hotel which was elegantly furnished. Lorrie had reserved the bridal suite. He was always full of surprises. They spent the days walking lazily down around the lake and resting up from their train travel.

Again they boarded the Northern Pacific and headed further west until they reached the twin towns of Moorhead, Minnesota and right across the river, Fargo, North Dakota. Lorrie's brother, Lester, met them at the station and drove them to his modest home. He had married after leaving Minnesota and Lorrie had never met his wife, Rosina. She was expecting their first child in a few months.

Lester was so happy to see his brother again. They had been very close, not only in age but they were also good friends. Lester couldn't wait to show Lorrie and Anna his grocery store. He was very proud of his little neighborhood store and tried to make it the best one in the whole town. Business was good but it had cost him quite a sum of money to procure the building, stock the shelves and set up business. He had been there for three years now. He liked the town and it was growing fast.

"Why don't you and Anna move up here, Lorrie?" he asked. "You could get a job teaching here easily."

"I just got hired to be the principal in Marshall for this coming school year," Lorrie said.

"You don't say! You're really coming up in the world there, brother," said Lester with admiration in his voice.

"That's what I've been working toward for quite a few years now," said Lorrie. "That's why I've been going to so much school."

"Oh, I just thought you liked school so much that you were going to keep on going forever," teased the older brother.

"Anna, what are you going to do, then?" asked Rosina. "I understand that you are a teacher, also."

"Well, I don't know yet. They don't really like to hire married women but I haven't checked into it yet. I was too busy with wedding plans!" laughed Anna.

"I was a teacher myself, before we got married. Now I help Lester in the store, but after the baby comes I guess I won't be able to do much of that for awhile.

The two young couples had a good time together for the next week. Lorrie helped his brother clerk in the store part of the time. They went dancing one evening as both Lorrie and Lester were considered "dancing fools" back in their hometown and enjoyed it so much. They also took in the opera one evening.

Before the wedding, Tomas had encouraged Anna and Lorrie to be sure to go and visit the Ruuds when they were in North Dakota so Anna had written them and told them that she and Lorrie would try and look them up while they were on their wedding trip. "You must be sure to come," Jorgen Ruud said in his reply letter. He sent directions on how to reach their place.

One morning bright and early, Lorrie and Anna started out in search of the Ruud farm with Lester's horse and buggy. They went south of Fargo along the Red River for some miles and then turned west. At one point they stopped to ask a farmer if they were on the right track and he said that he knew the Ruud farm and said it was still a few miles farther west. They passed field after field of wheat. The ground was so flat that they could see for miles. Neither of them had ever seen ground so flat!

At last they came to a farm that seemed to be the right one and they turned into the yard. They stopped in front of a big house that looked like it was an old one with a fresh coat of white paint. Two men stepped out of the barn at the sound of the approaching carriage and walked over to them.

"Is this the Ruud place?" asked Anna, not recognizing either of the men.

"That it is, ma'am," answered one of the men, looking at her intently.

"I'm Anna Olson....actually Anna Howe now...Tomas and Andrew's sister."

"Ah, Anna! We didn't recognize you. I'm Jorgan and this is Leif. Of course you wouldn't know us now. It has been over fifteen years since we last saw you and you were just a little girl then."

"We got your letter and were hoping you would come by and see us," said Leif. "Here, let me help you down and we must go into the house. What a surprise this will be for mother."

The two men led the couple up to the house and were met by two children who stared at them silently. " Letta, tell your mother and grandmother that we have company," said Jorgen. "Company from the old country," he added, laughing.

An old woman and a younger one came from the kitchen, drying their hands on a towel, to see who was there.

"Mama, remember little Anna Olson? Sister to Tomas and Andres?" asked Leif.

"Oh, my yes, but you have grown up now," Mrs. Ruud said in Norwegian.

Anna introduced Lorrie and Jorgen introduced his wife, Carrie, and their two children, Letta and Freddie. Leif said that he and his wife and children lived down the road on the next farm. Mr. Ruud was over there working on some machinery and he would be home soon for dinner.

After the noon meal, the men lingered around the table and talked for quite some time with Anna and Lorrie. Mr. Ruud said that he would take them on a drive all around his land. They owned this whole section now and were doing very well. They had had some very good wheat crops the last few years.

As they drove slowly around the section, looking at the wheat fields that would soon be heading out, he explained to them that this had once been part of a very large farm. One farmer had owned about 10,000 acres and was very successful in his bonanza farming operation for several years. Then he ran into some difficulties and had to split up the land about the time the Ruuds arrived in the area. They had scraped together every penny they had to buy this piece and now were finally doing quite well.

"Anna, you tell Andrew that he should come here and farm. The soil is unbelievably rich here in the Red River Valley," said Mr. Ruud. "Better than that Iowa soil," he joked.

That evening, Leif brought his family over after supper and they all sat and talked till quite late. Anna and Lorrie stayed the night and early the next morning they left to return to Fargo.

"You know, Anna, this flat land grows on one after awhile. It has a beauty all of its own," commented Lorrie as they drove by the endless fields of wheat.

"Yes, I was just thinking the same thing," reflected Anna. "I loved the mountains of my homeland but this is another kind of beauty. The soil is so rich and black and the crops look so lush and green."

They spent their last night with Lester and Rosina. The next morning, Lester drove them to the train station where they began their trip back home. The two of them spent much time reminiscing about their trip and all that they had seen.

"I love to travel," said Lorrie. "Let's do as much of it as we possibly can. Every summer we'll take a trip someplace. We'll live simply and save our money and spend it on traveling!" His excitement was contagious and Anna just smiled at him, this man who was now her husband and so dear to her.

"I'd like to see the whole world," Lorrie went on. "I guess I'm like you, Anna. You dreamed of seeing the world, too. You were very brave coming over to this country all alone."

"Well, I had family here to come to," she said. "I don't think I would have come otherwise.

Lorrie took Anna's hand and said, "And has your dream come true for you, then, Anna?"

"It is coming true right now, Lorrie," she answered. "I was reunited with part of my family and I found you and now we're starting a life together here. I would have to say that my dream is coming true."

"Do you miss your homeland very much, and your family back there?" he asked.

"Oh, yes, at times I miss them all very much but I love it here and this is my home now," she answered with a faraway look in her eyes so that Lorrie wasn't so sure that she was completely happy here.

"I will take you to Norway someday, Anna. I promise you that," Lorrie said with conviction. She just squeezed his hand without saying a word. Lorrie's love and devotion were overwhelming sometimes. He would promise her the world, that man! She leaned back in the seat and gave in to thoughts of her childhood home. The rhythm and sounds of the train carrying them homeward soon put her to sleep.

CHAPTER 10

For the remainder of the summer, Anna and Lorrie got settled in their little house. It was very small but they managed to make it a cozy place with the help of paint and some hand-me-down furniture from family and friends. Lorrie started his new job at the school in September and Anna passed her days helping out at the grocery store once in awhile.

Lorrie's sister, Elizabeth, announced that she and Conrad would become parents by Christmas, so the family was all excited about that. By Thanksgiving, Anna found that she, too, was going to have a baby so there was much to be thankful for around the table of the growing Howe family.

Anna's excitement and happiness was short-lived, though. One day about the middle of December, she awoke with cramps that increased in intensity throughout the day. That evening, Lorrie called for the doctor and after examining Anna, he declared that she was having a miscarriage and that it all would be over by morning. She passed blood and tissue during the night and by morning her cramps had ceased. She was very distraught and Lorrie was very disappointed, too, but he had to try and help Anna get through this.

So I have lost another baby, she thought to herself. She buried her head in her pillow and sobbed as if her heart would break in two. Maybe this is my punishment, she thought. Lorrie was not able to console her and she remained depressed for many weeks.

Elizabeth had her baby the day after Christmas. It was a boy and they named him Alex. He brought much joy to the Howe family but every time Anna saw the beautiful little baby, it was like a stab to her heart. She tried not to show her feelings but Lorrie knew how much she was suffering. He tried so hard to cheer her up that, out of love for him, she did her best to put on a happy face. By spring, he began to think that she was out of her depression but deep down inside her, she ached as much as ever.

One Sunday morning in church, the Reverend Oveson gave a sermon that seemed to be just what Anna needed. It was about putting your whole trust in the Lord in spite of adversities and to be thankful for what you do have. Anna felt like he was speaking right to her and she had to brush tears of shame from her eyes. She had been feeling so sorry for herself. Self pity was really a sin, the Reverend had said. It showed a lack of trust. That night Anna spent extra time in her devotions before she went to bed. Paging through her Bible, she came across the pictures once again of Samuel, her first baby. She removed the pictures and put them in her trunk so that Lorrie would not see them and ask about them. She prayed for forgiveness for being so self-centered and indulging in such self-pity. She turned her future over to the Lord and promised that she would trust Him for whatever was to come.

Anna went to bed with a much lighter heart that night and Lorrie could tell that there was something different about her. She snuggled next to her husband and felt a peace and joy sweep over her. She thanked the Lord for lifting the terrible veil of depression that had encompassed her for so many months. She fell into a blissful sleep with Lorrie's arm around her.

One evening before school was out, Lorrie mentioned to Anna that they should start planning their summer trip. "Where shall we go this year?" he asked.

"Oh, I wish so that we could go to New York and visit Sigrid!" exclaimed Anna.

"Well, maybe we could do that," Lorrie said, warming up to the idea.

"Could we really, Lorrie?" Anna asked as she jumped up and went to put her arm around him as he sat reading the evening paper. "Would we go by train? Could we afford it?"

"Well, let's just do it!" he said impulsively. "I'll check the train fares tomorrow and see how much it would cost to go all the way to New York and back."

And so it was that in late June they set out on a trip across the country by train. Their first stop was to make a visit to Andrew and Alice in Iowa. They hadn't seen them since the wedding the year before. They enjoyed their stay there so much. Lorrie had never spent much time on a farm before so Andrew was busy showing him all around. Little Berta, who was now seven, completely captivated Lorrie's heart. What a wonderful father he will make someday, thought Anna, as the yearning for a child came upon her again with sudden intensity.

While they had been planning their cross-country trip, Anna had mentioned to Lorrie that she would like to stop in Toledo and visit the Martin family. Lorrie readily agreed and so Anna had written Mrs. Martin and asked if they could just meet them at the train station during their stopover so that she could see them and of course, little Samuel. She anxiously awaited Mrs. Martin's answer and shortly before they left Minnesota, a letter came saying that she and Samuel would be at the station at the appointed time.

As the train labored ever closer to Toledo, Anna grew more and more anxious about the meeting with her small son. Finally they pulled into the station, almost right on schedule and Anna felt so weak that she could hardly get up from her seat. Lorrie asked her if she felt all right.

"I guess I'm just tired from sitting so much," she answered. I'm also very nervous and worried how this meeting is going to go, she added to herself. She stepped down from the train and her eyes scanned the platform. Then she saw Mrs. Martin walk toward them holding the hand of a little boy. Oh, how he's grown, she thought.

Anna was rendered speechless at the sight of the boy so Mrs. Martin held her arms out to welcome her former friend and the mother of her child.

"Anna, my dear, it's so good to see you again! You're looking very well and happy." Anna introduced her to Lorrie and she stooped down to talk to Samuel, who was somewhat shy. She tried to embrace him but he pulled back and clung to his mother's skirts. Anna stood and looked at Mrs. Martin with tears in her eyes. She knew that Anna had not told Lorrie about the child so she took Anna by the arm and walked away from the man and the child for a short distance.

"Anna, don't feel bad. He doesn't know you and he is shy with strangers at first," Mrs. Martin said, trying to comfort Anna in her disappointment.

"Of course, you're right," said Anna. "I was foolish to think that he would just run into my arms and give me a big hug. How I've longed for this meeting but I don't know what I really expected."

"Well, Anna, don't take this personally. Remember, he is only a little child." The two women walked back to join Lorrie and Samuel and they heard Samuel say, "I'm five years old now and I have a big tricycle, almost as tall as me, and I can ride it up and down our street really fast."

Mrs. Martin engaged Lorrie in conversation so that Anna and Samuel could visit a little. Anna asked him all kinds of questions and he soon warmed up to her. When the conductor gave the final "all aboard" call, Mrs. Martin asked Samuel if he could give Mr. and Mrs. Howe each a big goodbye hug. He obliged and when Anna felt his chubby little arms go around her neck, she thought she had never felt anything quite so wonderful before. She would savor that hug for the rest of her life.

Back on board the train, Anna felt weaker than ever and she leaned her head back and sighed. She closed her eyes and let the tears fall. She couldn't control them anymore. Lorrie looked over at her.

"Anna dear, are you all right? I didn't know that you were so close to that family." She wasn't able to answer him. If he only knew just how close I was, she thought to herself. She tried to sleep but the emotional turmoil that the day had wrought upon her was too much. She was very restless and made several trips to the back of the car. Lorrie was beginning to worry about her. Finally she fell asleep and slept for many hours, until the call for Pittsburgh awoke her.

"Are we already in Pittsburgh?" she asked incredulously.

"Yes, my dear, you slept through several stops. I guess you really needed the sleep so I didn't see any reason to wake you."

They would be changing trains here for the last leg of the journey to New York. They walked up and down the platform many times to get the kinks out of their bones. Anna was feeling better after her long rest but she would never be able to get the picture out of her mind of the little boy standing on the platform, waving goodbye to her. Whenever she thought of it, which was often, she would feel a stab of pain through her heart, an almost physical pain.

They were crossing the big, wide state of Pennsylvania now, with its lush, green rolling hills. This seemed to have a calming effect on Anna and she resolved to put the past behind her now and look toward the future; the immediate future, that of seeing Sigrid and her family again. Oh, how fun that will be, she thought. Lorrie was getting excited about seeing New York. He wanted to see everything there that he had ever read about. His excitement and curiosity about things was probably what made him a very interesting teacher, thought Anna.

The entire Anderson family was on the platform to greet them: Louis, Sigrid, Annie, Arthur and Sylvia. Anna could hardly contain her happiness at seeing all of them again. The children were so happy to have her back, if only for a short visit. The ride home was a noisy one, with everyone talking at the same time. Louis had borrowed his neighbor's extra large carriage so that they would all fit. The children had insisted on going along to the station and Sigrid thought it would be great fun for them.

By the time they reached the Anderson's home, all the children had decided that Lorrie was the greatest. Everyone thinks that, thought Anna, happy and proud of her husband. After they got settled in, everyone gathered around the dining table and Sigrid served coffee and cake. Anna remarked on how the children had all grown so much. Annie was thirteen now and stood as tall as her mother. She looked more like Anna however, and she was very proud of this fact. Arthur, now eleven, favored his father, and Sylvia, who was almost nine, was a bubbly and vivacious girl with rosy cheeks and blond hair.

Later they all went into the parlor at Sigrid's suggestion. She had a surprise to show them. "Remember how much I've always wanted a piano, Anna?" she asked. "Well, my dear husband gave me one for Christmas last year. Annie and I have both been taking lessons from the lady down the street. We've been practicing a little duet to play for you." Everyone found a seat and listened as mother and daughter played an unfamiliar but pretty song. Everyone applauded the duo and asked for more.

"We don't know any more," laughed Annie. "That's the only duet we practiced." Sigrid sat down and played, with one hand, a song that Anna and Sigrid used to sing back in their home in Norway: 'Pal sine hoene pa haugen utslepte, honunn sa lett over haugen sprang'. (Paul let his chickens run out on the hillside, over the hill they went tripping along). The words came to Anna, little by little, and by the end of the piece, she and Sigrid were singing their hearts out, much to the pleasure of the others.

"More! More!" shouted Lorrie and Louis in unison. Sigrid started another song that she and her sister knew well from childhood: ' A kjøre vatten, a kjøre ve', A kjøre tømmer over heia'. (I'm hauling water, I'm hauling wood, I'm hauling lumber from the valley). Anna joined Sigrid on the piano bench and the two sang lustily, almost in tears by the end. It brought back memories of Papa. He used to sing that particular song with such gusto when he was working out in the yard.

As Lorrie watched his wife and her sister singing and laughing, he thought that he hadn't seen Anna this happy in quite some time. I think this trip was a good idea, he thought to himself.

"I wish I was better at playing the piano," Sigrid said apologetically. "Annie seems to have a special talent at it so I'm sure she will surpass me in no time. Arthur and Sylvia will be starting lessons next year."

Anna asked Sigrid about her old friend, Emma Flaten. "Oh, she stayed on at the hat factory for awhile after you left and then she started work uptown in a women's dress shop and married the assistant manager. She did quite well for herself. They live over across town and I believe that she has one or two children by now.

Anna and Lorrie stayed with Sigrid and her family for a week, doing and seeing all the things that visitors do and see while in New York. Lorrie took it all in with a voracious appetite for seeing and learning new things. It was a sad day when the two had to say goodbye to Sigrid, Louis and the children.

"We will try to come out as a family to see you sometime," promised Louis. He and Lorrie had taken an instant liking to one another. The train ride home was long, hot and tiring. Anna thought to herself that it would be a long time before she would make that arduous trip again.

In the fall, Anna discovered that she was again pregnant. She and Lorrie were very happy about it but they didn't dare let themselves get too excited only to be disappointed again. By Christmas time they began to tell their families. By mid-January the doctor said that he felt that Anna had passed the three-month mark and that all should go well this time. Only then did Anna dare to start planning for the blessed event.

One Saturday Lorrie came home with a little package for her. He and his father had been on a day trip to Granite Falls on business for the grocery store. He had spotted something in a store window that caught his eye so he went in and bought it for the baby. As Anna opened the package, she saw that it was a beautiful little silver cup with the word "Baby" engraved on one side. It was gold on the inside and there were small rosebuds etched on the handle. She held it to her breast and shed a few tears of happiness as she hugged and thanked Lorrie. She put it up on a shelf in their little kitchen where she could look at it every day.

Anna was feeling good now; her morning sickness had gone away and she was happier than she'd ever been, anticipating the birth of this baby. She thanked God for her happy life and her wonderful husband. It all seemed too good to be true.

The people of southern Minnesota had recently been reading about an influenza that was beginning to affect some communities nearby. The Spanish Flu it was called.

"I hope it doesn't come here," Lorrie said, as he closed the newspaper and turned out the lights. "We don't want our school to have to close down like some places I've been reading about."

A week later, six cases of the flu were reported in their school in two days time. The board was debating whether or not to close the school for awhile when they heard of the first death. It was a nine-year-old child whose two siblings were also ill. Word went out that school would close until further notice. When news of another death circulated around, this time a middle- aged man, the town became really frightened. The characteristics of this illness were sudden fever, chills, headache, muscle pain, pneumonia and rapid death.

A few nights after the school closing, Lorrie came home from the grocery store saying that he was very tired and had a headache. During the night, he awoke after a restless sleep. He felt very hot and Anna felt his forehead and realized that he must have a very high fever. Oh, no, she thought, he can't be getting that flu! She became very worried. She sponged him down with cool, wet cloths. Then she dressed quickly and ran across the street to his parents' home and woke them up and asked them to come quickly. Mr. Howe went for the doctor. He returned shortly to say that the doctor was out on another call and would come when he could.

By morning's light, Lorrie's condition had worsened. When is that doctor coming? Anna thought to herself. She was becoming very alarmed. Lorrie now had the chills and his breathing was very labored. She sat by his bedside but didn't know just what to do for him. The doctor finally came shortly before nine o'clock. He had been to five other houses in town during the night! All the sick people seemed to have this same malady.

After checking Lorrie, Anna could see the concern in the good doctor's face. "There is nothing I can give you to treat this illness," he told her. "He is developing pneumonia now. Put mustard packs on his chest and cover him with many blankets and make him sweat. I'll check back later this afternoon."

Mrs. Howe insisted that Anna lie down in the front room and try to sleep a little. "I'll stay by his side while you try and get some rest, dear," she said. At noon, Mr. Howe came from the store to check on him. He sat with Lorrie so that his wife could make a bite to eat for them. Anna woke from a short nap and went quickly to the bedroom. She was alarmed when she saw her gravely ill husband lying there. She could tell that his condition was deteriorating rapidly. She shook him gently to try to wake him up.

"Lorrie, wake up! Can you open your eyes and look at me?" She pleaded. He opened his eyes but he couldn't seem to focus on her face.

"Lorrie, you must get better. You can't die on me," she demanded.

"Think of the baby and all of our plans." She was getting desperate.

"Of course he's not going to die, Anna, my dear," said Mr. Howe, trying to console her. "We'll take the best possible care of him and he'll soon be better." He was really trying to convince himself that this would happen. Deep down he was very frightened for his son.

Mr. Howe didn't go back to the store but stayed instead by his son's bedside. The doctor came by in the late afternoon. He looked very exhausted. As Mrs. Howe took his coat, he said that two more people had died. The sister of the nine-year old and also a baby from another family.

After examining Lorrie, he said that things did not look very good. The pneumonia might just do him in. "You better do some serious praying," he told the anxious family. "I'll be back first thing in the morning." With that, he returned home and tried to get some much needed rest before the next summons.

Anna and Lorrie's parents took turns by his bedside during the long night. In the morning, Lorrie was hardly able to breath. Anna sat by the bedside holding his hand, alternately sobbing and praying and imploring Lorrie to pull through this. "Yea, though I walk through the valley of the shadow of death, I will fear no evil, for thou art with me, thy rod and thy staff, they comfort me...." She prayed this passage aloud over and over again. In the afternoon, she was alone in the room with him and she had fallen asleep by his bedside, holding his hand.

All of a sudden she awoke. Something was not right here. It was too quiet. She looked at Lorrie; he was sleeping peacefully. Or was he? She looked at him closer and a coldness grabbed her heart as she realized that he was too still. Fear crept into every fiber of her being. She could not feel a pulse. She ran out of the room looking for his parents. The had both fallen asleep; Mrs. Howe in a chair and Mr. Howe on the sofa. She called out to them loudly and they awoke with a start.

"Come quick!" she called out and they ran into the bedroom behind her. They looked down at their son and Mrs. Howe gasped and Mr. Howe leaned close to him to see if he could feel him breathing. He looked back at the two women with the most devastated look.

"Our son. I think he's gone," he said as he laid his body across that of his son's, as if he could put life back into him.

"Nooooo! Noooo!" screamed Anna. "It can't be. He can't be dead. God wouldn't do that to me! We had so many plans and dreams. He's still alive! Go and get Dr. Paulson."

Mr. Howe grabbed his coat and ran down the block to fetch the doctor. Mrs. Howe just stood stock still by the bed and stared down at her son, unable to speak. Anna was rubbing his hand vigorously, trying to put some life back into him. She knew deep down that he was gone, but she couldn't admit it for then it would surely be true. In less that ten minutes, Mr. Howe returned with Dr. Paulson and they hurried into the bedroom.

"Oh, Doctor," said Anna. " I'm so glad you're here. I think Lorrie is better. Look how peacefully he sleeps." Her voice cracked and she broke down and sobbed. The doctor check his vitals and turned to look at the three family members waiting for him to say that everything would be all right.

"I'm afraid that Lorrie is gone." With this, the doctor broke down himself and cried unashamedly. He had known Lorrie since he was a child and he had always been very close to the Howe family. He cried in sorrow and also in frustration that he was so utterly helpless against this illness. Eight people had died in all now. No, nine with Lorrie. When would it end?

Mr. Howe had to lead his wife out of the room and got her to sit down on the sofa. She was in shock and couldn't do anything but stare and shake her head. Anna had fallen into the comforting arms of the good doctor and she cried hysterically. He could do nothing to calm her down. He led her to a chair in the other room and sat her down and Mr. Howe came and put his arms around his dear daughter-in-law and together they sobbed until they both ran out of tears.

The doctor had let himself out and went to inform Lorrie's sister and her husband. They had not been to see Lorrie when he took sick because Mrs. Howe said they should not come near him. They had to think of the baby. But now they ran next door with little Alex and left him with their neighbor and then they came running over to Lorrie and Anna's house. They hurried past everyone in the front room and stopped short at the bedroom door. Lorrie was lying there like he was peacefully sleeping. Elizabeth walked up to the bed and looked down at her beloved brother and saw for herself that he was indeed dead. She hadn't believed it when the doctor had first told them. She and Conrad stood crying together by the bed. She went out into the next room and looked at her parents and sister-in-law. She knew that she had to keep herself in check because someone had to take over here. She would have liked to just given in to her emotions and collapse in despair but she knew that she couldn't. Not yet anyway.

"Father, we have to take some action," she said, rather more sharply than she had meant. Mr. Howe gathered himself up and the two of them started making some arrangements quietly. Conrad was trying to comfort Anna and he kept looking at his mother-in-law, wondering when she was going to break.

The doctor had sent for the undertaker and so he arrived to take over with the body. Anna jumped up and would not let him do anything with Lorrie yet. She had to go in there by herself, she told him, so he let her alone in the bedroom for awhile.

Anna pulled up the chair close by the bed again and took Lorrie's hand, which was quite cold by now, and she began talking to him softly so that those in the other room could not hear her.

"Lorrie, dearest, what am I going to do without you? We're going to have a baby, don't you remember? I can't raise him alone. He needs a father.

Please, you must come back. Start breathing again!" she commanded.

She started crying and she knew that he was really gone but maybe if she pretended that he was still alive then maybe he would be! No, she told herself, he is really gone. She folded his arms across his chest and kissed his cheek and stood looking down at him for a very long time. In those last moments something died inside her very soul. She felt herself grow cold in her inner depths, a coldness that she didn't think would ever leave her. Finally, she went and bid the undertaker to come in.

Mr. Howe insisted that Anna come to their house to spend the night. He and Mrs. Howe helped Anna throw a few things in a bag and they walked slowly but resolutely over to their house. There was a finality to this act; she was leaving Lorrie and their home and their life together. Friends and family came to the house that evening to offer their condolences but they didn't stay long and they didn't seem to want to get too close to the family. Everyone was frightened of the terrible and dreaded illness that was taking so many lives so swiftly.

During the night Anna awoke, drenched in sweat and then she felt ice cold and tried to get up to get some more blankets to put over her. She could not find any and then she remembered that Mr. Howe had brought all their extra blankets over to cover Lorrie. She was too weak to look any more so she sank back down in her bed and tried to double up the blankets that were there. Towards morning, when she heard the first stirrings of someone who was up, she called out and Mrs. Howe put her head inside her door.

"What is it, my dear?" she asked softly, "Can't you sleep either?"

"I'm sorry to bother you but I am so cold," Anna answered, as her mother-in-law came closer to the bed. She could see that Anna was shaking with cold. She ran to get her husband and he could see fear in her eyes.

"Do you suppose that Anna is coming down with the flu, too?" she asked, almost at the point of hysteria. "She's shaking like a leaf!"

"Don't jump to conclusions, my dear," he said, trying to calm her fears. "It maybe is because she is in shock. We'll have Doctor Paulson stop by and check on her." He finished getting dressed and stopped by Anna's room. Mrs. Howe followed, bringing a quilt from their bed to lay on top of her. Mr. Howe felt a knot of fear in the pit of his stomach when he saw her but he didn't want to believe the thoughts that were creeping into his mind. He grabbed his coat and hat and went down the street to see if the doctor was in his office yet.

About an hour later Doctor Paulson came and, as he stood over Anna's bed and looked down at the young woman lying there, he didn't know when he had felt more distraught and helpless. It didn't take long to make his diagnosis, but he was stalling, trying to decide how he was going to tell his good friends that indeed Anna did have the same illness that took the life of their dear son.

"I'm afraid that Anna has the flu, too," he finally said to them. They gasped and Mrs. Howe started crying softly.

"We just can't lose her, too; and the baby!" she said to her husband and the doctor.

"Do your best to care for her and I will try to stop by this afternoon." With that he left the house, feeling like the weight of the world was on his helpless shoulders.

Mr. Howe had to see to funeral arrangements for his son. The night before, Conrad had sent a telegram to Anna's brother, Tomas, in Mankato, telling him that Lorrie had died of the flu. This morning, Mr. Howe sent another telegram saying that Anna also had the flu but that they should **not** come as it was too risky. The flu was spreading so fast.

Early that evening, Dr. Paulson stopped by to check on Anna. Her condition was unchanged. Her fever was quite high but Mrs. Howe was keeping Anna sponged down every hour to keep it from rising to a dangerous level. Mr. Howe sat with her during the night so that his wife could sleep. He was worried about her. She looked so exhausted.

The next day was Lorrie's funeral. The church was full of mourners, as the Howes were a well-known and loved family. Martha Peterson, the mother of one of the children who had just died a week ago of the same flu, volunteered to stay with Anna while the Howes both attended the funeral for their son. She was not afraid of contracting the disease like everyone else was.

The crowd at the church, though large, did not linger long after the service was over as everyone was in a hurry to get back to their homes and away from anyone who might be coming down with the flu. The whole community was in an extremely frightened state.

When the Howes returned home, there was a telegram waiting from Tomas and Bergit asking about Anna's condition. Mr. Howe went to the train station to send another wire to say that there was no change while Mrs. Howe went to take her place beside Anna's bedside. Anna's fever was high and she tossed and turned constantly. She seemed in a delirious state, talking about things that didn't make sense. She mumbled incoherently, often in her native tongue. Mrs. Howe had to strain to hear the words and yet she could not understand their meaning: "Papa...help me up... can't see... Sigrid... talk to Kjersti....Mama....apples all over....Lorrie come and get me....Jesus saves....Little Samuel..... God forgive....train..stop...Toledo...hot...so tired...Lorrie Lorrie LORRIE!"

"There, there, my dear," shushed Mrs. Howe. "Everything will be all right. Here, let me sponge you off again. You are so hot." After that, Anna calmed down for an hour or so. Her mother-in-law sat in the chair by her bed and dozed off. Mr. Howe came in and told his wife to go lie down and he would take over. He wondered to himself how much longer the two of them could keep this up. Would they get sick, too? He was so distraught over the loss of his son that he really didn't care at this point if he lived or died. But he wanted, with all his heart, for Anna to live. Anna herself probably wouldn't care if she lived or died either with Lorrie gone.

Towards morning, Anna started stirring again and mumbled something about milking cows and making cheese and other things he couldn't make out. Anna looked very flushed and he felt her forehead and it was burning up again. He went to get some cool water and returned to sponge her off again. "Please God, let her get well. We can't bear to lose her, too." He wept for his son and for his sick daughter-in-law. His tears fell on her already hot flesh. His wife came in just then and she took over the task and told him to get some sleep. After her body was cooled down, Anna slept for awhile again. I know I should be trying to get some liquids into her, thought Mrs. Howe. Next time she wakes up, I'll try. But the next time she awoke, Anna was thrashing violently and sobbing and crying out for Lorrie and Papa and Mama, and Mrs. Howe couldn't subdue her. "Get doctor...stomach hurts...the baby..."

Mrs. Howe called to her husband and he came stumbling into the room half awake. "Hurry and fetch Dr. Paulson. I'm afraid she is losing the baby," his wife said.

The doctor didn't get there until later that morning. "Two more have died," he told Mr. Howe as he shed his winter coat, "but no new cases in the last two days. That's the only good news lately." He hurried up to Anna's room.

He checked her over in silence and then turned to the Howes. "I'm afraid she is indeed losing the baby. She will have some uncomfortable cramps for awhile. I can give her something for the pain. Try and keep her fever down. The one good thing is that she has not developed pneumonia. At least not yet. Those who have recovered from this flu are the lucky ones who have not gotten that." He looked at his dear friends and said, "You two need to take care of yourselves, too. Shall I try to get some help for you?"

"No, no, don't bother anyone," said Mrs. Howe. "Some of the neighbors have dropped by with food, hot soup and things like that, so that has been a real help."

"Well, I don't want you two to get sick, too," he said as he left to go to the next house to tend to the ill.

Anna's fever seemed to be down but she slept fitfully. Whenever she would wake up a little, she would start sobbing, but then she would drift off to sleep again.

Mr. and Mrs. Howe, who were completely exhausted, finally moved their mattress into the room with Anna and put it on the floor beside her bed. They fell onto it and slept whenever she slept and woke up whenever she did.

In the morning, when Mrs. Howe was washing Anna and changing her drenched nightgown, she noticed that Anna was lying in a pool of blood and she knew that the worst had happened and that it was all over. She had lost the baby for sure. She cleaned Anna up and changed the bedding with her husband's help and then went to warm up some soup for Anna. It was hard to get the liquid through Anna's parched lips. She was so weak that she could hardly open her mouth. She got a few spoonfuls down and then she fell asleep again. This went on like this for another two days. Then one afternoon, Anna opened her eyes and looked at Mrs. Howe and asked "Mother Howe, how long have you been sitting here?"

Mrs. Howe jumped up and came closer to the bed to look at Anna. "Oh, for many days, now," she answered. "How are you feeling, Anna dear?"

"I don't know. How long have I been here, in this bed?"

"Since Saturday. That's about six days ago now," she answered.

"Lorrie. He died, didn't he?" she asked, with tears starting to form again.

"Yes, he did, dear," answered Mrs. Howe, her own voice choking up. Together they cried for the husband and son they had just lost. I wonder if she remembers that she lost the baby, Mrs. Howe was thinking to herself. Anna cried herself to sleep and slept until Dr. Paulson made a call.

He checked her over and smiled for the first time in days. "I think she's going to come out of this," he told the Howes as they waited expectantly for his verdict. "Her fever is down, almost to normal, and like I said before, she shows no signs of having pneumonia."

"You're going to make it, Anna," he said, patting her legs through the many layers of blankets. "You're going to be all right."

"What about the baby?" Anna asked, already knowing the answer.

Gently Dr. Paulson took her hand and said, "Don't you remember? I'm afraid that you lost the baby." Anna didn't say anything. She just turned her face into her pillow and sobbed softly. The doctor left and Anna fell asleep again.

Mr. Howe wired Tomas again to tell him that Anna was recovering and that she was going to be all right. However, she had lost the baby, he told them. Meanwhile, Tomas and Bergit had gotten a wire from Andrew saying that the flu epidemic had struck their house, too, and that their dear little Berta had died. The boys had also had it but they recovered. Alice was inconsolable. Berta was their ray of sunshine, the apple of their eye. Tomas decided that he would not let Anna know this sad news just yet. She had had quite enough of that for now.

CHAPTER 11

Anna's convalescence took quite some time. After she was out of danger and the epidemic had subsided, Mr. Howe hired a girl to help his wife around the house to catch up with all the things left undone for so long. Mrs. Howe and Anna spent many hours together, talking about Lorrie, and this seemed to help the both of them work through their grief. It was harder for Mr. Howe, as he chose to keep it all inside. His wife tried to encourage him to talk about Lorrie with her.

About three weeks into Anna's recovery, Tomas rode the train out to visit her. He was shocked at the sight of her. She was so thin and her hair had lost all its luster.

"I know I look terrible," Anna said to him. Her body had been covered with fever blisters, especially around the mouth. Those had almost healed up now.

Tomas hugged her. "You look wonderful to me, Anna. We almost lost you, too." The two of them had a good cry together over Lorrie and she told him that she had also lost the baby.

"Here it is, back to just me again," she said. "Sometimes I wonder if I was meant to come to this country. Perhaps I should have stayed in Norway and been a good daughter. Maybe this is my punishment."

"Don't have thoughts like that, dear sister," Tomas said. "Life everywhere has its ups and downs and good times and bad. God is not punishing you. Learn to trust Him 'with all your heart and all your soul and all that is within you'."

"There isn't much left within me these days, Tomas. I'm still trying to heal, inside and out. But," she went on, "I think trust in God is what got me through this. Every time I would awaken, I would see that plaque on the bedroom wall, 'JESUS SAVES' it said. Then I would drift off to sleep again. I think those words pulled me through."

Tomas finally had to break the news to her about Andrew and Alice's little Berta. She had succumbed to the flu the same week as Lorrie. The epidemic hit down there, too, quite hard. Two of their neighbors had died, also.

This news struck Anna particularly hard. She loved little Berta so much and so had Lorrie and everybody else. She ached for Alice and Andrew. She sent off a note to them the next day. Tomas left for home after staying only two days. He told Anna to come and stay with them when she felt up to traveling.

The Howes urged Anna to sell the little house that she and Lorrie had lived in. At first she balked at this idea. If she gave up the house and all her and Lorrie's things, what did she have left of their short life together? she wondered. Finally she decided that selling it was for the best and the Howes told her she could stay with them for as long as she needed. She was grateful for their offer.

Spring came to southern Minnesota but not to Anna's heart. She still felt a coldness inside of her that would not melt. She received a letter from Papa. He had heard about Lorrie from Tomas and he wrote some comforting words. He said that Mama was not very well. It was her heart, the doctor said. Everyone else was fine and they all hoped that she could come for a visit sometime or else come back to stay. It sounded like Papa expected her to do this now that she had lost Lorrie. He wanted to see her and comfort her. Anna put the letter down after reading it through several times and stared into space.

She was sitting out in the Howe's lovely back yard and it was a beautiful June day. What shall I do? she asked herself. I'm not strong enough yet to make that long, tiring journey. If I went back there, would I ever return to America? She didn't have answers to all these questions yet.

She leaned back in the chair and looked up at the beautiful blue sky and the fluffy white cloud formations. First they would go in one direction and then in another, changing shape all the while. She watched these clouds for a long time. My life is something like that, she mused to herself.

Mrs. Howe came out to join her, two glasses of lemonade in her hand. "Oh, thank you, Elsie. Just what I needed. It's getting quite hot."

Elsie Howe took the lawn chair closest to Anna and sat down with a big sigh and began sipping the cold beverage. Anna took a long look at this remarkable woman, Lorrie's mother, who had nursed her back to health and who had tried so hard to keep her son alive as well. Anna had thought that she seemed more depressed lately. Maybe her loss was starting to really sink in.

"What's the matter, Elsie? Talk to me," commanded Anna in her straightforward manner.

"Oh, it's just one of those days. Some are better, some are worse. You know that, I'm sure," she answered.

"Yes, I certainly do. Today as I was sitting here looking up at the clouds, they reminded me that I need to get my life together and get on with living. I have lived in this listless state for too long now," said Anna. When Mrs. Howe didn't say anything, Anna went on. "Tomas said that I should come and stay with them when I feel like traveling so maybe I will do that."

Mrs. Howe started to cry softly. "Why Elsie, what have I said?" asked Anna, reaching out for her mother-in-law's hand. As she stroked it, Elsie said,

"I've been thinking lately that you may feel it's time to leave us soon, and of course I don't blame you. You are a young woman and you should get on with your life, but you are all we have left of Lorrie. Oh, how I wish that you hadn't lost the baby. Then we would have had Lorrie's child with us." The two women were both crying now.

"Oh, Elsie, I have wished that every minute of every day since I got well. If only I had his baby. It would give me something to live for."

"I'm sorry to make you cry, Anna, but I've been thinking so much about that lately."

"Don't be sorry for telling me that, Elsie," said Anna. "I'm glad that we're able to talk about it and it's even good for us to cry together, I think."

"As you know, I can't talk this freely to John. He keeps everything to himself. I know that it's not good for him."

The two women talked for a long time, until the heat of the day drove them inside.

Anna started to make efforts to get herself back into the mainstream of life. She asked Mr. Howe if she could work in the store a few hours a day for something to do and to get out among people again. She felt that that was very important. The longer she put it off, the harder it would be.

She had lost so much weight that her clothes just hung on her, but with the increased activity she began to get her appetite back again. She and Elsie took long walks in the evenings. Often they would walk over to Elizabeth and Conrad's. Baby Alex was growing so fast and, though it hurt Anna to see him or any other baby, she loved him dearly and he would come to her now without crying.

When September came, Anna decided that it was time to move on. For the Howes it was like losing a daughter when she left, and there were many tears, hugs and promises to keep in touch. She packed her trunk once more with everything she owned in it.

She went first to Tomas and Bergit's. In October, she passed her 27th birthday. She also spent Christmas there but towards spring she went down to see Andrew and Alice. This visit was particularly hard as Alice was still so depressed about Berta. Anna tried to get her to talk about her loss but Alice just shut everything up inside her. One could see the profound grief in her once sparkling eyes.

Anna went out to see the Benson family. Mary seemed very happy and she said that things were going just fine. Ben was able to walk quite well now but his back and legs tired very easily. He had two hired men to help with all the farm work. He had kept his promise to quit drinking and so far he'd been successful. The girls had grown up so much since she had last seen them. Rose Ann and Sonja were attending the high school in town but Grace and Marie were still going to the country school down the road. Rose Ann planned to become a teacher and Sonja was undecided.

Anna and Mary talked about Anna's losing Lorrie and her two miscarriages.

"I feel so bad for you, Anna," said Mary as she wiped tears from her eyes. "Don't give up hope. Those things will come to you again. Just trust in the Lord."

"I don't think I'll ever find anyone that I could love as much as I loved Lorrie," Anna said. "Maybe I'll just be an old maid school teacher," she added wryly.

Anna also stopped by to see the Reverend and Mrs. Peterson. They were so glad to see her again. They had heard about her misfortunes and felt so bad for her, they said. Their children had grown up, too. Josie was planning to be a teacher and Lucas thought he might like to be one, too. Willie, the bright little boy who hadn't even started school yet when Anna stayed there, was already saying he wanted to become a scientist. He just might indeed do that, Anna thought to herself.

Anna tried to help Alice as much as possible that summer. In her depressed state she was unable to function properly and much of her work was going undone. If Anna hadn't planted the garden there wouldn't have been one. Andrew was so grateful for her help. When he and Anna were alone, he would confide his concerns about his wife.

"She can't seem to come to grips with her grief, Anna. I don't know what I'm going to do." He put his head in his hands and sobbed. "She neglects things around here and even the boys." Alfred was ten now and already a great help to his father, but George was only five and he needed a mother's attention.

Anna tried to pick up the slack where Alice was lacking, but she soon realized that it was too much of a burden for her. Alice just had to come to grips with the situation. Anna had a long talk with her one day and things seemed to go a little better after that, but Anna could see that Alice was just going through the motions most of the time. There lacked feeling and emotion in her interaction with her children and Andrew.

Anna knew that she would have to stay during harvest or Alice would never make it through on her own. There was all the garden produce to do something about, too. Then Andrew begged Anna to stay at least until after Christmas. She said she would. They got through the holidays, trying to make it as happy as possible for the boys.

Being around Alice all the time, in her depressed state, didn't help to lighten Anna's grief in any way so Anna decided that maybe it was time for her to move on. A plan had begun to formulate in her mind and she was becoming more and more convinced that she should pursue it. It would take a lot of courage, though.

She announced to Andrew and Alice one evening that she would be leaving soon. She was going out to see Sigrid once again. She had some money, she told Andrew, money that she and Lorrie had been saving. She wrote a letter to Mrs. Martin asking if she could stop and see them. She would like to stay with them for a day or two, she said. She didn't want to just see them for a few minutes at the station.

While Anna was waiting for a reply from Mrs. Martin, she made herself busy around the house and tried hard to get Alice interested in things again. A letter came one day from Sigrid. Her family was so excited that Anna was coming to see them. Still no letter from Toledo. She waited and waited. She was anxious to be on her way but Mrs. Martin's reply was very important to her. Finally at the end of April, her letter came. Anna hurriedly opened it up and scanned it. Yes, she could come and stay with them for a short time if she liked, it said.

Two weeks later, leaving her big trunk at Andrew's, Anna boarded the train for another journey back East. Mr. Martin met her at the station in Toledo and they drove to the house in one of those newfangled motor cars. It was the first Anna had seen up close. It was very noisy and a rather breezy ride. She didn't care for it very much. Mr. Martin seemed very proud of it, though. "It's the coming thing now, Anna," he said.

When she arrived at the house, Mrs. Martin met them at the door. She embraced Anna but not with the usual enthusiasm, Anna felt.

"I don't think Anna liked our new motor car," Mr. Martin said teasingly.

"Well, that's the first one I've been in so it's very new to me," she answered in defense.

"Anna, I'm sure you will want to go right to your room as it is quite late. Samuel, of course, is already sleeping. We'll talk in the morning, but first I want to say how sorry we were to hear about your husband but how grateful that you survived." She led Anna upstairs and showed her the guest room, not the one she used when she lived here before. Anna was grateful for that. She washed up and climbed gratefully into the comfortable bed. It had been a tiring trip, as usual. She needed her rest for tomorrow and for what she had planned.

She slept rather late the next morning so that when she came downstairs, Mr. Martin had already gone off to work and Samuel was dressed and busy playing with his toy train. He was shy with her at first but he soon became quite talkative when she showed a keen interest in his train. It was his pride and joy.

"Papa and I play with our train almost every evening," he told her. "I'm in the second grade now. Did you know that?" he asked.

"Well, yes, I guess I did know that. You are getting to be such a grown up young man." Anna said. "Do you like school?"

"Sometimes," he answered. "But I'd rather stay home and play with my toys and be with Papa 'cause we do such fun things always."

Amanda Martin came and interrupted them to say that their breakfast was ready. They ate hot cereal together and Samuel made Anna laugh many times by the amusing things he would way.

"You are such a delight, Samuel," Anna said, and she looked at Amanda who was looking back and forth between Anna and Samuel. She wore a concerned expression on her face.

"Well, you two, what shall we do today?" Amanda asked. "Would you like to go to the zoo? They have quite a good one here in a very nice park."

"Oh, yes, yes," cried Samuel. "I love to go to the zoo and see the monkeys. Have you ever seen real monkeys, Mrs. Howe?"

"No, I never have but I would like to very much," Anna answered.

"Oh, goodie, goodie!" Samuel exclaimed, as he jumped off his chair. "Let's go! Let's go!"

This being Saturday, Mr. Martin came home at noon and he joined them on the trip to the zoo and park. It was a very enjoyable day for Anna. She loved watching her son and seeing how he delighted in everything. He was a wonderful little boy, she thought. He was so fascinated with all the animals.

"He could stand and watch them for an hour at a time," said Mr. Martin, with pride in his voice. Anna could tell that he thought the sun rose and set on that child!

That evening, after Samuel had been sent off to bed and the grownups were having their coffee in the parlor, Anna got up from her chair and started pacing the floor in front of her hosts.

"You maybe have been wondering why I wanted so badly to stay with you for a couple of days. This is not going to be easy but I have been thinking about something for some time now," said Anna. She cleared her throat and went on. "I've lost everything that was dear to me in this world. First, I gave up my first born child, then I lost my dear husband. and I've also had two miscarriages. I am left with nothing." She paused and took a deep breath, knowing that what she had to say next would be very difficult to get out. "I've decided that I want my child back. I want Samuel back!"

First there was a stunned silence and then Mrs. Martin let out a gasp and said, "Oh, John, I was afraid of this happening!" She started sobbing hysterically and Mr. Martin tried to soothe her a little. He then turned to Anna.

"You can't mean this, Anna. You don't know what you are doing to us and most of all to Sammy!" He rose and began pacing the floor himself.

"I have given this much thought, Mr. Martin, and I would like my son back," stated Anna, her voice rising.

Mr. Martin tried to calm himself. "Anna, my dear, please sit down and get hold of yourself and let's talk about this calmly. Do you have any idea what this would do to Samuel? This is the only family that he has ever known. If you took him away, we would still be his mother and father in his eyes. You would never be his real mother, to him."

"Please, Anna," said Mrs. Martin. "Don't even think of doing such a thing to that dear little boy. It would break his heart and ours, too, of course. You promised you would never try and get him back."

"I know I did, but I was only a young girl in trouble then. I didn't know just how terrible things were going to turn out for me. I need him, don't you see?" Anna was beginning to cry, too, now.

"You can't take him away from his family just to help you in your sorrow over losing a husband and two unborn babies," said Mrs. Martin. "You have to think of Samuel. He would hate you, if you succeeded in taking him away from us!"

Anna was crying more now as she realized that this might be true. She didn't want to hurt her little boy.

"It would be a very serious mistake to disrupt his happy life here with us, Anna," said Mr. Martin. " You can see how he loves us and how we love him."

"Yes, I know that and you have been wonderful parents to him but I love him, too, and want him back very badly," Anna answered, trying to wipe the tears from her cheeks.

"Anna, please," begged Mrs. Martin, "you can't do this to him. Please think of him if not of us. What would you have felt like if you had been taken from your home at age seven and had to go live permanently with someone else, almost a complete stranger?"

Anna was silent as she thought about this, trying to put herself in this same situation.

"You are young yet; you will marry again and have other children of your own," Mrs. Martin went on, through her sobs. "We can't have any children of our own."

" Anna, you have to think of the child's welfare in this. It would completely devastate him," said Mr. Martin.

"You can see how close Samuel and his father are," added Mrs. Martin.

Anna had many things to consider and think about. Maybe this wasn't such a good idea after all. She had only been thinking about herself and how grief-stricken and lonely she was. How had she reached such a low ebb in her life! she wondered. Why had all this happened to her? She cried harder and harder, until she couldn't cry anymore. Mr. Martin was beside himself; with the two women crying, one louder than the other, he didn't know what to do next. He decided to just wait till they calmed down. He didn't dare let himself think what he would do if he ever lost Samuel. He loved that little boy more than anything in the world.

Just then they became aware of a small figure in the doorway. It was Samuel. "Why is everybody crying?" he asked. "Did something bad happen?"

"No, no, Sammy," said Mrs. Martin. "We were just talking about ....
grownup things. What are you doing out of bed?"

He came to sit on his mother's lap. "I had a bad dream and I went into your room and it was empty so I came down here," he answered.

"Well, you run along back up to bed now," said his father. Mrs. Martin led him out into the hall and watched him go upstairs. She came back and stood in the doorway. "Anna, you can't do this to him and to us," she pleaded. "Please, please, don't try and do this."

Anna rose and said that she had much to think about and that she was going up to her room. She undressed and went to bed but sleep wouldn't be coming for her this night. She finally sat up and turned on her bedside lamp and reached for her Bible. She turned first to the Psalms to try and find some comfort. Then she paged through other passages of scripture trying to find some direction. She laid back down and finally fell asleep, praying for God's guidance in this matter.

The next morning things were much clearer in her mind. She knew what she had to do. How could I possibly have thought that I could do this to that little boy, she thought to herself. And to his parents, too. I've not been thinking too clearly these days.

When she arrived downstairs she found the Martins in the kitchen. She could tell that they had not slept much last night either. Mrs. Martin looked imploringly at Anna as if to ask what she was going to do next. The Martins both knew that if Anna decided to press the issue, she could indeed get Samuel back. There had been no legal adoption. Only a verbal agreement. Mrs. Martin was very afraid and so was her husband.

Anna looked at both of them and said, "I'm very sorry for what I put you through last night. I don't know what I was thinking. I just can't turn my son's life upside down. I've decided to leave here immediately and I promise I will never come back and I'll never try to get him away from you again.

She could hear Mrs. Martin let her breath out, as if she had been holding it since last night. Mr. Martin made an audible gasp and she could see the tears in his eyes. Tears of relief and joy. Mrs. Martin was crying again but she turned to the stove to get some coffee for the three of them.

"I'll leave this morning," she said to Mr. Martin, "as soon as you can arrange a ride for me to the train station. My bags are packed."

"I'll take you myself," he said. He took a big sip of the hot coffee set down in front of him. He looked very tired and worn, Anna thought. What an ordeal I have just put them through.

"I'm sorry," she said again. "Please, please forgive me."

"We're trying to understand your actions, Anna," he said. "We realize what you have just been through. We wish for you a good future. You are a strong person and you will start all over again."

After they had eaten breakfast, Anna said that she would like to go right away. She didn't think that she could bear to see Samuel again. It would be too hard. Mr. Martin hurried to get his coat and go and bring the car around. It was as if he couldn't get her out of there fast enough. He didn't want her to change her mind if she saw the child again.

At the station they bade each other a reserved goodbye, yet Mr. Martin had compassion in his eyes for the young woman. He knew how she was hurting. He knew what it was like to want a child so much.

Anna could remember little of the ride from Toledo to New York. She had spent her time crying and sleeping. When Sigrid saw Anna for the first time, she was shocked at what she saw. Her sister was decidedly thinner and quite pale. Her eyes had lost their sparkle.

"Why Anna," exclaimed Sigrid, "you're nothing but skin and bones! We'll have to do something about that." As she hugged her sister, Anna started to cry again.

"It's not only my body that needs healing," said Anna, as she sobbed on her sister's shoulder. I can see I have a big job ahead of me, thought Sigrid to herself. Louis was waiting for them outside so she led Anna and the baggage man out the main door.

That night and for many days afterwards, Sigrid and Anna talked of many things, among them Lorrie's death, Anna's two miscarriages and Anna's feelings of loneliness and despair. The one thing that was bothering Anna the most was, of course, the incident with the Martins but she couldn't tell Sigrid about that. Or could she? Maybe it would do her good to tell someone her terrible secret. No, I don't think I could do that, she thought to herself. Not yet anyway.

Sigrid tried many things to perk up Anna's appetite and also her spirits. It was a slow process, as Anna didn't seem to want to try to overcome her deep despair.

"Anna, you must stop resisting all our attempts to help you. It's like you don't really want to get better. You can't let all this self pity just completely engulf you," Sigrid told her one day. This made Anna sit up and think about what she had been doing. She had fallen into this trap before and knew how hard it was to come out of it.

She knew what she had to do. It had worked before and why had she waited so long to do it? Was it because she thought she deserved to be in this depressed state and did she enjoy all this self pity? That night she knelt beside her bed and poured her heart out to God. Why hadn't she done this before? she asked herself. God has been waiting for me. She again asked for forgiveness and the strength to go on living. She asked for this deep despair to be lifted from her. She praised God and soon a song was forming in her heart and she felt lighter and freer than she had in a long, long time. She slept good that night for a change and woke up refreshed.

She took some pains with her dressing that morning and knew she had to do something with her hair. When she mentioned this to Sigrid, her sister knew that things were maybe beginning to change for the better. She helped Anna wash her long hair and she cut it some and styled it for her. That evening when Louis came home from work, he noticed the change immediately.

"Why, Anna, you look ravishing tonight!" he teased her.

"Well, I guess it's time I started to look like I'm among the living!" she said.

"Why don't we all walk down to the park tonight. There's a concert at the bandstand and it's such a lovely evening," said Louis. Both Anna and Sigrid seemed to think this was a good idea.

After their evening meal, the whole family started down the sidewalk in the direction of the park. It took about twenty minutes to walk there. Many people had already gathered around the bandstand. They spread their blanket on the ground and sat down to listen to the music which had already started. The children milled around, finding some of their friends there, also.

The music was so beautiful, Anna thought. There were Viennese waltzes and also some Strauss. The refrains tugged at her heart strings and it felt good, she thought, to actually feel something again. The chill that had been in her heart for so long was beginning to thaw.

The months that Anna spent in New York with Sigrid proved to be quite therapeutic for her. She began to take an interest in life again and was starting to plan her future. Louis had arranged for her to get her U.S. citizenship, so on September 10, 1914, Anna Olson from Norway became an American citizen at last! She was very proud of this.

Sigrid and Louis wanted her to stay in New York and find a job there, but the pull of the Midwest was tugging at her to return, so the following March she boarded the train once again and headed back to Minnesota. She didn't stop to see Andrew and Alice this time. She went straight to Tomas and Bergit's.

She spent the spring sending out inquiries for teaching positions. She would like to teach right in Mankato but she didn't hold out much hope for that. At the end of June, she received a letter from a country school in southern Minnesota saying that they would like to hire her for only the next year as the teacher they had was taking a one year leave of absence. She waited awhile before replying, in case she received another offer, a better one. Finally, not daring to wait any longer, she wrote and said that she would take the position.

The last week in August she took the train out to Burrsville and got settled in there before the school year started. She would have one room in a house in the tiny village. The house was owned by a plump, cheerful woman who lived there by herself and she enjoyed having Anna around, she said. "I enjoy having someone to cook for," she told Anna. Her husband had died years ago.

The schoolhouse was small and not very well equipped but it was clean and the people that she had met so far were nice. Children came from the country if they didn't live too far out so there were nineteen pupils in all, grades one through eight.

Things went well and the time went fast. Before she knew it, it was Christmas time. She went to spend her vacation with Andrew and Alice as she was only about 50 miles from them. She took the train part way and Andrew came and met her in a town northwest of there. They had a good time. Alice seemed to be doing better, at least she was trying. But Anna noticed that every time she brought up Berta's name, Alice would change the subject right away. She would not talk about the little girl. That's not healthy, Anna thought to herself.

Vacation time soon ended and Anna went back to her school. The children were all glad to be back and see her again. They all liked her so much. There was one little first grade girl that Anna was especially concerned about. She never gave Anna any trouble but she seemed so unhappy all the time. Her name was Sarah Thompson. Anna tried everything possible to cheer her up but to no avail.

She asked her landlady, Mrs. Morris, about the child, and she told Anna the story. Sarah's mother died in childbirth so she and her father lived alone on a farm near town. The father seemed to blame the child for his wife's death. He would even tell the child this so it was no wonder that she looked and felt so sad all the time. "It's a real shame, that's what it is!" said Mrs. Morris. "The poor child. She shouldn't be blamed for her mother's death. Can't that father see what he's doing to his little girl?" Mrs. Morris became more agitated the longer she talked about it.

Anna decided that she was going to have a talk with the girl's father so she told Sarah to tell him that he should stop in after school one day. About a week later, on a Friday, after the children had all left, Mr. Thompson came to the school to see her.

"Has my daughter been giving you some trouble?" he asked Anna.

"No, no, she's no trouble at all," Anna assured him. "Do sit down, I want to talk to you about something. I'm very concerned about Sarah, though. She seems so extremely unhappy all the time. I've never seen her smile or heard her laugh like little girls should be doing. She doesn't seem to have any friends, either. Can you shed some light on why she is so unhappy?" asked Anna.

He seemed to think on this for awhile and then said, "No, she has a home, plenty of food and clothing so I don't know why she should be unhappy."

"But is she getting any love, Mr. Thompson?" asked Anna.

"Any love?" he asked. "What do you mean?"

"I mean, do you ever hold her and cuddle her and tell her that you love her and that she is pretty? These are things a child needs to be truly happy."

"Well, I..ah...I don't tell her those things, no," he answered.

"Maybe this isn't something that I should say to you, Mr. Thompson, but I have been told that you blame Sarah for your wife's death. Is that so?"

He looked at her, surprised by her forthrightness. Then he hung his head and did not answer her.

"You can't blame a little child for her mother's death. It's just something that happened but it was no fault of Sarah's, just because she was born. You can't continue to blame her or you will ruin her life, if you haven't already."

Mr. Thompson had never been talked to like that before. He didn't know what to say.

"Have you been blaming her, Mr. Thompson?" Anna asked again, persistently.

"I suppose I have been," he mumbled almost inaudibly.

"That girl needs lots of love and no more blame put on her little shoulders." Anna went on. "She shouldn't have to carry that burden around any longer. What she really needs is a mother," Anna said boldly. "Have you ever thought of getting on with your life and remarrying?"

Well, if this isn't the gol darndest woman I've ever met, thought Mr. Thompson. She sure has her nerve. She seemed to be waiting for his answer. "I've loved only one woman and that was Sarah's mother and when she died I died inside, too, and have never thought about another woman since," he said defensively.

Anna rose from her chair behind her desk and walked back and forth in front of the man. "Mr. Thompson, let me tell you something. I was married once, too, and my husband died in the flu epidemic. I also thought my life was over, but now I've decided to choose life for myself instead of self pity and I'm trying to get on with this process of living. My advice to you is to put the past behind you and start loving your little girl and look for another woman to be your wife and a mother to that poor child."

Boy, that woman sure can get on the band wagon when she gets started, he thought to himself. She has alot of nerve, too, telling me to get married. As if it's any of her business. He was thinking all these things as he rode home. Sarah was already home when he came in the house. He looked at her, really looked at her, and he could see that she indeed looked about as unhappy a child as he had ever seen. Something stirred in his heart and he broke down and started sobbing right then and there. Sarah was so startled that she began to cry, too. She had never seen her father cry before, or show much of any emotion at all.

"What's the matter, Pa? What did the teacher say? Have I been bad?"

He gathered his child into his arms and sobbed as though his heart would break. He sobbed for his dead wife, and for himself and for this poor innocent child whom he had been blaming all these years for something she had not caused. Actually it was his fault that his wife died, he believed. She had told him to get the doctor but he had procrastinated and then it was too late. He never had admitted that to himself before, but that was the fact of the matter.

"Pa, why are you crying so?" she asked timidly. "What did I do?"

"You didn't do anything, dear girl. You didn't do a thing," he said as he held her and cuddled her and stroked her hair. "Sarah, can you ever forgive me? I've been blaming you all these years for your mother's death and it wasn't your fault at all. I'm so sorry, so sorry. Your teacher told me some things that I needed to hear. Things are going to be different around here from now on. I promise you, Sarah."

The little girl did something that she hadn't done in a long time. She smiled. Mr. Thompson thought, how much she looks like Katy when she smiles. A beautiful smile. "You're a beautiful little girl, Sarah. You look just like your mother."

Sarah went to bed that night happier than she had ever been in her short life. The next few days at school, Anna could already notice a difference in her. She actually smiled and was even laughing at recess time.

One day she came to school especially happy. She told Anna that she had a secret and then she would cover her mouth and giggle. She seemed very excited about something all day and could hardly concentrate on her school work. When school let out, she hung around and Anna asked her if she was waiting for someone.

"Yes, my papa is coming to talk to you," was all she would say.

About ten minutes later, Mr. Thompson came driving up in his old and rickety wagon and walked up to the schoolhouse door. He knocked timidly and stepped in. He nodded to his daughter and she left and went to wait outside.

"Why, Mr. Thompson," said Anna, "Sarah said that you wanted to talk to me. Is it about your daughter? I have noticed such a difference in her already and she's been especially happy today," Anna exclaimed.

"Well, yes," he said, "I took your advice and I had a long talk with her and we cleared up some things."

"I'm so glad you did that, Mr. Thompson. It has certainly changed her life already."

"I am going to take your advice about something else, too, Mrs. Howe," he said, looking directly at her. "I'm going to ask someone to marry me."

"How wonderful! You must have had someone in mind all along," Anna said.

"Well, n..n..no," he stammered, "I didn't, but after our talk last week, I thought of somebody. I came here today to ask you to marry me," he blurted out.

Anna could hardly find her voice. "Mr. Thompson, you can't be serious. You must be joking," she said incredulously.

"No, I'm not joking," he said defensively. "You would be the perfect mother for Sarah. You seem to understand her so well. And you were right, I need to start thinking about the future and forget the past.

"Mr. Thompson," she said, getting up from her desk. "I can't possibly marry you. We don't love each other and I..I'm still in mourning for my husband."

"Well, I realize that but we could learn to love each other in time. Think of Sarah, how good it would be for her?" he said.

"I can't marry someone just because he needs a mother for his child, Mr.

Thompson," she said emphatically. "You must get that notion out of your head. I don't mean to hurt your feelings," she went on, "but I don't think I shall ever marry again. You will need to start looking for someone else. There must be some nice young woman in this area who would want to marry you after a reasonable time of courtship."

Mr. Thompson looked hurt and she could see Sarah peeking in the doorway, trying to hear the conversation. "I just thought it was such a good idea at the time," he said, turning his hat around and around in his hands. "I'm sorry if I have upset you." With this he turned around and left the room quickly. Anna stood still for quite sometime, hardly believing what had just transpired.

At school the next few days, Sarah was quite cool toward Anna so one day at noon recess, Anna took Sarah aside and suggested they take a little walk. It was a nice spring-like day and the roads had finally dried up after a hard rain. They walked in silence for awhile, then Anna said to the girl, "Sarah, I know that you are very disappointed that I didn't accept your father's marriage proposal."

"I wanted so much for you to be my mother!" Sarah blurted out. She started sobbing and searched for her hankie.

"Sarah, you must know that two people have to know each other and love each other before they decide to get married. Someday your father will find someone who is just right for the two of you. You can't rush things like that."

Sarah finally stopped crying and she reached for Anna's hand. They walked for awhile longer. "Sarah," said Anna gently, "I can't be your mother but I can be your teacher and your friend." Sarah gave Anna a little smile and they walked back to the school.

From then on, Sarah blossomed into the delightful little girl she was meant to be. Anna only saw Mr. Thompson once or twice before the end of the school year. He came for the program on the last day but avoided her eyes. He hung around though after the others had left, waiting for a word with Anna. When it was only he and Sarah and Anna left in the room, Anna looked at him and he said, "I want to thank you, Mrs. Howe, for all you did for Sarah ..... and for me, too," he added.

Anna extended her hand and said good bye to him and wished the best for the two of them. He really was quite a nice man, she thought to herself, and he seems to be coming out of his grief at last.

The next day, Saturday, Anna came back to the school and packed up all her books and things and tidied up the room. One of the older boys who lived in town stopped by to help her load the boxes in a wagon. She took one last look around this room that had been filled with music, laughter, tears, much learning, and maybe even some healing. She closed the door and walked to the wagon and drove slowly back to her boarding house.

CHAPTER 12

Anna spent that summer at Andrew and Alice's. The whole farming area there was enduring a severe drought. It didn't look like Andrew would be harvesting any crop at all. The wheat that he planted didn't even come up as the spring had been so dry, too. The old timers knew better than to even put seed in the ground. "It's no use to plant seed in dry dirt," they said, but Andrew thought he would try anyway. He was an optimist. The corn was almost as hopeless looking. Hardly enough to use for feed. Andrew had had a good crop the year before so he thought that he wouldn't be too bad off. He could survive one bad year.

Besides the poor crop outlook in the area, the newspapers were writing more and more about the war in Europe. It had begun the year before and German troops were on the move, invading Poland and Belgium and moving into Russia and France. President Wilson declared to the Americans, however, that the US would remain neutral. After a German submarine sank the Lusitania though, killing 128 Americans, the US government began setting up training camps. The war, however, seemed far away and of no immediate concern to these hard-working immigrant farmers who were simply trying to eke out a living from their new land.

Andrew's neighbor, Peder Jorgenson, started to come around quite often. The family suspected it was because of Anna. She, of course, did not encourage him in any way.

One Saturday evening in August, the church that the Olsons attended held a basket social. This was to be a money-making event to raise funds for an organ. The whole family went, each one preparing a basket with special things to eat inside.

As the bidding progressed, it was finally Anna's basket that was up for bid. Peder came to life and watched the good-natured bidding and bantering among the auctioneer and the young men in the crowd. Finally he made his move. When the bidding was up to $5, he stood up and said, "$10!" The crowd was stunned and all eyes were on him. He glared at the other young men who were heretofore the highest bidders, challenging them to dare to bid higher. After the auctioneer said "going twice", one of the young men said "$10.50!" Peder raised that bid to $12. The auctioneer declared him the winner when no one else bid higher. He took the basket and sought out Anna. They went out on the lawn like several of the young couples had done.

Peder spread a blanket on the grass and they sat down. Anna had been taken aback to think that anyone would pay that much for the privilege of eating with her! She was speechless and, of course, Peder was, too. She opened the basket in silence and started taking out the carefully prepared food. She finally found her voice and thanked Peder for paying so much for her basket and thus contributing so much to the money-making event.

"I wanted very much to share your basket with you," he said shyly.

The other couples were casting curious glances now and then at Peder and Anna and he was proud to be eating with the prettiest girl there. He would have liked to have told her that but he was too timid to say what was on his mind. Anna had to carry the ball when it came to conversation and she found that they had some things in common. He liked to read and had read some of the same books as had Anna. Anna concluded, however, that he didn't have much experience in the art of small talk.

After the meal and a short program, Peder asked Anna if he might drive her home. Well, that took courage, thought Anna. She accepted his offer and eyebrows were really rising by now! By the time they reached the Olson farm, most of the people had the couple almost married, Anna thought to herself wryly. Such is life in a small community.

Peder helped her down from the wagon and she noticed that his palms were very sweaty. She thanked him and he said, "Good evening," and tipped his hat to her and went back to the wagon.

Andrew and the family had driven in shortly before the couple and Alice looked slyly at Anna when she came in the door. Anna just laughed and said, "Don't jump to any conclusions!" The boys started teasing, "Anna and Peder. Anna and Peder."

It was almost a week before Peder showed his face on the Olson farm again. He came one evening as Anna was starting to pack her things. She would be leaving soon to go to start her new teaching position. She had a job over in the next county west of there near the town of Asheville. Peder asked her if he could drive her to the train station the next day. Before she could answer, Andrew said, "That would be a good idea, Peder, as I will be kind of busy tomorrow." He winked at his wife who smiled at Anna and Peder.

"I guess that would be all right," said Anna, and she told him what time she would like to leave. He left without another word and Anna turned and looked at her brother with mock indignation.

"You two!" she exclaimed. "Trying to play matchmaker, aren't you?"

Andrew and Alice just laughed good naturedly. It was good to see Alice almost back to her old self again.

The next morning Peder was there promptly and he and Andrew loaded her bags and boxes in the wagon. On the way to the station Peder tried to make conversation. Anna tried to help him along, as she felt sorry for him. He could be a nice man if only he weren't so terribly shy, she thought to herself. He was actually rather nice looking. He will need to find himself a very talkative, bubbly girl, Anna was thinking, when he interrupted her thoughts by saying, "I don't know how to say this, as you know that I have a hard time saying what is on my mind, but I was wondering if you would be my girl!"

Anna's mouth must have dropped open a good three inches! She looked at him and he was staring straight ahead, hardly daring to look at her. She felt instantly sorry for the poor, young man. Before she could say anything, he went on, "You must know that I think you are the prettiest and nicest girl around."

"Peder," she said, "I..ah..don't know what to say. As you know, I'm still trying to get over the sudden passing of my husband and I can't think of getting involved with any other man right now and maybe not ever."

Peder looked crushed and she appreciated the courage it took him to even open his mouth to express his feelings like he had.

"I don't want to hurt your feelings, Peder. You are a nice young man but I can't think about anything like that just yet," Anna went on.

They rode in silence the rest of the way to the station and Peder got out and helped Anna down with great gentleness and he held her hand a little longer than necessary. She looked into his eyes and he looked heartbroken. She felt a lump form in her throat and she said to him, trying to be stern but at the same time gentle, "Peder, listen to me, I have been married before, you are several years younger than I am. I think it would be better for you to find some nice, young girl from around here and start courting her. I can't be the one you are looking for." As he started to protest, she put her hand close to his mouth to keep any words from coming and said firmly, "Peder, I cannot be that girl for you."

She started walking towards the ticket office, bought her ticket and turned toward him. He was standing in almost the exact same spot. He was too stricken to move. "Thank you very much for the ride to town, Peder. This will have to be goodbye." She extended her hand and after some hesitation, he took it and shook it and said almost inaudibly, "Goodbye, Anna."

Anna boarded the train and found her seat. She could see Peder turning the wagon around and heading for home. She felt a terrible emptiness inside her. She knew how it felt to lose someone you cared about and she didn't doubt that he cared about her a great deal, but she didn't feel anything for him and she knew that she could not have led him to believe otherwise. That wouldn't have been right. He would get over her and maybe he would have the courage now to pursue some other girl. Then, again, maybe he would never dare try again, afraid of getting hurt. She fell into a troubled sleep, dozing on and off until the next stop.

Her new school was called Lakeside #2 and it was in the heart of a bustling rural Norwegian community. She would stay at the homes of her pupils again. The first place was the Nelson's, Jake and Olivia and their two young boys. The oldest, Ernie, was in the second grade and the youngest, Ozzie, was four. Besides the four members of the family, Jake's mother lived with them, too. The situation was a bit unusual. The way Anna heard it, the senior Mrs. Nelson just up and decided one day that she was going to go to bed and never get up again. She wasn't in ill health and there didn't seem to be anything wrong with her but she said that she had nothing to live for anymore so she went to bed and was waiting to die!

The family didn't pay her too much attention other than to provide the necessary care of bringing her food and keeping her clean. Most of the work fell on young Olivia. She was hardly in her middle twenties but she looked older. She looked very tired and Anna felt almost guilty by adding to her work load. She tried to help her as much as she had time for. She insisted on washing and ironing her own clothes.

It was too far for Anna to travel to Andrew's every weekend so she had to stay put at the Nelson's. After several weeks, she asked Olivia about her mother-in-law. Olivia sighed and said, "Well, I think she did it to get back at me. She never did like me and didn't think that I was good enough for her only son. We ran off and got married when we were only seventeen and eighteen. When Jake's father died several years later, she had to come and live with us."

"Rather than learn to get along with me and help me," Olivia went on, "she chose to get attention by going to bed and staying there. At first it worked, at least with Jake, but he soon realized that she was just doing it to get his attention and to spite me so he refused to play her little game anymore. This makes her very bitter and angry at me. She wants the doctor to come out every week, naming a new ailment, but he won't come anymore, either. He says there is nothing wrong with her."

Anna was appalled and could hardly believe that someone would do such a thing. Who would want to stay in bed if they didn't have to? "How long has she been in bed without getting up?" she asked Olivia.

"Let's see, it must be a little over a year now," she answered, calculating in her head. "It's made it pretty rough around here, but what can we do? We can't let her die. We have to take care of her." Olivia was almost in tears, tears of frustration and anger.

Anna was indignant and had great compassion for the young, overworked woman. Taking care of an ungrateful, demanding old woman was hard on everyone in the family. The little boys were often cranky, wanting more of their mother's attention. Anna decided that she was going to try and remedy the situation. It would take some doing to think of how to go about it the right way.

Every day after school, Anna would stop by Mrs. Nelson's room and greet her. Gradually, she would stay a little longer and tell the woman a little bit about what they did in school that day. There was never much response from her but Anna didn't let this daunt her efforts.

One Saturday, after Anna had done her laundry, she stopped by Mrs. Nelson's room and pulled up a chair. The two women looked at each other for awhile, each sizing up the other. "Would you like me to read to you, Mrs. Nelson?" Anna asked, surprising the old lady.

"What would you want to do that for? I'm soon ready to die and nobody cares. I need a doctor, that's what I need."

"If you're wanting to die, what do you want a doctor for?" asked Anna. "A doctor's job is to make people well. I know," Anna went on, "because I was very ill during the flu epidemic just a couple years back and a doctor helped me get well. I didn't want to die."

"That's because you were young and had people who cared about you," the raspy voice said.

"I lost my husband in that epidemic, Mrs. Nelson, and almost lost my own life and I realized how precious life is," said Anna gently. The old lady closed her eyes and turned her face to the wall. The visit was over. I will keep trying, thought Anna.

In the evenings, Anna would read aloud to the two boys. Mrs. Nelson's door was open and she knew that the old lady could hear her. She deliberately left out the last chapter, the most exciting part of the story, in hopes that Mrs. Nelson would ask about it someday. She whispered to the boys that she would read it to them after they got into bed.

Several days later, when Anna stopped by Mrs. Nelson's room after school, the old woman told Anna to sit down. "I want to know what happened to the boy and girl in that story you were reading to the boys the other night," she demanded. So she was listening and taking some interest in something, thought Anna to herself.

"Oh, I read it to the boys after they got to bed that night. I'll bring the book down and you can finish it yourself," Anna said and then, before the woman could protest, she quickly left the room.

One day when Anna returned from school, she found Olivia hanging some bed sheets on the line and when she turned she could see that she was crying. "What's the matter, Olivia?" Anna asked.

"Oh, it's Jake's mother. I can't take this much longer!" she said as she sat down on the porch step. She started crying harder and Anna had to strain to catch what she was saying. "She..makes my life so....miserable. To..to..today she..she deliberately knocked over the bed pan when I... was helping her...relieve herself. It made... such a..mess..I had to wash... all the bedding." Olivia finally cried herself out. "She does these things on purpose all the time, just to make my life harder," she went on. "I can't live like this anymore but I don't know what to do. I am so tired all the time with taking care of the boys, cleaning and cooking and doing laundry and then having her to care for, too."

She shook her head back and forth and started to cry again.

Anna, more angry than she had been in a long time, strode to Mrs. Nelson's room and approached the bed and took the blankets and threw them off the startled woman. "Get up!" demanded Anna. "Get out of bed this minute!" Anna was almost screaming by this time. The woman looked almost frightened.

"What are you talking about, young lady" she asked. "You know I can't get out of bed, I'm too sick."

"You're no more sick then I am," Anna retorted. "Get up and get dressed and make yourself useful around here. Are you trying to work your son's wife to death? I've never seen anyone so...so ungrateful and useless in all my life! Maybe you should just lay down and die!"

With that, Anna left the room and went outside and walked to the barn to cool herself down. Olivia had heard some of the conversation from inside the house and she couldn't believe her ears. She didn't dare to go into the house and she didn't even dare to follow Anna. She had never seen Anna like that before.

Jake was getting ready to milk one of the cows. Anna grabbed the pail from him and pulled up the stool beside the big animal and, before Jake knew what was happening, she was pulling down on those teats with all her strength. She was venting her anger on this poor, old cow!

"Hey, what do you think you're doing?" he asked, as the cow started moving away in protest and milk was spraying on the floor. Finally she let go and stood up.

"I'm sorry, Jake, I am just so angry. He sat down on the stool and gently but firmly took over the job.

"Who are you so mad at?" he asked as she paced the floor in the stall. "I'm glad it's not me," he tried to joke.

"Well, in a way it is, but mostly it's your mother. She is making Olivia's life unbearable. Did she tell you what your mother did today?"

Jake was silent for awhile, considering his answer. "Yes, she told me. I don't know what to do with mother either. She's always been hard to live with, for as long as I can remember."

"Well, can't you tell her that she can't treat your wife like she does? I was just in her room and I told her to get up out of bed and make herself useful."

Jake looked up at Anna, surprised at what she had just told him. "You actually told my mother that?" he asked. "What did she do then?"

"I was so angry that I walked out and left a very surprised woman looking after me," Anna answered. Just then Olivia came into the barn and stopped near the two of them. Her eyes were red and puffy from much crying. The young couple looked at each other in desperation.

"Something has to be done, Jake," Olivia said. "If things don't change, I'm going to leave."

Jake stood up so fast that he almost tipped over the half-filled milk pail.

"Now, now, honey, don't say that," he said, trying to soothe her.

Anna interrupted and said, "I think it's your mother that should leave, Jake."

"But where?" he asked. "There's no place else for her. I'm the only child and she has no other family."

"Tell her you're going to put her in the county poor house unless she gets up and joins the living," Anna suggested.

"I can't tell her something like that," Jake said hotly.

"You sure can, Jake Nelson!" exclaimed Olivia. "Tell her that it's either her or me." Jake stood shaking his head back and forth.

"Jake, I think it's time that you laid it on the line to your mother," said Anna. "I know it's maybe not my place to say these things to you or her but I can see what is happening here even if you can't. She's pitting herself against your wife and your first obligation is to your wife and children. You must make her see and understand this."

"Yes, Jake," said Olivia, " you can't put this off any longer. Anna and I will take the wagon and go over to the neighbors and pick up the boys and leave you to deal with your mother. When we come back I want things settled."

Anna had not seen Olivia stand up to her husband like this before but things had taken a desperate turn.

When Olivia and Anna and the boys were returning to the farm, Anna asked Olivia, "If Jake's mother hasn't been out of bed for over a year, will she be strong enough to stand and walk?"

Olivia was silent for a moment and then said quietly to Anna, "I think she gets out of bed when no one is home. Several times I have thought that I've seen her looking at me through the window while I was working out in the garden. And once," she went on, " when I came into the house in a hurry and came into her room, I noticed the rocker was slightly moving back and forth. I felt of the seat and it was still warm so I think she had been sitting in it."

Anna was not too surprised to hear this. "So she has been just playing a game with you all of this time." Anna shook her head. "This makes me very angry and I'm sure you have been very angry for a long time about it."

"Yes, I have been all along," Olivia said emphatically, "but Jake is rather blind when it comes to his mother. I hope he's finally realizing what I have suspected, that she has just been trying to make my life miserable."

"What kind of a woman would do such a thing!" exclaimed Anna. "She must be a very miserable woman inside. Think of all the precious time she has wasted, not being a proper grandma to her two little grandsons."

They drove into the yard and tied the team to the hitching post as Jake wasn't around. When they entered the house, they could see that Mrs. Nelson's bedroom door was closed. She never wanted her door closed. "She doesn't want to miss out on anything," Olivia said.

Olivia started to prepare supper and Anna set the table, wondering if there would be one more person at their table tonight. Soon the door opened and Jake stalked out, closing the door after him. He looked at Olivia soberly and said, "Things will be different around here from now on." With that he left the house and went to tend to the horses. The two women looked at each other, a questioning look in both pairs of eyes.

Jake returned and washed up and said to Anna, "You can set another place at the table tonight." Supper was ready and Olivia looked expectantly at the closed bedroom door. Jake went and rapped lightly and said, "Mother, supper is ready and waiting."

The two boys stared wide-eyed at the grownups and then at the door. It opened slowly and then to everyone's surprise, Mrs. Nelson stood in the doorway, fully dressed and she had even combed her hair nicely. Jake went to his mother and extended his arm and led her slowly to the table. No one said a word for sometime.

"Grandma," exclaimed Ozzie, "aren't you sick anymore?" Everyone held their breath to hear the answer. Mrs. Nelson didn't say anything so Jake said, "Children, your grandmother is feeling much better now and will be joining in the family activities... and the chores," he added, looking at Olivia. "Aren't you, Mother?" he asked when she still didn't say anything.

Mrs. Nelson sat down and looked around at her family. "Yes, I guess I am," was all she said. Jake led the family in the table prayer, adding a special thanks for the returned health of his mother. Everyone said "Amen" to that!

Table conversation was a little forced to begin with. Anna started talking about school and Jake about the farm work. Soon little Ozzie, in a small and quiet voice said, "It will be fun to have a grandma again." Everyone's fork stopped in mid-air as they looked toward the little boy. Anna's eyes started filling with tears as she thought once again about how much time had been wasted between a grandma and her grandsons. She looked at Mrs. Nelson and she actually saw that her eyes, too, were misted up. I hope she realizes what she has lost and will make up for it in the future, Anna thought to herself.

Over the next few days, Mrs. Nelson became stronger but she remained very quiet. One evening Ozzie brought a book to her and asked, "Grandma, will you read me a story tonight?" Mrs. Nelson lifted the small boy into her lap and started reading the fairy tale, beginning 'Once upon a time'...... as Ozzie laid his head on her shoulder. When the story was finished, the sleepy child nestled in her lap and fell sound asleep. She rested her cheek against his forehead. That woman loves her grandchildren, it's plain to see, thought Anna. There is some good in her, as in everyone.

There was, however, still tension between the woman and her daughter-in-law. Mrs. Nelson helped with the household tasks but only spoke in short, clipped sentences to Olivia when necessary. Anna could not let this continue so in her straightforward manner she approached Mrs. Nelson one evening when the rest of the family was out in the barn.

"Mrs. Nelson," she began, "I'm so glad that you are up and about now and helping Olivia with all the work around here. I'm sure she appreciates it very much." When there was no response, Anna continued on. ""But do you know what she really needs and so do you, to make the relationship right between you? You need to ask for her forgiveness for all the time you made her tend to your every need when that wasn't even necessary."

Mrs. Nelson gave Anna a hard stare. "Now don't look at me like that," Anna said, as she got up from her chair and stood in front of the woman. "You can't go to your grave with this enmity between the two of you. Look what this is doing to your own son and the children. You think you're punishing her for marrying your son when you didn't approve of the match. Well, let me ask you this," Anna went on. "What is wrong with Olivia as a wife and mother? Nothing! She is a wonderful person and you're the one who is being punished for your attitude. You could have had such a warm, loving relationship with her and the rest of the family if you weren't so stubborn and pig-headed." Mrs. Nelson looked at Anna intently and thought to herself, what nerve this young woman has! Imagine telling someone these things!

"I know what you're thinking," said Anna. "You're thinking that I have no right to say these things to you and maybe I don't. I'm just a guest in this house. But I can see what's going on here and it's wrong and you have been trying to ruin the lives of your only family. You have wasted so much precious time. What if you died tonight and still had this guilt upon you? You must reconcile with Olivia and ask for forgiveness from both her and Jake, and also the boys."

Just then the boys came running into the house followed by Olivia. They stopped when they saw the two women in an apparent confrontation. "What's the matter?" asked Olivia.

"You ask your mother-in-law what is the matter, Olivia," answered Anna, as she looked pointedly at the older woman. Mrs. Nelson got up abruptly and left the room in a huff. She closed her bedroom door, a barrier between her wretched soul and the family that she obviously loved and needed.

There was not much sleep for Mrs. Nelson that night as she lay awake and agonized over the frank words thrown at her by this upstart of a young woman who had no business meddling in other people's affairs. But the truth could not be ignored and the Holy Spirit was working in the heart and soul of this embittered old woman, just as Anna had been praying to happen.

The next morning, when Mrs. Nelson didn't come out of her room for breakfast, Jake knocked on the door and asked his mother if she was all right. She said that she would like for Anna to come into her room. As Anna came in, Mrs. Nelson was sitting in the rocker with a worn Bible in her lap. She indicated to Anna that she should sit down on the bed. The elder woman took a deep breath, almost like a huff, and began.

"I have been awake all night thinking about the things you said. I hate to admit it, but you're right and I've been so wrong all this time. I don't know how to go about making amends. I am proud and stubborn, I will admit, and I don't know what to do next." With this, she put her head in her hands and cried tears of remorse.

Anna felt compassion for the woman but let her cry for awhile. Tears could be so cleansing. Finally she said, "Mrs. Nelson, I will first ask you to forgive me for talking to you in such a forthright manner but I thought that it was necessary and I cannot hold back when I see a wrong being committed. Some people think I am too forward."

Mrs. Nelson held out her hand to Anna and said, "You don't need forgiveness. I am thankful that you did what you did because I was getting deeper and deeper into a situation that I couldn't get myself out of. I'm not really such a mean old lady as you probably think, but I have too much pride and stubbornness to admit when I am wrong. I knew many years ago that I was wrong about Olivia. She is a wonderful wife for Jake, but I had made such a fuss about their marrying that I didn't know how to change my attitude toward her."

Mrs. Nelson started crying afresh and Anna put her arm around her stiff, unyielding shoulders. "Let it all out and turn that stubbornness and pride over to God and he will get rid of it for you," Anna told her. She sobbed some more and finally Anna could feel her relaxing against her shoulder.

"Perhaps it is time for you to ask first Olivia to come in here and then Jake," suggested Anna. Mrs. Nelson just nodded her head. Anna rose and left the room for a moment and then came back with a reluctant Olivia.

"Olivia," said Anna, " your mother-in-law has some things that she wants to tell you." With that, Anna left the room, leaving the two women alone to straighten out the many things that had been wrong in their relationship. She took the boys outside and they joined Jake in the barn, where he was tending to a horse who was soon going to have it's first foal.

"Ernie, go tell your Ma to come out here and help me, will you, please?" Jake told his son. Anna stepped between them and put a hand on Ernie's shoulder.

"Wait, Ernie," she said. "Your mother is in talking with your grandmother and I think they will need lots of time." She looked at Jake as she said this and he seemed to understand that something important was happening in the house.

"That's OK, Ernie. We'll do it later," he said to the boy as he gave Anna a quizzical look. "I think this horse is going to have some trouble later on today."

"I think perhaps that your mother is about ready to talk to you now, too, Jake," Anna told him, and she nodded her head toward the house. "The boys and I will stay out here."

Jake went directly to his mother's room and knocked softly on the door. "What's going on in there?" he asked, turning the knob. He was not prepared to see his wife and his mother hugging and crying on each other's shoulders. He just stood and looked at them, not knowing what to say. Finally the two women parted and started wiping their tears.

"Jake," said his mother, "this is not an easy thing for me to do, but I am asking your forgiveness, too, for all the years that I've made life miserable for the two of you. Olivia and I have made our peace and I am trying hard to change my ways. Things are going to be different around here, thanks to that upstart teacher who likes to meddle in other people's affairs." She actually smiled when she said this and Jake and Olivia had to laugh because it was so true and it greatly relieved the tension.

"Welcome back, Ma," said Jake and he took his mother in his arms and held her tightly. She started crying again, in relief and happiness.

Things really did change around the Nelson household. There was laughter and fun and Olivia looked so much happier. Mrs. Nelson actually was a real worker and she took much of the load of the housework from Olivia.

Three months had passed and it was time for Anna to leave and go on to the next family. She had come to dearly love the Nelson family, even the stubborn old mother-in-law! When it was time to say their goodbyes, Mrs. Nelson came to Anna and said, "Anna Howe, you are one feisty, young woman and I dare say that you will go far in this world. No one will step on you!" She gave Anna a hug and she added, "Thank you for helping me mend my ways and turn things around."

"Don't thank me, Mrs. Nelson, thank the Lord. You don't know how much praying I had to do for you!" They both laughed at this and hugged again.

"It feels so good to be 'well' again and enjoying life again," Mrs. Nelson said. The rest of the family said their tearful goodbyes, too, and Jake loaded her things in the wagon for the short drive over to the next family.

The rest of the school year went by quickly. During the middle of May, Anna got to experience the full wrath of Mother Nature as she had never seen it before. It had been hot and sticky weather for several days and it was quite miserable in the schoolhouse. The children were listless and getting crankier each day.

This one particular morning started out more miserable than usual. By noon, the sky looked strange and the air felt even stranger. Anna couldn't quite put her finger on it but she felt like something was about to happen. By afternoon recess time the sky was becoming darker and darker. One father had stopped by and picked up his two young children. He told her that he thought that a storm was coming and that she should be on the look out.

Anna didn't know quite what to do. Should she send the children home early or keep them at the school? An awful stillness seemed to come upon them. Not a bird could be heard and not a leaf moved on the trees. She shooed all the children inside and tried to keep them occupied and at the same time her mind was on the darkening sky.

All of a sudden, a wind started blowing across the prairie and as Anna looked out the window, she could see it leaving a trail of dust. It became louder and louder. The children all stood up and looked at her for direction. She glanced out the window again and she could see the big, black cloud coming closer and the sound was getting louder. She told the children to lie flat on the floor in the middle of the room and so they almost piled on top of each other trying to find a spot.

The noise was by now so loud that she could no longer be heard above the din. She, too, finally threw herself down on the floor next to the children. The noise sounds just like a train, she thought to herself. Then she heard glass breaking and a big thud on the roof above them. The children were screaming and crying. They couldn't hear her tell them to just stay down.

The noise seemed to be letting up a little and then she heard the rain and wind pelting the school. They all laid there for quite sometime and then Anna got up and ventured to the window. There was a big branch from the oak tree laying across the roof. There were small branches and leaves everywhere! The rain was letting up, too, now, so she told the children that they could get up. They all ran for the windows, several of which had been broken in the storm.

"Look out, children, for the glass!" Anna exclaimed, when she finally got her wits about her. She motioned them back from the broken windows and she found a large pail and started to carefully pick up the big pieces of glass. Then she took the broom and swept the rest of the pieces off to the side.

The children were strangely quiet, rather like they were stunned. Some of the little ones were crying softly, being comforted by the older ones. The rain had now stopped and they heard a wagon and team come racing up to the school. It was Mr. Anderson, the closest neighbor. He came bursting through the doorway. "Is everyone all right here?" he asked excitedly, taking in the room and the broken windows.

"We're all OK," answered Anna, still frightened by the ordeal. "I've never seen anything like it!" she exclaimed. "Was it a cyclone?"

"We call them tornadoes around here," Mr. Anderson told her, "but I don't know if it was that or just a bad wind storm. I can give some of the children a ride to their homes. If their parents are coming for them, I'll meet them on the way." Some of the children got up into his wagon, those who lived west of the school, and they started off. Some of the bigger children started walking home and Anna still had several younger ones there but the parents soon came for them, one by one.

That evening, Anna was still shaken, and news started passing through the community regarding the storm damage. About a mile east of the school, a barn had its roof blown off and some cattle were killed. Another farmer lost his hog barn and some hogs and there were many trees uprooted and branches down. School was called off the next day as the whole community pulled together for the clean-up effort.

There was only minimal damage to the school house roof and the broken windows were boarded up until replacement panes could be found. School resumed as usual two days after the storm. This was the last week of school and the end-of-the-year program was put on for the parents and townspeople on the last day. Anna said goodbye to all her students and their parents. They all hoped that she would come back next year. "I'm planning to," she replied.

The next day she packed up her belongings, which seemed to grow each and every year, and she was driven to the train station.

CHAPTER 13

Anna had many plans for the summer. First of all, she went to pay a visit to the Howe family. She caught a ride with the father of one of her students part of the way and then took a short train ride from there. The Howes were so happy to see her. Mrs. Howe kept herself busy with her two grandchildren who lived nearby, she said, but she worried about her husband. Since Lorrie's death, he didn't have the old zest for life or for his work. The grocery store business was suffering for it, she told Anna. "Things will have to change soon," she said, "or I don't know what we'll do."

One day as Anna was catching up on some old newspapers, she read in the Posten that the Hotel Minnesota, in Detroit, had burned the year before. That was where we spent our wonderful wedding trip, she thought to herself! This seemed to upset her very much. That afternoon, she took a walk over to the cemetery where Lorrie was buried. She sat down on the grass near his tombstone. She picked at some weeds and tall grass near the stone as the tears fell. She didn't try to stop them but had a good cry. She talked to Lorrie in a quiet voice about many things.

It was nearing dinnertime, but she was reluctant to leave. Mr. Howe came walking down the street, on his way home. He saw her there and he walked over by the family plot to join her. He didn't say anything but they looked at each other for a few moments and then he took his daughter-in-law in his arms and they both sobbed on each other's shoulder. Anna suspected that Mr. Howe did not let his guard down very often.

"Do you walk by the cemetery on your way home every day?" she asked him, after they had composed themselves somewhat.

"No, I couldn't bear that," he answered, "but for some reason today I felt the urge to do so. I could hardly believe it when I saw you here."

"Well, I felt the need to come here today, too. I had just read in the paper that the hotel where we spent our honeymoon had burned down and it made things seem so final. Even my memories are being taken from me!" Anna told him, a sob forming in her throat again.

They slowly left the cemetery, this place of broken dreams and sorrow.

By the time they reached the house, they had regained their composure, but Mrs. Howe could see that her husband had just gone through something, like a load had been lifted from him. Anna told her of their joint visit to the grave site. Ah, he needs to have a good cry sometimes and let it all out, thought Mrs. Howe to herself, suspecting that this is what had happened.

After about a week's stay with the Howes, Anna took the train to Mankato to see Tomas and Bergit. They had a good time catching up on everything and how those children had grown! Arne was now a tall 17-year-old and had a job at the Hubbard Mill. Tomas hoped that he would help him in the carpenter trade when business picked up a little. Hannah was 15 now and had the fair good looks of her mother. Sarah, at 12, had the promise of being a raving beauty. She was dark like Tomas and was going to be a tall girl. Teddy, on the other hand, was a short, roly-poly 9-year-old with a carefree nature. How dear this family was to her, thought Anna.

She was planning to spend two weeks here and then travel out to New York to see Sigrid. Tomas and Bergit suggested that maybe Anna should move to Mankato and try to get a teaching job or something there. They liked having her near them.

"Well, I promised the Lakeside School that I would come back next year so I think I had better do that, but maybe after that I will give it some thought."

Several days before Anna was to depart for New York, she got the bright idea that maybe Hannah should go with her! Was Hannah ever excited about this venture and she begged her parents to let her go. Tomas said that he didn't know if they could afford her train fare. Anna said that she would pay for the girl's ticket because Tomas and Bergit had taken her in so many times and they had helped put on the wonderful wedding reception for her and Lorrie. Finally she and Hannah had them convinced that this trip was a wonderful experience for their daughter, who was almost a young woman now.

The next days were buzzing with activity! Hannah scrambled around, trying to find enough clothes to make a decent traveling wardrobe and they borrowed a suitcase from a neighbor. Anna wired Sigrid, telling her of the additional guest.

The trip back East was more fun this time for Anna, having a traveling companion. Hannah was so excited about everything that it made Anna remember back to the time when she, as a young girl herself, had crossed the ocean and how wonderful it had been, seeing things for the first time.

Sigrid's children were so excited to finally meet one of their cousins. Arthur was the same age as Hannah and Annie was two years older and Sylvia was two years younger. Anna and Hannah stayed for a month and during that time, Hannah saw all the sights and was completely enamored of the big city.

A few days before they had to leave, Sigrid received a letter from Papa. It contained the sad news that their mother had died. "She died peacefully in her sleep one night," he wrote, " and the doctor said that it was heart failure." Reading between the lines, Sigrid and Anna could tell that Papa was quite distraught. He was lonely and he now had the sole responsibility of Kjersti.

Anna felt guilty when she was unable to shed any tears at first, like Sigrid. Why can't I feel any sorrow? she asked herself. I hardly knew her, she thought to herself; my own mother! Then she was able to cry along with Sigrid, just thinking about how sad it is when a mother and daughter don't have a close relationship, and now it was too late!

"I should have made a trip back to Norway," she told Sigrid through her tears. "Maybe Mama and I could have become closer. Now she is gone and so is the chance for us to have said the things that we should have to each other." Anna started crying afresh and Sigrid tried to console her.

"Maybe we both should have gone back for a visit, knowing that her health was not very good," said Sigrid. "Poor Papa, I wish he would come over here now but he can't leave Kjersti and of course he still has the others back there."

"Maybe we could convince him to come over for a short visit," suggested Anna. She and Sigrid wrote him a long letter that evening, expressing their sorrow and they also urged him to come and visit all of them in America.

Anna and Hannah were both reluctant to leave New York but they knew it was time for them to head back home. The trip back was a long one, but Hannah hardly seemed to notice. She was so filled with excitement over what she had just experienced. She had been looking out the train window for quite sometime when suddenly she exclaimed, "Aunt Anna, I know what I'm going to do with my life. I'm going to become a teacher like you and then I'm going to travel all over the country and see many things and places!" The young girl was almost bouncing off her seat with enthusiasm.

Anna looked over at her niece and saw herself as she was some years ago back in Norway. Young and excited about a future full of adventure. She took Hannah's hand and said, "Don't ever give up on your dream. Do what your heart tells you to do and don't give up on it."

Hannah looked at her Aunt and asked, "Did you dream big dreams when you were young? And did they come true?"

Anna thought for awhile and then answered, "Yes, Hannah, I had a dream to come to America and I did that and I believe that each day that I live, the dream is still unfolding. I don't know how or when it will end." Anna leaned her head back and closed her eyes as the train car bounced along the bumpy track. My life has been bumpy, like this track, she thought to herself, but it keeps moving right along.

"Do you think that Pa and Ma will let me go to college?" asked Hannah, interrupting Anna's thoughts. "Will you talk to them for me?"

"I'm sure that when the time comes, Hannah, they will find a way to send you to college. Your father is quite broad minded about girls getting an education so I'm sure we can convince him."

When they arrived back in Mankato, Tomas and Bergit had also received word about the death of Tomas' and Anna's mother. Tomas regretted, too, that he had never been able to see his mother again.

"That's what happens when we leave our homeland and go so far away. Maybe it's not always a good thing to try to seek a better life somewhere. The family suffers the consequences sometimes," he lamented sadly.

Tomas wrote to their father, asking him to consider coming to America for a visit. "We want to see you again and you have so many wonderful grandchildren to meet!" he wrote.

Before an answer arrived, Anna traveled back to her school of the year before, Lakeside #2. She stayed with several different families this time and the time went by quickly and uneventfully. At Christmas time, Anna had received a letter from her father saying that he had given some thought to coming to America, and Tollef and Margit had even said that they would keep Kjersti with them while he was gone. But he had been reading of so many ship sinkings by the German subs that he dared not come at this time.

All Americans were shocked when, on April 6, 1917, the US declared war on Germany. Congress stated that "the world must be made safe for democracy." This act had been prompted by a record number of sinkings of US merchant ships.

That summer, Anna went first to visit Andrew and Alice. Alice had just suffered a miscarriage and so she needed some help and emotional support. Her state of mind was still rather fragile after the loss of their only little daughter, Berta, four years earlier.

Anna noticed that there was much talk about the war among the men when they would get together. The country was not very prepared for a war but the government adopted a selective-service act that required all men between the ages of 21 and 30 to register for the draft. This made everyone realize just how the war "over there" was suddenly to affect them all very closely as sons and young fathers answered the call and made their way to towns and villages to register.

Andrew and Alice said many times how glad they were that their son, Alfred, was not old enough to have to comply with this new act of Congress. He was only fourteen. Tomas and Bergit's Arne was soon eighteen, and he, too, escaped it. But they could not quite still their concern that if the war dragged on, their sons would eventually have to enlist. It was a worry for many families.

The crops didn't look very promising this summer either. It was very dry and the dust blew almost every day. On top of that, there was a great infestation of grasshoppers. They were so thick that sometimes the sky looked all black. They could wipe out a field of wheat overnight. Anna could tell that Andrew was worried. He stayed up later at night, drinking coffee and figuring his expenses on paper. Then he would say to his wife and Anna, "We'll put our trust in the Lord, as always. We own our land and farm free and clear so we don't have it so bad. Things could be much worse."

Anna heard from Tomas and Bergit, suggesting to her that she should think seriously about moving to Mankato permanently and look for a teaching job there. The school there had been enlarged and they were adding more teachers as the town was growing so fast.

Anna gave this much thought and prayed about it for several nights and then finally, one morning at breakfast, she announced that she had decided to go to Mankato and live and look for a job. She thought that she should be going soon if she was going to look into a teaching job for the coming year.

A few days later, Andrew got her big trunk down once more and she filled that and several more crates and after some prolonged goodbyes, she was driven into town to meet the train once again. Andrew stayed with her while she waited for the train to come in. She took a long look at her brother and realized that he was beginning to look old. He worked too hard, she thought, as did most of the men in all the communities across the Mid-West, trying to fulfill their dreams of a better life for themselves and their families. Mother Nature often worked against them, though. She expends her wrath on the prairies with a vengeance with her blizzards, her relentless winds, tornadoes, floods, drought and prairie fires. The people try to prepare themselves and fight back but it is sometimes to no avail. Nature often has the last word.

She embraced her brother warmly and boarded the train. She settled down in her seat and after several miles, she laid her head back against the head rest and closed her eyes. Why do I have the feeling that this move is the beginning of a new chapter in my life? Anna mused. Or is it simply the continuation of my dream. The dream that brought me all the way across the ocean to this country. She felt the stirring of excitement inside of her and she looked forward to what lie ahead of her.

CHAPTER 14

Upon arriving in Mankato, Anna didn't waste any time. The very next day she walked over to the school and went into the principal's office and inquired about a job. She was told that all the positions were filled but she could fill out an application just the same. She did this and walked home, feeling disappointed. Well, what did I expect, looking for a job at this late date? she scolded herself.

At the house, Bergit tried to console her and told her to have faith that something would come up. "Maybe you could apply downtown at one of the stores," she said.

So Anna did just that. In the afternoon, she walked downtown and went into several stores, a department store, a drug store and a jewelry store. The drug store was, in fact, the store that Hannah had a part-time job in after school and on Saturdays. They said they didn't need any more help right now.

She had better luck at the department store. One young woman was quitting so they would be needing someone at the end of the month. The manager hired Anna on the spot and said that she could start training in three weeks. How lucky I am, she thought, and couldn't wait to tell Bergit and Tomas that evening. She made a few purchases of thread and buttons for a dress she was sewing and hurried home.

The family was excited over her news about getting a job in the store but they knew that she would rather be teaching. "Something may come up at the school for me sometime," she told them reassuringly. "This job at the store might be fun for awhile. It will be different, that's for sure!"

Three weeks later, Anna started working every day in the store. She enjoyed meeting the people and helping them find what they needed. As the Christmas season neared, new merchandise came in weekly.

The community was trying to get in the Christmas mood but with a war going on and the news coming back of many Americans already being killed, it was hard to be in a holiday spirit. Two young men from this very town had already lost their lives over in France someplace so it was hitting very close to home now.

Business picked up, however, a couple days before Christmas. It was as if the people decided to try and make this a festive holiday in spite of the hardships and fear of what was to happen to their families and their country.

Anna made some small purchases, something for each member of the family and wrapped them at the store. On Christmas Eve, the store closed early and when she arrived home Tomas was already there.

Smells from the kitchen assailed her as she stepped in the front door, promising a wonderful meal a little later on. The family was gathered in the parlor. They were reading a letter that had come from Sigrid that day. They read it aloud again so that Anna could hear it. Sigrid said how much she wished that they could all be together this Christmas. She was worried about the war and wondered how long it would go on. Reading between the lines, Anna could tell that she was concerned about Arthur, who was too young yet, but like his cousins would one day maybe have to go to war.

Bergit tried to lighten the mood by talking of other things and Anna put her packages under the tree, to the delight of the children. Soon it was time to gather around the dining-room table for their special supper. They would eat early and then get ready to go to church for the Christmas Eve services. Bergit had made sweet soup, spare ribs, mashed potatoes, and lefse. They would have their special Christmas goodies later.

At the church they had a wonderful service and several Christmas songs from the old country were sung. A fresh evergreen tree had been placed at the front of the church just the day before. Its pungent aroma filled the sanctuary.

When they left the church they discovered that it was snowing lightly. It was very pretty with the snow falling past the light of the gas street lamps. This beautiful night reminded Anna of a Christmas Eve back in Norway many years ago and she started singing and soon the whole family joined in.

They passed the house of an old woman who was housebound so they turned and walked up her sidewalk and stood by her front door and sang a couple more songs. They could see old Mrs. Juleson peering out from behind her curtains. She smiled and waved at them as they turned to leave.

When they got home, Bergit hurried to make some hot cocoa and put the sweets on the table. Then the children would be allowed to open one gift each. Anna had bought pocket knives for Arne and Teddy, an ivory-handled letter opener and matching trinket box for Hannah and a beautifully bound book of "Little Women" for Sarah. She loved buying gifts for others, especially the children.

Tomas picked up the big family Bible and opened it to Luke and read the Christmas story aloud as the family gathered around him. No one said a word for awhile afterwards, not wanting to break the spell of this wonderful night. Snow was still falling lightly outside and the fire crackled in the fireplace inside. They were all safe and warm and cozy and most importantly, they were a family so far untouched by the war. They had much to be thankful for.

One evening late in January, Mr. Stolle, the school principal, came to call. He wanted to talk with Mrs. Howe, he said. Bergit ushered him into the parlor and Anna joined them. Bergit excused herself and the two sat down. Mr.

Stolle began by saying, "Mrs. Howe, I'll get right to the point. One of our teachers has become ill and the doctor has ordered her not to come back to school the rest of the year. We were wondering if you would consider filling in for her. It would mean starting next Monday. We have been using a substitute but she can't stay with us any longer than the end of this week."

He finally stopped to take a breath and Anna said, "Well, this is rather sudden. Let me think a minute here." She got up and paced the floor like she usually did when she needed to think clearly.

Bergit came in just then with a cup of coffee for the principal and one for Anna. Anna motioned for Bergit to set hers on the end table. She kept pacing. She told herself that this was the break that she had been waiting for even though she did like working at the store.

Finally she sat down opposite Mr. Stolle and took her cup and had a sip of the hot beverage and then said, "Mr. Stolle, I've decided. I will accept your offer to teach til the end of the year."

"Splendid!" said Mr. Stolle. "That is a great relief to all of us at the school, Mrs. Howe." They drank their coffee and discussed some details and then he rose to leave. They shook hands on the deal.

"We'll see you next Monday morning then," he said as he went out the door, into the cold winter night.

Bergit came back into the room and Anna told her the news. "I won't be giving them very much notice at the store," she said, "but this is what I have been wanting for a long time. To teach in a city school. I'll have to break the news to Mr. Larson the first thing in the morning."

Mr. Larson, the store manager, was sorry to hear that she would be leaving. However, he said that giving only one week's notice was not really a problem as business was quite slow now this time of year. When the weekend came, she was a little bit nervous about starting her new job in the big school but on Monday morning she had calmed her fears and was eagerly awaiting the challenge.

She arrived early and Mr. Stolle led her to her classroom. She would be teaching the 3rd and 4th graders. There were twenty-two of them, he told her. Mr. Stolle gave her the attendance book listing all their names and she sat down to wait for them to begin arriving. Upon reading the list of names, she found that she would be having a boy named Samuel. She felt a deep sadness as she thought of her own dear little Samuel. She looked across the room at the large calendar. Tomorrow would be February 3, her Samuel's birthday. He would be eleven years old now. Oh, how she longed to see him. She had not heard from the Martins since she had last visited them and tried to take Samuel from them. She no longer received the annual Christmas letter and picture.

She was deep in thought and old memories when a woman's voice brought her back to reality. "Good morning, Mrs. Howe, and welcome to our school. I'm Miss Rice," she chirped, "and I teach the 1st and 2nd grade right next to you." Anna jumped up from her chair behind her desk and went to the doorway to acknowledge the greeting.

"I'm sorry, I guess I was daydreaming," apologized Anna. "It's so nice to meet you." Just then her first two students arrived and she introduced herself to them. By the time the bell rang, all the children were present and she began to take roll call, attempting to put a face to every name.

Her first day went by quickly. At suppertime that evening, she was feeling exhausted and a little bit discouraged. Tomas and Bergit both noticed this and commented on it. "Maybe you were just trying too hard today to make everything perfect," suggested Bergit. "Just relax and things will work out. The children are probably just testing you at this point," she added.

Anna took their advice and by the end of the week things were going much smoother. The children seemed to like her and what was more important, she genuinely liked the children. She had only two boys who occasionally gave her some trouble. Here in a city school she had a principal to whom she could send misbehaving pupils. Mr. Stolle was a firm disciplinarian but he was always fair. The kind of administrator that Lorrie would have been, Anna thought with sadness. To think of Lorrie sometimes was like a stab in the heart. Would it ever get better? Would she one day be able to think of him without feeling this real, physical pain?

With the coming of spring, Hannah was getting excited about her graduation from high school. She had made plans to attend the teachers' college here in town. It had not been difficult to convince her father that she should go on to school and become a teacher. In fact, both he and Bergit were delighted.

Anna could not believe how fast the past four months had gone. Mr. Stolle commended her on a job well done. She asked him if there would be any openings in the school next fall for her and he said not that he knew of just yet but they would certainly keep her in mind should anything arise.

Graduation Day was a beautiful Saturday afternoon. The town hall was all decorated with fragrant lilac bouquets in big, white wicker baskets. Bergit had made a dress for Hannah, a pale yellow organdy and she looked stunning in it. Hannah had finished second in her class of seventeen graduates. They all sat in a row along the width of the stage. The boys looked uncomfortable in their new suits and ties.

Hannah rose to give the salutatorian speech and Anna felt a lump in her throat as she listened to her niece give an eloquent but short speech. My, this makes me feel rather old, Anna thought to herself, to think I have a niece this age already and here I am, not even married yet.

After the ceremony, Tomas took his whole family up to the drug store where they celebrated with ice cream sundaes. Back home they all gathered in the parlor. A few neighbors and friends stopped by to congratulate Hannah and wish her the best in the future. Arne brought his new girlfriend over to meet the family. Her name was Sophia and she worked at the mill where Arne worked.

Summer arrived and Anna was planning to travel down to Andrew and Alice's but one evening Mr. Larson from the department store paid a call. He asked her if she would like to come back to work in the store. "One of my clerks ran off and got married," he told her, "so if you are looking for a job, we would love to have you back."

She said that she would think it over and let him know the next day. "You know, Mr. Larson, that if I'm offered a position at the school again, I will take that for sure."

"Yes, I understand that, but we will just take a chance on you staying for awhile. We'd like to have you back for however long it may be. You were so well liked by the other clerks and also by the customers. Until tomorrow then," he tipped his hat and left.

That night, Anna tossed and turned, trying to decide if she should take the job. She had wanted to go and see Andrew and his family but then on the other hand she knew that the extra income would be nice. She had been thinking lately that it would be nice to have a place of her own in which to live. She had not mentioned this to Tomas yet but she was getting rather tired of always living with another family. She prayed about it once more and then fell asleep.

In the morning, she awoke and she knew right away what she was going to do. She would take the job at the store and save her money and maybe try to find herself a little place to live. At breakfast she told Tomas and Bergit of her decision. Tomas almost hit the ceiling when she mentioned finding another place to live. "No sister of mine has to go out and find a roof over her head as long as I am able to provide one for her!" he exclaimed. "You can stay here for as long as you need to. It wouldn't look right for a young, unmarried woman to be living alone, especially when she has a brother right here." And that was final! Anna didn't bring up the subject again. But she did begin work at the store the next day, all the same.

A couple of times during the summer, Tomas and Bergit tried to play matchmaker. On two different occasions, an eligible bachelor was invited over for Sunday dinner. It was quite obvious to Anna what was going on and it probably was to the gentleman, also. She was not in the least bit interested in either one of them. One of the gentlemen seemed to take an interest in her, however, and he asked if he could accompany her to a social the next week. Anna declined, giving some feeble excuse and he never tried again.

That was the end of the matchmaking attempts as Tomas and Bergit could see that it was doing no good to try and find someone for Anna. "She will have to do it on her own," Tomas said in exasperation.

The war continued on in Europe but the news seemed to favor the Allies by the end of the summer. One day in early August, a letter came from Alice. She told them the sad news that Peder Jorgenson, their neighbor and the one who had been sweet on Anna, had been killed in July in France during the Battle of the Marne.

As Anna read this, she had to sit down and she reread it again. She couldn't believe it. Poor, dear, shy Peder, she said over and over again. She went out on the porch, letter in hand, and sat and thought about Peder and about all the young, innocent boys who were killed in a far-off land. She felt very sad. It was at times like this that she always thought about her father and how they would discuss things. She let the tears flow, tears for Peder, for her mother, and finally for Lorrie. Would he have had to go to war, too, if he had been still alive? she wondered.

Just then Hannah came home and ran up the steps. She looked at Anna and then at the letter in her hand and asked, "Have you had bad news, Anna?"

"Well, yes, Hannah. A young man who was your Uncle Andrew's neighbor was killed over in France a couple months ago."

"Did you know him very well?" asked Hannah.

"I guess you could say that I knew him quite well. About as well as anyone knew him. He was very quiet and shy. He came over to Andrew's quite often when I was there. He was trying to court me, but I had to discourage him, as I didn't feel anything special towards him. But whenever I thought of him, after that, I felt sad. I guess it's because he always looked so forlorn and lonely."

Anna sighed and then, to change the subject, she asked her niece, "How were things at the drug store today?" The two of them spent every evening discussing their jobs uptown.

"Things were very slow most of the day," said Hannah. "I just hope I will get to keep my job this fall on Saturdays."

Mr. Stolle and his wife were in the store one day and Anna took him aside and asked if there was any chance of an opening for her at the school.

"Not right now, Mrs. Howe, but you know that I will keep you in mind if there is."

It wasn't more than two weeks later that Mr. Stolle contacted Anna to tell her that Miss Erickson, the teacher that she had filled in for, had just found out that she needed surgery. She had resigned her job at the school just this morning, so if Anna still wanted it, the job was hers.

Her family was excited for her. "And it won't be just for a few weeks, it's a permanent position!" Anna exclaimed happily. She had finally made it, she thought. This is what I've wanted to do for so long, teach in a city school in America!

With the coming of September, Hannah started her classes at the teacher's college and Anna went back to her classroom at the school. The 3rd grade class this year was so large that they were put in a separate room and Anna had this class so all of the pupils were new to her. There were 18 of them. A perfect size for a class, she thought.

November 11, 1918, was a day to remember. The war ended in Europe and an armistice was signed. It was all over the papers the next day. People were relieved to have it over with and could now go on with their lives with more certainty.

On Thanksgiving Day that year, there was much to be thankful for. As Tomas led the table prayer that day, he thanked God that their country was at peace and that their family was all safe and together around his table. Arne had invited Sophia to join them and, after dinner, they made the announcement that they planned to get married! The wedding would be in the spring.

That afternoon, Sophia told the family about herself. She lived with her grandmother as her mother and sister had died of TB when she was only 10 years old. Her father had become a drunkard so her grandmother took her in and raised her. I guess this explains why Sophia always has such a sad and melancholy look about her, Anna thought to herself. She looks happy today, though!

At Christmas time, they heard from Papa but he made no mention of coming to America. They heard from Sigrid, too. She said that Annie was working in a nice store downtown and that Arthur would be graduating in the spring and wanted to be a building contractor. He would work for his father in the summer and go to school in the fall. How these young people are growing up, Anna thought!

Arne and Sophia's wedding took place the week after Easter on a fine April day. Bergit had helped Sophia make a simple but beautiful wedding dress of white voile. She carried a small bouquet of fragrant apple blossoms. She looked lovely, as all brides do on their wedding day. It was a simple and small wedding, held in the church that the Olson family attended.

Sophia's mother had married Charley Minsk, against her parent's wishes. He was Catholic and so Sophia had been baptized in the Catholic church. When Sophia's mother and little sister had died, her grandmother had turned against God, blaming Him for taking her daughter and granddaughter. Then her husband died, too, and she was left alone to take in and raise the young Sophia. She should have been taking the girl to church but she refused to set foot in the church again. She did, however, send Sophia to the Lutheran Sunday School. She did come to the church for the wedding but sat towards the back. She cried into her handkerchief the whole time.

The bride's father managed to stay sober long enough to come, too, but Sophia did not have him escort her down the aisle. She walked it alone, much as she had done her whole young life. Arne looked at her with so much love and tenderness as she met him at the altar, that Anna knew the two of them would be all right.

Her mind wandered back to her own wedding and thought of how Lorrie had looked at her the same way. She had felt very loved and cherished. But then that didn't last. She prayed that God would grant Arne and Sophia a long and happy life together. One that would not be cut short by death or tragedy.

As the couple were pronounced man and wife, Anna wondered if she would ever be a wife to someone again. It seemed unlikely. She still felt a coldness inside of her where those special feelings of love and desire should be. I guess I will just have to settle for a life alone, with my students and my nieces and nephews as my children. She felt tears beginning to form at the corners of her eyes and she wiped at them with a clean, fresh handkerchief.

CHAPTER 15

Anna was hurrying home from the library early one evening as it was beginning to rain. She was thinking how soaked she would be by the time she walked the remaining ten or so blocks. Just then a motorcar stopped on the street and a man jumped out and shouted, "Mrs. Howe, allow me to give you a ride or you will be drenched."

After a few moments, Anna recognized the man as Mr. Nielson from the lumber yard. "That would be wonderful, Mr. Nielson," she said, as he helped her into the passenger side of the car and he ran around to the driver's side and hopped in.

The side curtains were down so it was rather dark in the car. She had just recently met Mr. Nielson when he and his crew had brought over a load of lumber to her brother's house.

"I left home without my umbrella and was just thinking that I would be paying dearly for that mistake," remarked Anna as they pulled away from the curb.

 "How is your brother's building project coming along?" Mr. Nielson asked.

"Actually he hasn't gotten very far on it but he had planned to have his men help him tomorrow," Anna answered.

"He's a good carpenter, your brother is. He has built many of the newer houses in this town. I've sold him alot of lumber over the years."

They stopped in front of her brother's house and Mr. Nielson said, "Here, use my umbrella to get to the house. It's coming down harder now." She started to protest but he said, "Go ahead and take it. I have two more at home."

He opened the door for her and helped her open the umbrella. She thanked him and made a dash for the house. She burst through the front door and startled young Teddy who was sitting reading a book. Bergit came rushing from the kitchen, wiping her hands on a towel, to see what the noise was all about.

"Oh, it's you, Anna. I was worried about you walking home in this rain. I see you remembered to take your umbrella."

"Actually, no I didn't. This is Mr. Nielson's. He saw me walking along and offered me a ride in his motorcar," answered Anna, shaking the umbrella over the rug before putting it in the stand. Shaking her skirts she said, "I think my dress fared pretty well but my shoes were not so lucky. I should have worn my old ones but I never thought it would rain. It was such a nice evening when I left."

"Why don't you change your clothes and come into the kitchen for a cup of coffee?" suggested Bergit. "Teddy, go and see if your father is ready to come in and he can join us. He went out to try and cover the lumber so it wouldn't be so wet for tomorrow. Some of his men are coming to help in the morning. We'll have extra mouths to feed all day."

Several evenings later at the dinner table, Tomas mentioned to Anna once again that maybe it was time for her to start thinking of remarrying.

"I don't know if I'll ever be of a mind to do that," said Anna. "I don't know if I could ever feel about any man like I felt about Lorrie."

"Well, I know someone who is interested in calling on you," Tomas offered.

When Anna didn't say anything, Bergit asked, "And who is that, may I ask?"

"Jake Anderson. One of the new men who works for me. In fact, he was here on Saturday helping. Do you remember which one he was?"

Indeed I do, thought Anna. He kept looking at me in a way that I didn't care for. "I wouldn't be interested in him at all, Tomas," she said.

"He was rather nice looking," offered Bergit, "and polite enough."

"Don't encourage him, Tomas; I'm not going to allow him to call on me and that's that!" said Anna emphatically.

"He'll be here again this coming Saturday," Tomas said teasingly, " so you can take another look at him."

I will certainly try to be gone much of that day, thought Anna.

Sure enough, come next Saturday Anna had her day planned and it did not include serving Jake Anderson lunches so he could look her up and down again! She apologized to Bergit for not being there to help her but she had helped her bake some cake and pies the night before.

Anna's first order of business was to go down to the lumber yard and return Mr. Nielson's umbrella. She found him behind the counter engrossed in filling some order. When he looked up, he was surprised and pleased to see her.

"Well, Mrs. Howe, what brings you in here so early in the day?"

"I meant to return your umbrella sooner but my Saturdays seem to slip by too fast," she replied.

"That was nice of you but not necessary. It hasn't even rained since that night, has it?" He was trying to think of something more to say to keep her in the store awhile longer. His eyes fell upon a poster laying on the counter.

"Mrs. Howe," he said as she was turning to leave, "are you and your family planning to attend the big May Day dance next week?"

"Perhaps we will. We've talked about it some."

"Would you do me the honor of allowing me to come by and escorting you myself?" he asked nervously.

Anna was rather stunned but tried to remain unflustered. "Well, I'll think about it, Mr. Nielson, and let you know. Good day, then." With that she left the store and headed for the millinery shop.

When she returned home later that day she almost felt guilty when she saw that Bergit was still in the kitchen cleaning up after having given the men their afternoon lunch.

"I'm sorry, Bergit, that I left you with all the work today but I didn't want to have that Jake Anderson staring at me," Anna said.

"That's all right, Anna. I understand, and anyway Sarah and Teddy washed all the dinner dishes for me so that helped alot. Did you see how far the men got on the shed?" Bergit asked.

"No," answered Anna, "I'll take a look at it this evening. Do you have to feed them supper, too?"

"No. I suggested to Tomas that he let them go early so I think he was going to do that. What did you do all day, Anna?"

"Well, this morning I went to the millinery shop and ordered a new hat to go with the new gray dress I bought a few weeks ago. I think it will be very pretty. I can't wait to see it finished," Anna said excitedly.

Did you return Mr. Nielson's umbrella?" Bergit asked.

"Yes," answered Anna, hurrying on quickly, "and then I went to the library for a couple hours until that closed at noon. Then I went over to the school and worked in my classroom for awhile. On the way home, I stopped by old Mrs. Juleson's and visited with her for a short while, and of course she insisted on a cup of coffee."

"Is that all you've eaten all day?" asked Bergit.

"No, I brought a couple biscuits along and ate them in my school room."

Later that evening when Tomas joined the family in the parlor, he said to his sister, "Well, Anna, you missed out on seeing Jake today. I know that he wanted to know where you were but he didn't want to come right out and ask. He did ask, though, if we were all going to the big dance next Saturday night."

"And what did you say, Papa?" asked Sarah.

"I said that we sure were!"

Anna didn't say anything but a plan was formulating in her mind.

The next morning the whole family walked to church. It was a beautiful April morning. After the worship service, Anna saw Mr. Nielson in the crowd. He spotted her and came over to the Olson family.

Anna took him aside and said, "Mr. Nielson, about your invitation to the dance next Saturday-- I've decided to accept."

Mr. Nielson looked so pleased at this and said that he would be over to pick her up at half past eight. And so the matter was decided. Anna felt relieved whenever she thought about it the rest of the week because now she wouldn't have to worry about Jake Anderson! If he saw that she had an escort, he would leave her alone and be discouraged from thinking about her in the future.

The night before the dance, Bergit, Anna and Sarah helped each other decide what each one should wear for the big event. This would be Sarah's first dance and she was very excited. A boy that she liked would be there so she wanted to look especially pretty and grown up.

Anna was wondering if she should wear her new gray dress but Bergit and Sarah both thought it looked too severe and " teacherish".

"Why don't you wear this blue one," suggested Bergit. "It looks more suitable for a dance."

"I haven't been to a dance in so long that I don't know what people even wear anymore!" exclaimed Anna. "I just hope I can remember how to dance."

"Did you go to many dances when you were young, Aunt Anna?" asked Sarah.

For a fleeting moment, Anna had a flashback from her first dance in America, back in New York. She shuddered and quickly dismissed the memory.

"Lorrie loved to dance so we went every chance we got," she finally answered her niece. "He was good, too, and he taught me a new dance or two."

Tomas had been teaching Sarah how to dance several evenings during the past week. It was fun to watch father and daughter move around the room. Sarah was a tall, pretty girl, dark like her father and slim like her mother. She will have many beaus after Saturday night, thought Anna.

May Day dawned bright and beautiful. Anna actually felt a trickle of excitement as she thought of going dancing that evening. Maybe, she thought, my soul is coming alive again after a long dormant spell. Maybe the time has come to forget the past and look to the future. Maybe.

At exactly half past eight that evening, Anna looked out her upstairs window to see Mr. Nielson drive up in front of the house. She hurried to grab her shawl and hand bag. Thomas had let Mr. Nielson in and they were already busy discussing the construction business. Mr. Nielson stopped in mid sentence when he saw Anna come down the stairs. "My dear Mrs. Howe," he said, " are you ready to dance your feet off, then?"

"Well," Anna answered light heartedly, "I haven't danced in quite a long time, you know."

Bergit said, "You two run along then and we'll see you there. We're waiting for Sarah."

Mr. Nielson helped Anna into the motorcar and they started off for the dance hall. Nearing the building, Anna could see that many people had already come. There were a number of motorcars and many horse and buggies and wagons. You could see many of the townspeople walking up from all directions. They heard the music a block away where they had to park.

Upon entering the hall, Anna was impressed with how pretty it looked. There were baskets of lilacs everywhere and colored streamers were hanging from the ceiling. The best musicians in the county were hired for this event, Mr. Nielson told her. They found a place on one of the many benches which had been pushed up against the walls. They watched the dancers for awhile and looked to see who was all there.

When the band struck up a waltz, Mr. Nielson asked her if she would like to dance this one. At first she had somewhat of a hard time following his lead but she soon got the hang of it. He actually was quite good and she found that she really enjoyed whirling around and around the floor. After dancing the whole set they sat down, laughing and panting.

"This is certainly good exercise," Mr. Nielson said, "but I can tell I'm really out of shape!"

"Oh, me too," said Anna, trying to get her breath.

"After I rest a bit, I'll go and get us each a glass of punch," said Mr. Nielson.

"Ah, that would taste wonderful!" Anna said. "Oh, look, there's my nephew, Arne and his wife, Sophia. Doesn't she look pretty tonight!"

As Mr. Nielson left to get the punch, Anna also saw Tomas and Bergit come in. Where was Sarah? she wondered. Then she saw her enter with several girls her age and a few boys trailing behind.

Then to her horror, she saw Jake Anderson come in and look the place over like he was seeking someone. I suppose he saw Tomas and Bergit here and is looking for me. Oh, dear, she thought. Maybe he won't see me in this large crowd. She turned to make small talk with the lady sitting next to her. Then the lady's husband whisked her away to dance and the places next to her were empty. I wish Mr. Nielson would hurry back, she was thinking just as she saw Jake walking over to her. Oh, no, now he'll think I'm sitting here all alone like a wallflower!

"Good evening, Mrs. Howe," Jake said. "Are you enjoying the dance?"

"Yes, very much, Mr. Anderson," Anna answered.

As he leaned closer to her, she could smell liquor on his breath and she backed away from him. Thankfully Mr. Nielson appeared just then with two punch glasses.

"Here you are, then," he said as he handed her one of the glasses.

Jake had been about to ask Anna to dance but then he must have realized that Mr. Nielson was her escort for the evening so he excused himself and skulked away. He looked angry as he left the hall. He's probably going to join his cronies out back and have another drink, Anna thought to herself.

"I'm so glad you came back just then," Anna told Mr. Nielson.

"Was that fellow bothering you?" Mr. Nielson didn't know the man but for some reason, he didn't like the looks of him. "Did you know him?"

"He's one of the new men who works for Tomas," Anna answered. "He's been at the house a couple of Saturdays helping with the shed." Changing the subject, she said, "This is certainly good punch and really hits the spot."

The band struck up a polka and Mr. Nielson suggested they dance again.

"Well, I have only tried the polka once or twice before," said Anna, "but if you're willing, then so am I."

Halfway through the dance, Mr. Nielson said, "You're doing very well. You're a fast learner."

Tomas and Bergit came up to them on the floor between dances and Tomas suggested that they switch partners.

When Tomas had led Anna to the other side of the hall, he said, "I saw Jake come over and talk to you. I was ready to come to your rescue when I saw Mr. Nielson return."

"Yes, I think he was going to ask me to dance and I didn't want to. I smelled liquor on his breath, which doesn't surprise me."

" I understand he likes his booze."

"I can't imagine why you thought I would be interested in him, Tomas," she scolded.

"Well, I guess I was wrong. I know him better now and I won't encourage him as far as you are concerned. He is a good worker, though."

"Are you and Bergit having a good time?" asked Anna.

"Oh, yes," Tomas answered. "We love to dance. And you? Are you having a good time?"

"Why yes, of course. Mr. Nielson is a better dancer than I expected and it's fun to be here and see everyone having fun."

That dance ended and as they were waiting for the band to strike up the next tune, Anna noticed Jake coming in the door of the hall and heading in their direction.

"Oh, no, Tomas, here comes Jake heading our way."

Jake tapped Tomas on the shoulder and said, "May I cut in, Mr. Olson, and have a dance with your beautiful sister?"

Tomas grabbed Anna just as the music started again and said, "I'm afraid not, Jake, we're not through dancing yet." They whirled away to the farthest corner of the hall.

"Whew, that was close!" Anna exclaimed. "I hope that discouraged him." She saw Jake leave the hall again, probably for yet another swig from the bottle!

They danced two more dances and then met up with Mr. Nielson and

Bergit and they all went to sit down together along the wall.

As they watched, they saw Sarah dance by with a young boy slightly shorter than her. She looked their way and rolled her eyes upward. Anna and Bergit laughed at this because they knew just what she meant by that gesture. She had told them the night before that she supposed that the only boys she would get to dance with were either younger or shorter. Her mother told her to be patient and make the best of it. The day would come soon enough when a handsome young man would sweep her off her feet.

"I hope that day doesn't come too soon," Bergit said to Anna. "Sarah is too pretty for her own good and so impatient to grow up!"

Arne and Sophia came over to join their little group. Anna introduced them to Mr. Nielson. Arne said, "Aunt Anna, I must have this next dance!"

Arne's lead wasn't very easy to follow but Anna enjoyed dancing with him all the same. He was so dear to her. He was such a fine young man and so much fun, always kidding around with her.

"So, Anna, I see you have a fellow now! Isn't he kind of old for you?" he teased.

"He's not my fellow, Arne," she replied. "He's just a new friend who happens to be escorting me to the dance this evening."

"Well, you could have fooled me! Anyway it's about time you found someone and got hitched again, don't you think?" he asked.

"I'm not thinking along those lines yet, Arne. It's not as easy as you think. You are so young yet and haven't experienced the things that I have."

"You're still young, Anna. You can't be much more than thirty, are you?"

"I'm thirty-two, to be exact," she answered.

"The man I work for is about thirty, I think, and he is still a bachelor. Maybe I should steer him your way," Arne volunteered.

Anna said laughingly, "Why is everyone trying to match me up with someone all of a sudden? Is this a family conspiracy?"

Before Arne could answer, Anna said, "Oh, no! Here comes that Jake Anderson that your father was trying to match me up with and I know he's going to ask me to dance again and I absolutely will not dance with him."

Jake tapped Arne on the shoulder and asked if he could cut in. "Leave us alone, mister, this lady is all mine."

At that Jake looked confused. He didn't know who Arne was and was wondering who Anna really did come with this evening. She sure seems popular, he was thinking. He walked over to a group of girls who were sitting by the wall and asked one of them to dance. She accepted, and Anna thought, "Poor girl!"

When the set was over, Arne returned Anna to the rest of the family. He and Sophia went off to get punch and Mr. Nielson suggested that he and Anna go and get some, too. He wasn't going to take the chance of leaving Anna alone again. Tomas and Bergit followed them.

While they were standing and drinking their punch, Tomas saw Jake over talking to Sarah. "By thunder," he exploded, "that man better not be asking my daughter to dance."

They all looked in that direction and saw what Tomas had seen. It looked like Sarah was trying to refuse but Jake seemed to be insisting. Tomas handed his glass to Bergit and hurried over to where Sarah was sitting. Sarah seemed to be relieved when she saw her father standing there. She looked at him in silent appeal.

"Good evening, Jake," Tomas said, as civil as possible. "I came over to ask my daughter to dance." Turning to Sarah, he bowed and asked, "May I have this dance, young lady?

Relieved, Sarah jumped right up and almost fell into her father's arms. They danced away and Tomas looked back and saw that Jake was looking awfully mad. He asked one of the other girls and she refused, too. Finally he stalked out of the hall again.

"Thank goodness you came, Father. I told him 'no' but he kept on insisting. I didn't know what I was going to do. I think he was drunk, too. He sure smelled!"

"I'm glad I saw what was happening over there in time. He's been bothering Anna, too."

The two finished out the set and returned to the others. The last dance was announced so everyone went out on the floor for one last whirl.

As Anna and Mr. Nielson were dancing the last dance, he asked her if it would be all right if he called her Anna. It would sound so much less formal, he said. "And please, just call me Hans," he added.

Visiting with several other folks along the way, they made their way out the door. On the way to Hans' car, Anna spotted Jake lurking in the alley with a bottle in his hand. Raising the bottle, he called out, "Good night, Mrs. Howe, sorry we didn't get to dance. Perhaps next time or do you think you're too good for me?" She grasped Hans' arm a little tighter and they quickened their steps.

"Oh, I hope I never see that man again," Anna said. "I wish Tomas would get rid of him but he says he is a good worker."

Hans felt very protective of Anna and said, "I wish this incident had never happened. I hope it hasn't spoiled your evening altogether."

"Oh, no, Mr. Nielson....er... I mean Hans," she answered. "I had a lovely time. Perhaps I'll never see him again and that will be the end of that!"

"Well, I hope I can see you again, Anna. Maybe we could do this again sometime soon."

They reached the Olson house and Hans helped Anna out of the car. He escorted her to the front door. She thanked him again for the evening and let herself in. She could see Tomas and his family pulling up to the side of the house. Teddy, who stayed home alone, looked up as she entered. It looked like he had been sleeping in the chair.

"Is the dance already over?" he asked. "Where's Mama and Papa?"

"They're coming in the back door now," Anna answered. "We saw Arne and Sophia there."

"Yes I know. They stopped by here on their way."

"Well, Teddy, how did you get along by yourself then?" asked his mother.

"Just fine," he answered. " I guess I fell asleep about an hour ago."

"Well, you go on up to bed now," Bergit said. "There's church tomorrow, you know."

"That sounds like a good idea for all of us," Tomas said.

After Anna had undressed, she put on her dressing gown and went quietly into Sarah's room.

"Well, Sarah, how did you like your first dance? Did you have a good time?"

"I did until that Mr.Anderson came along," she answered vehemently. "Why did he pick on me anyway?"

"He probably did it because he knew it would upset this whole family and he wanted to spite me, especially because I always avoided dancing with him," Anna explained to her niece. "How about that boy you were interested in, did he ask you to dance?"

"No, he didn't even know I was there, I don't think! He only had eyes for Mary Callahan! I hate her!"

"Mary Callahan," said Anna "is a very nice girl and you musn't hate anyone, Sarah. But she is quite a bit older than you. Just how old is this fellow you are interested in anyway?"

"He's about eighteen, I think," Sarah answered softly.

"Well, I think that is much too old for you at this time in your life, dear Sarah. You better stick to the boys in your own grade."

"But they seem so young and immature to me!"

"I can understand that, dear, but you must be careful whom you associate with. Some bad choices can lead you into trouble. Believe me, I know!"

"What do you mean by that, Aunt Anna?" Sarah asked.

"Well, I can't go into that now but just take my word for it. Don't be so impatient to grow up. That time will come soon enough." Anna turned to leave the room. "I'll let you get to sleep now."

"Good night, Aunt Anna. Oh, I forgot to ask you if you had a good time with Mr. Nielson? Do you like him?"

"We had a good time and he's a very nice man. Good night, Sarah."

Anna returned to her room and slipped into bed. She lay awake for quite awhile, thinking about Lorrie and the baby she lost and also of the little baby boy she gave up. She wept softly into her pillow, although the tears didn't come quite so often anymore.   What is ahead for me, Lord? she thought. I am trusting in you.

The next morning Anna felt strangely refreshed, as if the tears of the night before had somehow cleansed the last dark places in her soul. She dressed for church and went down to join the family.

Only Tomas and Bergit were in the kitchen as yet. She sat down to coffee and eggs and bacon. She found she was very hungry.

"Did you work up an appetite with all that exercise last night, Anna?" asked Tomas.

"I guess I did. I'm not used to it," she answered.

Bergit was busy getting a roast in the oven for their dinner. "Did you enjoy going with Mr. Nielson, then, Anna?" she asked. "Too bad that Jake Anderson had to come around and spoil things."

"Mr. Nielson and I had a good time together and I'm going to try and forget all about that Jake!" she exclaimed. "I hope he doesn't come around the house here anymore, though, Tomas."

"I guess I won't have him help on this project again," Tomas said. "Anyway, we're soon done with it."

Teddy joined them and then Sarah came down a bit later. Hannah had spent the weekend with a friend so she wasn't home. There was much talk about the previous night and then they all got ready to go to church.

Anna didn't see Hans there and she found to her surprise that she was a bit disappointed. The family returned home and sat down to a nice roast beef dinner. In the afternoon, Arne and Sophia came over. Arne, of course, had to tease Anna about Mr. Nielson.

They also talked some about Jake and it suddenly struck Anna why it was that Jake repulsed her so. It was because he looked a little like that Joseph somebody from back in New York. The one she never wanted to see or think of again. She felt a cold sweat come over her. She rose and left the room quickly. She stepped out on the back porch and sat down on the top step.

Bergit followed her out and sat down beside her. She could tell that Anna was upset about something. "What's wrong, Anna?" she asked. "Don't you like having Arne tease you about Mr. Nielson?"

"That's not it, Bergit. I don't know what came over me. I'll be all right in a minute."

Bergit didn't seem convinced. "You're not getting sick, are you?"

"No, no, I'll be fine. I think I'll take a little walk by myself for awhile. I'll be back shortly."

Bergit let her go without further comment. Anna turned and walked down the street leading to the church. She didn't know exactly why, but she turned and entered the now empty building. She walked halfway up the aisle and sat down in a pew. The afternoon sun was streaming in the side window. She turned to her Lord in prayer. She had struggled for all these years with the terrible thing that was done to her and had not really come to terms with it. Perhaps it was because there was no one with whom she felt she could discuss it with. Then there was also the guilt of giving up her son and her longing to have him back.

As always, she prayed for forgiveness and guidance. Maybe, she thought, I need to accept the fact that God has indeed forgiven me and go on with my life. After a short time she left the church. It felt like a big weight had been lifted from her. She returned to the house and could smell coffee from the kitchen. They were all sitting around the table eating chocolate cake. Bergit looked up as Anna entered and could see that Anna looked better than when she left. In fact, there was something different about her that Bergit couldn't put a finger on. I'll have to talk with her later, she thought.

Anna enjoyed the cake and the closeness of the family sitting together laughing and teasing each other. This is what I'm missing, thought Anna. I want a second chance to have a family of my very own.

CHAPTER 16

That summer, Hans came to the house to see Anna occasionally, usually on Sunday afternoons. They would often take walks or a drive in the country. One hot, June Sunday afternoon they drove out to a lake east of town a few miles. Tomas and Bergit came along and so did Teddy. They went in Hans' car. They found a dock to sit on and they all took off their shoes and socks and dangled their feet in the water. This went a long ways to cooling them off. There were many townspeople at the lake that day, too; some swimming in the section of the lake considered safe for wading. Teddy soon got bored sitting with the grownups on the dock. He wanted to go swimming so Tomas and Bergit walked with him over to the other side where he put on his bathing suit and they watched him from the edge of the lake.

Anna and Hans continued sitting on the dock, too hot to think of moving. Hans was unusually quiet since they arrived at the lake. "You're so quiet today, Hans, is it too hot even to talk?" she asked jokingly. He gave her a little smile but continued to look out across the lake for a long moment. Then he said, "I'm sorry that I haven't been very good company this last hour or so."

Before he could go on, Anna interrupted him to say, "That's all right, one doesn't have to be talkative and entertaining all the time. Perhaps you're tired after that big dinner of Bergit's. We could go up on the grass there under that big tree and sit down. You can lean against the tree," she added laughingly.

"Yes, I guess we could do that. Here, let me help you up," he said after getting himself to a standing position. They carried their shoes and socks and climbed up to the grassy knoll overlooking the water's edge. Anna indicated that Hans should sit by the tree and he laughed and said, "Oh, I'm not really that tired." But he did sit there anyway and as he gazed back out over the water, he said to Anna, " You know, I haven't been out to this perfect spot for over fourteen years now."

Something about the way he said this made her look intently at him, waiting for more. He didn't say anything for awhile but she continued to look at him. He seemed to want to say more but didn't quite know how to start. She never liked uncomfortable moments so she finally said, "Why has it been that many years, Hans, and why have you been keeping track?"

Hans took a deep breath and said, "I'll tell you the whole story, Anna. Perhaps you have already heard that I was once engaged to someone. Her name was Cora and she was a lovely, young woman. We were very much in love and planned to get married." He paused here for awhile and then continued.

"One afternoon we were out to the lake here, to this very same spot, as a matter of fact. We had a very pleasant afternoon, and then I brought her home. That night, she got very sick and the doctor was called. He said that it was appendicitis and she had to be rushed to the hospital. The next day they removed her appendix and we thought everything was going all right but at the end of the week, she realized that she could not move her legs. We were all very upset, as we figured that the surgeon had done some damage to her spine when he was operating on her. She spent several more weeks in the hospital and then she was sent home in a wheelchair. When I went out to see her at their house, her father came out to meet me and he told me that I should forget about marrying Cora. 'You don't want to marry a cripple' he said to me. 'She can't marry anyone now so you might as well forget about her' he added. He also told me that she didn't want to see me and that I should never come out there again."

"Oh, Hans," Anna said, very moved by what he had told her, "I am so sorry. What did you do then?"

"Well, I was devastated, that's for sure. I tried to go back and see her several times after that. I'd go when I knew her father was gone, but her mother would stop me at the door and tell me to just go away. I begged her to let me see Cora, just to talk to her myself, but she wouldn't let me in. She said that Cora didn't want me to see her like she was, in a wheelchair with useless, lifeless legs." As he said this, he looked very sad and tears were forming in his eyes.

"I'm sorry, Anna, I shouldn't be burdening you with this. I haven't talked about it in so long to anybody." He wiped his eyes and was silent for sometime.

"Is that why you never came out to this spot again?" asked Anna.

"Yes, I couldn't bear to think of that last wonderful day that we had together. We sat here and talked about our future and about the house we would someday build. How our lives changed all of a sudden. I felt bad for myself, to be sure, but I felt especially bad for poor Cora. And to make matters worse, I couldn't even talk to her about it."

"Haven't you spoken with her at all this whole time?" Anna asked.

"Well, yes, I finally was able to get past her father and I convinced Cora herself that we needed to talk about it. She was adamant, though, that we could not get married. She encouraged me to forget her and go on with my life. About a year later, she moved away with her parents."

"And you've never heard from her since?" asked Anna.

"Not from her directly, but I did hear from someone who knew them. Cora's father had been taking her to many different doctors. They finally found out the reason for her paralysis. It was polio! Not a slip of the doctor's knife." Hans started putting on his socks and shoes. "Shall we go for a walk?" he asked, getting up off the ground.

They walked back down to the dock and sat on the bench at the far end. Anna was too moved by this sad story to say anything. As Hans looked out over the lake, he continued.

"I tried writing to her but my letters came back unanswered." He paused for awhile again. "I'm ashamed to tell you that after that I took to the bottle for comfort and almost drank myself to death. My mother and my sister didn't know what they were going to do with me. After about two years of this, Mr. Simmons, the man who owned the lumber yard got hold of me and straightened me out. He gave me a job. I had been working for a local carpenter but I lost my job because of my drinking." With this, Hans hung his head in shame and sorrow.

Anna put her hand on his arm in a comforting gesture. "Oh my, Hans," she said, "you have had a tough time of it, haven't you? So you don't even know where she is or what happened to her?"

"Well, I only know that she's in St. Paul, still living with her parents and still in a wheelchair." He shook his head back and forth slowly. "What a terrible thing to have happened to such a wonderful girl as she was. We had such plans and dreams."

Anna sighed and said, "Yes, our dreams don't always come true and our plans are sometimes changed suddenly, aren't they?" She felt the tears coming close to the surface and so she stood up and walked a ways on the dock, toward the shore. Hans got up and joined her and the two of them walked in companionable silence along the shoreline.

"Hey there, you two!" they heard someone call. They turned to look and it was Tomas. He came closer to them and they could see that he was out of breath. "Bergit and Teddy are on the other side and I said I'd come back here and check to see if you were wanting to head for home yet."

Hans checked his pocket watch and said, "Yes, I suppose we should do that." The three of them started for the car. "What have you two been doing then?" asked Tomas.

There was an awkward silence but Anna finally answered, "We've been having a good, long talk." Hans didn't say anything and Tomas thought that that was strange for him to be silent. He was usually so jolly and always joking around. They drove to the other side of the lake and found Bergit and Teddy, ready and waiting.

Bergit looked a little sunburned and Teddy was tired out from his day in the water and the sun. "We should have packed a picnic and we could have had our supper out here," said Bergit.

"When we left the house we were all so stuffed from your wonderful, big roast beef dinner that we weren't even thinking of food!" said Anna.

"I'm still not even hungry," said Tomas. "I think it's the heat."

When they arrived back in town and pulled up in front of the Olson house, Bergit invited Hans to come in and she said she would fix a bite to eat. Hans excused himself and said that he was still too full and he thought he would just go on home.

When the family was in the house and they were just resting in the parlor, Bergit asked Anna, "Did you and Hans have a good time this afternoon?"

"Well, he told me all about his former fiancée and what happened to her. Did you know all that, Bergit?"

"I guess we did but that's so long ago now that I really can't remember just what happened."

Anna told them what Hans had told her and they were all silent for awhile, each with their own thoughts. The children came in and broke into their reverie and were asking what was for supper. Bergit got up and headed for the kitchen.

A few weeks later, Anna was planning to take the train down to visit Andrew and Alice. Hans heard this and he suggested that he drive her down there in his car.

"Oh, no," Anna said, "that would be way too far for you to go just to take me down there!"

"Well, I would like to do it, Anna," he said, "and then I will mix a little business with pleasure. I need to stop several places and check out their lumber yards and I also have some business in Owatonna."

Anna was still hesitant. "Do you think it would look proper for me to travel all the way down there alone with you, Hans?"

"We'll make it in one day," he answered her with a slight smile. "I'll do my business on the way back."

So it was decided that Hans would drive her down and they would leave early next Thursday morning. Bergit, who must have had second thoughts about Anna's reputation, suggested that Teddy go along with them. "He would enjoy going to the farm and seeing his cousins," she said. Anna thought this a good idea, too. Teddy was so excited that he could hardly sleep for two days.

That's why, on the morning that they were to leave, he was so hard to get up! Bergit filled them up with a good breakfast and sent a basket of food for them to eat on the way. It was still dark when they left Mankato but the sun came up about a half hour later. It was a beautiful sunrise. Even Teddy was impressed and then he settled down to have a nap. They stopped in the little town of Waseca and Hans had to put some gas in the car. Teddy and Anna got out to stretch their legs. About noon, they stopped along the road to have their dinner of sandwiches and doughnuts.

"We'll try and make it to Albert Lea by suppertime," said Hans. "There's a nice lake there where we could stop and eat."

The afternoon's drive became very long and it was rather hot and dusty. Teddy laid down in the backseat again and fell sound asleep. Hans looked over at Anna several times and finally he said. "Anna, you haven't told me very much about your life, except about how you came to this country and a little about some of the schools you have taught in."

He wants to know about my marriage and what happened, thought Anna. Well, he bared his soul to me, so I guess I can do the same to him. She told him about how she met Lorrie and how happy they were together; how they, too, dreamed and planned of a wonderful life together, working and traveling and raising a family. She told of the influenza epidemic which took her young husband's life and, along with it, her life and dreams, too. Now, just like Hans, she just had her memories of a person whom she loved so very much.

"We have much in common, you and I, Anna," Hans said when she had finished and was quiet for awhile. He reached over and squeezed her hand. "How are you coping with it? The grief and depression and all that?" he asked her. "Obviously you didn't take to the bottle like I so foolishly did!"

Anna thought about this for sometime. "My faith in the goodness of God is very strong and I guess that is what keeps me going. I look to him for my strength to get through trying times. 'I lift mine eyes unto the hills. From whence cometh my help? My help comes from the Lord.' That's what has gotten me through the bad times." She looked down at her hands in her lap and at her wedding ring. Her thoughts were soon far away and Hans did not disturb her.

Finally she turned to him and asked, "Do you trust in the Lord, Hans?"

"Yes, I do now," he said hesitantly. "My mother made sure that my 'spiritual house' was in order before she moved, with my sister and her husband. After I quit drinking and started trusting God again, I prayed daily for peace of mind."

"And did He answer your prayers?" asked Anna.

"Yes, I believe that He did," Hans answered thoughtfully. "I no longer dwell on it and when I do think of it now, I don't have so much pain. Except that day by the lake, when I was telling you about it. That day was rather hard for me. I haven't talked about it for many years. Nobody asks about it and it seems like nobody wants to talk about things that cause sorrow. Have you found that to be true, too?"

"Well, yes, I guess there are only a few people who want to talk about Lorrie with me. There's Lorrie's mother, but his father doesn't want to talk about him. He's having a very hard time coping with it. Bergit will talk about it sometimes but Tomas usually avoids the subject."

"I find it refreshing to be able to talk to you about such things. I suppose it's because you've gone through something similar," Hans said.

"My sister-in-law, Alice, the one I'm going down to see, is one that won't face things and talk about them. I think it would help her get over the death of her little girl if we could sit down and talk about the child. But she always cuts me short when I bring up little Berta's name. When she had her last miscarriage, she wouldn't talk about that either but I know she was just dying inside, all over again."

"People are funny, aren't they?" said Hans. "They can't talk about what's most in their thoughts, even with their loved ones. What are we afraid of?"

When he said the word "we" she turned and looked at him, knowing that it must have been hard for him to be so frank with her. Again she touched his hand and she said, "Hans, I'm glad that we can talk like this. Maybe we can help each other."

He didn't answer, but just continued looking down the road ahead. Teddy finally started to wake up and he sat up and wondered where they were now and how much farther it would be. Hans laughed and said, "Oh, we will soon be stopping for our supper, my boy. I suppose you're starving again!"

As Hans had said, they found a pretty lakeside stop by Albert Lea and pulled over. They got out and spread their picnic on a blanket on the ground. The lemonade had long ago become very warm but everything tasted so good anyway. They walked awhile to stretch their limbs before the last leg of their journey.

"When will we get there, Mr. Nielson?" asked Teddy.

"Oh, I figure about ten o'clock this evening." They had to buy some more gas and then left the good gravel road for a less-traveled dirt road which would take them the rest of the way. Teddy was not tired anymore and he kept them laughing with his tales and funny stories. Hans threw in a few of his own and before they knew it, they were heading down the familiar road, at least to Anna, which led to Andrew's farm.

It was almost ten o'clock and the sun had set just a short while ago and the moon was shining brightly so the outline of Andrew's farm buildings were visible from the end of the driveway. Lights were on all over the house! The whole family came out to meet them when they saw the headlights come up the road. Andrew and Alice hugged Anna warmly and she introduced them to Hans. Teddy was a little shy at first with his cousins whom he hardly ever saw. George, who was only a year younger, soon remedied that by taking Teddy to the barn with a lantern to show him the new baby kittens. Alfred stayed to hear what the grownups had to say.

Alice had coffee waiting for them and it had never tasted better! She also had some fresh cake and when the boys came in from outside, they devoured a couple pieces each with some milk. After awhile the children were sent upstairs to settle down for the night. The four adults sat around the kitchen table awhile longer, catching up with all the news of family and getting better acquainted with this Mr. Nielson. Bergit had written them that she hoped that something would come of this relationship between him and Anna!

The next morning Alice fixed a big breakfast and then Hans said that he had to be leaving if he wanted to make his stops along the way. He would spend the night in Owatonna at a friend's house and then go back to Mankato Sunday afternoon. He said goodbye to Andrew and his family. Anna walked him to his car. The young boys were standing around admiring it and wishing that their Pa could afford one like it.

"Thank you again, Hans, for driving us all the way down here. That was so nice of you." Anna told him, shaking his hand. "We'll take the train back in about two weeks. We'll see you then. Goodbye."

Back in the house, Alice couldn't wait to talk to Anna about Mr. Nielson.

"Mr. Nielson sure seems like a very nice man, Anna, don't you think?" asked Alice.

"Yes, he is very nice, and I know what you're thinking," she said laughingly, "but he's just a good friend of the family!"

"And isn't he a good friend of yours, too?" asked Alice mischievously, hoping that Anna would open up to her.

"Well, yes, I guess he is a good friend of mine, too," she answered, "There, now are you satisfied?" She and Alice had a good laugh over this and were still laughing when Andrew came in the house. He asked her almost the exact same questions and this set the two women to laughing all over again.

"I can see that I'm not going to get any wiser, talking to the two of you," he said in mock disgust, as he left the house and went back to work.

The next two weeks went fast and Teddy had the time of his life. He said that he didn't want to go home and begged Anna to let him stay longer and he could take the train back home alone later. Anna said, no, he had to come back with her.

The night before they were to leave, Anna and Alice took a long walk down the road. It was a beautiful evening. They walked arm in arm in comfortable silence. Anna broke the spell by asking, "Alice, it seems that you have come to grips with Berta's death, now. Is it getting easier for you?"

Alice let her arm fall to her side and she looked at Anna in surprise for daring to ask such a personal and hurtful question. When she didn't answer right away, Anna knew that maybe she shouldn't have been so blunt with Alice, but she also knew that these things needed to be talked about.

"Alice, my dear," Anna began, "I know this is very painful for you, but I think it would help if you would express your feelings with someone. Do you and Andrew ever talk about Berta?"

Alice swallowed hard and almost felt angry with her sister-in-law. "It's too hard to talk about it, Anna. I just keep it all inside of me. Maybe that isn't the right thing to do but that's how I was brought up. Everyone always kept their innermost feelings to themselves."

"That's not good for us to do that, Alice. Let's you and I talk about Berta right now. I loved her very much and I can still feel her pudgy little hands on my face and hear her tinkling laughter." She heard Alice sobbing next to her but she kept right on. She didn't mean to be cruel but she wanted Alice to start to open up. "And I remember how cute she looked in that new, blue dress you made for her the last time I was here. She was such a sweet-natured child, too."

Alice was crying much harder now. "Anna, this is very cruel of you. I can't talk about her; it hurts too much!" Anna took the distraught woman in her arms and let her cry like she probably had never cried before in front of anyone. There they stood in the middle of a country road, with dusk falling around them, holding on to one another! Alice cried for quite sometime, completely wetting the shoulder of Anna's dress with her tears.

"Berta was so soft to...to hold, and so kind....kind-hearted!" Alice began. "She would cry so when a...a kitten would d..d...die. I just miss her so much, even after all this...this time!" She was hiccupping and sobbing at the same time now and Anna had to strain to hear her words. Keep talking, Alice, Anna thought to herself!

"And when she got sick I felt so helpless because I couldn't do...do anything for her. That last night, she looked at me with her big, brown eyes and said that she loved me and then she fell asleep and never.....never woke up!" Alice broke out in fresh, new sobs at this and Anna held her tight again. I bet Andrew never does this for his wife, she thought angrily. I must have a talk with him before I leave.

The two women started walking again, back towards the farm, as it was growing dark. They talked of Berta some more and Alice finally started to calm down.

"Goodness, I can't go into the house like this! My eyes must be all red. The family will know that I've been crying." Alice fussed.

"Well, so what if they do know that you've been crying," said Anna, her voice rising. "You have a perfect right to cry now and then and you certainly have something to cry about. To lose a child is the most painful thing there is," Anna went on. "Tears help clean the windows of our souls." Andrew maybe needs to shed a few also, together with his wife, she thought to herself.

They neared the house and Anna indicated that the two of them sit on the porch stops for a little while. Alice was glad of this. Maybe she could regain her composure. Anna put her hand on the other woman's arm. "Alice, I'm sorry if this was difficult for you, but I only hope that I did the right thing by making you talk about Berta and shedding some tears. That's nothing to be ashamed about. Crying is meant to be a cleansing thing."

Alice turned to Anna with a slight smile on her lips and said, "Anna Olson Howe, how did you get to be so wise? I'm older than you and I should be giving you advice! Anyway, you have your own grief to handle, but you don't seem to need any help. How do you do it?" she asked.

"I talk about it and I pray about it alot. But I have my bad days, too, Alice. Make no mistake about that!" exclaimed Anna. Just then they saw Andrew coming toward the house. He was finally finished with his chores for the night.

"Well, what have we got here? Did you two have a nice walk on this beautiful evening?" he asked as he sat down beside his wife. He put his arm loosely around her shoulder and drew her close. He felt her shudder and he thought it was because it was getting chilly but when he looked at her, he could see that she was crying.

"My goodness, what is the matter, Alice dear?" he asked. She could not answer, but only shake her head.

"Andrew, we need to talk," said Anna. She rose and indicated that he should follow her. Alice got up and went into the house. They walked over to the bench in the yard and sat down. Anna told Andrew all about the good talk and the good cry that she and Alice had had and she told Andrew that he needed to talk to Alice often about Berta and anything else that's bothering her.

"Women need a shoulder to cry on and someone to listen to them once in awhile," Anna went on. "Alice isn't used to doing this so you need to show her your feelings as well and draw her out. The two of you need to talk about the loss of your little girl or it will eat away at you."

Andrew hung his head and tears were forming in his eyes. "I know that, but every time I would try to bring up little Berta, Alice would turn away or change the subject. I just thought it was too painful for her to discuss it."

"Yes, of course it's too painful to talk about but it's even more painful not to talk about things like that," said Anna. "Did you ever talk to her about her miscarriage after it happened? That was very traumatic for her, as well, but no one ever wants to say anything that will make the other person feel sad!" Anna got up and started walking back and forth in front of her brother. "Why are we people so afraid of our feelings, anyway?" she asked.

"I suppose that's the way we were brought up, but I can understand that it's not the right way to be," said Andrew. Anna sat back down beside him and they reminisced for a long time about Mama and Papa and about their old home. Finally it started to get too cool and they had to go inside. Alice had the coffee on and the three of them sat by the table, like they had so many other nights, and drank the hot beverage before them, each with their own thoughts.

The evening had been emotionally draining on all of them and they were tired and so, even though this was Anna's last night with them, they all retired early. The next morning, Anna noticed that Alice seemed more at peace and not so jittery. She's not running away from her thoughts anymore, I hope, Anna mused. Perhaps she and Andrew had a good talk last night.

Alice rode along to town to take Anna and Teddy to the train station. When they said their goodbyes, Alice whispered "thank you" softly in Anna's ear and gave her an extra-long hug.

"I'll write you," Anna promised her sister-in-law. Then she turned and gave her big brother a hug, too, and then the two boarded the train. Teddy was reluctant to leave. He and George were no longer just cousins; they had now become fast friends.

Teddy was rather quiet and a little sad on the first leg of the journey home. Anna had her own thoughts, too, to occupy her mind. Among other things, she was thinking of Lorrie and how she wished that she was going home to him. How wonderful it would be if he was going to meet her at the station! I must quit thinking like that, she told herself. It can only happen in my dreams. Then she fell asleep until the next stop.

Anna may have been hoping and dreaming that it would be Lorrie who would meet her at the station but it was, in fact, Hans who was there. It was very late when the train chugged into Mankato. Teddy was looking out into the darkness, trying to make out the few figures on the platform.

"I don't see Papa anywhere," he told Anna. "Oh, but there is Mr. Nielson!" He will take us home in his car."

Sure enough, Hans was there alone to pick them up. In explanation he told them, "I told your brother that I could just as well come and meet you and he didn't argue!" He gave Anna a quizzical look as if he were asking, was that all right?

"Well, that was very nice of you to offer, Hans. We'll just get our bags and be on our way home. We're both very tired, to be sure!"

Hans ruffled Teddy's hair and then put his arm around the young boy's shoulder. "I thought that your uncle would keep you on the farm the rest of the summer as a hired man!" he teased.

"I wish he would have! They were soon getting ready to harvest the wheat. The big threshing crew was going to be coming in about a week. Boy, I sure wish I could have stayed for that!"

"Maybe you can go again next year and then you"ll be even bigger and will be of more help," Hans said to the boy.

"Wow! I sure hope I can. I loved it on the farm!" Teddy exclaimed.

They got in the car and were soon at the Olson house. Hans carried the heaviest bags up to the house and Tomas met them at the door and held it wide open for the trio.

"Well, well, the farmers are back again, are they?" joked Tomas.

Anna turned to Hans and thanked him for bringing them home. They shook hands and Hans left as it was late for everyone. Teddy kept up a running commentary of every thing they did from the time they arrived at Andrew's to the time they left! Finally his mother had to tell him to be quiet and he could tell them more in the morning.

It didn't take long before the whole household was settled down for the night. Anna was dog tired but as she lay in her bed, she couldn't go to sleep immediately like she thought she would. She felt a deep loneliness come upon her. I go from one family to another! How I wish I had a home and family of my own! She finally fell asleep, talking to God about the situation.

CHAPTER 17

The remainder of the summer passed quickly. Anna's niece, Hannah, was offered a teaching position in a small town, some miles west of Mankato, named St. James. She was happy to get this job because it was not too far away and the school was in the town itself. Tomas and Bergit drove her out there several days before school opened and helped get her settled. She found a room in the home of an elderly widow.

Anna returned to her classroom where she had a new batch of 3rd graders. She and Miss Rice, the 2nd grade teacher, began to spend some time together and soon became fast friends. Miss Rice, whose first name was Margaret, but everyone called her Maggie, had pretty blonde hair and light blue eyes. She also had the deepest dimples that Anna had ever seen!

Anna and Maggie set about that fall to update their wardrobes. Anna had seen a dress in the window of the Larson's Department Store that she would love to buy but she felt she couldn't afford it. "Maybe after I get my first paycheck, if it's still there, then I will buy it," she told Maggie.

Meanwhile, Maggie had a subscription to the Ladies Home Journal and they could tell by the fashion pages that the styles were changing and the hemlines were still going up. Anna had hemmed up a few of her skirts last year to about mid-calf but now they were going up even more!

"Where would they end?" she wondered aloud to her friend.

Maggie had been experimenting with her hair, too. She had cut it a little shorter than she had been wearing it and thought about getting one of the new permanent waves that the beauty shop was offering. Anna didn't care to go that far!

The young man whom Maggie had been rather sweet on before the war was drafted and went off to Europe and never came back. It was believed that he was taken prisoner but his family didn't know for sure. Maggie, not one to wait forever for anything, had now been seeing a young man named Mel. He was a foreman at the Hubbard Mill, where Arne worked.

"I'll have my nephew check him out," teased Anna.

"I understand Hans Nielson has been courting you all summer, Anna!" said Maggie.

"Oh, we're just good friends, Maggie!" Anna assured her.

Maggie, who was several years younger than Anna said, "Well, you can't afford to wait forever if you want to have a home and family. You're not getting any younger!"

Anna laughed at this at the time but later, alone in her classroom, it didn't seem so funny. She was getting older. In fact, next week was her birthday and she would be 33 years old.

The day of her birthday, she came home from school feeling rather dejected. Bergit had the table in the dining room all set with the good dishes and flowers on the table.

"My, what's all this?" Anna asked, as she walked by the table to go upstairs and change.

"Well, it's somebody's birthday today and we're going to have a little party," answered Bergit as she hurried back into the kitchen to check the kettles on the stove.

Anna quickly counted nine places set around the table. Bergit had put on the beautiful old, white hardanger tablecloth which she had brought from Norway. She only used this at Christmas time and maybe for a wedding or something equally special.

"Who's all coming?" she called to Bergit. "You've set nine places."

"Oh, just wait and see!" Bergit called back. "And you might want to change into something special while you're at it, and no, I don't need any help in the kitchen. Sarah will be helping me as soon as she gets home from the store."

Anna went up to her room, excited about the prospect of something special for her birthday, after all. She decided to lie down and rest for awhile. As she lay there, on top of her quilt, she wondered if Papa was thinking about her on her birthday. She dozed for a few minutes and then woke with a start. She got up and sat down before her dressing table and looked in the mirror. She took down her hair and brushed it and tried to think of some new way to wear it.

She heard Sarah come up the stairs so she called to her. "Sarah, if you have a few minutes, help me decide on a new way to wear my hair."

Sarah came up close to her and took the brush from her hand and started to brush and try different styles. What they came up with was some sort of a chignon in the back. Sarah hurried down to the dining room and snitched several flowers from the vase on the table and tucked them in Anna's hair. It looked very pretty.

"You are so beautiful, Aunt Anna," said Sarah as she stood behind her aunt and looked at her in the mirror.

"Oh, nonsense, Sarah!" she scoffed. "I'm just an old maid school teacher and I think I'm beginning to look it!"

They could hear Bergit calling for Sarah to come and help her so when she left, Anna went to her closet to pick out something to wear. She decided on the blue dress that she had worn to the last May Day dance when she went with Hans. She had to change her clothes very carefully so as not to disturb her hair.

Sarah came running up and told Anna that it would be fun if she stayed upstairs and not let anyone see her until they were all seated. Then Anna could make a grand entrance coming down the stairs! Anna thought that she would feel a little foolish doing that but the young girl looked so excited with her idea that she agreed to do it.

"I'll have everyone get seated when they arrive and then I'll come up and tell you when to come down!" She ran downstairs hurriedly at another call from her mother.

Anna took her time finishing getting ready. She found some pretty earrings and even put on some rouge and a dab of lip color. She surveyed herself in the mirror once more and remembered how she had always been taught not to be vain. She jumped up and went to sit in her rocker by the window. At least I can see who is coming before I walk downstairs, making my grand entrance!

In a short time, she saw Tomas come home from work and heard him come upstairs, supposedly to change. She was paging through a magazine when she heard a car drive up. She saw Hans get out and he walked to the passenger side and opened the door and out came Maggie. Oh, good, she thought. It will be fun to have Maggie. She got up and walked around the room a little, trying to pass the time, waiting for Sarah. She looked out the window again and saw Arne and Sophia coming up the walk. Let's see now, that should make about nine people, she thought to herself.

In about five more minutes, Sarah came bursting into her room and said, "All right, Aunt Anna it's time to go. They're all seated, wondering where you are!" The young girl was almost jumping up and down, she was so excited about her idea. Then she went down to take her place at the table.

As Anna placed her foot carefully on the top stair, she felt a rush of foolishness come upon her. This only served to bring a slight color to her cheeks. When she reached the point in the stairway where the seated guests would see her, she paused a little, and when Hans saw her, his mouth dropped open and he rose right up from his chair. He didn't know when he had seen Anna look more beautiful! He felt his throat constrict and his heart started to beat fast. Everyone turned to look at what he was seeing. They clapped and sang "Happy Birthday" as Hans went to the stairway and took Anna's hand and led her to her chair, which, of course had been placed right next to Hans' by Bergit and Sarah.

Anna didn't know when she had felt like such a queen except, of course, on her wedding day. Everyone commented on the new way she was wearing her hair and how nice--and young--she looked.

"Getting a year older has not hurt you one bit," commented her brother, as he looked at her in admiration.

She was getting almost embarrassed by all the attention and she could sense Hans looking at her often during the meal. He was rather silent for awhile, which was different for him, especially since everyone else was making jokes and having such a pleasant time.

The fact of the matter was, he was struck by the fact that he was in love with this woman, and when he saw her on the stairs, he knew for sure that he wanted her with all his heart. He was still a little speechless with this realization. He had liked and admired her before this but he never let himself feel too strongly about her because he didn't know if she could ever feel the same for him. He still didn't know that, but he knew one thing for sure. He was in love with her now and there was no changing that! Ever!

Hans finally found his tongue and suggested they propose a toast to Anna on her special day. Tomas had poured small glasses of homemade chokecherry wine for all the grownups and Hans raised his and said, "Here's to Anna, a most wonderful person, and may she have nothing but happiness from now on." He sat down again and looked deep into Anna's eyes and he saw tears beginning to form, but also a look of understanding. They had shared their misfortunes and he knew what lie beneath the tears.

Others made similar toasts and then Bergit suggested they all move to the parlor. She had Sarah and Teddy clear the table and when they had finished, Anna was handed several packages to open. The first one was from Maggie and it was a beautiful hair comb.

"Now that you've suddenly changed your hair style, you maybe won't have use for it anymore!" Maggie joked. Everyone laughed at this and Anna reach for the next gift. It was from Hans. He was not happy about the gift he brought. When he was in the store, looking around for just the perfect gift, everything he liked would have been considered too personal for a man to give a woman, unless she was his sister, wife or fiance. So he had had to settle for a box of chocolates.

"Oh, my favorite kind!" Anna exclaimed when she opened it. Hans was silent, wishing he could tell her that he had wanted to buy her other, more expensive things, more fitting to the way he felt about her. His heart ached with love as he watched her.

The evening ended early, everyone having to go to work the next day. Anna thanked everyone for coming and making this such a wonderful birthday. Hans lingered and was the last one to leave. He wished he could have taken her in his arms and held her close. Oh, why does love have to hurt so much! He said good night and they clasped hands. Anna whispered, "Thank you," and he turned and left, his heart bursting.

Anna helped Bergit clean up the kitchen and then they sat down at the table for a last cup of coffee. "Thank you, Bergit, for making this such a special birthday. When did you decide to do all this, anyway?" asked Anna.

"Well, just yesterday, I guess," answered Bergit. "You've seemed a little down lately so I thought this would help cheer you up."

"It sure did that!" exclaimed Anna.

"Hans seemed a little quiet tonight, didn't you think?" Bergit asked Anna.

Tomas came in just then and said, "I think he was struck dumb by your beauty!" He sat down at the table with the two women and Bergit poured him a cup of coffee. Teddy and Sarah had gone off to bed and the house was quiet, except for the chiming of the clock striking the half hour.

"I think that he is very smitten with you, Anna," said Bergit. "How do you feel about him? Not still 'just friends', I hope!"

Anna blushed a little and said with a laugh, "Well, yes, I still think of him as just a good friend. What's wrong with that?"

"Well, dear sister, for one thing," said Tomas, "I think he would make a good husband for you!" He wasn't at all prepared for her reaction to this comment. She stood up suddenly and as he looked up at her, he could see tears start to form in her eyes.

She said in a quiet and deliberate voice, "There's only been one 'good husband' for me and he's gone!" With that she turned to leave the room and go upstairs. Bergit and Tomas could only stare at each other in surprise. Finally Bergit called after her, "Good night, Anna, and happy birthday again."

Anna stopped on the first stair and then turned and came back into the kitchen. "I'm sorry, I'm just tired, I guess, and I do want to thank you again for the wonderful evening." With that she stooped to give Bergit a hug and then one to Tomas, too. "I know you both mean well, but don't get your hopes up that I will want to find a husband anytime soon." She retraced her steps and went up to bed.

Hans was having a hard time with his feelings. He wanted to rush right over to the Olson house and proclaim his love for Anna but he was afraid that she would not feel the same about him so he almost avoided her for the next couple weeks. He couldn't trust his feelings around her.

One day he sought out Tomas and said he would like to have a word with him in private. Tomas said that he would stop by the lumber yard on his way home from work. He came by shortly before suppertime and Hans was waiting for him. "Have a seat," he indicated to Tomas.

"I want to talk to you about something..ah.. personal, Tomas," said Hans nervously. "I want to talk to you about...about your sister, Anna." There, he had said it!

"Yes, what do you want to know about her, Hans?" asked Tomas good naturedly.

"You have probably guessed that I am rather--ah--fond of her, Tomas. In fact, I might as well tell you that I am completely head-over-heels in love with her! I wanted to ask you if you thought there was any chance there for me." Hans was pacing the floor in the small office, nervously stroking his beard.

This must be hard for Hans, to talk to me about this, thought Tomas to himself. He didn't know quite how to answer him. "Well, Hans, I really don't know what to tell you on that score!" But then he remembered what Anna had said to him and Bergit the night after the birthday party.

"Women are funny; you don't always know what they want," he continued, trying to stall until he thought of just the right thing to say. He didn't want to discourage the man completely but then he couldn't give him false hope either.

Hans was still pacing. "Well, do you think I would stand a chance at all? Does she ever say anything about me?"

Tomas chose his words carefully. "She thinks alot of you, I do know that, but I..ah..don't know if she is ready for any declaration of love yet. Maybe if you took it slow so as not to scare her off. You know, she was hurt deeply when Lorrie was taken from her so suddenly and after only a couple years of marriage. I think she is afraid of getting hurt again." He hoped that what he said was the right thing.

This seemed to satisfy Hans and he said, "Yes, I was thinking, too, that I may have to go slowly, but you know, neither she nor I are getting any younger and I have been so lonely for so long now and so has she, I thought that the two of us....well...we would be good for each other. I'll need to have lots of patience, perhaps."

When Tomas nodded at this, Hans went on. "This will be hard as I feel that I, myself, am finally ready to leave the past behind and go on. And I guess I'm a little impatient to do just that, especially with the way I feel about her." He ran his hand through his hair and began stroking his beard again.

Tomas felt sorry for the man. He was really in a dither. Tomas rose and said that he thought that everything would turn out fine, given a little time. He clasped Hans on the shoulder and wished him good luck. He didn't know what else to say or do.

When Tomas arrived home, supper was ready and he said he was sorry he was a little late, but he had had to stop by and talk to Hans about something . He looked at Anna intently when he said this and he wondered to himself what she would say if she knew what he and Hans were just talking about. He said no more about it and Bergit thought to herself, I'll find out more about this later.

Later that night, when she and Tomas had gone to bed, she asked what he had to talk to Hans about. Tomas was silent for some moments before answering.

"Well, I don't know if I should talk about it or not but that man is beside himself with love for my dear sister and he doesn't know what he should do about it." Bergit raised herself up on one elbow and looked at her husband. "He's so afraid of getting rejected, and that would simply break his heart, so he's almost afraid to declare himself to her. I told him to take it slow and see what happens."

Bergit lowered herself down again and let out a sigh. "I guess that was good advice. She doesn't seem ready to give up Lorrie's memory just yet. On the other hand, she's impatient to go on with her life. I think that she would love to get married again and have a family. I'm surprised that he confided in you with all this."

"I was, too," Tomas answered, as he snuggled up to his wife. "I'm glad I didn't have to go through such pain when I was courting you!" he teased.

"Oh, you!" she said, as she got up to open the window a bit. When she returned, she said, "We are so lucky, Tomas. We've had a good marriage and a good life together. I just hope Anna can find some happiness, too, that will last the rest of her life. I think Hans is the right man for her and I hope she realizes it soon."

Autumn went by quickly and a beautiful Indian summer lasted almost through the whole month of November. Arne, Sophia, Hans and Maggie joined the Olson family on Thanksgiving Day. After a traditional meal of turkey and all the trimmings, they were all resting in the parlor. Anna suggested they take a walk but Tomas had another idea. He wanted Hans to give him some driving lessons in his car. Tomas was planning to buy himself a small truck for his carpentry business come spring and he thought he should at least know how to drive a motor vehicle! He said that he hoped to buy an automobile someday, too, but he really needed a truck more.

His business was doing very well. His partner, Mr. Jenkins, was going to retire very soon because of his arthritis and they had several big jobs lined up for early spring. Arne was planning to quit his job at the mill and join his father in the business then.

Everyone got up and went outside. Hans told Tomas to get in the driver's seat and Hans got in on the passenger side. Teddy crawled in the back. No one else wanted to risk their lives by riding along, they told Tomas jokingly, so the rest of them started out on a walk. When they looked back, they could see Han's car jerking and stopping and starting! Arne said, "It will take some practice, getting used to shifting and all that. The clutch can be tricky, too. Hans let me try it a time or two last summer."

Anna declared, "I want to drive a car someday, too. Then I can take myself around wherever I want to go and not depend on someone else to take me there."   Sophia agreed but Bergit said that she didn't think she could ever learn.

Just then they saw Hans' car careening around the corner and heading right for them!   "That Tomas!" exclaimed Bergit.   "He's trying to show off and scare us at the same time."

As he slowed it down to put in the clutch and shift, he killed the engine right in front of all of them!   They had a good laugh but Tomas wasn't very amused.   He got out right then and there and said, "Those newfangled machines could get the best of me!   It's going to take some getting used to, that's for sure!"   He walked the other direction, where he was going back to the house, he told them.   Hans and Teddy took the car back and they were sitting on the porch steps when everyone else returned from their walk.   Tomas had gone in to take a nap.

Anna plopped herself down next to Hans and Teddy.   "That felt good to get some exercise after such a big meal," she declared.   Teddy ran off next door to see if the neighbor boy was home and Bergit, Maggie, Arne and Sophia sat down on the steps, too.   It was just too nice of a day to go in just yet.   It might be one of the last nice days for a long time once winter sets in, Anna commented. Hans asked Arne and Sophia about their work at the mill.   They said that they were scrimping and saving their money to buy that little Munson house across the street from where they presently lived.   For now they were occupying the three rooms on the second floor of Widow Benson's house.   It was cramped, but cheap, and they would put up with it until they had some money saved.

Later that evening, after a light supper of turkey sandwiches, Arne and Sophia departed for home as they both had to work early in the morning. Tomas had to go and feed and water his horses so Hans said that he'd help him.

"I'll sure be glad when I can get my truck and be rid of these horses," said Tomas.   "But I'll have to learn to drive the darn thing first," he added.

"For sure, you will enjoy having a truck, Tomas," Hans agreed.   When the two men had finished their job, Hans put his hand on Tomas' arm to detain him a moment longer.   "Has Anna said anything about me to you?" he asked.   "She seems different towards me but I can't just put my finger on what it is." He shook his head slowly.

"No, she hasn't said anything to me and I think Bergit would have told me if she had told her anything."

Ever since Anna's birthday party, their relationship had changed somewhat.   Hans, afraid that he would betray his strong feelings for her too suddenly, tended to keep his distance a little.   And Anna, sensing that perhaps Hans was feeling too much for her, and not really knowing what her own feelings were yet, was keeping herself somewhat detached so as not to give him false hopes. They had lost the closeness they had enjoyed during the summer.

Hannah came home for two weeks at Christmas. She liked her teaching job and she mentioned that she had been seeing a certain young man named Will Grant. Teddy started teasing her about him and she threatened to take the gift she had brought for him out from under the tree.

The house was a flurry of baking and cleaning. Anna was helping out at the Larson's Store during the holiday rush and everyday when she returned home, the wonderful smells of Christmas would assail her. Hannah and Sarah helped their mother bake many of the traditional Norwegian delicacies, like sandbakkels, rosettes, kringle, spritz, julekake and, of course, lefse and flatbread. There was enough to feed the whole town, Anna laughingly told them.

Christmas letters came from Norway, from Papa, from Tollef and Margit, and also from Barbro and Peder. The latter two letters were filled with news about their growing families. Anna read and reread them many times. Papa's letter was quite brief and he sounded lonely. No word about coming to America! Anna was disappointed that she didn't hear from the Martins anymore. No news about her Samuel. Let's see, he is twelve years old now, almost thirteen, Anna mused. The age of Teddy. They were both born the same year.

Arne and Sophia joined the family both Christmas Eve and the next day. Hans had been invited but he had decided to go to Chicago to be with his mother and sister and her family. He usually tried to go there every other Christmas. He took the train to St. Paul and then got on a faster one that would take him straight to Chicago. Anna had to admit to herself that she missed him much more than she thought she would!

On Christmas Day night, the whole family walked down to their church for the Sunday School Christmas program. Teddy was playing the part of one of the Wise Men. He had a small part to say and he did it with great gusto! The youngest children stole the show with their little recitations. They were so nervous and many would forget their one-liners. But they sang "Away in the Manger" loud and clear, under the direction of Mrs. Johnson who had been the Sunday School superintendent forever! She declared every year that this would absolutely be her last year of working with these rambunctious children but by the next November she would be back practicing for the next program!

After the program, the Young People's Society passed out all the gifts and then each youngster received a sack of peanuts and candy and also a shiny, red apple. In the sack of candy would always be some hard candy, including a piece of striped ribbon candy, and also one chocolate drop. These candies were highly sought after and once in awhile some lucky child would accidentally find two of them in his bag!

A couple evenings after Christmas, the Olson family was surprised by some 'julebukkers' at their door, dressed in disguise. There were only two of them and they were asked to come in and sit down. The family then had to try and guess who they were. Anna recognized Maggie's girlish giggle and so she was easy to guess. Then they soon figured out that the person with her was her friend, Mel. Tomas then served them a little glass of homemade wine and Bergit got out her large array of goodies.

"We've just begun," said Maggie, taking a small sip of the wine. "Why don't you all dress up and come with us?"

"Oh, yes, can we?" asked Teddy right away, excitedly jumping up from the floor.

"Oh, I don't know," said Bergit, setting down her tray. "What would we all find to wear, anyway?"

"Just find anything crazy, just to cover you up," answered Maggie. "You could cut up some old pillowcases for masks."

"Oh, please, let's go," begged Sarah and Teddy together.

"We thought we'd go over to Arne and Sophia's next," said Maggie.

That seemed to decide the matter. "Well, what do you think, Tomas, do you want to go?" asked Bergit, warming up to the idea.

"Well, I guess we could. We haven't gone julebukking for several years now," he answered, getting up from his chair. He clapped his hands and said, "Let's get ourselves ready, then!" This surprised Bergit somewhat because Tomas was usually content to settle down in his favorite chair every evening, read the paper and have himself a little nap!

It took almost an hour for everyone to find something crazy to wear before they were on their way. They went first to Arne and Sophia's. It didn't take them too long to figure out who most of them were as Arne recognized much of the old clothing they had found to wear. Arne and Sophia dressed up, too, and joined the group to go to the next place. Around midnight, it was time to call it a night. They had had such a good time, laughing and acting goofy!

When they got home and Anna had gone to bed, she lay there for awhile and thought about the evening. I wish Hans had been here, she said to herself. He would have had such a good time. When Hans wasn't around, Anna found herself missing him and when he was near, then she tried to keep a safe distance, emotionally. What's going to come of this friendship, anyway? she wondered to herself.

CHAPTER 18

In the spring, Arne and Sophia were able to buy their little dream house. Sophia's grandmother had died around the first of the year and left her house to her granddaughter. Sophia didn't want to live in that house because there had been too much unhappiness there so she sold it and she and Arne used the proceeds as their down payment.

Their new house needed some fixing and painting. Hans donated some used lumber and a few gallons of paint to help them along. Arne and Tomas spent several Saturdays over there working. One nice weekend early in April, Tomas, Teddy, and Hans helped Arne paint the outside. The women brought over coffee and sandwiches and watched the progress. Sophia was so excited and she already had plans for the different flowers that she was going to plant around the house. She wanted a white picket fence, too, if Arne and Tomas would have time to make one. They had been kept pretty busy lately. The house would be ready to move in by the next weekend, the men figured.

How exciting, thought Anna, to be fixing up and moving into your own little house. Her heart was filled with longing and the old feeling of deep sadness crept over her once again. Hans could not help but notice this but he didn't know what to say to her. When she was feeling sad, it affected Han's mood, also. He wanted to make everything right and happy for her.

At Easter, Hannah came home for a few days. Her boyfriend, Will, brought her home and spent a few hours meeting the family and then returned to his home. That evening around the supper table, Hannah dropped a bombshell by saying that she and Will were planning to get married in the summer! Everyone stopped eating and they first looked at Hannah and then at Tomas, who was clearing his throat. But Bergit was the first to speak. "Oh, Hannah, don't you think this is much too soon?"

Before she could answer, Tomas said, "You are so young, girl. And just how long have you known Will?"

Hannah very calmly and deliberately answered them as if she had rehearsed this speech for sometime, anticipating their reaction. "We've known each other since last September and I don't think we're too young. Will is twenty three and I will be nineteen, the age you were, Ma, when you got married. We love each other very much and Will makes a good living on his father's farm. He will be taking over the farm in a few years since his father is getting up in years. Will is the youngest in the family but all the other boys went off to the city." Here she stopped to catch her breath and to see what they all would have to say now. There was silence for some moments.

Tomas finally broke the spell by saying, somewhat hesitantly, "Well, then, I guess congratulations are in order!" Hannah breathed a sigh of relief and jumped up and went to hug her father. Bergit rose to hug her daughter, too, and there were a few tears shed by the women.

Later that night, after the family had gone to bed, Anna, who was sharing the bedroom with Hannah, came and sat down on the young girl's side of the bed. "Hannah, are you sure you know what you're getting into? Life on the farm can be very difficult. I certainly saw that when I stayed with the various farm families all the years when I taught in the country schools. Maybe you should wait and think this through some more."

Hannah got immediately defensive and answered, "Aunt Anna, maybe Will and I feel the same way about each other as you and Lorrie did. We're very much in love and we have talked this over for quite sometime now and we know this is right and that it will work out." At her reference to Lorrie, Anna was stopped from saying more. She went to bed but couldn't sleep. She was thinking of Lorrie and their wedding and their first little house.

Do you suppose I said these things to Hannah because I'm a little jealous of her getting married? thought Anna to herself. Getting married before me? Then she said aloud, "I'm sorry, Hannah, I wish you the very best and I trust that you are doing the right thing," but Hannah was already asleep and did not hear.

The next day, Hannah, Bergit and Anna were busy making wedding plans. Hannah and Will wanted to get married in August. Bergit said she would get started on a wedding dress. On Sunday afternoon, Will came to get Hannah to take her back to St. James. Hannah told him before he came in the house that she had told the family and that they had accepted it. He was relieved and he shook Tomas' outstretched hand. Anna had to admit that the young couple looked very happy together.

The first weekend in June, Tomas and Arne had a little break in their work so they were going to help Hans paint the outside of his house. This was to pay back Hans for the help and materials he had given Arne earlier. It was a rather hot day so Bergit and Anna brought over a large container of lemonade and ice.

Hans' house was a small two-story house that he had lived in as a youngster after moving from Chicago with his family. His father had worked at the newspaper office but had died when Hans was in high school. His sister, Ruth, was two years younger. He, his sister and even his mother had all had to go out and look for work to make ends meet. He and Ruth worked after school and on Saturdays. Their mother wouldn't let them quit school.

After high school, Ruth became engaged to a local boy who was attending the University of Minnesota, studying to be an electrical engineer. Hans got engaged also, to Cora, about this same time. Then she had her operation and became paralyzed. Ruth's engagement lasted for five long years before her fiance graduated and they could get married. He got a job in Chicago, so they moved there. After about two years, Ruth asked her mother to come and live with them. She had been born and raised there and still had family living in the area so she decided that she would go back. She hated to leave Hans alone, especially after what had happened to Cora several years earlier, but he seemed to be doing all right. He had quit his drinking and held a steady job at the lumber yard.

The years passed and Hans' mother had hoped that he would have found himself a wife to look after him. He traveled to Chicago occasionally to visit her and Ruth. Each time, his mother asked him when he was going to bring a wife with him. This last Christmas, when he had gone to visit them, he said that he was looking. That sounded encouraging, his mother thought. Before, he wasn't even looking!

The painting job was coming along fine when Anna and Bergit came back in the afternoon. They sat in the shade and watched the progress. Hans asked the ladies if they would like to see the inside of the house. They said they would, so Hans led them through the ladders and saw horses and in through the front door. It was a pretty house with plenty of windows and sunlight. She liked that in a house. The kitchen could use a little updating, Anna thought. It needed a woman's touch all over, Bergit thought. She sat on a chair in the parlor while he showed Anna the upstairs. It had two bedrooms with a dormer window in each one. It affected Hans immensely to have Anna actually in his house, upstairs yet! He wished that he could take her in his arms. She was so close to him as they moved from room to room. "Anna," he started to say, but when she looked at him, he couldn't finish what he wanted to say. He said, "Oh, nothing," and they headed downstairs.

The men were running out of paint. "One more can should do it," said Tomas from atop a ladder. Anna said that she and Bergit could go and get it.

"Tomas, can we take your truck?' she asked her brother. She had had a few lessons in driving the vehicle and hadn't done too badly.

"Well, I suppose you can, if you're careful!" he answered. Hans looked at Anna worriedly but she had already started for the truck. Bergit followed her and Hans came to crank it up for them. They got in and started off. It performed smoothly on take off but when they were out of sight and had to stop and shift at a corner, Anna had trouble. It killed on her and she had to restart it several times. It wasn't easy to crank but she was determined to manage without help. They went jerking down the street, to the delight of some of the townspeople. They left it running in front of the lumber yard and went in and told the young man who worked for Hans that they needed another can of white paint. After some time, when they went out to the truck, it was gone! They looked down the street and there it had rolled about a half a block away! The street slanted downward a little from where they parked and Anna hadn't set the brake. Luckily it hadn't hit anything! Tomas would have been very upset if anything had happened to his new truck. They got in and jerked their way back to the house, laughing all the way. They wouldn't tell the men just yet what had happened. Maybe someday!

Hans hired young Teddy to come in on Saturdays and help him out at the lumber yard. For his efforts, he got paid one dollar for the day. One Saturday Teddy heard Hans talking to another man about the Fourth of July celebration coming up. Later Teddy asked Hans if he was going to escort Aunt Anna to the dance. Hans said that he was and Teddy was thoughtful for awhile before asking, "Aren't you too old for my aunt, Mr. Nielson?" Hans just laughed at this, but later, after Teddy had left for home, he started to think about it. Maybe I am a little old for her, he thought to himself.

After he closed up and locked the door, Hans walked over to the store to buy some milk and eggs. He went past the Barber Shop and looked in the window. No one was in there except Iver, the barber. Hans found himself pushing open the door and stepping inside. Iver, who was using this slow time to sharpen his razors, looked up and saw Hans standing there, looking uncertain.

"Why Hans, is it time for another haircut already? How time flies!"

"Uh, no, I mean, ah....I don't know why I came in here, Iver. Just stopped to chat awhile, I guess. I looked in the window and saw you alone here."

"Well, sit down then. I'm just getting ready for a busy evening of haircuts," said Iver, continuing on with his work. This was Saturday and all the area farmers would be coming in for haircuts soon. He worked on for awhile and when Hans didn't say anything, Iver stopped what he was doing and came over closer to his friend and said, "Hans, is something wrong? If you stopped in to chat, you sure don't have much to say!"

Hans shifted in his chair uncomfortably. "Iver, do you think I look old?"
Iver was about to laugh, but then he realized that Hans was very serious.

"Well," Iver stalled, "that depends on what you call old."

Hans, sitting in the barber chair, was looking at himself closely in the big mirror. "You've told me many times that I should shave off my beard. Do you think that would make me look younger?"

"Well, it certainly would take a few years off your looks, Hans. I've seen it happen many times to other fellows around here. Look what it did for Bernie Larson, and Olander Johnson, too." Iver looked at Hans and asked, "Why the sudden interest in your looks, Hans? It wouldn't be on account of a certain young widow, would it?" Iver winked at Hans' reflection in the mirror.

Just then the door opened and the first of the evening's customers came in. Hans rose quickly from the chair and excused himself, saying that he had to get home with the milk.

At home, he made himself some supper and cleaned up. He rested awhile and read the newspaper. Then he decided to go back downtown to see what, if anything, was going on. He stopped in at the pool hall and soon was engaged in a heated game of poker. After losing a few dollars, he decided to leave there and walk down to the creamery where there usually was a large gathering of men on a Saturday night. As he looked around him, he saw that only one other man wore a beard. Of course, he was an old man. Or was he? Maybe the beard only made him look old! Hans ordered an ice cream cone and walked back to his house.

Here he sat on his porch step for awhile. It was such a beautiful evening. Hans felt an aching loneliness come over him. Here I am, a man of forty, all alone, not married, no family, he mused to himself. Finally he got up and went into the house. He climbed the stairs and undressed and went to bed. Only the thought that tomorrow he would see Anna cheered him up.

In the morning, Hans dressed up in his suit to go to church. As he was buttoning his jacket, a button came off in his hand. He looked at the clock and decided that if he hurried, he'd have time to sew it on. As he was doing some quick stitching, he thought, this old suit has seen many years, too. When was the last time I bought any new clothes? He couldn't even remember! After finishing the sewing, he cut the thread and grabbed his hat and hurried out the door.

After church, Hans talked to Anna and told her he would be by at the usual time and that maybe they would take a drive out in the country, this being such a nice day. Anna said that perhaps she could pack a picnic basket.

Later that afternoon as Hans and Anna were bouncing along down a country road, Hans turned to Anna and asked her, "Do you think I look old?"

This question, out of the blue, surprised Anna "Well, I guess I haven't thought about it, Hans. Why do you ask?"

"A certain young lad suggested that maybe I was too old to be escorting you to the Fourth of July dance." He tried to say this lightly, but there was an underlying question, if she thought this might be the case.

Anna laughed and said, "That wouldn't be Teddy, would it? He thinks anyone over twenty is old!"

"Well, I'm twice twenty so he must think I am really ancient!" They both laughed at this. Hans stopped the car and said, "This looks like a good place for a picnic." He had driven down a little-used road that took them up around the north side of the lake. They were on top of a small hill and there was a clearing in the trees. They spread a blanket and sat down. Anna opened the basket and Hans looked with appreciation at Bergit's fried chicken.

"I could smell that chicken all the way up here!" he laughed. Anna set out two plates and some silverware. Hans opened the jar of lemonade, the chunks of ice not quite melted yet. They ate slowly, relishing the beautiful day and just being together. They could catch a glimpse of the lake if they craned their necks.

After they had finished eating, Hans said, "Ah, that was mighty good," and he rolled over on his back to rest while Anna put the things back in the basket. She leaned back on her elbows and looked up at the sky, watching the funny shapes of the fluffy clouds. The birds were singing and it was a most peaceful setting. Hans rolled back up on his one elbow and looked at Anna.

"Anna, I think that it is about time we had a good talk. A serious talk." At this, Anna stiffened and shifted her position, like she was going to get up. Hans touched her arm and said, "Please, don't get up. Just listen to what I have to say." He sat up so that his eyes were level with hers. He cleared his throat and began a speech that he had been rehearsing for a long time.

"Anna, my dearest, you must know how I feel about you, and if you don't, I'm just plain going to tell you. I'm very much in love with you and have been for quite sometime now. I enjoy being with you and I think that you enjoy being with me." Anna started to say something but Hans stopped her. "Please, let me finish before I lose my nerve."

"I know that I am quite a few years older than you but I'm asking you, here and now, if you would consider becoming my wife." Hans stopped here and took a deep breath. He had hardly been breathing at all for the last few minutes. He took yet another deep breath and waited for her answer, hardly daring to hope. His heart pounded wildly in his chest. Still she didn't say anything!

He finally looked her full in the face. He saw tears there, in her eyes. That could only mean one thing, he thought. She doesn't feel the same way about me, and she doesn't know how to tell me. He tried to stifle a sob that was threatening to escape from his mouth. He got up quickly, and just stood there. Anna got up, too. She was very close to him. Without thinking, he reached out and took her in his arms and kissed her. This was their first kiss. Initially she yielded to his lips on hers, but then she put her hand on his chest and pushed ever so lightly, enough that Hans got the message. He let her go and they looked at each other, seeing the longing in the other's eyes.

"Hans, I ...ah...don't know...ah..what to say. I won't play coy with you and I guess I knew that this day would come sooner or later, when you would declare your feelings for me. I have known for sometime that you cared deeply for me. I care deeply for you, too, Hans." His heart skipped a few beats here. "But," she continued, "I don't know if I am ready yet to marry someone."

They stood on the blanket, looking at each other for a few moments. Then Hans said, "What are you trying to say, then, Anna? That you love me, too, but you can't marry me, or that you can't marry me yet? I need to know where I stand."

Anna looked into his kind, pleading eyes and said, "Hans, I don't know what I'm saying. I enjoy being with you but I don't know if it is love or not. I have to take it slow. Please be patient with me."

He saw the confusion in her face and, though he was disappointed with her answer, she had not actually said 'no'! He took her in his arms again and she leaned her head on his shoulder and he stroked her hair. "My dear, dear Anna," he said. "I won't rush you, but I hope that someday soon you will tell me what I have been waiting for and dreaming about for so long. That you love me and will marry me!" They stood like this for a some time and then, without a word, they gathered up the blanket and basket and returned to the car. They drove home in silence, each exhausted after so much emotion being revealed at long last.

When they stopped in front of the Olson house, Hans turned to Anna and took her hand. She did not pull away. "Think about what I have said, my dear," he said. "We could have a wonderful life together." With that, he got out of the car and came and opened her door and helped her out. He carried her basket up to the porch for her.

"I don't think I'll come in," he said. He squeezed her hand and turned and headed for the car.

"Goodbye," she called after him. "It was a lovely day." At those words, he stopped and turned to look at her. She was smiling and looked so beautiful that he wanted with all his heart to run back to her and take her in his arms again.

He waved at her. "It was a lovely day, indeed!" he said. He got into his car and drove off. On the way to his house he was thinking how he couldn't believe that he had finally summoned up the nerve to ask her to marry him! Well, now it's finally out in the open, he thought. I can only hope and pray that she will give me the answer that I've been longing for.

By the next morning, Hans had made some decisions. Before opening up his place of business, he walked down to the Barber Shop. Iver had just unlocked the door and raised the shades. He was surprised to see Hans there so early in the morning.

"What can I do for you this fine morning, Hans?" he asked jovially. Hans removed his hat and hung it on the coat tree. He marched to the barber chair, sat down and said to an astonished Iver, "Take it all off!"

Iver stepped closer to the chair and said, "What did you say, Hans?"

"Shave it all off! The beard, the mustache, the sideburns, everything!"

"Well, well, well," declared Iver. "This is certainly a surprise. Are you sure you really want to take this drastic step?"

"I'm sure, Iver," Hans answered. "Just go ahead and do as I said before I change my mind. And I've already taken some drastic steps lately so I may as well keep going."

As Iver prepared to do the drastic deed, he couldn't help but wonder what prompted this action. "Well, Hans, I'll bet that the love bug has bitten you, that's why these sudden actions! Love makes a man do strange and crazy things."

Hans didn't answer, he was too intent upon looking into the mirror at what was happening before his eyes. First one side of his face was revealed and then the other. He hadn't been bare faced for about fifteen years. He hardly knew the man staring back at him!

When Iver was finished, he waited for Hans to make some comment. But Hans merely paid him, grabbed his hat and left without a word! As.Hans walked down the street, he felt almost naked without his face covering. The people he met looked at him like they should know that man but they only nodded. After picking up his morning mail, Hans continued on over to Larson's Department Store.

He walked to the men's counter and said to Mr. Larson, "I'd like to look at a new suit." Mr. Larson, surprised as he was, tried to act like this was something Hans shopped for often.

"Come right this way, Mr. Nielson," he said cordially. Hans followed him to a row of men's suits hanging on a rack. Mr. Larson measured Hans' chest and his arm and trouser length. He pulled several possibilities from the rack and hung them out for Hans to see. Hans pointed to the light- colored one and said, "I like that one."

"A good choice, Mr. Nielson," said the store owner. This one is the newest and the light colors are the latest in fashion. Come this way," he continued, "and you can try it on."

When Hans had it on, Mr. Larson made the necessary notations for the altering and then suggested that perhaps Hans needed a new shirt and tie, also.

"Yes, I suppose I do. And how about some new shoes, too, while I'm at it?" he laughed.

A short while later, Hans emerged from the department store with several packages under his arm. The suit would be ready in a couple of days. He felt quite pleased with himself. As he passed several places of business, he couldn't help but look at his reflection in the windows. It was like looking at a stranger! When he got to the lumber yard, his helper, Jesse Jensen, looked up and then looked again in surprise.

"Is that you, Mr. Nielson?" asked the young man. "I must say, you look ten years younger!"

This was what Hans had been waiting to hear! It made it all worthwhile; the shaving of the beard, the purchase of all those new clothes!

"Yes, it's me, Jesse. A new and younger man!" he joked.

Hans avoided seeing Anna until the Fourth of July as he wanted to surprise her. Tomas had stopped in one day but Hans told him not to tell Anna about his 'new' look. The only thing that Tomas said when he got home that evening was that there was a "new man" working at the lumber yard now.

"That's funny, Hans didn't mention that he was getting a new man," declared Anna. Tomas only smiled and said, "You'll soon meet him."

Thursday was the Fourth and the town was having a parade. Hans didn't want to take the chance of running into Anna so he stayed at the lumber yard and watched the parade from there. After the Olson family arrived back home, Anna remarked that she thought it was strange that Hans wasn't at the parade.

"I hope he isn't sick or something," she said.

"Oh, I'm sure he's not sick, but maybe he was just busy," Tomas said, trying to keep a straight face.

Bergit fixed a light supper that evening and then the whole family went upstairs to get ready for the dance. Even Teddy was being allowed to go along this year. He wasn't interested in dancing with any girl but he thought it would be exciting to watch and find out why the grown ups had so much fun at these events.

Sarah and Anna were the last ones to get ready. They were helping each other with their hair. Anna heard an automobile drive up and looked out to see Hans' car park in front of the house. When she glanced out the window a second time, she exclaimed, "Why, that's Hans' car but who is that man coming up the sidewalk?"

She turned to put the finishing touches on Sarah's hair and then they both headed downstairs. Anna stopped on the bottom step as she could see a strange but yet somehow familiar man in the parlor talking to Tomas. It sounded like Hans but she didn't see him.

"Come in here, Anna," Tomas said. "Your escort is here!"

She cautiously stepped into the room and when the man turned and looked at her, she suddenly realized that it was indeed Hans. But he looked so different. She put her hand to her mouth and said, "Oh, my, is it really you, Hans? What have you done to yourself?"

Slightly embarrassed, Hans answered, "I just thought it was time to update my looks a little. A certain someone said that he thought I was too old for you." He looked at Teddy as he said this and the boy ducked out of view. " I thought, well, maybe if I shaved off the beard, it would make me look not so old. Iver, down at the Barber Shop has been after me for years to do this."

"I hardly recognized you," Anna said and Bergit nodded her agreement. All the while Tomas had been silent and trying not to laugh, but now he said, "I saw Hans a couple days ago but decided not to say anything and spoil his surprise."

Anna couldn't help staring at Hans. He was really quite handsome, she thought. He still had a full head of hair, dark brown and wavy. His eyes were such a deep blue that they looked almost black. They always had an expression of kindness to them, and, sometimes a mischievous twinkle, like now.

"Why Hans, I do believe you have a new suit of clothes on, too," said Bergit. "You really look quite dapper."

"Thank you," Hans said with a mock bow. "Well, let's all get to the dance then, before they start without us."

They all scrambled for their hats, shawls and handbags and off they went, laughing and in high spirits. They all managed to pile into Hans' car. When they arrived at the hall, it was lit up brightly. Inside it was decorated in red, white and blue streamers and bunting. Sarah and Teddy went to find their friends and the four grown ups found a place to sit along the wall.

They had hardly sat down when Hans stood and took Anna's arm and said, "Let's not waste any time. Let's get out there and start kicking up our heels!" And kick up their heels they did. They hardly sat out a dance for the whole first hour. Then they paused to have some punch. They took it outside where it was cooler. They walked aways and stood sipping the cool, sweet liquid.

"Oh, my, this tastes so good," remarked Anna. "I was getting very warm, weren't you?"

"Indeed I was!" answered Hans, trying to loosen his tie a little.

"I haven't told you how nice you look in your new suit, Hans, " Anna said, rather shyly.

"Thank you, Madam," he said. "I guess I was in need of some new duds."

"I like the new lighter colors in men's suits for the summer. It makes you look cooler, even if you really aren't," Anna told him.

They went back into the hall when they heard the band start playing again. Hans danced with Bergit while Anna danced with Tomas.

"You and that 'new man' in town make a nice-looking couple, Anna!" teased Tomas. "He looks much younger than that 'old man' you used to be seen with!"

Anna just laughed but she had to agree with him. At the next break, Anna went looking for Teddy as she wanted to have a dance with him and Hans found Sarah.

"Would you care to dance with an older fellow, young lady?" Hans asked the young girl, taking her hand and leading her onto the floor.

"I'd be honored to, Mr. Nielson," she answered, laughing. "I can't get over how different you look!"

"Well, I hope it's for the better," he said.

"Oh, yes, it certainly is!" she answered, quickly adding, "But, I mean, you looked nice before, but, ah, you just look younger now." She thought she better stop as she knew she was probably saying more that she should.

Hans just laughed and said, "I hope your aunt thinks I look better than before!"

"You really like her, don't you?" asked Sarah, forgetting herself. She really shouldn't be getting so personal with her questions.

He looked at Sarah seriously and answered, "I really do," and then, lightening up, he asked, "So where is this young man that you think is so wonderful? Is he the one you've been dancing with most of the time?"

"Oh, no, that's just a friend. The one I want to dance with doesn't seem to dare ask me."

"Give him time, Sarah," suggested Hans. "He'll come around before the evening is over if he knows what's good for him!"

On Hans' way back to find Anna, he ran into Iver, the barber. "Now I know why you wanted a new look, Hans," he teased. "I saw you and Mrs. Howe dancing together all evening."

"Yes, Iver, I have to thank you. I think she was properly surprised and pleased with the results of your efforts. I should have taken your advice long ago!" he added as he continued through the crowd.

He found Anna talking with Maggie Rice and her young man, Mel. They had just come and they stopped talking when Hans approached. "Why, is it you, Hans?" asked Mel as he slapped the older man on the back.

Anna beamed and Maggie said, "I think I will have to have a dance with this 'new man' in town!" Hans and Maggie started onto the floor to the tune of a waltz. Mel asked Anna if she would care to dance.

"I guess I would rather sit for awhile, Mel, if you don't mind. My feet are beginning to hurt. Hans has been keeping me going almost steady up to now!" she exclaimed. They found a place to sit down and they watched the couples.

"How come you and Maggie were so late in getting here?" Anna asked.

Mel hesitated a little and looked a little sheepish. "Well, I guess I'll let Maggie tell you," he said, and then he changed the subject. "So, Anna, how long have you been seeing Mr. Nielson?" he asked.

"Oh, about a year now, I guess," she answered.

"You make a nice-looking couple." he said as Hans and Maggie came back to join them. They moved down to make room for them.

A conspiratorial look passed between Maggie and Mel and Mel finally said, "Maggie, Anna was wondering why we were so late in getting to the dance and I said that maybe you would like to tell her." Hans and Anna leaned over to see Maggie better and to hear her explanation.

She blushed a little and said, "Well, we, ah, took a drive over by the lake and Mel, ah.... well, he asked me to marry him," Maggie finally blurted out.

"Oh, Maggie, I'm so happy for you!" said Anna, as she stood and came over and gave Maggie a hug. Hans stood, too, and went to shake hands with Mel.

"You're the first people we've told," said Maggie. She looked excited and happy and so did Mel.

"So when will you be getting married?" inquired Anna

"We think maybe at Christmas time, during school vacation," answered Maggie.

"Oh, a Christmas wedding, how beautiful!" exclaimed Anna.

The band leader announced the last dance of the evening so Hans grabbed Anna and led her onto the floor. It was a slow tune and Hans held Anna close as they let the music flow through them. Anna didn't seem to mind that he was holding her so close. It somehow felt so right with him. She was very quiet, thinking of Maggie getting married and thoughts of Lorrie even came and went through her mind.

"A penny for your thoughts, Anna!" said Hans, holding her at arms length to look into her face. "You seem far away."

"Oh, I was just thinking of Maggie and Mel....and other things," she replied.

After the dance was over, the whole family piled once again into Hans' car. Everyone was tired but they all agreed that it was the best dance ever. Even Teddy thought it was all right. Hans and Anna lingered on the porch after the rest of them had gone into the house. They sat on the top step as they so often did. It was after midnight but it was still warm and the moon was bright and full. The sky looked like an explosion of light, there were so many stars. The two of them sat in silence for quite sometime, just enjoying being together . Conversation wasn't always necessary.

"Well," began Hans, "that was quite a surprise to hear that Maggie and Mel are planning to get married, wasn't it?"

"Yes, I was rather surprised. They haven't even known each other a whole year yet."

"Sometimes it doesn't take very long to know that you have found the right one," said Hans, looking at Anna. He took her hand in his and stroked it gently. "I know that I have found the one for me and I hope that you have, too." With this he stood up, pulling her up along with him. He folded her in his arms and kissed her longingly. She didn't resist. This felt so good and right, she thought for the second time that evening.

"Anna, do you have an answer yet for my proposal of marriage?" he asked hopefully.

"Not yet, Hans, but I promise I won't make you wait much longer. It isn't fair to you."

"It's not a matter of being fair, Anna. Either you want to marry me or you don't. I'll wait for you as long as it takes." He kissed her once again and then she said that she had better go on in.

Everyone was in bed so she undressed quietly and laid down but couldn't sleep. She got up and sat in her rocker and looked out at the moonlight which was lighting up the whole front yard. "What shall I do, Lord?" she whispered. She prayed for guidance in this important matter. She knew that she had to be absolutely sure before she could marry someone again. She turned it over to God and then climbed into bed once again and fell right to sleep.

The next day Anna was telling Bergit about Maggie and Mel getting married and Bergit asked Anna if she and Hans were ever going to take that step. Anna told her that Hans had proposed a short while back and that he had brought it up again last night.

"Why didn't you tell me this before!" exclaimed Bergit. "What did you tell him?"

"I told him that I wasn't ready to marry anyone yet but now I don't know for sure just what to do. He's being patient, waiting for my answer, but I know it isn't fair to make him wait too long.

"Well, how do you really feel about him?" asked Bergit. "I think you two would make the perfect couple. He adores you and I think that you love him, too."

"Well, maybe I do love him, but I'm not sure. What is love, anyway? I like being with him. I'm lonesome for him when he's not around. We're very comfortable together. I'm just very happy when I'm with him." I also like the feeling of him holding me and even kissing me, she thought to herself.

"It sounds like love to me," said Bergit, handing Anna a towel to dry the breakfast dishes. "What's holding you back?"

"I keep thinking of Lorrie and how I felt about him and it's not the same feeling, so maybe it's not love at all," Anna said, sitting down on a chair and giving a big sigh.

Bergit took the chair opposite her sister-in-law and looked her right in the eye. "Anna, listen to me. You loved Lorrie in one way, but there are different kinds of love. That was a 'young love'. Perhaps this is a more mature love, but love nonetheless. Just a different kind. Lorrie was impulsive and full of life and you liked that," Bergit went on. "But Hans is mature and more deliberate. He's the kind of man you can depend on."

Anna was thoughtful for awhile. "Perhaps you're right. But I don't want to marry him just because maybe this might be my last chance for happiness. I want to be very sure about this, that I really do love him. I've been praying about it in earnest lately. God will answer my prayers one way or another."

CHAPTER 19

Hannah came home about the middle of July. She had stayed in St. James for six extra weeks to teach the parochial school there. She said that she could use the extra money. Bergit had the wedding dress ready for the final fitting and the hemming. The wedding would be on the 24th of August.

The next few weeks flew by. There was much baking to do for the reception after the wedding. It would be held in the church basement after the ceremony. Will came from a large family and Bergit didn't think she could handle so many people at the house. This had been a very hot August so far and perhaps the basement would be a cooler place for the doings.

The day of the wedding turned out to be blessedly cool, however. Will's family started arriving in the morning and Bergit fed them coffee and doughnuts. She had been up until way past midnight the night before frying doughnuts and rolling them in sugar. They were devoured quickly by everyone.

The ceremony took place at two in the afternoon. The church was full of flowers from Bergit's garden. A large lunch was served and then Will's family started to head back to St. James. The newly-married couple planned to spend their wedding night at the best hotel in town and then head on out to St. James and the little house that Will had prepared for them on the family's farm.

Bergit and Anna were exhausted that evening. They had worked so hard making all the food and preparations that they went to bed early. The next morning, Hannah and Will stopped by to say goodbye. Will's older brother had loaned them his car to drive back to the farm. After hugs and good wishes and promises to come and see them on the farm, the happy couple drove off.

"Well," sighed Bergit, sitting on the porch step, "only one more daughter left to marry! It sure is lots of work getting ready for a wedding, isn't it?" She looked at Anna, and then added. "I may have one more wedding to get ready for before Sarah's, isn't that right, Anna?"

Anna just smiled and shrugged her shoulders. "Time will tell, Bergit," she answered.

In the fall, another year of school started for several members of the

Olson family. Sarah was starting her junior year of high school and Teddy was now in the eighth grade. Anna returned to her same classroom, but with all new students. The first couple weeks were always hectic, just getting to know all the children.

Anna's friend Maggie was full of wedding plans and could hardly keep her mind on her teaching. She asked Anna to go shopping with her for a wedding dress.

"Aren't you going to make yourself one?" asked the ever- practical Anna.

"No, I don't know how to sew well enough so I've been saving up to buy one, just a simple little frock, of course," she answered.

One afternoon late in October, when Anna came home from school, Tomas was already home and met her at the door. He had a worried look on his face.

"What's happened, Tomas?" asked Anna, equally as worried by now.

"Hans had an accident this afternoon at the lumber yard and he's in the hospital!"

Anna's knees grew weak and she had to sit down. "What happened? Is he badly hurt?"

"He was walking up on the platform where the lumber is stacked and he stepped on the end of a loose board and it came up and hit him right on the side of his head. It knocked him down and he fell about ten feet to the floor. His assistant found him there and called for the Doc. He couldn't get him to come to so he said that he would have to be taken to the hospital."

Anna rose and asked, "How is he now? Is he still unconscious?"

"I don't know. The last I heard, there had been no change. I thought that I would wait for you and we would go to the hospital together."

"Yes, I certainly want to go there right away." They told Teddy where they were going as Bergit wasn't at home.

On the short ride to the hospital in Tomas' truck, Anna was wringing her hands, worried about Hans. The vehicle had hardly made the stop when she jumped out and ran up the steps to the forbidding-looking building.

When Tomas joined her she had found out which room Hans was in and they both took off down the hall, almost running.   When they neared the room, there were two nurses and a doctor standing in the hall.   One of the nurses asked them if they were family.

"No," Tomas answered, "but we are his closest friends. He has no family living around here."

Anna was getting very worried. "How is he? May we see him?" she asked, almost in a panic.

The doctor stepped forward and said, "Mr. Nielson has just started to come to. You may go in for a short while." The doctor followed them into the room and they all stood around the bed looking at the patient.

"Hans," cried Anna. "Can you hear me?"

At this, Hans opened his eyes a little and closed them again. "Anna," he said softly and reached out his hand. Anna, not caring what anyone thought, grasped his hand tightly and brought it up to her face.

"Hans, I was so worried about you!" she said. Hans didn't respond so she squeezed his hand very hard and then he opened his eyes again and smiled faintly. "My angel," he said, and then he closed his eyes again. The doctor came closer to the bed and checked his vitals.

"I think he's going to be all right. We'll let him rest now." The doctor left the room, followed by one of the nurses. The other nurse seemed to be waiting for Tomas and Anna to leave before she did.

"Can I just sit here and wait?" asked Anna. "In case he wakes up again soon and asks for me?"

"Well, I guess that would be all right. But don't disturb him if he wants to sleep."

Anna sat down in the only chair and said to Tomas, "You go on home and I'll stay here for awhile. You can come back later and get me."

Tomas started to protest but Anna said determinedly, "I want to be here."

So Tomas left for home and Anna began her vigil at Hans' bedside. It began to grow dark outside the window. She walked up to the bedside many times, just to make sure that he was still breathing. She would take his hand and look deep into his face. His forehead was bandaged where the plank had apparently hit him. How dear he is to me, she found herself thinking. Oh, what if he had been killed!

After several hours, she heard Hans moaning and she hurried up to the bed once again. "Hans," she said, "can you hear me? It's me, Anna."

He nodded his head slightly. "Oh, my head hurts something awful!"

"Well, it should! You had quite a little accident from what I hear," she said.

"I remember that board coming up to hit me but after that I don't know what happened."

Just then, Jesse, his assistant at the lumber yard came in the door. He removed his hat and said, "Good evening, Mrs. Howe. How is he?"

"He's talking and I think he'll be all right. His head really hurts, he said." They heard footsteps hurrying down the hall and Tomas and Bergit stepped in the room, anxious expressions on their face. Anna repeated the same thing to them. After about a half an hour, a nurse came in and said that visiting hours were over and that they would have to leave. Anna was reluctant to do so but complied anyway. She went home with Tomas and Bergit in the truck. She was exhausted and went up to her room right away and got ready for bed. She fell on her knees by the bed and thanked God that Hans wasn't hurt any worse. She prayed for a quick and complete recovery for him. She lay awake in bed for quite sometime, thinking. It was quite plain to her now what her true feelings for him were. She couldn't bear to think anymore about life without him. He would have the answer that he was waiting for soon.

In about three days time, Hans was out of the hospital and back to work a week after his accident. He was plagued with headaches off and on but the doctor assured him that they would diminish.

Two Sundays later, when Anna talked with Hans after church, she told him that when he came calling in the afternoon, she had a surprise for him. He arrived earlier than usual. The family were all resting after their big Sunday dinner. Anna motioned for him to follow her quietly out the front door.

"Let's drive out by the lake today, Hans," Anna suggested. It was a bright, sunny day but quite cool, but Hans didn't make any objection. Anna was rather quiet during the drive, so Hans didn't say much to interrupt her deep thoughts.

"Let's drive up around the back of the lake," she said. Hans drove until he found the exact same spot that he had proposed to her sometime ago. He stopped the car and turned to look at her, wondering what she wanted to do next. It was too cool and windy to be outside of the car for very long.

"You're probably wondering why I wanted to come up here today, especially when it's rather cold," started Anna. "This is where you asked me a very important question a few months ago and this is where I want to give you my answer."

Han's stomach turned into a knot of apprehension. What was she going to say? He hardly dared to breath, waiting for her answer.

"Let's get out and walk a little, shall we?" Anna suggested. Hans got out and came around and opened the door for her. He grabbed the blanket from the back seat and draped around their shoulders as they started up the hill. When they reached the top, they stood looking out over the lake for awhile. He waited for her to speak first.

"Hans, when I went to see you that first night in the hospital, I knew right then just how much you meant to me and that I couldn't go through life without you. And I guess that's what love is," continued Anna, "wanting to spend the rest of your life with someone."

Hans' heart skipped several beats and he was breaking out in a sweat, in spite of the cool air. He removed the blanket from his shoulders and looked full into Anna's face. "What are you trying to tell me, Anna, my dear?"

"I'm telling you that I do want to marry you, Hans!" she exclaimed. An exclamation of joy came from deep within Hans and he grabbed Anna by the shoulders and pulled her close to him.

"My dear, you don't know how happy this makes me!" He let out another whoop which could have been heard around the lake.

Anna clasped his hands and said, "I've been foolish to have kept us both waiting so long to be together but I wanted to be so sure."

"I understand, dearest," Hans said, drawing her close again. "I knew that you just weren't ready yet, not as ready as I have been for quite some time now!" They both looked at each other and then laughed with pure joy at their new-found happiness.

"Let's go and tell everybody!" said Hans, taking Anna by the hand and leading her back down the hill to the car.

They drove back into town, talking excitedly all the way. They came to a sudden halt in front of the Olson house and they both hurried up the porch steps, bursting through the door.

"My goodness!" exclaimed Berglt, who was sitting in a chair in the parlor. "What's the matter?" She jumped up and looked at the pair standing in front of her.

"Anna has just made me the happiest man in the world!" exclaimed Hans as he danced Anna around the room. " We are going to get married!"

Tomas came from the kitchen, hearing the commotion and the children came running down from upstairs. There was much hugging and tears of joy and some back-slapping. Tomas went to get the decanter of homemade wine and some glasses.

"This calls for a toast, even if it is the Sabbath!" he said, pouring four small glasses of wine. "So what finally brought this young lady to her senses, Hans?"

"Well, I guess I have my accident to thank for that," he said, laughing and putting his arm around Anna. She nodded her head and said that she had to agree with him that that's what did it.

About an hour later, Arne and Sophia came over to have supper with the family and they got in on the good news.

"We have some good news to share, too," said Sophia. "You know that we've been hoping to start a family and that never seemed to happen so we have decided to adopt and we heard yesterday that a baby could be waiting for us in a matter of weeks!"

"Oh, how wonderful!" exclaimed Bergit, hugging Sophia and Arne at the same time. "Oh, this is just too much good news in one afternoon," she said, laughing. She went to the kitchen and started bustling about getting supper ready for the group. Anna and Sophia joined her and there was lots of talk about weddings and babies!

Anna and Hans decided to have their wedding in early June, shortly after school was out. He said that he couldn't wait any longer than that! Anna sat down that very evening and wrote to Sigrid and also to her Papa in Norway, relating the good news. She told both of them that she hoped they could come for the wedding. She posted the letters the next morning and hoped for their answer in their Christmas letters.

At school the next day, Maggie was excited for Anna upon hearing the news. "It's about time you two got hitched. You're perfect for each other," she said.

Christmas was fast approaching. Anna helped out at the Larson's store again on Saturdays and some evenings. There came a letter from Andrew and Alice saying that they were very excited about the coming marriage and that they would be coming for the wedding. They had been thinking about coming for Christmas but decided to postpone their trip until June. Anna waited every day for a letter from Papa.

She and Hans had such a fun time during Christmas vacation. They went to Christmas programs, caroling, julebukking, and then to Maggie and Mel's wedding. It was a small but very pretty wedding. The couple couldn't afford a honeymoon but spent the rest of vacation getting settled into their little home. Anna helped Maggie with curtains and things.

The day before New Year's, a letter finally came from Norway. She ripped it open and sat down to read. She scanned it quickly at first. "Papa's coming! Papa's coming!" she cried, jumping up and running into the parlor to tell Bergit. She calmed herself down and reread the letter aloud to Bergit. Papa said that he would be coming in May. Kjersti would go and stay with Tollef and Margit.

"Oh, just think!" exclaimed Anna, sitting down and hugging the letter to her breast. " We're going to see Papa again after all. I really didn't think that I'd ever see him again." Tears streamed down her cheeks.

When Tomas came home he was filled in on the good news and he was very moved, too. It had been so long since he had seen his father. "Let's see, it must be about twenty-five years now since we left Norway," he said to his wife.

Hans came over that evening and he heard the good news as soon as he came in the door. It was so good to see Anna so happy and excited. Oh, he thought to himself, I don't know how I'm ever going to wait till June!

The winter went fast, though. Hans was busy making some repairs and changes in his house. He fixed up the kitchen and had new cupboards made for Anna. He and Tomas did some painting when the weather got warmer so they could have the windows open.

The women were busy with sewing dresses for the wedding. Anna would have a simple dress this time around. She splurged and bought new shoes to match and a little hat. Bergit and Sarah both needed something new, also, so the sewing machine was whirring almost every evening.

Arne and Sophia didn't get their baby as soon as they had expected. The first baby promised to them had something wrong with it at birth so they had to wait for another. Finally, on March 17, St. Patrick's Day, they were told that they could come and pick up their baby! How excited they were! It was a boy and a good-sized one at that. Almost nine pounds and very healthy. He was definitely worth the long wait, Arne told them. They named him Ronald Thomas and that very evening, the whole Olson family paid a visit to Arne and Sophia's to meet the new addition to the family.

Holding a newborn again brought tears to Anna's eyes and an ache to her heart. Hans saw this and put his hand on her shoulder and whispered, "Maybe we'll be having one of our own soon enough." Anna smiled and patted his hand. She hoped that she would still be able to have children. She wasn't getting any younger.

CHAPTER 20

On the last day of classes, Anna didn't know when she had been so anxious for school to end. The wedding day, June 14, was only about two weeks away. She was so excited, not only about the wedding, but about seeing her father again and Sigrid coming, too. There were many details to tend to before the big day so she kept herself very busy.

Hanging in her room was her dress that she would be wearing for the wedding. She and Bergit had finished it weeks ago. Being this was a second marriage, she felt she couldn't wear white so she had chosen a pale green voile with tiny flowers on it. She had hung it on her curtain rod so that she would see it the first thing in the morning and the last thing at night. The matching shoes and hat lay near by.

Every day for the next two weeks she, Bergit and Sarah were busy cleaning, baking, polishing and shining! Bergit was a very particular housekeeper and wanted everything perfect. Anna didn't want her to wear herself out getting ready for the big event so she tried to help her as much as possible. There would be lots of cooking to do, too, once the family started coming.

Sigrid and Papa would be coming a week before the wedding. Sigrid's daughter, Sylvia, was coming along. Her oldest children, Annie and Arthur, could not come as they both had jobs, and neither could Sigrid's husband, Louis. Andrew and Alice would wait until just the day before to come so as not to make too much added work for Bergit.

The wedding cake was going to be a white cake with lemon filling and white frosting, Anna's favorite, but Anna also wished that she could have a kransekake, or ring cake. This is a special cake used in Norway for weddings or other special occasions. It's very good and also makes an impressive centerpiece. It is made up of an almond-flavored dough, baked in graduated-sized rings and then layered on top of one another.

Lillie Larson, wife of Mr. Larson from the store, said that she would like to make just such a cake for Anna's wedding. She said that her husband could order the special little tins needed for the baking and he could also get the tiny Norwegian flags used to decorate the cake after it is assembled. Anna was so excited when Mrs. Larson offered to do this! Papa and Sigrid, too, would be so surprised to see this Norwegian favorite. Neither Anna nor Bergit had ever made one themselves. It was too difficult without the special tins.

Soon the big day arrived. Not the wedding day, but the day of Papa's arrival! He, Sigrid and Sylvia would be arriving on the train in the early afternoon. Anna was so nervous all that morning. She tried to keep herself as busy as possible. The family had a quick meal at noon. Tomas took the rest of the day off and about an hour before the train's scheduled arrival they could stand it no longer and they all piled in Hans's car and went down to the station to wait. What if it came early and no one was there to meet them!

As it turned out, the train was indeed a few minutes early. Anna felt so nervous and excited. Hans had to try and calm her down. Anna could tell that Tomas was feeling the same way but he tried not to let on. What would Papa look like now? It had been about fifteen years since Anna had bid him farewell on the pier in Christiania.

The train finally came to a complete halt and the steam was hissing and the brakes screaming. They all seemed to be holding their breath as they watched the passengers start to descend the train steps. First there was a family with small children and then a couple of businessmen and then a very old lady who needed help getting down.

"Oh, where is he!" exclaimed Anna, who could stand it no longer. What if they missed their train, she thought to herself!

Just then she spied Sigrid and a young girl emerge from the train doorway. They stopped and looked about the platform and when they spied the family standing there, they waved and then turned back to help an elderly man down the steps. It was Papa!

"Oh, Papa, Papa!" cried Anna as she ran forward to meet them. Tomas hurried after her. The rest of the family held back a little to let the sister and brother greet their father first.

When their father reached the platform he straightened himself and looked up to see his daughter and son, whom he had not seen for many years but recognized them nevertheless. He simply held open his arms and they both fell into his embrace at once. There were tears of joy and a lot of talking and laughing, but the trio kept looking at each other as if they couldn't believe their eyes. None of them thought that this day would ever come. The rest of the family got their turn to greet the elderly man and Hans was introduced to him last. Papa shook his hand and said in Norwegian, "a very good choice, a very good choice." They all laughed again at this.

Hans gave part of the family a ride home and then came back for the other half and the baggage. Papa, who was now seventy-four years old, was very tired out from that long train ride. He was encouraged to go upstairs and rest for awhile. He resisted at first but then gave in and ended up sleeping for about two hours! The rest of the family was anxious for him to awaken and join them but they knew they had to be patient and let him rest.

Sigrid filled them in on his trip from Norway and his stay in New York. He had arrived in America about a month ago, she said. He was having a hard time getting used to the big city and American ways. He was enjoying his new-found grandchildren, though. Sigrid's daughter, Sylvia, had grown up tall and lovely, and like her mother, she was fair with blond hair. She had just graduated from high school and was planning to find a job when she returned to New York. She said that she was so happy that her mother let her come along on this trip out west. She couldn't believe how vast it all was!

When Papa came down and joined the family once more, Bergit served coffee and some big, frosted molasses cookies. She made the coffee extra strong because she knew that was how her father-in-law liked it--strong with lots of cream and sugar!

They passed the next couple of hours listening to him tell about everyone back in Norway; Barbro and her family were doing well, still in Drammen. Tollef and Margit were getting along fine, too. Their oldest son, Arne, having the same name as Tomas's oldest son, had married and had a child. It was not unusual for cousins to have the same name as it was customary to name them after their grandfathers. Their other son, Knut, was planning to marry soon. Their oldest daughter, Signe, was going to stay with Barbro in Drammen for awhile and perhaps become a professional seamstress. Young Caren was still in school and her dream was to go to America someday! "Just like her two aunts," Papa said, looking at Anna and Sigrid.

Arne, Sophia and the baby joined them for supper and Papa became acquainted with still more of his family. Arne handed him the young baby and when he held him, he got tears in his eyes and was quiet for awhile. "I'm an old man now," he said, "but I decided I had to make this trip to America, even if I died trying. I needed to see all of you again and meet my grandchildren. And now," he continued, "this little great- grandchild. Life goes on and on, even when our time on earth is done. On to the next generation." Turning to Anna he added, "I guess I had to fulfill my dream of adventure after all. I really didn't think that I would ever make this trip. Your letters over the years finally wore me down."

"I'm glad they did, Papa," Anna said happily, "It really means so much to me to have you here, especially for my wedding."

The family stayed up late that first evening, talking and reminiscing and just enjoying being together. Finally Papa could stay awake no longer so he went upstairs to go to bed.

The next day, the baking started in earnest! Sigrid and Sylvia were a big help. Goodies by the dozens were stirred up and baked. It took one person just to keep washing up the dishes and drying them, only to have them used once again. The house smelled wonderful after a full day of baking and that evening the tired women and the rest of the family gathered around the big dining- room table, sipping coffee and sampling a few of the fresh-baked goods. The grown ups were talking in Norwegian for the sake of Papa so the grandchildren were often at a loss at what was being said, but they hung around anyway. There was such an atmosphere of joy and happiness at being together that they didn't want to miss that!

Papa was given Teddy's bedroom right across the hall from Anna. Teddy and Sarah were spending their nights at their friends' homes to make room for the extra company. One morning as Anna was ready to go downstairs, Papa called her into his room. He hadn't gotten up yet so he motioned for her to sit on the edge of the bed.

"Anna, it's hard to get a few moments alone with you. Sit a spell and we can have a little talk."

She sat down carefully and took his outstretched hand and father and daughter looked at each other for some time, savoring the moment.

"I've missed you so much, Papa, and I was so afraid that you weren't ever going to come and that I'd never see you again!"

"Well, I just had to come, my dear. You know, everyone back home said that I shouldn't make the trip, that I was too old and that it would be too hard on me. And I also worried about Kjersti. What would become of her if I came over here. But finally I decided, so what if the trip killed me, I needed to come and see the rest of my family. And I'm so glad that I'm here now."

"Have you been awfully lonely since Mama died?" asked Anna. "And how has it been going with Kjersti?"

"Yes, I was very lonely without your Mama. Kjersti seemed to know, though, just what to do in the kitchen. She's been cooking for me but she doesn't like cleaning very much! I have a lady come in once in awhile to do that."

"Did Mama suffer very much at the end?" asked Anna.

"Well, not exactly," answered Papa. "She just kind of slipped away gradually. She was in bed about three weeks before she died. I've been wanting to tell you that she talked about you at the very end, Anna. She had me draw close and she said, 'I know I haven't been a very good mother, especially to Anna.'" Anna stifled a sob as her father went on. "Then she said, 'Do you think she knows that I really did love her?' That's the last thing she said to me. She died about an hour later."

Anna and her father were quiet, each with their own memories, both shedding tears of sadness and remorse. Then Papa brightened and cleared his throat and said, "I sure like that man of yours. I can see that you two will be happy." Then he went on, "I was so sorry when I heard about your first husband's death. It broke my heart, I felt so bad for you. And I was so far away. It's not good for families to be so far from each other."

"Do you wish that I had never come to this country, Papa? Should I have stayed there with you and Mama?" Anna asked. I need to know how he really feels about it, Anna thought to herself.

Her father was silent for awhile and then he squeezed her hand slightly and said, "No, I'm glad that you came here, Anna. I always knew that you wouldn't be satisfied just staying there, living the life that would have been expected of you. It looks like life has been good to you here, for the most part."

Anna withdrew her hand and got up and walked back and forth as she said, "Yes, it has been pretty good, most of it anyway."

"I so enjoyed reading all your letters about your life here, your teaching experiences and everything," Papa said. "I've missed all our little talks, though."

"Yes, I have too, and I wished that I could have talked things over with you every evening, like I used to do," Anna said pensively.

"Well," said Papa, as he sat up on the edge of the bed and dangled his legs over the side, "I guess I better get up and see what this day brings. When are Andrew and his family coming? Then I will have seen all my family here in this country."

Not quite all, Anna thought to herself. She hadn't thought of Samuel quite as often as before, but ever since her father came, the boy had been foremost in her thoughts again. Perhaps it's because she wondered what her father would think if he knew what had happened to his beloved daughter so soon after her arrival in this country.

The wedding day was fast-arriving. It was to be held outdoors in the back yard. The peonies were almost in full bloom and there were many of them and this would make a lovely backdrop for the ceremony. Many of the neighbor ladies volunteered to bring bouquets of their own peonies for the house.

Several days before the wedding, Tomas came home and told Anna that he had found a way to have a piano for the outdoor ceremony. Mrs. Casperson down the block had told him that he could use her piano if he could find enough help to get it over to the Olsons'. He said that he was going to make a little cart for it and wheel it down the sidewalk. He was out in his shed for quite sometime that evening before he came in and said that the cart was ready and that the morning of the wedding, he and about three other strong men would go over and get the piano. Anna was delighted with this news! She had been wishing for a piano but thought it too much of an undertaking to get one there.

"Oh, and by the way," said Tomas, "Mrs. Casperson said that she would play it for you if you needed someone."

Anna went over to her house the next morning and the two of them picked out some music. Things are coming together, thought Anna. I just hope the weather holds for another few days, she thought to herself. She made a quick trip over to Mrs. Larson's house, too, to check on the kransekake. Mrs. Larson was in kind of a dither because the tin pans for the cake had not arrived until just that morning! But her sister-in-law was going to help her and they would deliver the special cake the morning of the wedding, she said.

One day left before the wedding! The weather was still good and things were coming along fine. Andrew and his family would be coming in on the afternoon train. Tomas and Arne started moving some of Anna's things over to Hans' house. Anna hadn't been over there recently and Hans said that he had a surprise for her that she couldn't see until after the wedding. Tomas and Arne wouldn't give her any hints as to what it was when they returned from the house to get another load of her things. The trunk was the last thing that they moved.

"This big trunk has moved around quite a bit, don't you think, Anna?" Tomas said teasingly. "Maybe it will stay put now for awhile."

Just the evening before, Anna had picked up and reread a letter that had come about a week ago from Lorrie's parents. She had written to them to let them know of her impending marriage. They said that they were happy for her and wished her the very best. She read it over several times and it was important to her that they knew about her remarrying and it relieved her to have their blessing. It seemed to be the closing of a chapter in her life that she had to finally let go of now. She put the letter in her trunk, closed the lid and felt ready to put those memories behind her.

Anna, Papa and Sigrid went along to meet the train. Andrew and his family were the first ones off. Andrew came hurrying up to the group awaiting them and Papa embraced him for a long while. Andrew had tears of joy streaming down his face and so did Papa.

"Now I have seen all my children. I am truly a very fortunate man," he said. Many a parent had bid farewell to their grown children on a pier in the old country, never to see them again!

Andrew drew his own family close and introduced his father to them, first to his wife, Alice, and then to his two sons, Alfred and George. Alfred was a big, strapping eighteen-year-old now and George was thirteen.

Teddy had walked down to the station because he was so excited to see his cousin, George, again and the two boys set out walking back to the house. They had much catching up to do! Teddy would no doubt show him the town on their way home.

The Olson house was bulging now with all the family gathered together! The supper table was crowded that evening but no one seemed to mind. Bergit had outdone herself cooking up a splendid meal. Sylvia and Sarah cleared up the dishes and washed them while the grownups lingered over their coffee, talking and catching up on everyone's news.

Every once in awhile Anna would feel butterflies in her stomach when she would remember that tomorrow was her wedding day! Then she would look at Hans, who was, of course, invited for supper, and he would give her a little wink and squeeze her hand under the table. This did not go unnoticed by the rest of the family.

"Well," Tomas declared, looking at the couple, "tomorrow night at this time you will be Mr. and Mrs. Hans Nielsen!"

Anna blushed and Hans beamed and everyone laughed and started pushing themselves away from the table. Hans and Anna went out on the porch to get some fresh air and to be alone for a few minutes.

"Well, Anna," said Hans as they clasped hands, "tomorrow will be the happiest day of my life! I"ve waited so long for this day."

"Yes, it will be a happy, happy day for me, too, Hans," declared Anna.

"I will leave you, then, for the last time. I have some things to do at home." He gave her a lingering kiss and said, "I'll see you tomorrow. I hope you can get a good night's rest."

"Good night, and remember, Hans," she called after him, "don't come too early. The groom can't see the bride before the ceremony!" He just waved and smiled at her and jumped into his car.

When Hans entered his house, he tried to look at it as Anna would see it when she moved in. She hadn't been there for some time now so she hadn't seen some of the new things that he had added. He had discarded the old, rickety kitchen table with one that a friend had offered to him. He had refinished it and it now stood gleaming and new looking. The chairs don't look too good, he thought to himself, but it's too late to do anything with them now.

His biggest surprise for Anna would be the new bedroom set that he had purchased. It was a beautiful set in a rich cherrywood. The bed was a four poster and there was a dresser and a chest of drawers to match. It had been delivered about a week ago and it was hard to keep it a secret. He had not slept in it yet because he wanted to wait till he and Anna could sleep in it together for the first time. He had moved his old bed into the other bedroom upstairs. They could use that as a guest room.

He found some clean sheets and made up the new bed. He wished he had some nice, new bedding but that would have to wait until Anna moved in. This house needs a woman's touch, he thought. New curtains and maybe some new rugs and all that kind of thing. Some of Anna's belongings were already standing around waiting for her to decide where to put them. Her trunk stood along one wall in the big bedroom.

Later that evening, back at Tomas and Bergit's, Anna walked into the kitchen to find Tomas, Andrew, Sigrid and Papa sitting drinking coffee so she joined them. They were talking about Mama. Her three older siblings all had much different memories about her than Anna did so she merely listened without comment.

Finally, after some time, they realized how quiet she was but they attributed it to her being preoccupied with the upcoming day. Papa looked at her with gentle eyes and she knew that he knew what she was thinking of.

"Well, Anna," said Andrew jovially, "do you have any thoughts of backing out at the last minute?"

"Not on your life, brother dear; I have waited too long the way it is!" she exclaimed. Bergit came with more coffee and said that she agreed with that statement.

Along about eleven o'clock the household started settling down for the night, one by one, each with their own thoughts about the next day.

Anna knelt by her bed and let herself be quiet for some time. Then she prayed, "Dear Lord, thank you for sending me this wonderful man that I am about to marry. I'm sorry that I didn't realize earlier that this was an answer to my prayer, but I'm very sure now that this is someone that you have sent to me to be my life's partner."

She lay awake for awhile. Her window was open wide and a nice breeze was stirring the curtains. She could see the moon and the stars and it was like they were twinkling in happiness just for her. She drifted off to sleep with happy thoughts of the morrow.

CHAPTER 21

Anna was lying in bed early the next morning when she heard her half-opened door squeak. Her eyes popped open to see Bergit stick her head in and say, "I just came to say 'good morning' to the bride! It's going to be a beautiful day!" She walked over to the window and raised the shade all the way up. Then she sat down on the bed beside Anna. "Oh, I didn't wake you, did I?" she asked, now feeling contrite. "I've been up for so long I forget that it might still be early for most people!"

"No, I was just starting to wake up. Goodness, what time is it anyway?" she asked, sitting up and trying to see her clock.

"It's only about 7:30," answered Bergit. "I just wanted to get a few moments alone with you. Things will be buzzing around here after a short while."

"Yes, I need to think about what I have left to do," said Anna.

"Well, we don't want you to do much of anything this morning," said Bergit. "This is your very special day and I think that everything is pretty much in readiness as far as you are concerned." She paused a moment or two before going on. "I just wanted to tell you how happy I am for you and I just know that you and Hans are so right for each other."

"Yes, we are 'very right' for each other," declared Anna, "and I know that now, with all my heart." Bergit rose and Anna jumped out of the bed. "And Bergit, I don't know how to thank you for all you've done for me over the years." Bergit started to protest but Anna went on. "You took me in and made me feel like a member of this family. And now you've worked so hard to make this such a wonderful day for me. You're the best sister-in-law ever!"

"I think of you, Anna, as the sister that I never had and we've enjoyed having you a part of our family." The two women looked at each other and then embraced, a little too quickly so as not to let the tears flow. "I need to get breakfast started," said Bergit, wiping at her eyes with the corner of her apron.

"I need to get dressed, too, and I'll be right down to help you."

"No, no, remember you are not to help with anything this morning," Bergit reminded Anna. "Sigrid will help. I heard her up a few minutes ago." She left the room and hurried downstairs.

Well, then, Anna thought to herself, I might as well enjoy myself for a few hours. She dressed and sat at the dressing table and worked with her hair a little. I wonder how I should wear it, she wondered. She got up and picked up her hat and put it on her head. She held her dress up next to her and looked at herself in the dresser mirror. Her face glowed and her eyes sparkled in excitement.

Sigrid peeked in just at that moment and she exclaimed, "Oh, Anna, you will be such a beautiful bride!" She stood behind Anna and they looked at their images in the mirror. The two sisters hugged and then Anna said, "I was just wondering how I should wear my hair today." She sat down again and removed the hat and Sigrid started playing with the rich, luxurious head of auburn hair. She tried several styles with and without the hat but they couldn't decide.

"I'll maybe wait and have Sarah help me. She's always been good at hairstyles," said Anna.

"And I better run down and help Bergit," Sigrid said, starting for the door.

"Sigrid, I'm so glad that you are here. Little did we know that when you came for my first wedding, that you would be coming for another one," reflected Anna.

"Well, Anna, that's how life goes sometimes," said Sigrid. "Not always like we plan it. And I'm glad that I can be here again for you. And I'm so very happy that Papa could come. I know that it certainly makes it even more special for you." The two embraced again and Sigrid left her younger sister to get dressed.

Over the next hour, the rest of the family drifted in and out of the kitchen, eating their breakfast of pancakes and chokecherry syrup in shifts. Anna was almost too excited to eat but she managed one pancake and a cup of coffee. She excused herself and said that she was going to run over to Mrs. Casperson's to check on something about the music. Her friend, Maggie, was going to be the soloist and she was very happy that there would be a piano to accompany her!

When Anna got outside, Tomas and Andrew were wheeling the cart out of the shed.

"When Arne gets here, we'll be going over to get the piano," he called to Anna. "Mr. Henderson said that he would help, too, so we should have enough help."

When Anna returned from the Casperson's, Arne drove up in the truck. It was full of chairs and some tables that they had borrowed from the community hall. The men started unloading them and asked her how she wanted them arranged.

When they were almost done with that task, Mr. and Mrs. Larson drove up and they said they had the kransekake in the back seat and where did she want it? Anna called to Bergit and they decided to put it on a small table on the edge of the lawn and cover it up with a light- weight dish towel. It wouldn't do to bring it in the house and then try to move it again later. Mrs. Larson set it up and put all the little Norwegian flags on it and some greenery around the base. It looked so impressive and when Sigrid saw it she almost cried.

"Oh, I haven't seen one of those since I left Norway!" she exclaimed. The day before, she and Bergit had made another cake, a white one with lemon filling and white, fluffy frosting. That would be brought out later with all the other food.

Mrs. Petersen from next door came over with a dishpan full of plates and cups that Bergit had asked to borrow. "My, it sure is a lot of activity around here this morning!" she exclaimed. "You'd think that something important was going to happen," she joked.

The men went down to get the piano and Anna joined the women inside. Bergit had Sylvia and Sarah busy making sandwiches, putting thin slices of ham and roast beef on white and dark buns that were freshly baked the day before. The girls put some of them on a plate for the family to quickly eat for their noon meal and the rest were stacked in cake pans and covered with towels and put in the ice box to keep cool until the afternoon. Bergit was filling large enamel coffee pots with water and was making the egg coffee mixture to have ready for the lunch after the ceremony. There were salads in several of the neighbors' iceboxes, also.

"Let's see now," said Bergit, "is everything taken care of then? You all can grab a sandwich whenever you're hungry and there are cookies in the jar. That should hold everybody until lunch this afternoon." Bergit went to sit down for awhile. She looked tired but flushed with excitement. Tomas came in and saw her sitting there. He grabbed a couple of sandwiches in his big hand and came to sit next to her.

"You aren't working too hard now are you, Bergit? You don't want to be all played out for the ceremony," he admonished lovingly.

"Oh, I'm all right," she answered. "Everybody is pitching in and things are about ready. I thought I'd sit for awhile before going up to change and maybe I'll help Anna a little if she needs anything." She got up and got herself a sandwich, too, and a glass of milk.

After Anna had eaten, she went upstairs and Sarah followed her. She was going to help do her hair before dressing. It was rather warm upstairs this time of the day. Papa was in his room, resting. The house was fairly quiet, considering all the people in it!

Sarah was excited about the wedding. Anna had asked her to be her maid of honor so she was a little nervous. She combed out Anna's long hair and then began to try different styles. They decided on a loose up-sweep with some curls hanging down on the sides. She helped Anna put her dress on and then she went to get her own on. It was a pale yellow and the style was similar to Anna's except that Sarah's had flounces on the bottom. She had gotten new ivory-colored shoes with a strap and a button on the side and a small heel. She was seventeen now and a real beauty and looked very much a woman.

The ceremony was to begin at two o'clock. Anna looked out her window and she could see the minister of their church and his wife walking up the sidewalk. She looked at the clock. One twenty! Soon, oh soon it would be time. Her heart was pounding. She didn't remember being this nervous at her first wedding but maybe she had forgotten. I wonder how Hans has been doing this morning, she thought to herself. I'm sure he's as nervous and as excited as I am.

She heard the other members of the family going downstairs, one at a time, as they got ready. Bergit and Sigrid popped in to take a look at the bride and they oohed and aahed over her appearance. Sarah came in and Anna was surprised anew at this young girl's beauty and loveliness.

"Oh, Sarah, you are going to be the most beautiful maid of honor there ever was!" exclaimed Anna. The two looked each other up and down.

Sarah said, "Aunt Anna, you are the most beautiful bride I've ever seen."

"Well, then, girl," laughed Anna, " you haven't seen very many brides!"

"Aunt Anna," said Sarah thoughtfully, "how do you know when the right man comes along?" Sarah was very interested in boys by now but didn't have any one particular fellow.

"Well, Sarah, I may not be a very good one to answer that question!" she said laughingly. "The right man for me was right here and I didn't realize it for quite sometime."

"But how will I know for sure?" she persisted. Anna realized that this was no idle question and she decided that she had better take the time to answer it carefully.

"Most importantly, you put the matter in God's hands and ask him to lead you to the right person. Finding a life's mate is too important a matter to try and do it yourself. It's the most important decision you will ever make. If you're not happy in your marriage then you won't be happy with your life as a whole."

This answer was getting pretty deep and Sarah had a frown on her face when Bergit came in the room once again. She looked at her daughter and then at Anna and said, "Why the serious faces? It's soon time to go down. Most of the guests are here. We'll get them all seated and then when you hear the piano start playing, that's your cue to come outside. Sigrid just got Papa down and he's waiting for you."

The three women went downstairs. Everyone else was outside, waiting for the ceremony to begin. Bergit went to sit by Tomas and Sigrid. Anna peeked out the back kitchen window and looked at all those assembled, about fifty people in all. There was her family, their closest neighbors and some friends of hers and Hans'.

She glanced nervously at the clock. It was time! She heard Mrs. Casperson start to play the piano. She slowly opened the back screen door and Papa was there waiting for her. He gave her a quick hug and they started walking up towards the front of the little congregation. Sarah and Jesse, Hans' assistant at the lumber yard and now his best man, were already up there and Hans was standing looking toward his bride-to-be. Why, he doesn't look nervous at all, Anna thought to herself. Just happy!

Papa handed Anna over to Hans and then took a seat by Bergit. The preacher started the service amidst the flowers and the chirping of the birds. It was all very lovely. After a short sermon, Maggie sang "O Perfect Love" and by the time she finished the third verse, there wasn't a dry eye in the audience. Everyone knew of the previous experiences of both the bride and the groom and they were all so happy for the two of them.

When they were saying their vows and Anna was placing the gold band on Hans' finger, she looked up into his face and saw such love there that it almost took her breath away. She knew without a doubt that this man would love and cherish her until death parted them.

"Hans Olaf Nielsen, do you take this woman present to be your lawfully wedded wife? If so, say 'I do'," intoned the preacher.

"I do!" answered Hans, loud and clear.

"Anna Olson Howe, do you take this man present to be your lawfully wedded husband?" Almost before the preacher could finish, Anna said "I do!"

He placed his hand over the joined hands of the couple and said, "What God has joined together, let no man put asunder. I now pronounce you man and wife."

The pianist started playing again and the couple turned and walked down the aisle. The guests started getting up and went over to the newlyweds and shook their hands and offered them their congratulations and best wishes. With this done, Tomas was waiting to take the wedding party in Hans' car over to the photographer's studio to have the official wedding portrait taken. They excused themselves from their guests and while they were gone, Bergit, Sigrid and Sylvia were busy getting the food placed outside on the tables. They uncovered the two cakes and everyone was looking with interest at the kransekake. The big coffee pots were carried out by Andrew and Arne and everything was in readiness when the party returned. Hans and Anna led the lunch line, each of them too excited to be hungry, but they took some of the food anyway to be polite.

After some of the guests had started leaving, with mostly just family left, Hans and Anna were urged to start opening their gifts which were on a long table in the shade of the big oak tree. The biggest box was from Tomas and Bergit and family. It was a beautiful Victorian-style table lamp with a fringed shade in the most delicate light-colored rose.

"Oh, this is just beautiful!" said Anna, looking at Tomas and Bergit.

There were many lovely and useful things. From Norway there was a set of silver spoons from Barbro and her family and a hardanger embroidery tablecloth from Tollef and Margit. Papa had brought these with him. Sigrid had made a set of bed linen and with lovely, intricate embroidery work on it.

After opening all the gifts, the newlyweds prepared to leave. Teddy brought down Anna's bag and amid hugs and laughter and well wishes, Anna and Hans drove off. They were only going downtown to spend their first night in the hotel there. Hans had reserved the bridal suite. Hans had wanted to take Anna on a honeymoon to Chicago but she didn't want to leave as long as Papa was still here. Maybe they would go later. Their first night together was full of love and tenderness and they savored this special time together, at last.

Late the next morning, after a lovely breakfast served in their room, they went to their little house. Hans carried Anna over the threshold and he was excited for her to see everything that he had done.

"Oh, Hans, the table!" she exclaimed. "It's beautiful!" Hans had put a bouquet of flowers on it and it did indeed look lovely. She had seen the new cupboards before so she quickly moved to the next rooms. They were freshly painted and things looked very nice and clean. She was already thinking of little touches that she could add. Maybe some new curtains on those windows, she thought. He steered her upstairs and she gasped when she saw the new bedroom set.

"Oh, Hans! I didn't know you were going to buy a new bedroom set! How beautiful!" She ran her fingers over the rich cherrywood. She turned and gave him a big hug. "I love it!" she said as she ran into the other bedroom. There he had set up his old bed and put a nice old quilt on it.

"This can be our guest room until....well...until maybe we might need it for something else like a.....a nursery," Hans stammered out.

"Oh, I sure do hope so!" said Anna with feeling. "Perhaps Papa can come and stay with us for awhile before he leaves. He could have this room."

"That's what I thought you would say," laughed Hans. "See, I am reading your mind already!"

They spent the rest of the day putting things away and getting settled. Tomas and Andrew came over with the wedding gifts later and invited them to come back to the house for supper if they would like.

"Unless you'd rather be alone," Tomas winked at Andrew.

"We'll see," answered Anna. "Maybe we'll come." She looked at Hans and he had an expression that said, whatever you want to do will always be all right with me.

As it turned out, Hans and Anna decided to spend the rest of the day just by themselves in their cozy little house. They ate some sandwiches that Tomas had brought over which were left over from the reception. He also brought some cake. They put the wedding gifts away and went up to their bedroom. They placed the new lamp on the new nightstand and when they turned it on, it put the whole room in a rosy glow.

"Oh, isn't it lovely!" exclaimed Anna, as she looked around her new bedroom.

Hans was glad that he had hooked up to the city's electric generator a few years back. It was worth it for just this magic moment. He took Anna in his arms and they could both have almost wept with joy. They both knew how fragile love and happiness were and they meant to never take it for granted.

CHAPTER 22

Anna enjoyed setting up housekeeping in her own little home at last. Papa came to stay with them for his last week before he and Sigrid and Sylvia left. They were going to stop at Andrew's for about a week and then head back to New York. Papa would be leaving from there to go back to Norway sometime in August.

When Anna said goodbye to her father this time she would not let herself think that this would probably be the last time she would see him. Perhaps someday she could go back to Norway to see him and her homeland again. She would not let herself be sad. She was too happy in her new marriage. She also knew how happy her father was to be able to make this trip and see his family one more time. This was something to be thankful for.

Bergit came by often and she helped Anna make new curtains for several of the rooms and also a bed coverlet for the new bed. Hans was greeted with some new improvement each day when he came home from work. He was also greeted with the aroma of something good for supper each evening.

The summer flew by and it was soon time for school to begin again.

Maggie had stopped by Anna's one day earlier with the news that she would not be coming back to school as she was expecting a baby. She and Anna rejoiced over this. Anna hoped that this would be the case for her sometime soon, too.

Back in her classroom, Anna didn't enjoy teaching as much as she used to. She was too anxious for the day to end so she could get back to her new home and her husband.

Hans and Anna never did go on a honeymoon but they were planning to go to Chicago at Christmas time. Anna was very excited about this. She hated to leave her family during the holidays but she was anxious to meet Hans' family. She shopped for gifts for her family early and brought them over the week before they were to leave.

Finally the day arrived. They took the train from Mankato to St. Paul where they got on another train. They were traveling first class so they had a sleeping berth in a Pullman car.

"Oh, just imagine being able to stretch out at night and get a good night's sleep!" Anna exclaimed. "I've traveled so many times by train but always have had to sleep sitting up."

When they arrived at Union Station in Chicago, Hans' sister Ruth and her husband, John, were there to meet them. Hans' mother was waiting for them at home. Ruth and John and their two children, Betsy and Stuart, lived in a brownstone apartment on Wisconsin Street and Mrs. Nielson lived in the same building. Her small flat was on the main floor and Ruth's family occupied the second floor apartment. They were only three blocks from Lake Michigan.

Hans' mother opened the door for them and she gave Hans a quick hug but she was more interested in meeting this woman who seemed to be making her son so happy. Hans and Anna had sent her their wedding photograph. After only a short time, she decided that not only was Anna lovely to look at but she was a very lovely person, indeed. Anna and Ruth hit it off right away, too. The children, Betsy, who was almost nine and Stuart, who was seven, were excited to meet a new aunt.

The family had a wonderful Christmas together. Anna enjoyed the sights of the big city. It was all lit up for the holiday season. John, who worked for Illinois Power and Light as an engineer, took Hans and Anna down to his office one day. They also went to see the Chicago Board of Trade and they stopped in some of the big department stores for a look.

After a week, it was time to board the train again and head back home. Mrs. Nielson gave Anna an extra big hug and said into her ear, "Thank you for making Hans such a happy man! You two are well suited for each other and I wish you much happiness." There were many tears, but also promises to see each other again soon.

When they arrived back home, there was some mail from Norway and also a letter to Anna from Toledo, from the Martin's. She waited till she was alone to open it and when she did, a picture dropped out. It was of Samuel, standing so tall and grown up in a suit. It was his confirmation photo, Mrs. Martin explained in the letter. Anna had not had a picture or any letters from Mrs. Martin for quite a number of years now.

She took the picture and sat down in the rocker by the bedroom window and stared at it for a long time. Tears welled up in her eyes. Here was her son whom she couldn't claim and couldn't even see anymore. How she longed to hold him and stroke his head and tell him how sorry she was for giving him up, but it had seemed the right thing to do at the time.

She heard Hans come back into the house so she quickly opened her trunk and put both the picture and letter in a box with other photos. This would be the only secret between her and Hans. She thought it better this way. She dried her eyes and went downstairs to greet her husband and to start supper.

"So, what did the family from Toledo have to say, then?" he asked, after they had eaten and were sipping their coffee.

"Only that they are getting along fine and that Samuel was confirmed recently. How time flies!" she tried to keep her voice even as she cleared up the dirty dishes and brought them to the sink so Hans couldn't see her face.

"Well, that's nice that they still keep in touch with you now and then," he commented, as he picked up the evening paper and began to read.

Anna was quiet for a long time as she washed up the dishes. Hans put down the paper and came and took the dish towel from the towel rack and started drying them for her.

"And why is my usually talkative wife so quiet this evening?" he asked good naturedly.

"I....I was just thinking about tomorrow Going back to school and all," she answered, hating the deception that she would always have to maintain on this subject.

Anna retired early that night but didn't sleep well. She kept thinking of the image of that tall young man in the photo. He would be fourteen now, almost fifteen, she thought to herself. She tossed and turned and hoped that she wasn't keeping Hans awake. He didn't say anything about her restlessness in the morning so he must have slept well.

In February, Maggie had her baby, a little girl, so Anna made a kettle of soup and brought it over to the house several days later. She sat and rocked the baby for a long time. How good it felt to hold a newborn! They named her Lenora Anne.

In March, Hans and Anna were invited over to Arne and Sophia's for Ronnie's first birthday.   Tomas, Bergit, Teddy and Sarah were there, too. As Ronnie sat in his high chair, Sophia placed a big piece of birthday cake in front of him. Instead of sticking his finger in it to taste the fluffy frosting, he took his little arm and batted it right off the tray! It flew about six feet in the air and landed frosting side down on a velvet chair nearby! First there was silence and then everyone burst out laughing except Sophia and Arne! They didn't think it was very funny. Ronnie started laughing, too, at his great trick.

"I think he's going to be a great baseball player, like Cy Young!" exclaimed his Grandpa.

While Sophia and Bergit cleaned up the chair, Anna fed the birthday boy some cake, a little bite at a time, and he loved it. The men started talking about the baseball scandal that had recently been uncovered. The Chicago White Sox were accused of throwing some games for money. Baseball had become a great American pastime and it was every young boy's dream, including Teddy's, to play the game in the big leagues.

As Anna sat back and watched the child run around after he finished eating, she thought to herself, how complete my life would be now if I could have a child again one day. Hans saw her looking pensively at the little boy and his heart went out to her as he knew what she was thinking about. He hoped, too, with all his heart, that they would be able to have a child. But if they didn't, he would still have Anna, and he would be content.

On the way home, he put his hand on Anna's and said, "I know how much you would love to have a little boy like that running around our house. I hope that it happens soon!"

"Oh, I hope so, too" she said, giving his hand a squeeze. She hoped it with all her heart.

Anna didn't have too much longer to wait. Several weeks after the birthday party, she woke up feeling nauseated and after several days of this, she just knew what was wrong! Her prayers had been answered. She was going to have a baby! That evening after one of Hans' favorite meals, she broke the happy news that had been ready to burst out of her since he came home.

Han's reaction was first one of disbelief and then relief and than sheer giddiness! He danced Anna around the room and hugged her and they both wept tears of joy. Anna wouldn't let herself even think about the possibility that she wouldn't be able to carry this pregnancy to full term.

The elated couple was not able to keep it a secret very long because they were both so full of joy and excitement. The first ones to be told were Tomas and Bergit. They were so excited for Hans and Anna that they could hardly stand it!

Everyone in town soon heard the good news, as things like this travel very fast in a small community.   All the townspeople congratulated them and were genuinely happy for them. Anna started to feel better after about three months and she busied herself sewing little baby things. She wouldn't be going back to school now, of course.   The doctor said that the baby would be born around Christmas time.

She and Hans started gathering up things that the baby would need. Arne and Sophia were using the baby crib that Tomas and Bergit had had for their children, so Hans just went out and bought a new one at the furniture store in town and it was delivered to Anna one day without her knowing a thing about it. It was a beautiful crib. It had some little animal decals on it and she was just finishing up a crib quilt when it arrived. She had the delivery men put it up in the spare bedroom and she put the new quilt on it and it was all ready for Hans to see when he arrived home at noon for dinner.

She led him upstairs and they looked with joy at the little room which was now ready for the new occupant. Anna patted her stomach and said, "It won't be too long now!"

Actually it was about six weeks later that their precious little baby boy came into the world! He made his entrance, after a somewhat lengthy delivery, on the day after Christmas. Hans called for the doctor when the pains first started but after examining her, he said that it would be a long time yet.   Finally, late in the evening the baby was born. As Hans and Anna looked down at him, they thought that they'd never seen anything so precious and beautiful. He was so perfect. They named him Frank after Han's father.   For his middle name, they chose Arnold, a variation of Anna's father, Arne.

Anna was made to stay in bed for almost two weeks. She was so ready to get up long before that but Hans insisted that she listen to the doctor. Bergit would come over every day and help out for awhile and Hans also had hired someone to come and be with his wife until he would get home.

Baby Frank grew into a strong and sturdy little fellow. His parents were so proud, as new parents are! They were going to get to show him off to some more members of the family soon as Hannah and Will invited the whole family to come and visit them. So on a beautiful June day, Hans, Anna, Tomas, Bergit, Teddy and Sarah and, of course, little Frank, crowded into Hans' car and they started off bright and early. It was a two hour drive. Hans and Anna had not been out to Hannah and Will's before.

They arrived at mid-morning and were greeted by the smell of fresh coffee. Hannah had had a baby girl two months before Frank was born so she and Anna had some comparing to do. The men had time to look around the large farm before dinner time. In the afternoon as the two babies napped, the women took a walk along the stream which flowed through the farm yard. They sat for awhile on the long, lush grass.

"I can see, Aunt Anna, that you seem just as happy as Will and I are," said Hannah. "Remember when you had a talk with me about getting married too young and about how hard life could be on the farm?"

"Oh, that!" exclaimed Anna, remembering that lecture with embarrassment. "I guess I was wrong, wasn't I?"

"We're very happy with our life out here and, sure, sometimes there is lots of work to do but I have good help with Will's mother living so close by."

Bergit beamed proudly at her grown daughter. "I just wish you lived closer to me, Hannah. I'd like to see more of you and Will and little Ellen."

"I think you married a fine man and he seems like a very hard worker," said Anna.

The babies were both awake and trying to out- cry each other when the women returned to the house. After much talk of babies, husbands, recipes and such, Hannah made a light supper and then the family loaded up for the return trip.

"It's been a wonderful day," Anna said to Hannah and Will. She kissed baby Ellen goodbye and after everyone had given and received their farewell hugs, the group started off for home.

After putting the sleeping Frank in his crib, Hans put his arm around Anna and said, "You know, I really enjoy being a part of your large, wonderful family. I realized now how lonely I was before you came into my life."

"Family is everything, isn't it," reflected Anna. How full and happy her life was now. Thank you, Lord, for all my blessings, she said prayerfully. She never failed to give God the thanks each and every day.

Later that year, Arne and Sophia were hoping to adopt another baby and just before Thanksgiving, they received word that they would be getting one soon, maybe by Christmas. As it turned out, the baby was born on Frank's first birthday and they were able to go and get their new little daughter before New Year's. They named her Katherine Elizabeth and she was a very tiny little thing.

"That's a big name for such a wee one!" exclaimed her Grandfather Tomas. Everyone was standing over her cradle, admiring her when Anna could hold in her good news no longer.

"We're going to have another baby, too," she blurted out, and everyone erupted into squeals of delight.

"Oh, all these babies in the family! Isn't it just wonderful!" exclaimed Bergit.

Hans and Anna's baby was expected in June and they were hoping for a girl this time. Their hopes came true on June 24th when little Margaret Anne made her appearance after a quick delivery.

"She was in a hurry to join this happy family!" exclaimed the proud, new father. "Just look at her. Isn't she just beautiful?"

Indeed she is, thought Anna, as she cuddled her close to her breast. Now my life is really complete. I have truly found my 'dream'. Two beautiful children, a husband who loves and cherishes me and who is a wonderful father and a good provider. What more could I possibly want?

CHAPTER 23

Life was good for Hans and Anna in the twenties. The lumber business was bustling and Hans had hired two more men to keep up with his growing business. Frank and his little sister, Margaret, were growing and thriving. Tomas and Arne were kept very busy in their carpentry business and now had a crew of five men.

In 1925, the Ford Motor Co. came out with a new model automobile. It was the first of the cars to have glass windows. It also had electric start (no more cranking!) Hans was very excited about this model so he decided to sell his car and buy this new one. Arne bought the old one from him. Tomas finally broke down and bought one, too, that year. Hans came driving home in his new purchase one evening and Anna and the children hopped in and they drove around town in it. These new models had just come in by rail that very day.

"Mr. Sheldon said that I could have any color I wanted as long as it was black!" joked Hans. Anna was busy thinking that she could make some nice curtains for the windows.

Little Frank sat in his Daddy's lap and 'helped' steer. "This will be easier for you to drive now, Anna. You just turn the key and it starts!" explained Hans.

"How much did it cost?" asked Anna.

"Six hundred dollars," answered Hans. I paid half down and I'll pay fifty dollars a month until it's paid. Don't worry, Anna," he went on. " We can afford it. And I got a hundred from Arne for the old one, too," he added.

By the end of the summer, Hans was thinking that he would like to build a new house for his growing family. The one they were living in was getting too small, he told Anna. She liked their first little house, but she had to agree that it would be nice to have a little more room. Especially another bedroom and a bigger kitchen.

In the fall, when Tomas and Arne's business slacked off a little, they started digging the basement for the new house. It would be a grand house, Hans informed Anna. A big, square two-story with four bedrooms and even a bathroom!

By the time winter had really settled in, they had the house fully enclosed and they spent the winter months working on the inside.

"It should be ready by April or May," Hans told his wife. She was excited about it now and liked to go over to see the progress about once a week.

That Christmas, they celebrated Frank's fourth birthday and little Margaret was almost two. What a fun Christmas they all had with Arne and Sophia with their three children and Hannah and Will, who came up for several days, too. When Arne and Sophia's adopted daughter was only a year old, Sophia surprised everyone, including her doctor, by becoming pregnant so they now had another little girl added to their growing family. They named her Amanda, but always called her Mandy.

Tomas and Bergit's house was bursting at the seams when they all got together Christmas Day! Hannah was expecting again come summer so there would soon be one more.

Sarah, who had gone to work at the Larson's Department Store full time after she graduated, was now married and had a child. She married Bert Larson, the grandson of the owner of the store. He was a wonderful young man and when he came back to town after graduating from business college in St. Paul, he started working in the store. He was about five years older than Sarah and when he had left town several years before, she had been just a young girl. His father wanted him to come back and take over the store eventually. The elder Mr. Larson was too old now to help out anymore and Bert's father wanted to be able to retire soon.

Bert and Sarah fell madly in love and they made a very handsome couple. They had a darling little boy named Robert, but he was always called Bobby. They were planning to buy Hans and Anna's old house as soon as the new house was ready.

Finally the big day came! Family and friends from all over town came to help load furniture and unload it into the new house. Everyone was eager to see the big, new house on the edge of town. It was one of the nicest houses to be built in a long time. The women came to help, too. They brought food and coffee and they helped Anna clean up the old house. Then they all helped Sarah and Bert move their things. It was a very tired group of people when that day was over!

Hans and Anna were too tired to even enjoy their new surroundings. They just fell into bed, which someone had thoughtfully made up for them but the next morning Anna awoke early, excited to take a good look at everything and start unpacking boxes. Her favorite feature of the house was the beautiful open stairway with the oak stair railing. It's lovely finish was smooth as satin to the touch. Anna also loved the big bay windows and all the light they let in. The children were fascinated with the bathroom and, of course, Anna really appreciated that, too The kitchen was a large, square room with lots of cupboards and a pantry and a kitchen sink with running water! Their oak table looked very nice in the middle of the room and they also had a formal dining room. They would have to purchase some more furniture to fill up this big house, Anna noted.

Anna's trunk was put in the big upstairs hallway, under the double windows. Perhaps this is its final last resting place, thought Anna.

That summer they had to work hard to get the yard in shape and they planted many trees. Apple trees, plum trees, evergreens and Anna's special request, a weeping willow and an oak tree in the back yard.

Late one afternoon, Hans pulled up in front of the' house with the lumber yard's delivery truck. He and one of his men came up the front walk carrying a rolled-up rug. Anna opened the door for them and without a word, they carried it right up the stairway and into Hans and Anna's bedroom. Anna followed them up and when she saw them unrolling the rug, she thought that it was the most beautiful carpet she had ever seen, and she knew it must be a very expensive one, also.

She watched without saying much but after Han's man left she turned to her husband and asked, "Hans, why do you want to put such a beautiful and expensive rug in the bedroom where nobody will see it?"

"Anna, my dear," he answered, "when I saw this rug in the window with it's delicate pink roses, I thought of you and knew I had to buy it. We will see it and enjoy it every day of our lives in this room."

It was a soft, mauve color and it matched the curtains, the bedspread and the lamp. She had to admit that it really transformed this large room and made it very cozy and inviting.

Anna loved entertaining and had many friends and family over for holidays and Sunday dinners. Their first Christmas in this house filled the rooms to overflowing. Andrew and Alice and their boys came for a few days and it was such fun to see them again. This was the first time that they had come for Christmas.

"We always said that we were going to come up for Christmas sometime so we finally decided to just do it!" Alice said.

Alfred, their oldest, was farming with Andrew now and was planning to get married soon. George wanted to go to college and was saving up his money to attend the University of Iowa. He was extremely interested in science and would pursue something in that field.

An eight-foot Christmas tree was placed in the living room in front of the bay window and it was piled high with gifts by Christmas Day. Tomas and Bergit and all their family came, including Hannah and Will and their children. Teddy was home from college for the holidays. He was attending the University of Minnesota in Minneapolis now. He had gone his first two years at the college in Mankato and had lived at home.

On Christmas Day evening, as family members filled her living room and dining room, and little children were running all around, Anna sat back and rested after a busy day of cooking and looked at her family. Andrew was sitting next to her and she said to him, "Look at our big, wonderful family! If only Papa could see us all now. His grandchildren are all grown up and are either married with children of their own or they are pursuing some interesting paths in their lives."

Andrew had to agree. "I'm so glad he got to come to this country at the time of your wedding." He was silent for awhile and then he added, "It would be so good to be able to go back to Norway for a visit but I don't know if that dream will ever come true for me. Do you think you'll ever get back there, Anna?" he asked.

"I don't know. Hans says that he'd like for us both to go someday but he's so busy at the lumber yard. He wants me to go, though, sometime. We'll just have to see."

Later that evening when the guests had left and Andrew's family were all settled down in various rooms in the house, Anna and Hans were in their bedroom getting ready to retire after a long, wonderful day. Anna was sitting at her dressing table, brushing her hair with the new ivory comb and brush set that Hans had just given her that day.

"You know, " said Anna reflectively, "every time that I think that my dream has come true, it just keeps unfolding more and more. How many more wonderful things has God got in store for me?"

Hans came up behind her and wrapped his arms around his wife and said, "Anna, my dear, you deserve the very best that He has to offer, and I hope that your dream never stops unfolding."

"Hans, you have been so good to me. You've made my dream come true." She stood and they held each other for a long time before they both sought the warmth of their bed.

Hans had not seen his mother since they had gone to Chicago the first year that they were married. Hans came home with a letter from her one day and they were surprised to read that his mother and her granddaughter, Betsy, were planning to come and visit them in June.

"I can't believe that Mother is actually going to make that long, tiring trip. She always said before that it would be too much for her," Hans said to Anna.

"Well, it says here that she's anxious to see her grandchildren and also our new house so I guess she wants to come no matter how hard it is on her," reasoned Anna.

"Something like your father making that big trip here," Hans said. "When you really want to do something, I guess you just do it and suffer the consequences later."

Frank and Margaret were excited to meet this grandmother that they had heard of but never met. When the day of her arrival came, they were excited to get to the train station. But when she got off the train and had been hugged by Hans and then Anna, they suddenly became very shy and drew back. She understood and let them warm up to her gradually. They loved their cousin, Betsy, who was now fifteen and full of fun, and had energy enough to play with them and chase them around the big house and yard.

"Ruth would have loved to have come along," Mrs. Nielson said, "but she didn't think that she could get away just now. She hopes to come someday, though."

Mrs. Nielson visited with several ladies who were her friends when she lived there so long ago. After two weeks, it was time for her and Betsy to return to Chicago. The family went to the station to see them off. The children had, by this time, formed a great attachment with their new-found grandmother and cried when she had to leave.

"I'm so glad that I got to meet those two adorable children and to see your magnificent house," she told Hans and Anna as she embraced each of them. "I may not get back again, but I hope you will come and see me again in the big city."

The little family stood on the platform as the train chugged out of the station. "It seems that we are always saying good bye to someone here," mused Anna. "It can be a sad place sometimes."

"Yes, but we also say 'hello' to many people here, too; then it is a happy place, isn't it?" Hans said as he put Margaret on his shoulders and took Frank by the hand and they walked the short distance to their car.

Late that Fall, Anna received a letter from Sigrid. In it she suggested that she and Anna make a trip back to Norway the next spring to see their Papa and celebrate his 80th birthday with him. Anna was very interested but didn't think that she could leave her family for such a lengthy trip.

In Sigrid's Christmas letter, she talked about it again and urged Anna to think seriously about going with her. On New Year's Eve, Tomas and Bergit had come over to spend the evening with Hans and Anna. The children had gone to bed and the four adults were sitting around the kitchen table, playing whist and drinking coffee. The subject came up about Anna going to Norway. Tomas said that he thought that she should go.

"I'd love to, but I don't see how I can get away with two small children," Anna said. "Why don't you go, Tomas. It's been such a long time since you left there. It would be nice if you could see Tollef again and Eric and Barbro."

"Yes it would," Tomas said longingly. "But I don't know how I could go and leave my work for so long. We're so busy in the spring."

The group was silent for awhile, concentrating on their card game. Then Hans said, "I think you both should go! Your work will wait until you get back, Tomas."

"And Anna, I could look after Frank and Betsy for you when Hans is at work," volunteered Bergit.

"Dear Bergit," said Anna, "you are always so willing to help me out. Why don't you and Tomas go?"

"Why don't we all go?" laughed Hans, jokingly. The four of them talked until way past midnight without coming to any decision.

"It's fun to talk and dream of going, isn't it?" she remarked to Hans as they were clearing up after their company had gone. "But I'm sure nothing will ever come of it. I guess Sigrid will have to go alone."

Later, when Hans and Anna had gone to bed, Hans turned to Anna after being quiet and thoughtful for some time.

"Anna, are you still awake?" he asked. When she stirred, he continued, "I want you to take this trip back to your homeland. We'll work something out with the children and everything."

The more Hans talked to convince her, the more she thought that maybe it was possible, but when she would lay awake at nights and think about it, she would tell herself that it just wouldn't work out. Then the next day, Hans would have to start all over again!

After another plea from Sigrid, it was finally decided that Anna would go! Tomas, however, decided against it. With this decision finally made, Anna grew very excited about the idea. Bergit and Sophia would take turns caring for the children during the day and Hans said that he would get along just fine with them the rest of the time. Hans was able to cook from his many years of being a bachelor, he said, and Bergit would do their laundry.

With everything taken care of, Anna left on April 15 by train for New York. She and Sigrid sailed from there to Norway on April 20. They were on the Norwegian steamship 'Viking' and it seemed very luxurious to them when they thought back to the ships they had come over on many years ago. This ship was a new one and very fast. They made the transatlantic trip in just under four days!

They docked in Oslo, which had just recently changed its name from "Christiania". Barbro and her husband were there to meet them. They had a car and after showing the two women around Oslo a bit, they drove down to Drammen, where Barbro and Peder lived. Their two daughters were grown up and no longer lived at home. One was married and the other was working in another city.

After a couple of days, Peder drove the women up to Hönefoss where they would catch a train for Nesbyen. Barbro was going to accompany her two sisters. It was so much fun for the three of them to be together once again. They laughed and cried and reminisced the whole time. Anna couldn't get enough of looking out the train window at the beautiful scenery.

"This is a mighty pretty country that we left, isn't it?" Sigrid asked Anna.

"Yes, it is, but when I was young, I couldn't wait to get away and see what the rest of the world was like!" Anna laughed.

"Will we even know Tollef and Margit anymore?" wondered Sigrid. They were to meet them but the train was early so the women went into the station and sat down to wait. Soon a couple came in the door and looked around and something about the man made Anna just know that it was Tollef. She jumped up and hurried toward him.

"Tollef, is that you?" she asked, and before he could answer, she held out her arms for his embrace.

"Little Annie, can this grown woman really be you?" he said as he held her away to look at her. She laughed and motioned toward Sigrid. With tears streaming down his face, the big man embraced his other sister whom he had not seen for about thirty some years!

Anna could hardly recognize Margit. Her appearance shocked her. She looked so old and tired, something like Mama, thought Anna. But she still had her same ready smile and tinkling laughter and the years soon dropped from her face as the women talked a mile a minute. Tollef went to get the wagon and the five of them set off for their father's little house.

Papa was all dressed up and waiting and Kjersti was nervous because she knew something different from her daily routine was about to happen. She was wringing her hands when she heard the wagon drive up. Papa was nervous and excited, too, but he just sat in his favorite chair in the kitchen and waited for the new arrivals to come in the house. Tollef opened the door and let Anna pass by into the room first. She ran to her father and he stood up and embraced his youngest daughter, the one so dear to his heart. He started crying and then he turned to Sigrid and embraced her, too. He had to sit down, it was getting too much for him. Just to think that his two American daughters were here, in this house after all these years!

Kjersti was standing quietly in the corner when Margit went to her and took her by the hand and gently urged her forward to greet her sisters.

"Kjersti, do you remember your sister Anna? And your sister Sigrid?" asked Tollef. Kjersti slowly shook her head negatively. Anna went up to her and started talking to her and she thought that she saw a flicker of recognition in the woman's eyes. Kjersti had changed markedly in the years that Anna had been gone. Let's see, Anna quickly calculated in her head, she would be about 46 years old now, wouldn't she? She looked older than her years.

Kjersti backed away from the group and just watched silently. Everyone sat down and Margit put the coffee cups on the table and poured the coffee that Kjersti had made earlier. Kjersti wouldn't join them; instead she went into the other room and sat in the rocker and rocked swiftly back and forth.

After awhile, Papa and Kjersti went with the rest of the family out to Tollef's where the three women would be staying. There was to be a birthday party that evening for Papa.

All of Tollef and Margit's children came with their families. They were all married except Caren, the youngest. She was working in a dress shop in Gol. Arne, the oldest, lived nearby and farmed with his father. He was the only one who remembered Anna. The others had been too young. Knut and his wife had twin boys and lived in Gol, also. Signe and her husband were both teachers in nearby Torpo. Eric and his family came, too, and it was a wonderful reunion but Papa was in tears most of the evening. He was so moved by having most of his family around him and knowing that this was the last time they would be.

Anna and Sigrid planned to stay for ten days. They visited old friends and places that were dear to them. They would go into town every day to see Papa, too, and sometimes he and Kjersti would go with them on their visits.

One day Tollef suggested that Anna and Sigrid ride with him up to their saeter in the mountains. The two women jumped at the chance to do this. On the way up, the three of them sang old childhood songs which brought back many memories. The day was cool but bright and sunny. Looking out over the valley one could see the early spring flowers in full bloom.

"This is really a beautiful country, isn't it?" said Anna, almost reverently.

"What if we had never left here. What would our lives be like now, do you think?" asked Sigrid.

"I don't know, but I'm sure it would not be as happy a life as the one I have," replied Anna. "Do you ever regret leaving, Sigrid?" she asked her sister.

"No, I never regret leaving, but I used to get lonesome for all this at times," she said as she expanded her arm to indicate the valley below.

The two stood on the mountainside and gazed out for a long time until Tollef called to them. He had finished his task and asked if they were ready to go back down.

"Oh, I could stay up here for hours!" exclaimed Anna. "I used to love it so when I was a child."

"Yes, I remember that," said Sigrid. "You would go up here any chance you could get. We all thought it was so that you could get out of all the work back at the farm!"

On the way down, they talked about the apple picking, the big garden that their mother had and all the other tasks which they had to help with.

"It was a good life," Sigrid said, and Tollef agreed, but Anna remained silent, thinking about Mama and Kjersti and a sadness crept into her heart.

Before they knew it, the ten days were up, and it was time to leave. It was extremely hard to say goodbye this time, especially to Papa. They knew they would never see him again. Papa tried to make it easier for everybody by reminding them that they would all see each other again in the hereafter.

Anna approached Kjersti, and half expected her to pull away, but instead she allowed herself to be embraced by Anna and even responded by hugging Anna back. Through her tears, Anna looked for a long moment into her sister's eyes. It was like looking deep into her soul; there was a longing there and something else, a feeling of distress and anguish. It was almost as if her soul wished to leap out of this body and mind that held it captive. Anna hugged her again, hard, and could barely keep from sobbing.

Anna and Sigrid boarded the train and waved a last farewell. Barbro had left several days earlier as she couldn't stay any longer. The two sisters sat without speaking for many miles. They looked out the window, each with their many conflicting emotions: sadness and regret at leaving, but thankfulness at being able to make the trip and seeing their family and homeland once more.

Barbro and Peder met them in Oslo and drove them to the hotel where they would stay overnight, before boarding their ship in the morning. They all had a meal together that evening and then Barbro and Peder said their goodbyes and left for Drammen. They said that they hoped to make a trip to America sometime in the future, perhaps when Peder retired from his position at the university.

Upon arriving in New York, Anna stayed only one day with Sigrid and then she left for home, dreading the long, tiring train trip but excited to see her family again. A couple of long days later, there they were, awaiting her arrival at the train station. The children ran to their mother, each wanting to be hugged first. Hans stood patiently, awaiting his turn.

"How did everything go then, Hans?" she asked after the excitement died down and they were in the car driving home.

"Oh, we got along quite well, didn't we children?" he said. "But we missed you very much and it's so good to have you home!" He reached over and squeezed her hand.

"Yes, this truly is my home, isn't it?" she said, looking over at him and then in the back seat at her two dear children. I never want to leave them again, she thought to herself.

CHAPTER 24

By the end of the decade, the Twenties were losing their "roar" and this golden period in American history was beginning to decline. Still, the future looked bright when Herbert Hoover became President early in 1929. However, in October of that same year, the country suffered the worst business crash in its history. Anna remembered it well. It was just a week after her 43rd birthday. Hans and Tomas had been talking worriedly about the economic situation the night of her birthday party.

After the stock market crash, the country sank steadily into the most acute depression in its history. Millions of people went broke and many businesses went bankrupt. Many banks failed, including one in town and the other one closed for a time. By the end of 1930, more than 6 million Americans were out of work. Hans had to reduce his help at the lumber yard by letting three of his men go. This bothered him very much. He read the papers religiously every day to keep up with events.

Sigrid wrote that conditions in New York were very bad. Her husband and son still had a job with construction but projects had been severely cut back or put on hold. How long could this last, everyone wanted to know. She told of the long soup lines to feed the hungry and of once-prosperous businessmen selling apples on street corners.

Hans was clearly worried but the Hoover administration assured the nation that prosperity was "just around the corner." Actually things got worse. Farm prices fell lower than ever before and Andrew wrote to say that he didn't know how long he could hang on. Many of his neighbors were already in danger of losing their farms.

With business slacking off for Hans, Anna went back to teaching in the fall of 1932. Hans hated to see this happen but Frank and Margaret were now ten and eight and Anna said that this would not be a problem for her. In fact, she rather enjoyed teaching again, she assured her husband.

That November, Roosevelt was elected President, mainly because of his vigorous and optimistic campaign speeches advocating a "New Deal for the common man," he said. Hans and Tomas talked and argued politics every time the family got together. Anna and Bergit were getting tired of it. However, the day of Roosevelt's inauguration, the family was huddled around their radio and heard the new President say, "The only thing we have to fear is fear itself." This sounded hopeful for struggling families.

During the summer, Hans kept reading in the papers about the World's Fair in Chicago. The theme was "A Century of Progress" and he was very interested in it. Every evening after supper, he would read aloud to Anna excerpts regarding this great event. "It sure would be fun to go and see it," he would say every time, but Anna dismissed this as wishful thinking. Ruth and his mother had been writing and urging Hans to come and bring the family as it was such a spectacular event. It was going to be held over into the summer of '34.

That spring, business picked up a little for Hans and also for Tomas. Hans kept talking about going to Chicago. He hadn't seen his sister or mother for a long time and the children hadn't seen their Grandmother since her visit back in '27. She was anxious to see them again, she wrote. Anna finally started taking his 'wishful thinking' a bit more seriously as he wouldn't let it rest. Anna argued that they couldn't afford the trip and Hans countered that statement with the different ways that they could save money.

"We would be staying at Ruth's and so we wouldn't be spending money on lodging and John says he can get us some free tickets for admission," Hans would say.

Finally Anna gave in and found herself caught up in the excitement of the proposed trip. The children, now ages twelve and ten, were the perfect age to take to such an event, Hans told Anna. They could hardly contain their excitement. The trip was planned for the end of July.

Meanwhile, the city planned for a modest celebration for the Fourth of July in spite of the economic times. One had to have some fun, reasoned the city fathers. There would be a parade and a dance as usual. There would also be baseball games and horseshoe and races and contests of all sorts. Hans and Anna were put in charge of the various races and had to secure prizes to be given to the winners.

Anna and Margaret went downtown to pick out the prizes that would be needed. The business places donated many of them and others were purchased by the celebration committee. For the boys' foot race they were given a baseball mitt and for the girl's foot race, an embroidery scissor. A vest chain was donated for the fat man's foot race and the winner of the men's egg rolling contest would receive a pocket knife. There would be a tug of war between the City Slickers and the Country Folk and the winning team would be given a box of cigars. A box of candy was purchased for the winner of the ladies' baseball throwing contest. Margaret was so excited over all these prizes that when they got home, she laid them all out on the dining- room table for her brother and father to see. Hans was pleased with all the prizes that Anna was able to secure and Frank hoped that he would win the boys' foot race so he could get the baseball mitt.

The celebration started early in the morning with the parade and then some speeches and the big dinner. The races were next and Frank came close to winning the mitt but not close enough. A concert put on by the Community Band took place in the park and then the baseball game. It was a long day and everyone went home to rest up for the dance later. Hans and Anna were almost too tired to attend but decided they would go for awhile. Frank and Margaret were old enough to stay by themselves, but they wished they were old enough to go to the dance.

"In a few short years you will be old enough to go dancing, Margaret," said her mother, as she was getting dressed. Margaret watched her put on her good dress and fix her hair.

"Mama, you're so pretty," said the girl wistfully. "I hope I'm that pretty when I grow up."

Hans overheard his daughter and he said, "Princess, you and your Mama are the two prettiest girls in this town and you always will be." Margaret seemed to be satisfied with this and Anna just smiled.

"Hans, you always know just what to say to the females, don't you?" teased Anna.

"Oh, I know a pretty girl when I see one and, believe me, they aren't all pretty!" he laughed.

They left the house in a jovial mood and, despite their tiredness, looked forward to an evening of fun with their friends. Maggie and Mel were going to meet them there.

Early on the morning of July 20th, the family packed the car and set off on their long-awaited trip to the big city. Hans had bought new tires for the car and had it checked over. This would be the longest road trip they had ever made in a car. Anna had packed a big picnic basket with food to last all the way down. They drove as far as Andrew's the first night and stayed for a couple days. Alice wanted them to stay longer but they assured them that they would stop again on the way home.

The next day, they drove as far as Galena, just across the border into Illinois. It was a beautiful, little town with huge, magnificent houses. They found a park and slept in their car because they didn't want to spend their money on a hotel room. It was not very comfortable trying to sleep this way but they thought for one night they could put up with it. They started out very early the next morning, hoping to reach Chicago by that evening.

Ruth and her family had moved since the last time Hans and Anna had been there. They now lived in a house a few blocks west of their old place. Mrs. Nielson lived with them. They still lived on the same street, however, so it wasn't too hard to find except that it had grown dark before they entered the city.

Ruth was so relieved to see them drive up in front of the house. Mrs. Nielson had been almost sick with worry and couldn't stop her tears from flowing once she saw them safe and sound. The family was so tired from the trip that Hans suggested that they save all their questions and visiting till the next day. They all just wanted to go to bed, he said.

The next morning, everyone was up early and had a nice, big breakfast together. It was Saturday so John didn't have to go to work.

"We thought we'd let you rest up today and then tomorrow we'll go to the Fair," John said. "Just wait, kids, till you see the big Ferris Wheel and all the other rides. There's a Sky Ride that you'll want to go on, I'm sure!"

John and Ruth's son, Stuart, still lived at home. He was going to school at the University there. Betsy was married now and lived across town. They would get to see her sometime during their stay.

That afternoon, they all piled into John's car, except Grandma, and they drove down by the lake and downtown to see all the tall buildings. From there they could see the area where the Fair was and they could see all the big rides. It looked so exciting, Frank and Margaret thought.

The next day, John took them down to the Fair. Aunt Ruth stayed home because she had been there several times already, and Grandma didn't care to go. She had been there once for a short while and said it was too much walking for her. The Fair site was on reclaimed land, with several lagoons, about 6 miles long and 6oo feet wide along Lake Michigan, Uncle John told them.

The exhibits of science and industry were what appealed to Hans and John but the children were anxious to go on some of the rides. They all went on the Ferris Wheel and the men and the two children went on the Sky Ride. Anna didn't think she would like that! She was glad she didn't go after hearing Margaret's reaction to it. She had been terrified but the men and Frank loved it.

Ruth had sent her Kodak camera along with John so he took many pictures of the family at different sites at the Fair. At noon, he treated the whole family to hamburgers at the White Castle. They cost a nickel apiece and neither Frank nor Margaret had ever had a hamburger anyplace but at home before. In fact, eating out was a rare treat for them and for most people during those hard times.

They saw a lot of interesting and fun things during the afternoon but were tired and ready to go back to the house when Uncle John suggested they leave. Aunt Ruth had a good supper ready for them, although they weren't very hungry. They had had Good Humor ice cream bars on a stick shortly before leaving the Fair grounds. Another first for Frank and Margaret.

That evening John and Hans were discussing the Fair and John said that it had been a real economic success for the city of Chicago. Its construction and operation, together with the many people that came to see it, brought many dollars and much-needed jobs to the area. The city had been in bad shape prior to the Fair.

"What about the crime in this city that we hear so much about?" asked Hans. "We read so much about your gangsters and the recent St. Valentine's Day Massacre."

"I guess this city is always going to be remembered for its gangsters and bootlegging, but I think it had reached it's peak with the Massacre," John stated.

"I'm glad we live in a small town, don't you, Hans?" asked Anna. "We don't have to worry about crime and things like that."

"It probably is a better place to bring up a family," said Ruth, "but we do like it here in Chicago and John has such a good job, too."

After resting up on Monday, Hans and Anna and the children wanted to go back to the Fair one more time. John had to go to work so he dropped them off in the morning and told them which bus to take back to the neighborhood. Frank just had to go on the Sky Ride again and Hans wanted to see more of the science exhibits. Margaret was fascinated with the house made of marbles in the Children's Isle. At noon, they begged their parents to eat at the White Castle so they could have those wonderful hamburgers again! They topped it off with a glass of ice cold Coca Cola and thought it the most wonderful meal they had ever eaten. Later in the afternoon, they all had an ice cream bar again, hoping to get the lucky stick that meant that their next one was free.

Soon it was time to catch the bus to go back to Ruth's. That evening Betsy and her husband came over for supper. The next morning the family packed up and started their long drive back to Minnesota. Ruth promised that they would try and drive up and see them in the next year or so.

The drive home seemed to go fast as the children were so busy talking about all the great things they had seen and done. When it was all quiet in the back seat late in the afternoon, Hans looked over at Anna, who was resting her head back on the seat, but not yet asleep.

"I'm glad that we decided to make this trip, even though we maybe couldn't afford it. It will be the highlight of their childhood," he said, indicating the two in the back seat.

"Yes, they certainly will talk about and remember this for a long time," said Anna, dreamily. "I had a great time, too."

They spent their last night on the road at Andrew and Alice's and were persuaded to stay an extra day. They had so much to tell them! Alice listened wistfully.

"I wish we would do fun things like that once in awhile," she said. "We just can't afford it and anyway, Andrew never has time, with the farming and all. I don't mean to complain, but farming is not an easy way of life."

Anna had always known that and was glad that she had not married a farmer. She looked hard at her sister-in-law and saw that she did look very tired and worn.

"I wish you could have gotten away and gone with us," she said to Alice.

"We never get anyplace, it seems. You think that you're going to get caught up with the work and then there's just more to do. It never ends!" Andrew came into the house then so Alice turned to the stove and grabbed the coffee pot and poured him a cup.

"Andrew, you should take Alice on a trip sometime," said Anna to her brother. "You need to get away yourself, too, I think."

"Well, if times weren't so tough maybe we could," he said, sipping the hot coffee. "Alfred could handle things here himself for a little while but there's no extra money right now. Maybe someday."

Two days later, the Nielson family was back in their own home and the children could hardly wait to see their friends and tell them all about their fine trip. They would talk about this the rest of the summer and then some.

Tough times continued to plague the nation during the thirties. President Roosevelt's "New Deal" projects, such as the WPA, the CCC, and the TVA, were implemented and helped provide the relief and recovery that were needed. To make things even worse during that time, severe drought conditions were present over the nation's mid- section. This devastated the agricultural areas and many farmers and small-town businesses went under. This area of the plains became known as the Dust Bowl as the winds would whip the dry, fine powdery soil into great black clouds.

Anna wrote to Andrew, concerned about him and his family. He answered that he was still able to hang onto his farm, because he didn't owe anything on it, but many of his neighbors had to sell out. Farm auctions were a common occurrence. Sometimes the daytime skies would be almost black as night, he said, with all the dust blowing around. Alice could hardly bare it anymore, but what could they do? They needed rain desperately.

The extreme heat was another unbearable factor in the mid-thirties. It was too hot to sleep some nights, and many a family carried their mattresses out on their lawns to try and get some relief from the heat! Hans and Anna and the children spent several nights sleeping out on their porch.

Frank, now a young teenager, would overhear his parents talking about money problems sometimes so he decided he would try and help out. He went into every business place in town, looking for small jobs that he could do. Nobody had any work for him. Finally, at the Larson's Store, he was told that he could come in on Saturdays and work as a stock boy and help bag and carry out groceries. He would have to work on Saturday nights, too, as that was when all the farmers came to town and their wives would shop for their grocery needs for the week. Many of them would bring in eggs and butter to trade for things they needed.

In the later thirties, things started to improve somewhat but by then, Americans were reading in their newspapers about the gathering war clouds in Europe. Germany, Italy and Japan were aggressive countries determined to build great empires by armed force. Hans and many others grew worried when they read these things. Most Americans tried to ignore the warning signs and they believed that the United States could remain safe across the broad

Atlantic.

In the fall of '39, world-wide conflict began. Germany struck and conquered Poland in a quick stroke and two days later, Great Britain and France declared war on Germany. The next spring, German armies overran Denmark and Norway, The Netherlands, Belgium and France.

"The Americans are going to have to get involved and help Great Britain," said Hans one evening to Anna, "or we're going to be next!"

That's exactly what happened. After Roosevelt won the 1940 election for his third term, the US started giving or leasing defense goods to any country that needed it for their own defense. Many Americans were put to work making planes and tanks and destroyers. About a million Americans were conscripted into the armed forces. The United States stood on the brink of war.

Anna was worried about her family back in Norway as the Germans were occupying the country. She had not received any word from them since before the invasion. Hans and Anna both worried about their own country being pulled into the war. Frank was now of an age that he may have to serve in the armed forces. He had graduated from high school in the spring of '39 and was now attending college there in town.

On Thanksgiving Day, 1941, the whole family was gathered at Hans and Anna's. They all tried to be thankful for the blessings that they did have but there was worry and anxiety about the future. And there was still no word from Norway.

One evening about a week later, Hans suggested that they call up their friends, Maggie and Mel, and all go to see the new motion picture in town, "Gone With the Wind." Everyone was talking about the film and it would take their minds off their worries and concerns. After the long movie, they all decided that it was the best one they had ever seen. They went to the drug store for some ice cream afterwards. Each one of them made it a point not to mention world events so it was a very pleasant evening.

The next morning Hans and Anna, Frank and Margaret all went to church together. When they came out of the building after the services, a man came running up the walk all out of breath, shouting something about a place called Pearl Harbor. When people began to question him, he said that it was just on the radio that the Japanese had bombed America's naval base at Pearl Harbor, in Hawaii. Everyone froze and didn't seem to know what to do or say. They just all looked at each other, fear and dread in their hearts, knowing that the "other shoe" had finally dropped.

The Nielson family hurried home to turn on their radio. Anna fixed something to eat but no one was really hungry. There was anger and frustration at this turn of events. How could this happen, they wondered, and what would happen now?

CHAPTER 25

The draft notice lay on the kitchen table. Anna felt her heart sink when it came in the mail that morning. She just knew what it was. It was like she had been waiting for it but hoping against hope that it would never come. Frank would open it when he came home from classes later that afternoon. It had been six months now since the Pearl Harbor attack which had pulled the US into the war. Many local men and boys had already been drafted. Anna considered Frank still a boy, even though he was now a young man and in college. Perhaps he could get a student deferment. She knew others who had done that.

Shortly before supper, Frank came bounding in the back door and put his books on the kitchen table and looked over the mail. His eye caught the official-looking letter addressed to him and he looked up at his mother. She was watching him and he knew what she was thinking. His hands trembled as he opened the thin envelope. He scanned it quickly at first, then sat down and read it slowly. Anna came and stood behind him and, putting her hands on his broad shoulders, read it also. He was to report to the induction center in Minneapolis on May 23. Only two weeks away!

Hans came home just then and saw the two of them reading the letter. By their stricken faces, he knew what it was. He felt a sick feeling in his stomach.

"Pa," Frank managed to say, "I have to go. I've been called up." He handed the summons to his father. Hans almost backed away from it but he took it and read it. He looked at his son who had an expression of desperation and fear mixed with resolve.

"Perhaps you can get deferred," Anna said, hopefully.

Frank was silent for awhile and then he said, "No, I'll go. I've been expecting this and how could I stay here and study when my friends are going off to fight? Jack just got his papers yesterday, and Billy went last week."

Supper was unusually quiet, with only Margaret doing the chattering. The others had their own thoughts. Frank went out that evening to be with his friends and didn't come home till late. Hans and Anna laid awake for a long time, talking and thinking.

Alice had written last week that George had been drafted. He was going to try and get a farm deferment. Bergit was worried about Teddy, that he would have to go. Arne was just past the draft age so he was safe, but Teddy was thirty-five so still eligible. Teddy lived in Minneapolis and had a wife and two small children now.

The next two weeks went by way too fast. Frank finished his second year of school a few days before he had to leave for Minneapolis. "I'll finish school when I get home, Ma," he said, trying to reassure Anna.

Frank was catching a ride to the city with two friends and he would stay overnight with Teddy and then report to the induction center. "I'll call you as soon as I know anything," he said to his parents as they said goodbye to him early that morning.

"I'll be praying for you, Frank," said his mother.

"I'm counting on that!" Frank replied with a smile of bravery as he jumped into the car and the trio sped off.

Anna didn't know when she had felt so empty. After Hans and Margaret went off to work, she climbed the stairs slowly and sat down in her rocker and almost without thinking, reached for her Bible. She read some passages that had given her comfort in the past and then she prayed for her son with all her heart. She also began thinking about another son, Samuel, so far away. I wonder if he will have to go, too, she thought to herself.

The next evening, as they were sitting around after supper, the telephone rang. Anna jumped up to answer it, just knowing that it was Frank. He said that he was being sent to an army camp in Mineral Wells, Texas, where he would receive his basic training. His buddy, Jack, would be going there, too. That seemed to help, knowing that the two would be going together. He would be leaving by train the next day. Hans and Margaret each took turns talking and then they said their goodbyes.

"I'll write you," were his parting words.

"Be sure to send your address," Anna shouted into the phone before he hung up.

Although the family missed Frank, they tried to be cheerful for each other. Anna went over to Bergit and Tomas' one afternoon soon after Frank left.

"I was going to come over and see you today," exclaimed Bergit, when she saw her sister-in-law. " We heard from Teddy last night. He's been drafted, too, and he has to leave next week! He's going into the Navy Reserve and will go to someplace in Idaho, near Coeur d'Alene." Bergit started crying. "How can they expect him to go when he has a wife and two children?" she wailed.

Anna tried to comfort her but to no avail. She finally left and walked uptown. They didn't take their car unless absolutely necessary. Gas was being rationed and also they had to save on the tires as well. Everyone was also receiving ration books and could only buy an item if they had a stamp for it, such as sugar and coffee, among other things. Meat was also in short supply. It was a little hard to fix meals nowadays. It took some careful planning.

That evening Hans was reading the paper and it listed the first war casualty from their town. Anna was filled with dread. Would they be reading their own son's name in the paper someday, too?

Their first letter from Frank came about two weeks after he had left. It was sure hot in Texas, he wrote. It had been a long trip by train and bus to get down there. Mineral Wells was near Fort Worth but they weren't allowed to go anywhere until after the six weeks of basic training. He gave them his address and urged them to write. Anna sat down that very night and wrote him a long letter and Margaret said she would write him the next night.

A letter came from Sigrid, inquiring about everyone. She was wondering if they had received any word from Norway. It had been over two years now since anyone had heard from their family back there, ever since the Germans had taken over the country.

The hot summer passed slowly but soon it was time for Anna to go back to her teaching job at school. Frank had finished his training in Texas and was then sent to Ft. Benning, Georgia. He had expected to get a leave to come home after Texas but for some reason he didn't. He would be going to officer's training school for the next three months.

Teddy had been home for ten days after he finished his training in Idaho. He and his wife and children had driven down to see his parents before he left again. He was being sent to the South Pacific.

Anna stopped by Bergit's one day in late September after school to see if she had Teddy's address yet as she wanted to write him. She wrote Frank a couple times a week and he said that he really appreciated getting letters. Bergit was lying down and told Anna that she didn't feel very well. She had pains in her stomach all the time now. Anna said that she should go to the doctor.

"Oh, I think it's just nerves, worrying about Teddy and all this war stuff going on," she said.

"Perhaps you're right, but if it keeps on too long, you go see Doc Simpson," Anna admonished her. She copied down Teddy's address and left.

That night at supper, she told Hans, "I don't like Bergit's color. I think it's more than nerves."

She settled down to do some mending. Hans would read aloud to her from the paper, mostly concerning the war.

"This war has certainly taken over our lives almost completely, hasn't it?" she asked. "It's all anyone ever talks or thinks about!"

Just then Margaret came bursting in the front door. She was crying. Anna jumped up and went to her.

"What's the matter, dear?" she asked, alarmed.

Margaret went and threw herself down on the sofa and it took awhile before she had composed herself enough to tell them what was wrong.

"It's Joe," she said, "he's gone and enlisted in the Air Force!" She started crying afresh and Anna just let her cry it out for awhile.   Joe Benson was her boyfriend. They had been dating for about six months.

"Well, you must have known, Margaret, that this day was coming," she said, sitting down beside her distraught daughter.

"Not so soon. He didn't have to join up. He could have waited until they made him go!" she wailed.

Well, you know that if you enlist, you have a say in what branch of the service you want to join," said Hans.   "He knew that he would have to go sooner or later."

Margaret cried herself to sleep that night and was red-eyed the next morning as she went off to work. She worked at the telephone office as a bookkeeper and sometimes operator.

Early in October they got a call one evening from Frank. He said that he would have ten days leave and was coming home! He would be home on Friday of the following week. After hanging up, Anna and Hans danced around the kitchen table in their excitement. It would be so good to have him home again!

Alice wrote again and said that George wasn't able to get his farm deferment and he was now in the Air Force, at a base in Kansas. A place named Coffeyville. He had a few weeks left there and then she didn't know where he would be going. She enclosed his address in Kansas.

"One more to write to," she said to Hans, as she added this address to her list.

The day that Frank was to arrive, the family was waiting at the bus depot in town. There were several other families waiting for their sons, too.   When they saw Frank step down from the bus in his uniform, they hardly recognized him! He looked so much older. When he removed his pointed army cap they could see that his hair was cut very short. He spied them and ran through the crowd of people waiting. Anna embraced him for a long time and then Hans and Margaret each got their turn. Anna and Margaret were crying.

"Hey, if I'd known I'd have this effect on you, I wouldn't have come!" Frank said jokingly, trying to lighten the moment.   They all laughed and linked arms and walked to their car. That night at home, they sat and listened to Frank tell about all his experiences. Anna couldn't take her eyes off him. He seemed more mature and had a new confidence about him.

"So, Margaret, your boyfriend left you to join the Air Force, I hear," Frank said to his sister. Anna thought that this would start her crying again as it had been only about a week since Joe left.

"Well, he's not my boyfriend anymore!" Margaret stated. "We broke up just before he left." This was news to Anna!

"Smart girl!" Frank said as he playfully boxed her shoulder. "He could be away for a long time. There's more fish in the sea."

"The trouble is, all the good 'fish' have either enlisted or been drafted. It's just us girls and old people left!" Margaret complained.

Frank made the most of the time he had at home. He stayed up late but rose early, so as not to miss too many waking hours. On the Sunday he was to leave again, the family went to church together and then had a delicious roast beef dinner at home. That was Frank's favorite meal and Anna had been saving up coupons to buy a roast.

His bus was to leave in mid- afternoon. They took him down to the depot in the car. When he returned to Georgia, he would find out where he would go next.

"I hope it's not overseas," Hans said. "The longer you can stay in this country, the better."

Anna's last words to Frank again were, "I'll be praying for you!" He smiled and waved from the bus window. The three rode home in silence, their hearts heavy with sadness and dread.

The next Sunday they went over to Tomas'. Bergit did not look well but she didn't say anything about not feeling good. Anna took Tomas aside when Bergit was in the kitchen making coffee and said, "Has Bergit gone to the doctor yet?"

"Not yet, but I'm going to get her there this week sometime whether she wants to go or not. Her stomach pains never let up and I'm getting worried," Tomas said. "She passed some blood yesterday," he added under his breath as he heard her coming into the room.

This alarmed Anna to the point that she couldn't say anything for awhile. After Bergit had poured coffee for the four of them, she sat down with a sigh and Anna could see that she was perspiring quite a bit. However, Bergit made it clear that she did not want to discuss her state of health so Anna didn't say anything.

That evening, Anna wrote letters to Frank, Teddy and George. About a week later, a letter came from Frank. He had been sent back to Texas, to a camp near Tyler. He was now a Second Lieutenant and would be an instructor there at the Infantry Training Replacement Center. Teddy wrote shortly after and he was somewhere in the Pacific but he didn't say where. His unit's job was to make drinking water out of sea water.

In their last letter from Alice, she said that George was in New York waiting to be shipped out overseas. She said that Andrew was having trouble finding men to help with farm work as so many of them had been drafted or had gone to work in the defense plants.

Anna volunteered to have Thanksgiving at her house that year as she knew that Bergit was in no shape to make a big dinner. Everyone offered to bring food, using their ration stamps to get certain items. Arne and Sophia came with their children and they brought the pies. Bergit brought the cranberry sauce and vegetables. Anna roasted a big turkey. When Hans prayed the table prayer, he thanked God that no one from their family had become a war casualty and he asked for God's protection over them.

Early in December there came a letter from Norway. Finally! This was the first letter they had received since Norway had been taken over by the Germans. Anna was almost too excited to open it! It was from Tollef and Margit. They said that they had written numerous times but had finally decided that their letters weren't getting through being they had heard nothing from America for the past two years. They hoped that this letter would make it. It had been posted about four months ago, Anna noticed.

Margit said that everyone was doing as well as could be expected except that Papa was quite ill right now with pneumonia. She went into town everyday to help care for him. There were many shortages due to the occupation. The Germans took everything for themselves. Margit said that they longed for news from America and hoped that this "mess" would all be over soon.

After Anna had read the letter several times, she wondered how this letter had managed to pass censorship. She sat down that very evening and wrote a long letter back, hoping that this one would get through.

It was hard to be cheerful that Christmas of '42. At least Frank was still in the States. George was somewhere in North Africa and Teddy was still in the South Pacific.

"We sure have our family scattered all over the globe, don't we?" Anna remarked one evening.   Hans had brought home a world map which they had tacked on the wall and they could follow events and war news and the general where- abouts of their loved ones.

Margaret heard from Joe once in awhile but she never answered his letters. He had been sent overseas to England recently but he couldn't say what he was doing over there. Hans figured that he was taking part in those flying missions across the Channel. Margaret was not dating anyone since Joe left because, like she said, all the boys were gone! She said that it sounded like Joe still considered her his girl. She would have to write him and set him straight.

Before she got a chance to do just that, she heard from Joe's mother that they had been informed that Joe was missing in action. His mother was frantic with worry. He was her only son and her husband was a drunk. Margaret felt sorry for her and would spend some time with her now and then.

Dr. Simpson had diagnosed Bergit as having ulcers, but she seemed to be getting worse so he suggested that she go see a specialist in Minneapolis. She didn't feel up to the trip but Tomas insisted that they go as he was clearly very worried about her. When they returned four days later, Tomas came over and reported the bad news to Hans and Anna. It was stomach cancer! Anna had had a suspicion that this might be the case but didn't say anything to anyone. Evidently Tomas had also been thinking along these same lines but had never said the word to Bergit. The prognosis was not good. The disease had progressed too far and she had only a short time left! Anna's heart took a leap in her chest as she heard this devastating report. How could they all get along without their dear Bergit? she wondered to herself.

Anna visited Bergit every day and sat by her bedside after helping around the house with the meals and laundry. Anna found herself hesitating at the bottom of the staircase before going up to Bergit's room. There was a stench, the smell of death, which met one as they climbed the stairs and Anna was trying to prepare herself once again for this smell.

Bergit was very sick now and the doctor had told her that when the pain became more than she could bear, she could enter the hospital and they would give her morphine.

One day as Anna sat in Bergit's darkened room, Bergit surprised Anna by saying, "Let's talk about death." Anna rose and started to protest but Bergit silenced her by saying, "I'm not stupid, Anna; I know I'm not going to live much longer and I want to talk about it. Why is everyone so afraid to talk about it?"

After some moments, Anna said, "You're right, Bergit. We don't like to talk about it because we don't want it to happen. We can't bear to lose you." Anna could hold her tears back no longer and sobbed quietly by her sister-in-law's bedside.

"What do you think happens when we die, Anna?" asked Bergit after a long silence.

Anna thought about how she should answer this. "Well, I believe that our soul goes up to Heaven to be with God at the moment of death and that things will be more wonderful up there than we could ever imagine." Anna rose and paced the floor of the small bedroom. "I believe that our life on earth here is but a small speck of time and that we will live in paradise for an eternity."

"I believe that, too, with all my heart," said Bergit, reaching out her hand to Anna. Anna sat down again and Bergit continued on. "I wanted to live a few years longer, though." She was sobbing softly by this time. " I wanted to see my grandchildren grow up and see Teddy get back safely from the war." She rested for a few moments. "I don't know how Tomas will get along without me. He is so dependent on me. You will watch over him, won't you, Anna?"

Anna couldn't speak for awhile, because of the lump in her throat, but could only squeeze Bergit's hand in reassurance. Finally she said, "I don't want to lose you yet, Bergit. You've been like a sister to me. Closer, in fact. You took me in when I needed a place to live and made me part of your family. You were always there for me."

The two women just sat there then, unable to speak any longer, and held on to each other. Tomas came home from work early and came up to the bedroom. He held a letter in his hand.

"It's from Teddy!" he said excitedly. "He can get a ten day leave and will be home in a few days." Tomas had written to Teddy about his mother's grave illness and hoped that he could come home.

"Oh, I am so happy that I'll be able to see him again!" exclaimed Bergit. Tomas and Anna looked at each other solemnly. Later Anna followed him out of the room and they went downstairs.

"Tomas, you need to talk to Bergit about her dying. This is no time for small talk. Talk about what's really important."

"I can't face up to it with her," Tomas said, burying his face in his hands. "I can't bear to lose her, and if I talk about it to her, it just seems so final then."

"It won't go away if we pretend it's not going to happen," Anna said. "Bergit pointed that out to me today. We're wrong if we think that we're doing her a favor by shielding her from the truth. She knows the truth and the truth is, she's dying and we all have to face up to it."

Brother and sister sat in the kitchen and cried softly, no need for words between them. Finally Anna rose and gave Tomas a hug and said that she had to be going home now. She would come again the next day.

CHAPTER 26

Teddy arrived that weekend. His wife, Caroline, and his two children were with him. Bergit was in much pain but she refused to go to the hospital and would not hear of taking morphine. At least not yet. She wanted to be fully aware of everything as long as Teddy was there. Hannah had come several days earlier and planned to stay for awhile. Sarah, who lived right there in town, spent most of every day now with her mother.

After a week, Teddy had to leave. He said his final farewell to his mother, both knowing that they would never see each other again. They each tried to be brave for the other.

"I hate to leave you, Ma," said Teddy, " but it's wartime and I guess I don't have any choice."

"I'm just so glad I got to see you once more," she said weakly. "You come back safely now to your family. I pray for you many times a day."

Teddy held his mother for a long while and then joined his waiting family by the front door. Tomas gave him a farewell hug and then they took off. Teddy had to get his family back to Minneapolis and then fly back to the South Pacific, to Canton Island. It would be a long and trying journey.

A week later, with family gathered around her hospital bed, Bergit took her last breath and, with a slight smile on her face, joined her Maker. She was laid to rest on a cold, bleak February morning. Scores of friends and loved ones had gathered to mourn her passing.

That night, Hans and Anna clung together in their bed. They had both lost someone they loved very much. Death was striking too close to home. Also on their minds were Frank, and their nephews Teddy and George.

The spring and summer of '43 passed slowly. They followed the war news and were thankful that Frank was still in Texas and not overseas. Tomas was having a hard time without Bergit. Hans and Anna had him over for many meals and he would spend the evening with them. Sarah would include him every Sunday in her family's activities. Sarah and Bert had three children now. Bobby was sixteen already and the two girls, Coralie and Becky, were ten and eight. Sarah was praying that the war would end before Bobby reached draft age!

No more letters came from Norway. At Christmas time, Anna received a letter from Mrs. Martin from Toledo. She wrote that her husband had died the previous summer from a heart attack. Samuel had been drafted but had not passed his physical. She did not state why. What was wrong with him? Anna wondered. She was glad that he had not had to go into the service. That was a relief. She wrote Mrs. Martin and conveyed her condolences and casually asked about Samuel, why he hadn't passed his physical. She didn't receive any more news from her so she had to content herself with the fact that at least he was safe.

It was difficult to muster up any Christmas cheer that year. They all missed Bergit so desperately and the war news was not encouraging. The fighting in Europe raged on and the Japanese proved to be formidable foes in the Central and South Pacific.

Everyone tried to do their bit for the war effort. Rationing and shortages were a way of life. Aluminum cans were saved and flattened and turned in at community centers. Tin foil was supposed to be saved, also. Margaret and her friends actually peeled off the tin foil of their gum wrappers and saved it.

There was no further word on the fate of Joe Benson. He was still listed as missing in action. In May of '44, Frank wrote saying that he would be moving to Camp Carson, Colorado, near Colorado Springs. Still in the US, Anna thought with relief!

The following week, the big news was the Allied invasion of Normandy. It had been a success but at great cost in lives. Teddy wrote and he was now in Hawaii and Frank was moved again, to Kansas this time. Closer to home, Anna thought! Her elation was short lived as the next letter carried the dreaded news. Frank's 44th Division was being sent to Boston and they would be shipped overseas from there. Oh, when was this madness going to end? Anna would say every day.

She prayed harder and harder. This war was getting everyone down. Almost everyone in their community knew of someone who had lost their life and tensions were building. More and more gold stars were appearing in the windows of homes across the land. Their hopes had soared after the D-Day invasion but still it dragged on and on. When would those Germans surrender completely?

It was two months before they heard from Frank. They were surprised that he could tell them where he was. He was in northwestern France, in Cherbourg. His was the first convoy to land in that coastal town after the Germans had surrendered there. He had visited the beaches of Normandy and he stated that he wondered how anyone survived that attack! The embankments were so steep and the men had to try to scale them without getting shot down.

Anna, to keep herself from going crazy with worry, had to remind herself many times a day that God was looking after Frank and that he would be all right. It was sometimes hard for a mother to let go and turn her child's life over to God and trust that He would take care of him. She would end each prayer with, "Please forgive my lack of trust, Lord, but I am a mother who loves her son with a fierce love. That's the way we mothers are."

In December of '44, two letters arrived from Frank on the same day. His Division moved across northern France. In November,' they had liberated the city of Strasbourg, which was on the border of France and Germany. He said that his thoughts and prayers would be with them all at Christmas time and he hoped that by next Christmas he would be home again with them.

Anna had Tomas' children and grandchildren over on Christmas Day. The house was filled with people and children and that helped to make it more cheerful. They tried hard for the children's sake to make it as merry as possible under the circumstances.

When everyone else had left, Tomas lingered awhile and Anna said, "Let's sit down and have one more cup of coffee." So she and Tomas and Hans sat by the kitchen table and talked of Norway, Bergit and Christmases past. They tried to avoid the subject of the war, but their thoughts were always on their sons Frank and Teddy, who had been absent for so long now. It was a helpless feeling to have their boys so far away and at the mercy of people like Hitler and Hirohito. Their wasn't much they could do but pray and wait, pray and wait!

Another letter from Frank came early in January. He had spent Christmas In Strasbourg. He and most of his group had gone to Christmas Eve services in the great Strasbourg Cathedral. The people of the city were so grateful to the American soldiers that they just couldn't do enough for the men. The mayor of the city had even sent a Christmas card to Frank's Division! Frank said that his group would be moving again soon, to the south.

Little did Anna know that this would be the last letter from their son for a long time. However, in mid February, there came a telegram from the War Department. Anna didn't dare to open it for fear of what it would say. She took it and ran down to the lumber yard where Hans was. She came bursting into his office gripping the letter and looking pale as a ghost.

"Hans," she gasped, out of breath, "this just came and I don't dare to open it." She collapsed in his chair and he took the telegram in shaking hands, his heart almost stopping with fear. He opened it and began to read aloud. "We regret to inform you that your son is missing in action......" Anna stopped listening there. Not dead, but missing! She felt some hope. Hans took the rest of the day off and they returned home where they read the telegram over and over again. Frank had been reported missing on February 15 and feared captured. Frank in the hands of those Germans! Anna couldn't comprehend what might possibly happen to him.

Hans called their pastor and he came by and the three of them prayed for a long time and tried to give each other strength and hope. Margaret was called and she came home early to receive the disturbing news.

The next two months were the darkest days of Anna's life. She threw herself into a working frenzy in the evenings and Saturdays, cleaning everything from basement to attic, while Hans reacted differently. He could hardly muster up enough ambition to go to work in the mornings and many times he didn't even bother to go. They waited for word every day.

On April 10, they received a letter from a British chaplain saying that Frank had been taken prisoner by the Germans but had been freed by the Allies and was now in Belgium in a hospital there! They would hear more later. Anna read this with much joy and ran once again down to tell Hans the joyous news.

"Our prayers have been answered!" she shouted as she met him in the doorway of his office. She waved the letter and said that Frank was all right. He had to sit down to read and his hands were shaking so much that Anna had to hold them still so he could see the words! They hugged and wept and once again Hans left work early. They walked over to the telephone office where Margaret worked to tell her the great news. She and the other girls working there all wept with joy and relief. It was a happy ending to a very trying situation.

However, Frank was not out of danger quite yet. They received a letter from him about a week later. He was in a hospital in Liege, Belgium, but would soon be flown to England to a hospital there. He was injured very seriously, the nurse said who was writing the letter for him, and he would probably be in the hospital for a long time yet.

"At least he's not in the fighting anymore," said Hans with apparent relief. Anna was concerned about his injuries and what they were. Had he lost an arm or a leg? Perhaps when he got to England, they would receive an address where they could write to him.

On May 8, 1945, the radio was blaring the news that most of the world had been waiting for a long, long time. The war in Europe had finally ended! The Germans had surrendered to the Allies! Everyone dropped what they were doing when they heard this news and they went out into the streets and hugged anyone who was near! The rest of the day and evening there was an air of celebration. People couldn't calm down, they were so excited. Hans and Anna got in their car and drove over to Maggie and Mel's and then they went over to see Tomas.

When Margaret came home later that evening after being out with her friends, she said, "I wonder if Joe will be coming home now. Perhaps he was taken prisoner and will now be freed," she said hopefully. Perhaps she liked this boy more that she had let on, Anna mentioned later to Hans.

Frank wrote that he would be returning to the States the end of May but would have to be in a hospital there. He would let them know where he would be sent. He said that he had been injured in the head and the leg but didn't say any more than that.

A few days after Memorial Day, Frank called from Kansas. He was now back on American soil! Anna cried with relief and said that she and Hans would come down to see him as soon as possible. Within the week, the two of them were on a bus heading for Kansas, to an army hospital there.

When they walked down the hospital corridor, heading for Frank's room, Anna didn't know when she had been so nervous. She didn't know in what condition they would find their son. The nurse showed them into the room and then left quickly. Frank was sitting up in bed and his face lit up when he saw his parents. They hurried to his bedside and he reached out his arms to receive first his mother and then his father. They hugged him gently, as if he was very fragile. All three were in tears and could hardly speak for some time. Frank found his voice first.

"I'm going to be O.K., Ma." He reached for her hand and she grasped it tightly. Hans could only sob louder.

"It's been very hard on both of us, " Anna told him, "but it is so wonderful to actually see you again. We feared many times that we might not have that chance." They spent the rest of the day with him as much as they were allowed.

They stayed overnight at a hotel and came back to the base the next day. The nurse wheeled Frank outside in the backyard of the hospital and the three of them sat in the late-morning sun and talked. Frank finally began to tell them of his experiences overseas and how he was captured.

"The day I was captured," he began, "was a day I've relived a thousand times over and over again in my head. I walked into a machine-gun nest. My patrol was bringing out trenching tools to the rest of our guys. I signaled that I would go ahead and check things out. I thought I was walking towards our own men but I soon found myself looking at two Germans in a foxhole who were just as surprised as I was!"

"They started shooting at me and I was hit many times. Nine times, I was later told. These two young men, just boys really, took care of my wounds and I was taken with them back to their unit. I had a head injury and a bad leg injury and many other injuries. It's a miracle that I survived at all!"

"It's because I was praying for you constantly, I think," Anna interjected here. Frank squeezed her hand and continued.

"I was taken to Lindberg, Germany, and kept prisoner there. I was questioned at length but was treated fairly well. I received adequate medical care. About six weeks later, I and some other prisoners were put on a train but didn't know where we were going. Soon we heard airplanes overhead and they were strafing the train. Several people were hit and some killed. The train stopped and it stood on the track for a long time. We didn't know what was going on but figured that it was American or British planes. Our hopes soared and when the German guards didn't reappear, we slowly started to get up and leave the train. Those who could walk, that is. Three men carried me on my stretcher. We walked from the train to a village nearby. We heard that there was an allied armored-tank division there so we sent one of our group to go and contact them. We were then liberated! There was a British chaplain there who got my name and address and said he was going to write to you."

Anna said, "Yes, we received word from him. What happy news that was!"

"Then I was taken by ambulance," Frank continued, "to Belgium and spent about a week there and then I was flown to England. The doctors there were amazed that I survived after being hit nine times! Luckily, none of my vital organs were hit. Thanks to those two young Germans who took such good care of me after trying to kill me!"

Frank paused for awhile, and was lost in thought. "You know, I can still see their faces as clear as day. They were just kids, maybe 16 or 17. I remember thinking that Hitler must be running out of men, now he's recruiting boys. At least they had been trained well in first aid!"

When they returned to Frank's hospital room, Anna noticed his worn New Testament book under some newspapers on his nightstand. She picked it up and Frank commented that he had received that when he was in training camp in Texas.

"When I went overseas, I kept it in my shirt pocket all the time. I read it almost from cover to cover, sitting in various foxholes." He took the book from Anna's hands and paged through the worn pages. "You know, the two verses that went through my head a hundred times a day, especially when I was a prisoner, were the ones you quoted most of the time, Ma.   The first verse of Psalms 46, 'God is our refuge and strength, a very present help in trouble' and 'I lift mine eyes unto the hills, from whence cometh my help? My help comes from the Lord'."

" I taught you well then, son," said Anna. "Those verses have helped me through many difficult times."

That afternoon, Frank's doctor came by and they had a good visit with him. He said he expected Frank to recover fully with maybe only a slight limp from the bad wound in his leg. After bidding their son goodbye, they returned to their hotel room and picked up their baggage. They walked to the bus station where they would catch the bus that evening for the long, tiring journey back home.

They had to go way to the back of the bus to get two seats together. There were many service men aboard and by their happy expressions, they were going home, too.

Hans immediately fell into an exhausted sleep and Anna dozed off and on. When she turned to look out the window, her gaze fell on the face of her sleeping husband. When did he go and get old on me? she thought to herself with a start. I guess this last year had really aged him. Anna thought back on their life together. They had been married 24 years now and Hans was going to be 68 years old soon. I thank you, Lord, she prayed, for this wonderful man you sent me.

If Lorrie hadn't died, she continued thinking to herself, that would be him sitting there now, beside me. I wonder how our life would have been all these years. She fell back to sleep and dreamed crazy dreams until they stopped at a town for a coffee break.

When they returned home, there was a letter awaiting them from Norway. It was from Tollef and Margit. Anna just skimmed it at first. Papa was dead! Oh, no! She sat down and read it more thoroughly. Papa died of pneumonia way back in October of 1944. Almost a whole year ago, thought Anna! And I didn't know it. Margit said that it was no use to have written sooner because she knew that her letters weren't getting through. But now, she exclaimed, those bloody Germans were gone and she hoped things could return to normal soon. She and Tollef moved into town to live in the little house with Kjersti after Papa died. Arne and Knut were taking over the farm. The husband of their youngest daughter, Caren, had been involved in the Resistance and was badly injured in an explosion. He lost some fingers and the sight in one eye. Margit also wrote that she had just heard from Barbro and that neither she nor her husband were in very good health.

After reading the letter, Anna wept for her Papa and for her dear family and all that they had endured. They are all getting old, she thought to herself, and won't be around very much longer. She wished she could see them all again.

That summer the war continued in the Pacific. Japan just would not give up. Most Americans were surprised, however, when they heard on the news, in early August, that the US had dropped an atomic bomb on the city of Hiroshima and three days later, another one on the city of Nagasaki.   Finally, on September 2, 1945, the Japanese surrendered and World War II ended, three years, eight months and 22 days after Pearl Harbor.

CHAPTER 27

Anna was determined to make Christmas of '45 the happiest since before the war. The whole family was there. Frank had been released several months earlier. Teddy and his family drove down from Minneapolis and Hannah and Will and their family came, too. They all were staying at Tomas'. It was such a pleasant surprise to hear from Alice and Andrew saying that they were coming, too, and that George would be coming along. Alfred would stay at home and take care of the chores. Sarah and her family would be joining all of them on Christmas Day at Anna's. Arne, Sophia and their three children came that day, also

There were twenty seven people in all. Hans and Frank set up planks on sawhorses in the parlor and Anna covered these with long, white tablecloths and they borrowed extra chairs from their neighbors. Andrew and his family had come a day early so Alice was a big help to Anna in preparing all the food needed to feed this bunch. They baked hams the day before and put a big turkey in the oven Christmas morning. The whole group went to early church services and then the women put the potatoes on to cook afterwards. Sarah brought the vegetables and Sophia had made the pies. Anna had made lefse, flatbread and many assorted goodies the week before.

When everyone was seated around the various tables, Hans suggested that they all join hands and he prayed a rather lengthy prayer, thanking God for all their blessings and for the safe return of Frank, Teddy and George. Then everyone dug in and what a feast it was! The table was heavy laden with food of all sorts. Everyone was in such a festive mood. Everyone except George, that is. Alice said that her son was not the same after he came home from the war. She thought that in time he would return to normal but this had not yet happened.

After this big meal, there were many dishes to do! It took almost two hours to clean up and get ready for the gift exchange. And what a pile of gifts under the tree! The week before, Hans and Frank had gone out and picked the biggest tree that would fit in their parlor. Hans had also come home with several strings of some new kind of bubble lights. It was starting to grow dark outside so they turned on the lights and all sat around wherever they could find a place to sit, some on the floor and some on the stairs. Margaret played some Christmas carols on the piano and they all sang along.

Hans had arranged for the neighbor next door to dress up as Santa and he came just at the right time and passed out all the gifts. After everyone had opened theirs, there was quite a pile of paper and boxes strewn around! Anna's favorite gift was from Frank. It was a rhinestone pin in the shape of a butterfly. He said when he saw it in the jewelry store, he had to buy it because when he had been in the prison camp he kept thinking about butterflies for some reason and wished that he had been one so that he could have flown to freedom.

Later that evening while the young people were playing parlor games, Anna noticed that George was off by himself, deep in thought. She went up to him and gave him a big hug and said how glad they were that he had come home safely. George responded with only a slight smile and a nod of his head. Alice told Anna later that he wouldn't talk about any of his experiences. When she had pressed him about it, he had only said that he had seen such terrible things that he couldn't get them out of his mind. Actually, he was a member of the Allied Forces units who, in April of '45, moved up from Italy and advanced into southern Germany. They came upon the concentration camp in Dachau and the atrocities that he saw there he just couldn't talk about. They did, however, liberate over 30,000 prisoners, some barely alive. They had been starved, severely beaten, and subjected to brutal medical experiments that were hardly believable.

Andrew and Alice stayed for several days after Christmas, but after they left, the house was terribly empty. Anna threw herself into doing volunteer work at the hospital. She no longer taught and she needed something to do with her spare time.

When Frank had come home from the service for good, he went to work with Hans at the lumber yard. Anna hoped that he would go back and finish his college education but Frank said that he didn't think that he would do that.

"After what I've gone through, Ma," he told her, "I just wouldn't be able to sit in a classroom again."

Anna noticed a restlessness about her son that hadn't been there before. Perhaps that is the way it is with soldiers when they come back from such a terrible war. They aren't the same people that they were before.

There had been no word about the fate of Joe Benson yet and it was presumed that he was dead. Margaret felt bad about this but didn't talk about it much. There were numerous young men for her to date now that the war was over. There were many dances and the young people were always ready for a party. She had many beaus, as she was a very pretty girl, tall and slim with a head of luxurious chestnut hair, like her mother's.

Frank started to date a young woman named Betty Skari. She worked at the drug store and Frank would go over there often for a soda in the afternoon. She was a very nice girl and it soon was apparent that their relationship was getting serious.

Anna still missed Bergit very much. She would think about her many times a day and this would prompt her to call Tomas and invite him over for a meal or something. One particular evening when she called him to invite him over for supper the next evening, he said that he had plans already. He was having supper at Edith Casperson's house. She had been widowed a couple of years earlier and just lived down the block. Apparently she and Tomas had been keeping company of late!

She told this to Hans later when he came home from work. "Well, good for him," Hans said. "It's no fun to live alone and be lonely all the time! I know how that was before I talked you into marrying me," he teased her. He came up behind her and wrapped his arms around her. How I love this woman still, he thought to himself. She turned around and gave him a peck on the cheek and continued to prepare the evening meal.

That summer, in June, Hans and Anna celebrated their silver wedding anniversary. Their friends at church put on a big affair for them including an open house in the church basement and a program. It was well attended as they were a well-liked and highly esteemed couple. Their friends all chipped in and bought them a beautiful silver service set, which was the custom at that time.

Tomas showed up with Edith Casperson and this was the first time that Anna had seen them together. It rather hurt, seeing Tomas with another woman besides Bergit, but Anna told herself that she'd have to get over that and she greeted Edith warmly.

When the immediate family arrived home, Anna put their new silver service set on her buffet and she kept it shined up for many years to come and used it on many occasions. That evening Frank and Betty announced their engagement and said that they planned to get married at Thanksgiving time.

"What an exciting day!" Anna exclaimed.

Hans told her later, up in their bedroom, that he wished he could afford to give her the gift that he had been wanting to give her for a long time. A trip to Norway for the two of them!

"Oh, Hans! I don't expect anything that grand. I know these past years have not been very good for business. When I say that I'd like to visit Norway once more, it's mostly just wishful thinking. But you are such a dear for thinking about it."

In October, Anna's family planned a big celebration for her 60th birthday. It was held in their house, but she was not allowed to lift a finger in the preparation of any food. This was a very difficult thing for Anna to do. Margaret finally had to chase her out of the house and send her over to her friend Maggie's house for a few hours the afternoon of the party.

That evening there were sixty people who came and went at the open house affair. " One for every year of your age," Frank told her.

Frank and Betty's wedding was the day after Thanksgiving. It was a very cold day and there were even some snow flakes in the air. The wedding and reception took place in Betty's church out in the country and then the happy, young couple went on a honeymoon to Minneapolis.

When they returned, they set up housekeeping in a small house out by the mill. Frank hoped to build a house someday.

The late forties were good years economically for the American people. Farm prices were high and the crops were good for several years in a row. The lumber business was booming, too. When all the service men came home, they got married and then wanted to build small homes and raise families.

Margaret started dating a fine young man by the name of Ted Davis shortly after Frank's wedding and in 1948 they were married. He had been in the service and had completed his college education under the GI bill and now worked for the mill as assistant manager. They also found a small house to live in until they could afford a larger one.

Frank and Betty now had two small children, born one right after the other. A boy, Roland and a little girl, Patricia. Margaret and Ted followed suit soon after with a son born in 1949. They named him Stan.

Things continued to boom in the early fifties, and that spring, Hans announced that he and Anna were going to take a trip to Norway.

"Oh, Hans," she exclaimed, "do you really think we can?"

"Well, we're not getting any younger and we may as well go now while we're both still in good health. I want to see that beautiful country of yours!"

So in June of that year, they took a train to New York and stayed a few days with Sigrid and Louis and then they set sail on the day of their 30th wedding anniversary. He proudly told the captain and everyone else on the ship that he and his "bride" were going on their second honeymoon!

They first visited Barbro and her husband, Peder. Barbro was suffering greatly from arthritis and Peder had a bad heart but it was so good to see them. They then traveled on to Nesbyen where they got a warm welcome from Tollef and Margit. And even Kjersti smiled at them and seemed to remember Anna. She was leery of Hans, though, but after a few days, she warmed up to him.

"I just have a way with women!" Hans bragged good naturedly.

They toured the fjords and the mountains and Hans could now understand why Anna would say that her country was so beautiful. He enjoyed being out on their little farm and they took him up to their summer farm where the cows were now grazing. Looking down on the valley and all the wild flowers was spectacular.

Anna was concerned about Tollef. He didn't look well and she mentioned this to Margit.

"Well, you know he's over eighty years old now," said Margit. "His heart isn't so good either. The doctor told him to slow down so he has been taking it easier these last years. Ever since we moved to town anyway. It was hard to take it easy on the farm."

All too soon it was time to say their goodbyes and leave for the States. Anna knew this would be the last time she'd see her brothers, Tollef and Eric, and her two sisters and all their families.

In New York they stayed with Sigrid again overnight and then headed for home. The train made a stop in Toledo and Anna found a telephone book near the ladies rest room so she looked up the name of her other son, Samuel. There it was, Samuel Martin, with his address and telephone number. She jotted it down on a piece of paper she had in her purse. I don't even know if he's married or not. Maybe I have more grandchildren!

She decided to place a call to Mrs. Martin and this was what she was about to do when Hans came looking for her. He said it was time to get on board the train again but she said she wanted to make a quick call to Mrs. Martin. She dialed and was almost afraid to hear her voice. She told Hans to wait for her by the train.

After four rings, a voice answered that Anna wasn't familiar with. It was the maid, she was informed, and Mrs. Martin was unable to come to the phone as she was ill.

"So how was Mrs. Martin, then?" asked Hans as they got themselves settled in their seats once more.

"I didn't get to talk to her. The maid answered and she said that Mrs. Martin was ill."

"What about her son?" asked Hans.

"I don't know," said Anna. "I don't think he lives with her. Perhaps he is married and has a home of his own now."

For the rest of that day, Anna couldn't get thoughts of Samuel out of her mind. I must write to Mrs. Martin when I get home and ask some questions of her, she thought.

Frank, Betty and the kids and Margaret and Ted and little Stan were all at the train station that Sunday afternoon when their parents returned home. They all went over to Frank and Betty's for a light supper. They were now living in their new house.   Hans and Anna had so much to tell them all and Anna could hardly wait to get the Norway pictures developed to show them.   Margaret surprised them all with the news that she was expecting again, early in the new year.

Roland, who was five now, was such a little character. He had them all laughing most of the time with things he would say. Patty, only a year younger, would try to imitate everything that her brother did and said.   Stan was almost two now and he was so cute and chubby. Oh, these grandchildren are so precious, she thought to herself many times over.

That night when she and Hans were getting ready for bed, she said to him, "That trip was so wonderful, Hans, and I'm so glad we could take that trip together, before we get too old. But isn't being home with our children and those dear grandchildren just the best thing ever?"

Hans had to agree with that and he held her close to him in bed and said that having her beside him all these years was also the best thing ever. They fell asleep with thoughts of thankfulness for their happiness and hopes that it would remain so for many years to come.

Several days after they returned from their trip to Norway, Anna sat down and wrote to Mrs. Martin. Two weeks later, she received a letter with Samuel's return address on it! He said that his mother was very ill and that he was answering her correspondence. He said that he was married but had no children, and that he was still at the Libby plant. Anna read this letter over and over again and then put it in her trunk.

Margaret and Ted's new baby, a girl, was born on a stormy day in early February. They named her Barbara Annette. Anna and Hans took care of Stan while Margaret was in the hospital for a week. That was quite a job, taking care of a very active two-year-old at their age They were very glad when Ted took him back home over the weekend. Anna went over there for the first few days that Margaret was home. The baby was so cute and seemed to just eat and sleep all the time. What a little darling!

Anna had been after Hans to retire but he said that as long as he felt good, he was going to help Frank at the lumber yard and he continued to go there every day.

One day in June of '52, he went along with Frank to St. Paul to attend a convention related to the business. They would be gone for three days. Anna kept herself busy but on the second morning, when she was just doing some ironing, she heard a knock on the front door. She passed by the hall mirror and tried to pat her hair into some semblance of order and she peeked out the side window to see who it might be. There was a strange man standing there but yet he looked oddly familiar. She opened the door and looked at the man inquiringly.

"Yes? May I help you?" she asked, all the while trying to place this man.

"Are you Anna Olson Nielson?" the man asked, looking somewhat nervous.

Just then it hit Anna. Could this be her son Samuel?

"Yes, I am," she said, warily, "and who are you?"

"I guess you wouldn't remember me. It's been so long. I'm Samuel Martin."

Anna took his outstretched hand and finally found her voice to invite him in. "My goodness, what brings you to Mankato, Mr. Martin?" she asked as she ushered him into the parlor and indicated that he should have a seat .

He sat, with hat in hand, looking uncomfortable and nervous. "I've come to talk to you, Mrs. Nielson." He looked around as if to see if they were alone.

"Can I offer you a cup of coffee first? she asked, stalling for time.

"Yes, that would be nice," he answered, obviously relieved himself for the delay.

Anna hurried off into the kitchen and had to grab the edge of the table as she was feeling weak. She finally got a cup of coffee poured for him and managed to bring it into the parlor without spilling it. She sat down on the sofa and waited.

He took several sips of his coffee first before saying anything. Then he said, "My mother passed away a couple of months ago. Shortly after I wrote you that letter."

"Oh, I'm so sorry for you," Anna said sincerely.

"Are we alone here, Mrs. Nielson?" he startled her by asking.

"Yes, my husband is gone for a couple days."

He seemed relieved as he continued. "Just before she died, my mother said she had something very important to tell me." He paused and swallowed hard before continuing. "She said that she and my father were not my real parents."

Anna could hardly breathe as she waited for what he would say next. Her palms were growing sweaty and her heart was thumping in her chest.

"She said that my mother was Anna Olson, a young girl that used to work for them. That's you, isn't it, Mrs. Nielson?"

Anna didn't answer but just looked hard at him for some time.

Before she could answer, he continued. "I know this is a shock to you and I'm not here to make trouble but I need to know for sure if it's you. It was indeed a terrible shock to me to find out that the Martins weren't my real parents."

"Yes," Anna said, almost inaudibly, and with tears starting to flow. "I am your mother." There was silence for a few moments, with the ticking of the clock the only sound. It was as if the world was standing still at this moment.

"Would you like to talk about it?" he asked gently, and she knew she had nothing to fear from this man, her son.

"It was a long time ago," she began, "and I was young and just new in this country. I went to work for your parents, the Martins, and I was...ah... pregnant and I didn't think that I could raise a child alone. They wanted a child so badly." Here she stopped and tried to control herself.

"I shouldn't have given you up and I regretted it every day of my life since, but at the time it seemed the best thing to do." She started sobbing again. "Can you ever forgive me?"

Samuel rose and came to sit next to her on the sofa. He put his arm on her shoulder. She looked up at him and said, "Oh, Samuel, my son!" She put her arms out to him and enfolded him in her embrace. They both wept, she with relief that she could finally embrace her son and he with compassion and understanding for this woman who was his real mother.

They talked and talked for a couple of hours and then Anna went into the kitchen to fix something to eat for the two of them. He followed her and sat at the kitchen table. He couldn't get enough of looking at this woman who was his mother. She took out the family album and showed him pictures of her children, grandchildren and also of her brothers and sisters, his aunts and uncles.

He spent much time pouring over these pictures and asking her all kinds of questions. Finally the question that she had been dreading came.

"What about my father? You don't seem to have any pictures of him. It said on my birth certificate that his name is Joseph Morrissey."

Anna hadn't heard that name spoken in almost fifty years! It gave her quite a jolt, hearing it again. Her mouth went dry and she couldn't speak. She could only nod.

"Can you tell me about him?" asked Samuel.

If she told him the truth, that she hardly knew the man and that he had raped her, how would that make him feel for the rest of his life? Anna wondered to herself. What shall I tell him?

"Well, that was...ah...a long time ago, Samuel," she began. "And he never did know about you, nor that I was even pregnant."

"What kind of a man was he and what did he look like? I thought that the next time I go to New York, I would try and look him up."

"Oh, no, you mustn't do that!" said Anna, horrified. She rose and started pacing the floor.

"Why not?" asked Samuel, "Maybe he'd be pleased to find out that he had a son."

"Like I said, he didn't know a thing about you and you mustn't try to find him," she said, almost frantically.

Should she tell him the truth and maybe then he would drop this idea of looking for him? No, she couldn't do that to her son. He would be devastated, knowing how he was conceived. She sat down opposite him again.

"I don't know much about him, Samuel," she said, looking down at her hands and not at her son. "He was a friend of a friend."

"You mean you hardly knew him and you weren't in love with him?" he asked incredulously.

"That's right," she said weakly. What more could Anna say?

They both were silent for several minutes. He seemed to be digesting this. He realized that she wasn't going to say anymore about the man who was his father so he dropped the subject.

"Samuel, I want you to know something. When you were about five years old, I came to Toledo and tried to get you back but then I realized that I would be taking you away from the only parents and home that you had ever known and I knew that I could never do that to you, no matter how much I wanted you back. So I left and never saw you again except for some pictures that your mother would send me occasionally."

This touched him deeply and he knew that this woman loved him very much and always had. They talked away the afternoon and she made supper for him. He said that he was staying at the hotel in town. He had come by train the night before.

Anna said that he could stay here with her but he declined. "I have to get back to Toledo tomorrow night and I'll be leaving on the early morning train."

That evening, Anna told him all about her life in Norway and about her coming to this country as a young woman. He seemed eager to absorb any information she was willing to give him about his new-found family.

"I have never told my husband about you. That's the only thing I have ever kept from him. Please forgive me for that. In fact, your parents and the doctor were the only other people to know. I am surprised that your..... your mother told you the truth."

"I guess she thought that that was the right thing to do. She was a wonderful mother and I loved her dearly. My father, too. It was really hard on the two of us when he died so suddenly," Samuel said.

"Does your wife know about this and where you are?" asked Anna.

"No, she thinks I'm on a business trip. I just couldn't bear to tell anyone, at least not until I had talked to you."

It was very late that night when Samuel rose and said that he better be going. Mother and son embraced for a long time.

"Will I ever see you again?" asked Anna, near to tears again.

"I don't know. I'll keep in touch with you but I don't want to upset the life that you have here," he said kindly.

"I'm so very glad that you came. You don't know what this means to me to be able to see you, and talk to you and hold you. It was the hardest thing I ever did, giving you up, and I don't know if it was for the best but what's done is done and we can't change that."

"I understand and I'll never hold it against you..... Mother."

When he called her "mother" she started crying all over again. They embraced once again and then he was gone.

Anna didn't sleep well that night and in the morning light, she wondered if it had all been a dream. But there in the kitchen was his cup that he had drunk coffee from and the dishes from their supper together. She couldn't concentrate on anything all day and kind of wandered around the house in a daze, straightening up things that didn't need straightening.

The next day, Hans and Frank came back in the early afternoon and Hans came into the house and gave her a hug and asked how she had gotten along without him around. She told him that she had had a visitor. Samuel Martin from Toledo came, she said.

And what did he want?" asked Hans casually.

"He told me that his mother had died and wanted to talk about.... things," she answered, trying to be equally casual.

"Oh, that was nice. Did you two have a good visit?" Hans asked absently, looking over the mail.

He didn't even notice that Anna didn't answer him. Later she asked him about his trip and the convention and he forgot completely about her visitor. That's just as well, Anna thought to herself.

CHAPTER 28

The mid-fifties continued to be good years for Hans and Anna. Their children prospered and their grandchildren were a source of pleasure. Margaret, however, had suffered two miscarriages and Anna knew her pain. Anna hoped that her daughter would be able to have more children someday. Frank and Betty had two children and seemed to feel that their family was complete.

One day after work, Hans and Frank backed their small truck right up to the house and as Anna watched, they unloaded a big box and set it on the porch.

"Hans, what in the world do you have there?" asked Anna, coming out the front door. Before he could answer, she could read the words on the box. It was a television set.

"I told you it was about time that we got one of these," he said to her. "I stopped at the Gambles store yesterday and Mr. Hoganson said that he had one left and would save it for me. They're going like hot cakes!"

Frank and Hans removed it from the box and carried it into the house and set it down in the parlor.

"Where do you want it, Ma?" asked Frank.

"Well, let's see, I'll have to think about it for awhile," she answered.

"I'll come back this evening and we'll get the antennae put up on the roof and get it all hooked up," their son said, and he left them admiring their new possession.

It was a big Stuart- Warner console and very nice looking, Anna thought. They decided just where they would put it and after supper Frank came back and helped Hans get it moved and set up. That night they watched some television programs on their very own set. Frank and Margaret had each had one for several months now.

Over the next years, their favorite programs to watch were, "The Ed Sullivan Show", "The Amateur Hour", and "I Love Lucy". Anna also liked Lawrence Welk's music.

"Now there's a man with a good beat," she would say.

One day in the summer of '56, there came two letters on the same day from Norway. Anna opened Margit's first. There was sad news. Tollef had died the month before of a massive heart attack. Margit was left to care for Kjersti but she said that the two of them were getting along all right.

The next letter was from Annetta, Barbro's youngest daughter. She had bad news, also. Her father, Peder, had also died recently and her mother was very crippled up now with her arthritis. Anna put the letter down and thought about this for awhile. Tollef is the first one of us to go, she mused to herself. And now Barbro is widowed and not doing too well either. Who will be next?

Annetta also wanted to tell them that her youngest daughter, Julianna, was coming to the United States in the late summer to attend school there! In fact, she would be coming to Minnesota and going to school at Gustavus Adolphus College in St. Peter, Minnesota.

"Why, that isn't very far away!" Anna exclaimed to Hans. "We'll get to see her real often! I wonder if she realized just how close she will be to us?"

"Well, I suppose she planned it that way, Anna," said Hans dryly. "She knew that it would be a comfort to her to have family close by in a strange country. A comfort to her mother, too, I dare say."

"Yes, I suppose you're right. She planned it that way. Oh, I have to go and call the girls right away. Won't it be fun to have her here!"

Anna phoned Margaret and Betty and told them the exciting news and then sat down and wrote a letter back to her niece, Annetta.

Julianna arrived in mid-August and came right to Mankato first from Minneapolis where her plane landed. Teddy and his family drove her down on a Saturday afternoon. She stayed a week with Anna and Hans and met all her relatives. She was only a year younger than Becky, Sarah and Bert's youngest, so the two of them became fast friends. Becky was attending college in town and living at home.

Frank took a day off and drove Julianna to St. Peter to get settled in there. Anna went along for the ride. Julianna would be staying in a dormitory on campus. She met her roommate, a nice girl from a dairy farm nearby.

Julianna spoke English quite well but she hoped that it would improve even more by studying in the States. It had already improved in the past week with all the communicating with her many relatives. Frank and Anna returned home that evening with much to tell everyone.

Word came from Sigrid that Louis had suffered a stroke and had to be put in a nursing home. This was very hard on Sigrid but he was completely helpless and she was not able to care for him at home.

"It seems lately that each letter contains some bad news, doesn't it?" Anna remarked to Hans one evening.

"Well, you know, Anna," he answered philosophically "your family are all quite a bit older than you so these things are to be expected now. That's the way of life."

Margaret's news, a few weeks later, was like a breath of fresh air. She was expecting again and had passed her third month without incident.

"Oh, how exciting to have a baby in the family again!" exclaimed Anna.

"You always say that, Anna," Hans teased. "You would like to just keep having one grandchild after another, wouldn't you?"

This new grandchild turned out to be their last one, however. It was a girl and they named her Kari. She was a sweet one and Anna tried to spoil her as often as she could! As she grew, she always held a special place in Anna's heart. Perhaps because Anna knew that this was the last grandchild. The two had a special bond between them.

Julianna spent as much time as possible with her family in the surrounding area. She would often go to visit Hannah and Will as they lived near to her roommate's family. In the summer months, she returned to Norway, and Becky accompanied her there one of those times.

"My, the young people sure do get around nowadays, don't they?" Hans mentioned to Anna one evening.

"Yes, they surely do, and I think it's wonderful," Anna responded. "I know that I'd be doing the same thing if I was young again."

"I'd say you got around some yourself in your day, my dear," Hans teased.

"Yes, I guess I did," answered Anna, reflectively. "And two trips back to Norway even!"

They received a call from Arne one evening to say that Tomas had just died. Oh, no, not dear Tomas, thought Anna. He had been living in a nursing home for the past two years.

"He just died peacefully in his sleep this afternoon," explained Arne, near to tears, when he came to see them later that evening.

Anna tried to comfort him. "Your father lived a long, full life. Why, he would have been 90 years old this summer now," she reminded him.

Tomas was laid to rest beside his beloved Bergit a few days after Easter.

"He has it good now, where he is," Anna told Tomas' children and grandchildren who were gathered together at Arne and Sophia's after the funeral. He and your mother are probably talking together right now!"

On the way home, she remarked to Hans pensively, "That makes two of them gone now. Tollef and Tomas." Anna did not fear death but the passing now of two of her siblings gave her cause to think of it more frequently.

Julianna graduated in June of '60 and her mother, Annetta, came from Norway for the occasion and spent about two weeks in the area. Then she and Julianna left for New York where they stayed with Sylvia a few days before returning to Norway.

Julianna returned to her home somewhat reluctantly, as she had found a boyfriend at college and the two of them were getting quite serious but she felt that she had to go back to Norway. That was her home, although she had learned to love it in the States. She was torn between love and loyalty. Becky was telling Anna all about it shortly after Julianna and her mother left.

"Oh, dear, I wonder how that will all turn out," Anna said, shaking her head back and forth. "Maybe she'll be back."

"That's what I think, too, Aunt Anna," said Becky.

Anna finally talked Hans into retiring. He was, after all, 83 years old now! Anna retired herself, too, from her volunteer work at the hospital and from teaching Sunday School. She had taught Sunday School for over 30 years!

She and Hans both still felt well so they enjoyed some traveling. They had their first airplane trip when they flew to New York to visit Sigrid and her family. Sigrid lived with Sylvia now. Louis had died several years previous, after another bad stroke. Sigrid was getting up in age, too, now. She was several years older that Hans.

One winter, Hans and Anna went down to Arizona for a month. Many of their friends were now doing this so they had to go down there and see what was so great about it all. Hans didn't care for it much. He liked it best at home, he said, and they never went there again.

Their oldest grandson, Roland, graduated from high school in '65 and he immediately enlisted in the navy. Anna was rather upset about this. The Viet Nam war was going on and she didn't want to think about having a grandson going off to war.

"But, Grandma," Rollie told her, " I know I'll get drafted sooner or later and I want to be in the navy so I just thought I'd enlist and get what I want."

"I'm getting too old to worry about another loved one involved in a war," said Hans. But he read the newspapers avidly every day anyway.

Becky kept Anna up to date on Julianna. She had married a former boyfriend in Norway but Becky said that she didn't think she was very happy. I still think she wishes she had come back and married Wally Lund. He finally got married himself but I think he was waiting for Julianna to make up her mind.

Anna listened to this real-life soap opera and hoped that Julianna had made the right decision.

"You know, Becky," said Anna, "it's better to follow your heart sometimes," rather than your head, but one doesn't usually know if that's the right thing until it's too late."

Becky herself was getting married that summer. All of Anna's grand-nieces and grandnephews who lived around here were married now. How time flies, Anna thought. I am just the old great aunt now! Our home used to be the center of all the family's activities and now we go to Sarah's or Arne's. Hans and I just rattle around in this big, old house. It's getting to be too much of a job for us to keep this place up, she continued thinking to herself. Hans didn't want to move, though.

Rollie was stationed out in San Diego and he seemed to like the navy. Anna wrote to him often. Here I am, writing to another young man in the service again, she thought, recalling the years when she wrote faithfully to Frank and her two nephews.

That fall, on Anna's 79th birthday, Hans got bad news. He hadn't been feeling well and had been to the doctor. The test results were in and he and Anna went back to the doctor's office.

"Mr. Nielson, I'm sorry to have to tell you that you have a cancerous tumor of the kidney and it has advanced quite far already," said the intense young specialist.

Hans just sat there, stunned, and Anna felt as if someone had pierced her heart with a sharp object! They went home and when Frank and Betty and Margaret and Ted and their two girls came over to see Anna on her birthday, it was a subdued gathering indeed. Hans tried to be philosophical about it all after he recovered from the first shock.

"Well, you have to die of something, you know," he told them.

Frank brushed this remark aside. "You're not going to die, Pa. You're going to fight it. Maybe they can do surgery or something."

On Hans' next visit to the doctor, he was told that, because of his age, surgery was not recommended. There was, however, something new they could try on him but it may or may not be successful. It was some kind of chemotherapy that was just in the experimental stage. "It will either kill you or cure you," the doctor had told him. They would start him on it the next day.

Hans entered the hospital for several days while this new treatment was administered and then sent home. When he returned to the doctor's office three weeks later, he was given good news. It looked like the treatment had done its job! He and Anna were elated and hopeful and they went to share the good news with their children.

They all had a happy Christmas together that year. Anna wanted them to all come over once again to the "big house" as it was called, and so they all gathered around the old, familiar dining-room table. There was Frank, Betty and Patty, and Margaret and Ted, Stan, Barb and Kari. The only one missing was Rollie. He was out at sea someplace but no one knew exactly where.

Their happiness at Hans' condition was short lived, though. He was not feeling well by the middle of January and his next visit to the doctor showed that the cancer had indeed returned and was spreading to his lungs. There was nothing more that could be done.

Hans was able to stay at home until toward the end of March and then he began to feel really ill and weak. He was hospitalized and never did return to his beloved home again.

Anna spent many hours every day at his bedside. They had many long talks, the two of them. One day, when Margaret came up to the hospital to see her father, she paused in the doorway. Her mother was sitting close by the bed, holding Hans' hand in hers and the two of them were silent. As Margaret watched her parents, a lump formed in her throat. Here are these two dear, old people, holding on to each other, knowing that this would be the end of a long, loving marriage, the end of an era.

Margaret felt almost like an intruder. She just stood there, tears forming in her eyes as she watched this scene. These two had been young and vibrant once, living and loving each other for many years. They had been spending these last weeks saying goodbye to each other in their own way. There was no despair here; each knew with certainty where they were going when death claimed them.

Margaret turned and stood in the hallway for awhile, giving in to the sobs that were forming in her chest. She had a good cry and finally wiped her tears and then stepped into her father's room.

Her mother looked up. "Oh, Margaret, it's good to see you. I was wondering if you were coming soon. He's resting right now. We had a wonderful talk earlier but I guess it wore him out."

For the next few days, Hans was mostly in and out of consciousness. On that next Sunday, early in the evening, the whole family happened to be all there at one time. Frank and Betty, Margaret and Ted and Anna were all standing around Hans' bed.

The nurse had just been in and taken his blood pressure and said, "His pressure is very low. It won't be long now."

Anna sat down in the chair next to the bed and took his frail hand in hers. It felt rather cool. She rubbed it and then brought it up to her lips. It was then that they heard him take his last breath, a gasp really, and then he was gone. Anna sat there still holding his hand. Everyone was crying and the nurse came in and disconnected all the tubes and things. She left the family in there alone for awhile and then the doctor came by and he pronounced him dead and he lifted the sheet over Hans' face. He ushered the family into a small conference room. Frank put his arm around his mother's thin shoulders and gave her a hug.

"I'll be all right, everyone," said Anna calmly. "And now your father's all right, too. No more suffering for him."

The necessary arrangements were made and then the family returned to their homes and their grief. Frank said that he'd stay with his mother that night but she said she'd be all right alone. Her granddaughter, Barbara, who was twelve, came over, however, and said she would spend the night with her grandma. Anna didn't argue. Perhaps it would be nice after all to have someone in the house, especially tonight.

Hans was laid to rest in the family plot on April 9, 1966, two months before his eighty-ninth birthday. The family and the community had lost a wonderful and loving man. The church had been full to capacity with the many friends that Hans had acquired over his many years of living and doing business in this town.

Anna insisted on answering all the expressions of sympathy herself. She said she needed to keep busy so she spent the next few weeks writing notes to hundreds of people. She wrote a short letter to Samuel to tell him about her husband's death and she received a letter back from him shortly, telling her how sorry he was at the news. He said that he would try to come and see her that summer, if possible. His wife was not feeling well right now.

Anna also wrote to Rollie. He was not able to make it home for his grandfather's funeral and he had sent her a long, wonderful letter earlier. He had been in the navy now for almost a year. He was "seeing the world" he told his grandma, but he hoped that he wouldn't have to go over to Southeast Asia. Anna hoped so, too.

About a month after Hans' death, Frank and Betty decided to sell their house and move in with Anna. Frank had always loved that dear, old house; better than the one he and Betty had built for themselves not so many years back. Anna didn't protest this, as she really didn't want to leave this house but she couldn't stay there alone either.

They made the large parlor into a bedroom-sitting room with a small bathroom in it for Anna. They wanted to put new carpet in there but Anna said that she wanted them to bring down the mauve, flowered rug from her bedroom upstairs. The rug that Hans had brought home for her so many years ago. They brought it down, plus the beautiful bedroom set and her trunk and old rocker and made the room as cozy as possible for her. She loved it and she wouldn't even have to climb those stairs anymore!

Anna turned eighty that fall. "I'm still in pretty good shape for an old gal, aren't I?" she would tell her family. It was true. She was still slim and agile and she stood almost as tall and straight as ever. Her hair was thinning a little but it was now a beautiful shade of gray and she always kept it looking nice. Hans had always insisted that she go and have it done at the beauty shop every week.

The only complaint that Anna had, health wise, was her knees. She would tell others, "My knees went and got old on me!"

Anna liked going to the Senior Citizen's Center several afternoons a week. She liked to play cards and just visit with her many friends there. Several of the others spoke Norwegian and she found, in these later years, that she was wanting to speak her old language more often.

Over the next couple years more sad news came from Norway. Two more of Anna's siblings had died. Barbro and Kjersti had died the same year. That just left Eric in that country. Back home, Sigrid had died in New York the year before. It was just Anna and Andrew left now here in this country. He was getting up there in years, almost 92 years old now. He was still in fairly good health and lived on the farm with his son. His dear wife, Alice, had died five years earlier.

My family is almost all gone now, mused Anna to herself. But look at the generations that are coming up to replace us! Like Hans used to say, "That's the way of life!"

CHAPTER 29

In the summer of 1968, Rollie returned from Viet Nam, safe and sound. What a relief, thought Anna. One more young man home safely from a war fought far from home. That fall, he enrolled at the University of Minnesota in Minneapolis to study pharmacy. His father had rather hoped that he would have taken an interest in the lumber business.

"If I can't cut it in pharmacy, Dad, I'll come back and work with you," he had said.

Anna's other grandson, Stan, Margaret and Ted's only son, was going to school down in Ames. His plans were to go into engineering. Anna was very proud of her grandchildren. They all were going on to higher education and this was good, she thought.

Patricia, Frank and Betty's oldest daughter, got married in June of 1969. In fact, she picked June 14, the same wedding day as Hans and Anna's so many years ago. It was a large affair. She married a nice, young man named Paul Hanson. He was the new dentist in town. She met him when she went to have her teeth checked. Something clicked and they were married two years later!

Anna remained almost as active as ever in her church ladies aid group and with the senior citizens. She even served as president of the latter group at age 83. They had a very busy, active time that year. She pushed through some new programs which included daily exercises at the Center and also some lectures on the latest books. They also had many card parties and potlucks. She also started a program where senior citizens would go to the school and read to the youngsters there. Anna especially enjoyed doing this as the old "school teacher" in her still had an interest in school children.

Anna heard from Samuel several times a year. His wife had become very much an invalid these last years and Anna felt sorry for him. Too bad that they had had no children. She wished that she could see him but it wasn't easy for him to get away. He was going to retire in the next year and take his wife down to Florida where they would live year round, he wrote.

The week before Thanksgiving of 1969, the family received a terrible shock.   Rollie was killed in an automobile accident on his way back to Minneapolis! He had been alone and apparently he had fallen asleep and had left the road and hit a telephone pole in the ditch.   Frank and Betty were devastated and so was the rest of the family.

Their only son, thought Anna. And to think that he came back unharmed from the Viet Nam War only to be taken in a car accident on the highways of his home state. The funeral was the worst thing that Anna had ever had to endure. Here I've lost two husbands and had two miscarriages and lost most of my sisters and brothers, but this is the most difficult thing I've ever gone through, she thought to herself.

The thing that made it the hardest, Anna pondered, was that not only did she lose a grandchild but she could do nothing to alleviate Frank and Betty's grief. She, as the parent, could do nothing to "make it all better".

"A child shouldn't die before his parents or grandparents!" Anna stated over and over again. "It's not right that this should happen!"

The weeks following Rollie's death were the darkest that Anna could ever remember. Of all the things that she had suffered, this was by far the worst. She spent many hours praying and pleading with God to alleviate her despair and to grant comfort and hope to her son and daughter-in-law.

It was a very subdued Christmas that year. They all were invited over to Arne and Sophia's. Betty was in no shape to entertain. Frank was a very broken man, grieving for his only son. Anna ached so for the two of them. They had many long talks together, which was good for them, and Anna prayed fervently for the family.

In the spring, it was like a breath of fresh air when Patricia announced that she was expecting. New life! That's what the family needed right now.

Barbara, Margaret and Ted's oldest daughter, graduated from high school in May and she wanted to be an airline stewardess so she set off for Minneapolis to apply at Northwest Airlines. She could stay with Teddy and Caroline.

"I want to see the world, Grandma," she would say to Anna. Anna could understand that so she could only wish her well.

Patricia and Paul's baby was born in October, almost on Anna's birthday. Only two days off. It was a girl and they named her Beth Ann. She was a delight, especially to Betty, who threw herself into becoming a grandmother with great enthusiasm. It helped alleviate the pain somewhat, taking care of a new infant.

Beth was followed by another sister, named Kristin, born two years later. The following year, Patricia and Paul and their two little girls moved away from Mankato, much to the dismay of Patricia's parents. Anna missed them very much, too. Paul had gotten an offer to be the only dentist in a town about three hours away and he thought it a great opportunity for them.

Margaret and Ted's oldest daughter, Barb, got married in 1974 to a fellow she had met in college named Dan Schmit. The whole family loved him as he was so friendly and outgoing. Stan nicknamed him "Dan, the Man" and he especially endeared himself to Anna. He was always joking with her and yet he had such a soft side to him. Frank joked that it was maybe good to get a little German blood mixed into the family!

A couple months after her cousin's wedding, Patricia had another little girl! They named this one Jana. Betty wished that she lived a little closer to her growing number of granddaughters.

The next spring, Kari, Anna's youngest granddaughter, graduated from high school. She enrolled in college down in Ames that fall. She was interested in journalism.

Before Christmas that year, Anna's daughter and daughter-in-law, Margaret and Betty, were already starting to talk about a big birthday party for Anna the next fall, for her 90th birthday. The following spring, the plans started in earnest! Anna just scoffed at the idea of having anything very big.

"Just keep it small," she would say, but this seemed to do no good. The girls thought that this milestone called for a big celebration.

And a big affair it was! The party was held at the Senior Center and attended by many friends and family. Anna was kept busy for weeks just opening her cards and reading and enjoying each one. Her granddaughter, Kari, at that time announced to Anna that she planned to write the history of her life for a paper that was due at school in January. They would need to have many long visits together.

True to her word, Kari came up from Ames about every other weekend for the next two months. Anna would talk and Kari would write and sometimes record on her little tape recorder her grandmother's words. She spent her Christmas vacation typing up the paper and showed it to Anna before she returned to school. Anna was pleased with it.

This paper, however, was only a short version of the account of Anna's life that Kari planned to write someday. In that one she would include everything and it would be long, indeed. Too long for a college term paper!

The next two summers Kari worked on this project with Anna's help and input. The two had come to an agreement about something. The contents would not be revealed until after Anna's death. This was the way Anna decided that she wanted it to be and Kari would honor this request. Kari finished the final draft the summer before she returned to Ames for her last year of school.

"I'm ready to go now, Lord," Anna would say every evening as she said her prayers. "My children are getting old themselves, my grandchildren are all doing well and my great-grandchildren are growing up, too" she continued her conversation with her Lord. "It's time for me to leave this world. I'm getting tired out and weary." Hans' words echoed in her mind. "It's the way of life".

CHAPTER 30

August 4, 1979

Three years later, on August 4, 1979, Anna passed away peacefully in her sleep in her own bed. The morning of the funeral was a beautiful day. The whole family was there. At the church, Kari kept looking at the door, as if watching for someone.

"C'mon, Kari, we need to line up now. Who is it you are watching for?" asked her mother.

"Oh, I'll tell you later," said Kari, as she went to stand by her brother, Stan. The family passed by the casket once more before the lid was closed forever. Each of the mourners took one last look at the body of their loved one lying there. As they were ready to enter the church sanctuary, Kari took one last look toward the door. Just then a man entered rather uncertainly. She broke out of line and hurried over to him and conversed with him briefly before returning to her place.

"Who is that?" asked her brother.

"I'll tell you later," she answered, as the group started down the aisle, following the pallbearers and the minister. The beautiful white casket was now in place at the front of the church. The family filed into the pews reserved for them.

The hymn, "Beyond the Everlasting Hills" was sung. Margaret could not trust herself to sing aloud but she followed along. These words could not have been more perfect for her mother, she thought. No wonder she chose this hymn. The words went: "Beyond the everlasting hills, Above the starry skies, My spirit seeks the home of peace, Where tears shall dim no eyes. There shall I find again the love Of those I cherished here; And friendship's ties shall holier be, And bonds of love more dear. There shall I see thee, O my God, Creator, Saviour, Friend; And with angelic voices join In worship without end. Amen."

Pastor Saunders ascended to the pulpit and looked out over the sanctuary of Our Savior's Church. It was packed with family, friends and flowers.

"Anna Olson Howe Nielson was born October 20, 1886 in Norway . She immigrated to America in 1905. She worked for a time and then attended Mankato State College. She taught in several schools until her marriage to

Lawrence Howe in 1912. He died in 1913. She married Hans Nielson in 1921. They had two children. Frank, born in 1922 and Margaret, born in 1924. She had four grandchildren and five great-grandchildren. She was preceded in death by her husband Hans and her grandson, Roland. Blessed be her memory."

Pastor Saunders removed his glasses and looked down at the family seated before him. He paused for awhile, seeming unable to continue. Finally he started to speak.

"Today I am officiating at the funeral of not only a member of this congregation but of one of my best and dearest friends. When I came to this congregation ten years ago, Anna's son, Frank, was the president of the council and he invited me and my family to his home for dinner. There is where I first met Anna. She and I immediately hit it off. I can't explain why, but she and I established a rapport which lasted all these years. You might say we were 'kindred spirits'. Have you ever met someone whom you felt this way about? It's as if your hearts and souls are exactly on the same wave length. That's the way it was with Anna and me. Many of you probably felt the same way about her."

"When I went to visit her with a concern or problem or maybe just a feeling of being a little 'down', I would always leave feeling much better. She had a way of getting to the heart of the matter and showing you what was really important. And, my friends, what was most important to Anna Nielson was her Lord, Jesus Christ, and she never made any bones about it! She was never hesitant to speak of her faith. We all, family and friends alike, will miss her sorely. But the body which rests in that casket over there does not contain Anna, only her shell. She is home in heaven with her Savior, where there is no sadness. She is with the two people she loved most, her Lord and her beloved Hans. She believed most fervently that she would be reunited with all her loved ones. Her parents, her brothers and sisters, and her grandson Roland, who died so tragically just ten years ago."

"So, my friends, our grieving today isn't for Anna, but for ourselves. We have to go on living without her. Her passing has left a great void in all our lives. Only Christ can fill that void, and someday we will be reunited with her in heaven."

"As most of you know," Pastor Saunders continued, "Anna died peacefully in her sleep in her own bed. This is exactly how she wanted it. She prayed about it often. Isn't that just like our Anna to have that all arranged with her Lord? I've never known anybody who so fervently believed in answered prayer. What an example she was to me and to all of you. She told me that she prayed for me every day, And I'm sure that she prayed for many, many others every day. What a prayer list she must have had!"

"She would ask me sometimes if I felt that someone had been praying for me and when I would think about it, I would have to say, yes, I could just feel it. It's hard to explain but some of you have perhaps had that same feeling. In fact, I'm sure Anna herself was praying for most of you out there every day."

The pastor continued for several more minutes and then the last hymn , "I Know of a Sleep in Jesus' Name" was sung by the congregation.

As the family was following the casket down the aisle, Kari turned her head and sought the face of the man who had entered the church late. Their eyes met and she could see that he had been weeping.

Before leaving for the cemetery, Kari sought him out among the crowd standing in front of the church.

"Mr. Martin," she said, "won't you please ride with us to the cemetery."

"Yes, I'd like that. Thank you very much," he said.

She led him to the family car and introduced him around.

"This is Mr. Sam Martin," Kari explained. "He is the son of the family that Grandma worked for back in Toledo years ago." They all shook his hand and they got into the cars reserved for them.

The ceremony at the cemetery was very hard for the family. It was their final goodbye to the person most dear in their lives. The young great-grandchildren skipped and played around the tombstones, not really comprehending the somberness of the adults. Margaret and Frank were the last to leave the cemetery. They held onto each other, this brother and sister, wondering how they would ever get along without their dear mother in their lives. They now were the head of the family, so to speak.

The mourners returned to the church where the Ladies Aid served a hot noon meal to everyone. The family mingled with one and all, accepting everyone's deepest sympathies. The grandchildren and great- grandchildren started to leave to return to the house. Frank and Betty, Margaret and Ted were the last to depart the church. They put as many of the flowers in their car as they could and brought them to the house.

"Mr. Martin," said Kari, as they got out of the car in front of the house, "could you help me carry a box from my car there into the house?"

"Of course, Miss Davis. That's the least I can do. You have been so kind to me."

"Call me Kari. Here, it's this one right here, " she said as she opened her trunk.

"Whatever is that? " asked Kari's father as he opened the door for them.

"You'll see soon enough," answered Kari. "It's a surprise."

Everyone was finding comfortable chairs and kicking off their shoes. It had started to get awfully hot by what was now almost mid afternoon. Beth, Kristin, and Jana ran upstairs to change into shorts and then outside to play. The twins were taken upstairs to be put down for a nap.

Margaret and Betty were bustling in the kitchen to find cold drinks for everyone. Frank carried in the large envelope containing all the sympathy cards and laid it on the coffee table. He didn't have the energy or the desire to look at them all just yet. Maybe tonight.

Kari had her box put on the dining-room table and she stood nervously waiting for everyone to assemble in the adjoining living room. Stan brought in a tray of ice cold glasses of lemonade. Barbara returned from putting her twin boys to bed and Patricia came in from outside where she had been telling the girls to stay in the shade and play quietly.

It was a beautiful summer afternoon in this peaceful neighborhood. How could everything seem so normal, thought Kari, without Grandma here. Life goes on, just as Grandma said it would.

"Is everyone here now?" she asked. "Oh, wait, here comes Pastor Saunders up the sidewalk. Let him in, Stan. I asked him to come."

The pastor was offered a cold drink and a chair.

"I'm so grateful to be invited to come here with the family,"·he said. " I didn't feel like going anyplace else for awhile. I feel kind of at loose ends as I'm sure you all do, too."

Stan said, "Kari, are you going to show us what is in that box? You look nervous as a cat!"

"Well, I am nervous, and I'll show you what's in here now if you wish." She took a quick look at Mr. Martin and thought to herself, here goes!

"As you all know, I have been busy writing Grandma's life story for the past three years. It started out as a term paper for my English II class at the University. I got an 'A' on it, I might add. Then I decided to expand on it and have it published and given to family and friends. So I went to the head of the English department to find out how I could go about this. They said that they could do it there for me for a reasonable fee."

"So, anyway," she continued, "I have one for each family here, but before I hand them out, I have something to tell you and it's not going to be very easy."

Kari took a deep breath and reached for her glass of lemonade.

"Boy, is it hot in here or is it just me!" she exclaimed.

"Well, it is warm, Kari," said her Aunt Betty. "Just sit down and relax for awhile."

"You see," Kari began, "when Grandma told me her life story she told me something that she had never told anyone before. She had wanted to many times in these last years but it never seemed like just the right time."

Everyone was looking at each other, wondering what this secret could have been.

"As you know," Kari continued, " when Grandma first came to this country, she stayed with her older sister, Sigrid, for a couple of years. Then she headed west and stayed in Toledo, Ohio for awhile and worked for the Martin family." Here Kari nodded at Mr. Martin.

"What you don't know is that when Grandma left New York she was, ah, ...this is the hard part.... she was...... pregnant." She could hear the intake of breaths around the room but no one said a thing.

"She had the baby, a boy, while at the Martins and if you are wondering what happened to that boy he is right here in this room. Samuel Martin here is Grandma's son." She let this sink in as all eyes were now on Mr. Martin but no one was able to utter a word for a few seconds.

When Frank finally realized what this meant, that this stranger in his living room was his half brother, he rose and approached Mr. Martin and extended his hand. Margaret was too shocked to move and she looked to Kari for further explanations.

"I'll continue if you are all over the initial shock," said Kari. "The reason Grandma never wanted to tell anyone is that her condition came about in such a painful way, as you will find out as you read her story. In fact, I think I will explain no further and let you all read it for yourselves tonight or whenever you have time."

No one seemed to know what to say. Poor Mr. Martin looked very uncomfortable, as if he felt somehow to blame for this unexpected revelation. Margaret, trying to suppress her own feelings for the moment, could see his predicament. She went over to him and said, "Mr. Martin, why don't we go someplace where we can talk privately? Frank, you come along, too."

Margaret led them to Anna's room and offered him the rocker while she sat on the trunk.

"Whew," said Frank as he sat down on the edge of his mother's bed, "that was quite a shock to us. I'm sorry if our reaction has caused you any embarrassment of any kind. I guess we will have many questions to ask you. Maybe we should read her story first. I really don't know what to do or feel right now." He got up and started pacing the floor of the little room.

"I can understand your feelings, Mr. Nielson," said Mr. Martin.

"Please," said Margaret, "we must stop being so formal. Call us by our first names, Frank and Margaret, and we'll call you Samuel"

"Thank you, Margaret," said the elder man. "Perhaps I should be leaving now so that you all can come to terms with this situation. I'm staying in a motel here in town and maybe I could stop back tomorrow before I leave."

Margaret, ever the gracious hostess, started to protest, but Frank interrupted and said, "Perhaps that would be best, Samuel. We aren't quite ourselves right now. That will give us a chance to read the story tonight and why don't you stop by in the morning."

"Yes," said Margaret, "come by for coffee and we'll have a long chat then."

They rose and left their mother's room and Samuel poked his head into the living room to say goodbye to the rest of the family and Pastor Saunders.

Frank and Margaret walked him out to his car parked along the street. As he drove away, Frank put his arm around his sister's shoulders as they walked slowly back to the house. The house which would never be the same now with Anna gone. They sat down on the top porch step and Margaret, finally letting the emotions of the day overtake her, let the tears flow freely and unashamedly. Frank, usually never showing his emotions, joined her in this natural, cleansing act.

After a few minutes he took out his hankie and they took turns using it. They could hear the voices of the little girls playing in the back yard. Things sounded and looked so normal but yet their world had just changed dramatically that day. Not only had they said their final farewell to their beloved mother, but they also had the shock of finding out that they had a brother. They'd had one all these years and never knew about him.

Frank stood up and said his sister, "Well, I think we have some serious reading to do. Let's go in." Margaret stood up and they went in to face the family.

Later that evening, after the family had all left, Frank felt compelled to enter his mother's room. Betty, tired out from the past few days, had retired to their bedroom early. He turned on the lamp on the nightstand. As a child he had been so fascinated with that lamp. He would run his fingers under the fringes on the shade and make them sway and dance in the light.

He moved to the trunk and lifted the lid. He reached for a pack of letters tied with a red ribbon. After studying them for a moment, he knew that these were the letters he had sent home during the war. He opened and read a couple of them. Then he reached down to the very bottom of the trunk and pulled out another small bundle of letters, these tied up with a piece of blue yarn.

Looking them over, he noticed that they were all postmarked Toledo, and that the first ones were addressed to Anna Olson. He opened one, with the earliest date, December, 1907. It was from Mrs. Martin and in it she told Anna all about baby Samuel. "He is a very bright and happy child," she assured Anna, "and he is thriving and growing like a weed."

As Frank continued reading all the letters, he realized that this was Mrs. Martin's attempt to keep Anna informed of the well-being of her little son. His heart ached for his mother and her attempts to keep this secret to herself all these years.

"Why, Mother, didn't you share this with us?" he said aloud, looking about the room as if his mother were there. "Did you ever tell Dad?"

Frank returned the letters to the trunk and shut off the lamp. When he reached his bedroom, Betty had fallen asleep sitting up reading the booklet that Kari had left for them. He switched off her reading lamp and took the booklet and sat down in the soft, bedroom chair and turned on the floor lamp. He was quite tired after the emotional day but he felt he just had to read this tonight.

He hardly moved in his chair at all, so mesmerized was he by his mother's story, until he came to the chapter when Samuel, as a grown man, sought out his birth mother. Here the tears really started to flow from Frank's eyes. He rose and went into the kitchen and poured himself a glass of cold water. Again he felt moved to go to his mother's room.

Moonlight was streaming through the ruffled curtains and illuminated the flowers on the carpet. He went to the trunk once more and reached in for the shoebox which contained all the old family pictures. He took it to the rocker and turned on the lamp again and rummaged through the box until he came to pictures of Samuel. One was of him as a baby, another one at about two years of age, and still another as a young man on his confirmation day.

As Frank looked at these pictures, he could just feel all the heartache that his mother must have felt when she received them. Compassion and understanding overcame him and he could hold back the tide of tears no longer. He knelt down by his mother's bed and great heaving sobs came from somewhere deep within him.

"How terrible it must have been for you to give up your son," he cried aloud. "I love you and miss you so much. Did I tell you enough how special you were to me?" His tears fell on the quilt that had been on the bed for many years. He had the feeling that his were not the only tears that had fallen there.

After some time, he returned the box to the trunk and went back to his room. It would soon be morning, he thought to himself.

Frank and Betty were sitting at the kitchen table finishing their breakfast the next day when Margaret let herself quietly in the side door. She looked at Frank and could tell that he had spent somewhat of the same kind of night as she had.

"Did you read all night, too, Frank?" she asked as she poured herself a cup of coffee and joined the pair.

"I read up to the chapter when Samuel came to this house looking for her. I couldn't read anymore, it affected me so."

"Yes, that was hard on me, too," she agreed. "I wondered if Dad ever knew about this secret."

"I wondered the same thing myself. They never kept anything from each other."

"Do you think Samuel will come over this morning?" Margaret asked her brother.

"I don't know, but I hope so," Frank answered, getting up from his chair and looking out the window. He stood there awhile, sipping his coffee and reflecting on all he had read the night before.

Just then a soft, hesitant knock was heard at the front door. Frank and Margaret both jumped up and hurried toward the sound. Samuel stood there looking tired and unsure of himself.

"Oh, Mr....ah...Samuel. How good to see you. We were just wondering if you would come by this morning," said Frank, as he ushered the man into the kitchen and offered him a chair.

"How about some breakfast, Mr. Martin?" suggested Betty, standing by the stove ready to dish up a plate for him.

"Oh, no, no," he said. "I ate at a coffee shop near the motel. But I will take a cup of coffee, if you don't mind."

"So, Samuel, what kind of a night did you have?" asked Frank, sitting down next to him. "My sister and I didn't get much sleep. We were reading all night, it seems."

"Well, yes, so was I," he answered. "I didn't finish it all yet but I was very moved by what I read. Especially the part where she came to Toledo when I was about 5 years old and she tried to take me from my parents." He slowly stirred the cream in his cup and went on. "I knew then how much she loved me and how hard it was for her to give me up."

"The chapter where you came here as a grown man in search of your mother really undid me," Frank admitted. "We were wondering if she had ever told our father."

"No, I don't think that she ever did, from what she told me that day," Samuel said.

Everyone was silent for awhile and Betty broke the spell by passing around the doughnuts.

"She was a remarkable woman, our mother was," stated Frank, as he looked at Margaret and Samuel. "I wish she were here right now to see the three of us together."

"Perhaps she is looking down on us right now," volunteered Margaret, and a reverent silence prevailed again.

"Perhaps she is, perhaps she is," Samuel said, nodding his head.

After visiting for about an hour longer, Samuel rose and said that he needed to head back as he had a long trip ahead of him. They all walked him out to his car and after some clumsy attempts at a proper goodbye, Frank reached out to his brother and clasped him in a big bear hug.

"I wish that I had known you all these years, Samuel, but maybe we can make up for lost time," said Frank, releasing him and Margaret took her turn hugging her new-found brother.

"Yes, I hope we can meet again soon. You two have accepted me very well, under the circumstances. I know it was a terrible shock to you."

"Yes, it was," Margaret admitted, "but I think we have fully recovered now. Reading her story helped us to understand things, I think."

With that, Samuel got in his car and drove away, smiling and waving back to his brother and sister standing on the curb.

Neither Frank nor Margaret could speak for some moments. They merely linked arms and walked back into the house. Without planning it, they walked into their mother's room. Margaret sat down in the rocker and picked up the worn and tattered Bible.

As she thumbed through the pages she said, "This book was the mainstay of Mother's life and so shall it be for ours."

"So it shall be, so it shall be," Frank agreed, nodding his head.